THE HUNTING PARTY

LUCY FOLEY

HarperCollins*Publishers*

HarperCollins*Publishers* Ltd
1 London Bridge Street,
London SE1 9GF

www.harpercollins.co.uk

This paperback edition 2019
18

First published in Great Britain by HarperCollins*Publishers* 2019

Copyright © Lost and Found Books Ltd 2019

Lucy Foley asserts the moral right to
be identified as the author of this work

A catalogue record for this book is available from the British Library

ISBN: 978-0-00-829715-2

Typeset in Sabon by Palimpsest Book Production Ltd, Falkirk, Stirlingshire

Printed and bound in the UK by CPI Group (UK) Ltd, Croydon CR0 4YY

MIX
Paper from
responsible sources
FSC™ C007454

The Hunting Party

Lucy Foley studied English Literature at Durham and UCL universities and worked for several years as a fiction editor in the publishing industry, before leaving to write full-time. *The Hunting Party*, an instant *Sunday Times* and *Irish Times* bestseller, is Lucy's debut crime novel, inspired by a particularly remote spot in Scotland that fired her imagination.

Lucy is also the author of three historical novels, which have been translated into sixteen languages. Her journalism has appeared in *ES Magazine*, *Sunday Times Style*, *Grazia* and more.

/LucyFoleyAuthor
@lucyfoleyauthor
@lucyfoleytweets

Also by Lucy Foley

The Book of Lost and Found
The Invitation
Last Letter from Istanbul

For AC, my partner in crime.

Should old acquaintance be forgot
And never brought to mind?

NOW
2nd January 2019

HEATHER

I see a man coming through the falling snow. From a distance through the curtain of white he looks hardly human, like a shadow figure.

As he nears me I see that it is Doug, the gamekeeper.

He is hurrying towards the Lodge, I realise, trying to run. But the fallen, falling snow hampers him. He stumbles with each step. Something bad. I know this without being able to see his face.

As he comes closer I see that his features are frozen with shock. I know this look. I have seen it before. This is the expression of someone who has witnessed something horrific, beyond the bounds of normal human experience.

I open the door of the Lodge, let him in. He brings with him a rush of freezing air, a spill of snow.

'What's happened?' I ask him.

There is a moment – a long pause – in which he tries to catch his breath. But his eyes tell the story before he can, a mute communication of horror.

Finally, he speaks. 'I've found the missing guest.'

'Well, that's great,' I say. 'Where—'

He shakes his head, and I feel the question expire on my lips.

'I found a body.'

Three days earlier
30th December 2018

EMMA

New Year. All of us together for the first time in ages. Me and Mark, Miranda and Julien, Nick and Bo, Samira and Giles, their six-month old baby, Priya. And Katie.

Four days in a winter Highland wilderness. Loch Corrin, it's called. Very exclusive: they only let four parties stay there each year – the rest of the time it's kept as a private residence. This time of year, as you might guess, is the most popular. I had to reserve it pretty much the day after New Year last year, as soon as the bookings opened up. The woman I spoke with assured me that with our group taking over most of the accommodation we should have the whole place to ourselves.

I take the brochure out of my bag again. A thick card,

expensive affair. It shows a fir-lined loch, heather-red peaks rising behind; though they may well be snow-covered now. According to the photographs, the Lodge itself – the 'New Lodge', as the brochure describes it – is a big glass construction, über-modern, designed by a top architect who recently constructed the summer pavilion at the Serpentine Gallery. I think the idea is that it's meant to blend seamlessly with the still waters of the loch, reflecting the landscape and the uncompromising lines of the big peak, the Munro, rising behind.

Near the Lodge, dwarfed by it, you can make out a small cluster of dwellings that look as though they are huddling together to keep warm. These are the cabins; there's one for each couple, but we'll come together to have meals in the shooting lodge, the bigger building in the middle. Apart from the Highland Dinner on the first night – 'a showcase of local, seasonal produce' – we'll be cooking for ourselves. They've ordered food in for me. I sent a long list in advance – fresh truffles, foie gras, oysters. I'm planning a real feast for New Year's Eve, which I'm very excited about. I love to cook. Food brings people together, doesn't it?

This part of the journey is particularly dramatic. We have the sea on one side of us, and every so often the land sheers away so that it feels as if one wrong move might send us careering over the edge. The water is slate-grey, violent-looking. In one cliff-top field the sheep huddle together in a group as though trying to keep warm. You can hear the wind; every so often it throws itself against the windows, and the train shudders.

All of the others seem to have fallen asleep, even baby Priya. Giles is actually snoring.

'Look,' I want to say, 'look how beautiful it is!'

I've planned this trip, so I feel a certain ownership of it – the anxiety that people won't enjoy themselves, that things might go wrong. And also a sense of pride, already, in its small successes . . . like this, the wild beauty outside the window.

It's hardly a surprise that they're all asleep. We got up so early this morning to catch the train – Miranda looked particularly cross at the hour. And then everyone got on the booze, of course. Mark, Giles and Julien hit the drinks trolley early, somewhere around Doncaster, even though it was only eleven. They got happily tipsy, affectionate and loud (the next few seats along did not look impressed). They seem to be able to fall back into the easy camaraderie of years gone by no matter how much time has passed since they last saw each other, especially with the help of a couple of beers.

Nick and Bo, Nick's American boyfriend, aren't so much a feature of this boys' club, because Nick wasn't part of their group at Oxford . . . although Katie has claimed in the past that there's more to it than that, some tacit homophobia on the part of the other boys. Nick is Katie's friend, first and foremost. Sometimes I have the distinct impression that he doesn't particularly like the rest of us, that he tolerates us only because of Katie. I've always suspected a bit of coolness between Nick and Miranda, probably because they're both such strong characters. And yet this morning the two of them seemed thick as thieves, hurrying off across the station concourse, arm in arm, to buy 'sustenance' for the trip. This turned out to be a perfectly chilled bottle of Sancerre, which Nick pulled from the cool-bag to slightly envious looks from the beer drinkers. 'He was trying to get those G&Ts in cans,' Miranda told us, 'but I wouldn't let him. We have to start as we mean to go on.'

Miranda, Nick, Bo and I each had some wine. Even Samira decided to have a small one too, at the last minute: 'There's all this new evidence that says you can drink when you're breastfeeding.'

Katie shook her head at first; she had a bottle of fizzy water. 'Oh come on, Kay-tee,' Miranda pleaded, with a winning smile, proffering a glass. 'We're on holiday!' It's difficult to refuse Miranda anything when she's trying to persuade you to do something, so Katie took it, of course, and had a tentative sip.

The booze helped lighten the atmosphere a bit; we'd had a bit of a mix-up with the seating when we first got on. Everyone was tired and cross, half-heartedly trying to work it out. It turned out that one of the nine seats on the booking had somehow ended up in the next carriage, completely on its own. The train was packed, for the holidays, so there was no possibility of shuffling things around.

'Obviously that's my one,' Katie said. Katie, you see, is the odd one out, not being in a couple. In a way, I suppose you could say that she is more of an interloper than I am these days.

'Oh, Katie,' I said. 'I'm so sorry – I feel like an idiot. I don't know how that happened. I was sure I'd reserved them all in the middle, to try to make sure we'd all be together. The system must have changed it. Look, you come and sit here . . . I'll go there.'

'No,' Katie said, hefting her suitcase awkwardly over the heads of the passengers already in their seats. 'That doesn't make any sense. I don't mind.'

Her tone suggested otherwise. *For goodness' sake*, I found myself thinking. *It's only a train journey. Does it really matter?*

The other eight seats were facing each other around two tables in the middle of the carriage. Just beyond, there was an elderly woman sitting next to a pierced teenager – two solitary travellers. It didn't look likely that we'd be able to do anything about the mess-up. But then Miranda bent across to speak to the elderly woman, her curtain of hair shining like gold, and worked her magic. I could see how charmed the woman was by her: the looks, the cut glass – almost antique – accent. Miranda, when she wants to, can exert *serious* charm. Anyone who knows her has been on the receiving end of it.

Oh yes, the woman said, of course she would move. It would probably be more peaceful in the next carriage anyway: 'You young people, aha!' – though none of us are all that young any more – 'And I prefer sitting forwards as it is.'

'Thanks Manda,' Katie said, with a brief smile. (She sounded grateful, but she didn't look it, exactly.) Katie and Miranda are best friends from way back. I know they haven't seen as much of each other lately, those two; Miranda says Katie has been busy with work. And because Samira and Giles have been tied up in baby land, Miranda and I have spent more time together than ever before. We've been shopping, we've gone for drinks. We've gossiped together. I have begun to feel that she's accepted me as her *friend*, rather than merely Mark's girlfriend, last to the group by almost a decade.

Katie has always been there to usurp me, in the past. She and Miranda have always been so tight-knit. So much so that they're almost more like sisters than friends. In the past I've felt excluded by this, all that closeness and history. It doesn't leave any new friendship with room to breathe. So a secret part of me is – well, rather pleased.

I really want everyone to have a good time on this trip, for it all to be a success. The New Year's Eve getaway is a big deal. They've done it every year, this group. They've been doing it for long before I came onto the scene. And I suppose, in a way, planning this trip is a rather pitiful attempt at proving that I am really one of them. At saying I should be properly accepted into the 'inner circle' at last. You'd think that three years – which is the time it has been since Mark and I got together – would be long enough. But it's not. They all go back a very long way, you see: to Oxford, where they first became friends.

It's tricky – as anyone who has been in this situation will know – to be the latest addition to a group of old friends. It seems that I will always be the new girl, however many years pass. I will always be the last in, the trespasser.

I look again at the brochure in my lap. Perhaps this trip – so carefully planned – will change things. Prove that I am one of them. I'm so excited.

KATIE

So we're finally here. And yet I have a sudden longing to be back in the city. Even my office desk would do it. The Loch Corrin station is laughably tiny. A solitary platform, with the steel-covered slope of a mountain shearing up behind, the top lost in cloud. The signpost, the National Rail standard, looks like a practical joke. The platform is covered in a thin dusting of snow, not a single footprint marring the perfect white. I think of London snow – how it's dirty almost as soon as it has fallen, trodden underfoot by thousands. If I needed any further proof of how far we are from the city it is this, that no one has been here to step in it, let alone clear it. Toto, I've a feeling we're not in Kansas any more. We passed through miles and miles of this wild-looking countryside on the train. I can't remember the last time I saw a human structure before this one, let alone a person.

We walk gingerly along the frozen platform – you can see the glint of black ice through the fallen snow – past the tiny station building. It looks completely deserted. I wonder how often the 'Waiting Room', with its painted sign and optimistic shelf of books, gets used. Now we're passing a small cubicle with a pane of dirty glass: a ticket booth, or tiny office. I peer in, fascinated by the idea of an office here in the middle of all this wilderness, and feel a small shock as I realise it isn't empty. There's actually someone sitting there, in the gloom. I can only make out the shape of him: broad-shouldered, hunched, and then the brief gleam of eyes, watching us as we pass.

'What is it?' Giles, in front of me, turns around. I must have made a noise of surprise.

'There's someone in there,' I whisper. 'A train guard or something – it just gave me a shock.'

Giles peers through the window. 'You're right.' He pretends to tip an imaginary cap from his bald head. 'Top o' the morning to ya,' he says, with a grin. Giles is the clown of our group: loveable, silly – sometimes to a fault.

'That's Irish, idiot,' says Samira, affectionately. Those two do everything affectionately. I never feel more aware of my single status than when I'm in their company.

The man in the booth does not respond at first. And then, slowly, he raises one hand, a greeting of sorts.

There's a Land Rover waiting to pick us up: splattered with mud, one of the old kind. I see the door open, and a tall man unfolds himself.

'That must be the gamekeeper,' Emma says. 'The email said he'd pick us up.'

He doesn't look like a gamekeeper, I think. What had I imagined, though? I think, mainly, I'd expected him to be old. He's probably only about our age. There's the bulk, I suppose: the shoulders, the height, that speak of a life lived outdoors, and the rather wild dark hair. As he welcomes us, in a low mumble, his voice has a cracked quality to it, as though it doesn't get put to much use.

I see him look us over. I don't think he likes what he sees. Is that a sneer, as he takes in Nick's spotless Barbour, Samira's Hunter wellies, Miranda's fox fur collar? If so, who knows what he makes of my city dweller's clothes and wheeled Samsonite. I hardly thought about what I was packing, because I was so distracted.

I see Julien, Bo and Mark try to help him with the bags, but he brushes them aside. Beside him they look as neat as schoolboys on the first day of the new term. I bet they don't love the contrast.

'I suppose it will have to be two lots,' Giles says, 'can't get all of us in there safely.'

The gamekeeper raises his eyebrows. 'Whatever you like.'

'You girls go first,' Mark says, with an attempt at chivalry, 'us lads will stay behind.' I wait, cringing, for him to make a joke about Nick and Bo being honorary girls. Luckily it doesn't seem to have occurred to him – or he's managed to hold his tongue. We're all on our best behaviour today, in tolerant holiday-with-friends mode.

It's been ages since we've all been together like this – not since last New Year's Eve, probably. I always forget what it's like. We fit back so quickly, so easily, into our old roles, the ones we have always occupied in this group. I'm the quiet one – to Miranda and Samira, my old housemates, the group extroverts. I revert. We all do. I'm sure Giles, say, isn't nearly such a clown in the A&E department where he's a senior registrar. We clamber into the Land Rover. It smells of wet dog and earth in here. I imagine that's what the gamekeeper would smell like, too, if you got close enough. Miranda is up front, next to him. Every so often I catch a whiff of her perfume: heavy, smoky, mingling oddly with the earthiness. Only she could get away with it. I turn my head to breathe in the fresh air coming through the cracked window.

On one side of us now a rather steep bank falls away to the loch. On the other, though it's not quite dark, the forest is already impenetrably black. The road is nothing more than a track, pitted and very thin, so a false move would send us plunging down towards the water, or crashing into the thickets. We see-saw our way along and then suddenly the brakes come on, hard. All of us are thrown forward into our seats and then slammed back into them.

'Fuck!' Miranda shouts, as Priya – so quiet for the journey up – begins to howl in Samira's arms.

A stag is lit up in the track in front of us. It must have detached itself from the shadow of the trees without any of us noticing. The huge head looks almost too big for the slender reddish body, crowned by a vast bristle of antlers, both majestic and lethal-looking. In the headlights its eyes gleam a weird, alien green. Finally it stops staring at us and moves away with an unhurried grace, into the trees. I put a hand to my chest and feel the fast drumbeat of my heart.

'Wow,' Miranda breathes. 'What was that?'

The gamekeeper turns to her and says, deadpan, 'A deer.'

'I mean,' she says, a little flustered – unusually for her – 'I mean, what sort of deer?'

'Red,' the gamekeeper says, 'A red stag.' He turns back to the road. Exchange over.

Miranda twists around to face us over the back of the seats, and mouths, 'He's hot, no?' Samira and Emma nod their agreement. Then, aloud, she says, 'Don't you think so, Katie?' She leans over and pokes me in the shoulder, a tiny bit too hard.

'I don't know,' I say. I look at the gamekeeper's impassive expression in the rear-view mirror. Has he guessed we're talking about him? If so he gives no indication that he's listening, but all the same, it's embarrassing.

'Oh, but you've always had strange taste in men, Katie,' Miranda says, laughing.

Miranda has never really liked my boyfriends. The feeling has, funnily enough, generally been mutual – I've often had to defend her to them. 'I think you pick them,' she said once, 'so that they'll be like the angel on your shoulder, telling you: she's not a good'un, that one. Steer clear.' But Miranda is my oldest friend. And our friendship has always outlasted any romantic relationship – on my side, that is. Miranda and Julien have been together since Oxford.

I wasn't sure what to make of Julien when he came on the scene, at the end of our first year. Neither was Miranda. He was a bit of an anomaly, compared to the boyfriends she'd had before. Admittedly, there were only a couple for comparison, both of them projects like me, not nearly as good-looking or as sociable as her, guys who seemed to exist in a permanent state of disbelief that they had been chosen. But then, Miranda has always liked a project.

So Julien seemed too obvious for her, with her love of waifs and strays. He was too brashly good-looking, too self-confident. And those were her words, not mine. 'He's so arrogant,' she'd say. 'I can't wait to hand him his balls next time he tries it on.' I wondered if she really couldn't see how closely he mirrored her own arrogance, her own self-confidence.

Julien kept trying. And each time, she rebuffed him. He'd come over to chat to us – her – in a pub. Or he'd just happen to 'bump into' her after a lecture. Or he'd casually be dropping in to the bar of our college's Junior Common Room, ostensibly to see some friends, but would spend most of the night sitting at our table, wooing Miranda with an embarrassing frankness.

Later I came to understand that when Julien wants something badly enough he won't let anything stand in the way of his getting it. And he wanted Miranda. Badly.

Eventually, she gave in to the reality of the situation: she wanted him back. Who wouldn't? He was beautiful then, still is, perhaps even more so now that life has roughed a little of the perfection off him, the glibness. I wonder if it would be biologically impossible not to want a man like Julien, at least in the physical sense.

I remember Miranda introducing us, at the Summer Ball – when they finally got together. I knew exactly who he was, of course. I had borne witness to the whole saga: his pursuit of Miranda, her throwing him off, him trying and trying – her, finally, giving in to the inevitable. I knew so much about him. Which college he was at, what subject he was studying, the fact that he was a rugby Blue. I knew so much that I had almost forgotten he wouldn't have a clue who I was. So when he kissed me on the cheek and said, solemnly, 'Nice to meet you, Katie,' – quite politely, despite being drunk – it felt like a big joke.

The first time he stayed at our house – Miranda, Samira and I all lived together in the second year – I bumped into him coming out of the bathroom, a towel wrapped around his waist. I was so conscious of trying to be normal, not to look at the bare expanse of his chest, at his broad, well-muscled shoulders gleaming wet from the shower, that I said, 'Hi, Julien.'

He seemed to clutch the towel a little tighter around his waist. 'Hello.' He frowned. 'Ah – this is a bit embarrassing. I'm afraid I don't know your name.'

I saw my mistake. He had completely forgotten who I was, had probably forgotten ever having met me. 'Oh,' I said, putting out my hand, 'I'm Katie.'

He didn't take my hand, and I realised that this was another mistake – too formal, too weird. Then it occurred to me it might also have been that he was keeping the towel up with that hand, clutching a toothbrush with the other.

'Sorry.' He smiled then, his charming smile, and took pity on me. 'So. What did you do, Katie?'

I stared at him. 'What do you mean?'

He laughed. 'Like the novel,' he said. '*What Katie Did*. I always liked that book. Though I'm not sure boys are supposed to.' For the second time he smiled that smile of his, and I suddenly thought I could see something of what Miranda saw in him.

This is the thing about people like Julien. In an American romcom someone as good-looking as him might be cast as a bastard, perhaps to be reformed, to repent of his sins later on. Miranda would be a bitchy Prom Queen, with a *dark secret*. The mousey nobody – me – would be the kind, clever, pitifully misunderstood character who would ultimately save the day. But real life isn't like that. People like them don't need to be unpleasant. Why would they make their lives difficult? They can afford to be their own spectacularly charming selves. And the ones like me, the mousey nobodies, we don't always turn out to be the heroes of the tale. Sometimes we have our own dark secrets.

What little light there was has left the day now. You can hardly make out anything other than the black mass of trees on either side. The dark has the effect of making them look thicker, closer: almost as though they're pressing in towards us. Other than the thrum of the Land Rover's engine there is no noise at all; perhaps the trees muffle sound, too.

Up front, Miranda is asking the gamekeeper about access. This place is truly remote. 'It's an hour's drive to the road,' the gamekeeper tells us. 'In good weather.'

'An *hour*?' Samira asks. She casts a nervous glance at Priya, who is staring out at the twilit landscape, the flicker of moonlight between the trees reflected in her big dark eyes.

I glance out through the back window. All I can see is a tunnel of trees, diminishing in the distance to a black point.

'More than an hour,' the gamekeeper says, 'if the visibility is poor or the conditions are bad.' Is he enjoying this?

It takes me an hour to get down to my mum's in Surrey. That's some sixty miles from London. It seems incredible that this place is even in the United Kingdom. I have always thought of this small island we call home as somewhat over-crowded. The way my stepdad likes to talk about immigrants, you'd think it was in very real danger of sinking beneath the weight of all the bodies squeezed onto it.

'Sometimes,' the gamekeeper says, 'at this time of year, you can't use the road at all. If there's a dump of snow, say – it would have been in the email you got from Heather.'

Emma nods. 'It was.'

'What do you mean?' Samira's voice has an unmistakable shrillness now. 'We won't be able to leave?'

'It's possible,' he says. 'If we get enough snow the track becomes impassable – it's too dangerous, even for snow tyres. We get at least a couple of weeks a year, in total, when Corrin is cut off from the rest of the world.'

'That could be quite cosy,' Emma says quickly, perhaps to fend off any more worried interjections from Samira. 'Exciting. And I've ordered enough groceries in—'

'And wine,' Miranda supplies.

'—and wine,' Emma agrees, 'to last us for a couple of weeks if we need it to. I probably went a bit overboard. I've planned a bit of a feast for New Year's Eve.'

No one's really listening to her. I think we're all preoccupied by this new understanding of the place in which we're going to spend the next few days. Because there *is* something unnerving about the isolation, knowing how far we are from everything.

'What about the station?' Miranda asks, with a sort of 'gotcha!' triumph. 'Surely you could just get a train?'

The gamekeeper gives her a look. He is quite attractive, I realise. Or at least he would be, only there's something haunted about his eyes. 'Trains don't run so well on a metre of snow, either,' he says. 'So they wouldn't be stopping here.'

And, just like that, the landscape, for all its space, seems to shrink around us.

DOUG

If it weren't for the guests, this place would be perfect. But he supposes he wouldn't have a job without them.

It had been everything he could do, when he picked them up, not to sneer. They reek of money, this lot – like all those who come here. As they approached the Lodge, the shorter, dark-haired man – Jethro? Joshua? – had turned to him in a man-to-man way, holding up a shiny silver phone. 'I'm searching for the Wi-Fi,' he said, 'but nothing is coming up. Obviously there's no 3G: I get that. You can't have 3G without a signal . . . Ha! But I would have thought I'd start picking up on the Wi-Fi. Or do you have to be closer to the Lodge?'

He told the man that they didn't turn the Wi-Fi on unless someone asked for it specifically. 'And you can sometimes catch a signal, but you have to climb up there' – he pointed to the slope of the Munro – 'in order to get it.'

The man's face had fallen. He had looked for a moment almost frightened. His wife had said, swiftly, 'I'm sure you

19

can survive without Wi-Fi for a few days, darling.' And she smothered any further protest with a kiss, her tongue darting out. Doug had looked away.

The same woman, Miranda – the beautiful one – had sat up in front with him in the Land Rover, her knee angled close to his own. She had laid an unnecessary hand on his arm as she climbed into the car. He caught a gust of her perfume every time she turned to speak to him, rich and smoky. He had almost forgotten that there are women like this in the world: complex, flirtatious, the sort who have to seduce everyone they meet. Dangerous, in a very particular way. Heather is so different. Does she even wear perfume? He can't remember noticing it. Certainly not make-up. She has the sort of looks that work better without any adornment from cosmetics. He likes her face, heart-shaped, dark-eyed, the elegant parentheses of her eyebrows. Someone who hadn't spent time with Heather might think that there was a simplicity to her, but he suspects otherwise; that with her it is very much a case of still waters running deep. He has a vague idea that she lived in Edinburgh before, that she had a proper career there. He has not tried to find out what her story is, though. It might mean revealing too much of his own.

Heather is a good person. He is not. Before he came here, he did a terrible thing. More than one thing, actually. A person like her should be protected from someone like him.

The guests are now in Heather's charge, for the moment – and that's a relief. It took no small effort to conceal his dislike of them. The dark-haired man – Julien, that was the name – is typical of the people that stay here. Moneyed, spoiled, wanting wilderness, but secretly expecting the luxury of the hotels they're used to staying in. It always takes them a while to process what they have actually signed up for, the remoteness, the simplicity, the priceless beauty of the surroundings. Often they undergo a kind of conversion, they are seduced by this place – who wouldn't be? But he knows they don't understand it, not properly. They think that they're roughing it, in their beautiful cabins with their four-poster beds and fireplaces and underfloor heating and the fucking *sauna* they can trot over to if they really want to exert themselves. And the ones he takes deer-stalking act as if they've suddenly become DiCaprio in *The Revenant*, battling with nature red in tooth and claw. They don't realise how easy he has made it for them, doing all the difficult work himself: the observation of the herd's activities, the careful tracking and plotting . . . so that all they have to do is squeeze the bloody trigger.

Even the shooting itself they rarely get right. If they shoot badly they could cause a wound that, if left, might cause the animal to suffer for days in unimaginable pain. A misfired headshot for example (they often aim for the head even though he tells them: *never* go for it, too easy to miss) could cleave away the animal's jaw and leave it alive in deepest agony, unable to eat, slowly bleeding to death. So he is there to finish it off with an expert shot, clean through the sternum, allowing them to go home boasting of themselves as hunters, as heroes. The taking of a life. The baptism in blood. Something to post on Facebook or Instagram – images of themselves smeared in gore and grinning like lunatics.

He has taken lives, many of them in fact. And not just

animal. He knows better than anyone that it is not something to boast about. It is a dark place from which you can never quite return. It does something to you, the first time. An essential change somewhere deep in the soul, the amputation of something important. The first time is the worst, but with each death the soul is wounded further. After a while there is nothing left but scar tissue.

He has been here for long enough to know all the different 'types' of guests, has become as much of an expert in them as he is in the wildlife. But he isn't sure which variety he hates more. The 'into the wild' sort, the ones who think they have in a few short days of luxury become 'at one' with nature. Or the other kind, the ones who just don't get it, who think they have been tricked . . . worse, robbed. They forget what it is they booked. They find problems with everything that deviates from the sort of places they are used to staying in, with their indoor swimming pools and Michelin-starred restaurants. Usually, in Doug's opinion, they are the ones who have the most problems with themselves. Remove all of the distractions, and here, in the silence and solitude, the demons they have kept at bay catch up with them.

For Doug, it is different. His demons are always with him, wherever he is. At least here they have space to roam. This place attracted him for a rather different reason, he suspects, than it does the guests. They come for its beauty – he comes for its hostility, the sheer brutality of its weather. It is at its most uncompromising now, in the midst of its long winter. A few weeks ago, up on the Munro, he saw a fox slinking through the snow, the desiccated carcass of some small creature clamped in its jaws. Its fur was thin and scabrous, its ribs showing. When it spotted him it did not bolt immediately. There was a moment when it stared back at him, hostile, challenging him to try to take its feast. He felt a kinship with it, a stronger sense of identification than he has had with any human, at least for a long time. Surviving, existing – just. Not living. That is a word for those who seek entertainment, pleasure, comfort out of each day.

He was lucky to get this job, he knows that. Not just because it suits him, his frame of mind, his desire to be as far from the rest of humanity as possible. But also because it is very likely that no one else would have had him. Not with his past. The man sent to interview him by the boss had seen the line on his record, shrugged, and said, 'Well, we definitely know you'll be good for dealing with any poachers, then. Just try not to attack any of the guests.' And then he had grinned, to show that he was joking. 'I think you'll be perfect for the job, actually.'

That had been it. He hadn't even had to try to excuse or explain himself – though there *was* no excuse, not really. A moment of violent madness? Not really: he had known exactly what he was doing.

When he thinks about that night, now, hardly any of it seems real. It seems like something glimpsed on the TV, as though he were watching his own actions from a long way away. But he remembers the anger, the punch of it in his chest, and then the brief release. That stupid, grinning face. Then the sound of something shattering. Inside his own mind? The sense of feeling himself unshackled from the codes of normal behaviour and loosed into some animal space. The feel of his fingers, gripping tightly about yielding flesh. Tighter, tighter, as though the flesh was something he was trying to mould with sheer brute force into a new, more pleasing shape. The smile finally wiped away. Then that warped sense of satisfaction, lasting for several moments before the shame arrived.

Yes, it would have been difficult to get a job doing much of anything after that.

NOW

2nd January 2019

HEATHER

A body. I stare at Doug.

No, no. This isn't right. Not here. This is my refuge, my escape. I can't be expected to deal with this, I can't, I just can't . . . With an effort of will, I stopper the flood of thoughts. You can, Heather. Because, actually, you don't have a choice.

Of course I had known it was a possibility. Very likely, even, considering the length of time missing – over twenty-four hours – and the conditions out there. They would be a challenge even to someone who knew the terrain, who had any sort of survival skills. The missing guest, as far as I know, had nothing of the sort. As the hours went by, with no sign, the probability became greater.

As soon as we knew of the disappearance we had called Mountain Rescue. The response hadn't been quite what I'd hoped for.

'At the moment,' the operator told me, 'it's looking unlikely we can get to you at all.'

'But there must be some way you can get here—'

'Conditions are too difficult. We've haven't seen anything like this amount of snow for a long time. It's a one-in-a-thousand weather event. Visibility is so poor we can't even land a chopper.'

'Are you saying that we're on our own?' As I said it I felt the full meaning of it. No help. I felt my stomach turn over.

There was a long pause at the other end of the line. I could almost hear her thinking of the best way to respond to me. 'Only as long as the snow continues like this,' she said at last. 'Soon as we have some visibility, we'll try and get out to you.'

'I need a bit more than "try",' I said.

'I hear you madam, and we'll get to you as soon as we are able. There are other people in the same situation: we have a whole team of climbers stuck on Ben Nevis, and another situation nearer Fort William. If you could just describe exactly your problem, madam, so I have all the details down.'

'The guest was last seen at the Lodge, here,' I said, 'at . . . about four a.m. yesterday morning.'

'And how big is the area?'

'The estate?' I groped for the figure learned in my first few weeks here. 'A little over fifty thousand acres.'

I heard her intake of breath in my ear. Then there was another long pause on the end of the line, so long that I almost wondered if it had gone dead, whether the snow had cut off this last connection to the outside world.

'Right,' she said, finally. 'Fifty thousand acres. Well. We'll get someone out there as soon as we can.' But her tone had changed: there was more uncertainty. I could hear a question as clearly as if she had spoken it aloud: *Even if we get to you, how can we be certain of finding someone in all that wilderness?*

For the past twenty-four hours we have searched as far as we can. It hasn't been easy, with the snow coming down like this, relentlessly. I've only been here a year, so I've never actually experienced a snow-in. We must be one of the few places in the UK – bar a few barely inhabited islands – where inclement weather can completely prohibit the access of the emergency services. We always warn the guests that they might not be able to leave the estate if conditions are bad. It's even in the waiver they have to sign. And yet it is still hard to process, the fact that no one can get in. Or out. But that's exactly the situation we find ourselves in now. Everything is clogged with snow, meaning driving's impossible – even with winter tyres, or chains – so our search has all been done on foot. It has just been Doug and me. I am beyond exhausted – both mentally and physically. We don't even have Iain, who comes most days to perform odd jobs about the place. He'll have been spending New Year's Eve with his family: stuck outside with the rest of them, no use to us. The Mountain Rescue woman was at least some help with her advice. She suggested checking first the sites that could have been used for shelter. Doug and I searched every potential hideout on the estate, the cold stinging our faces and the snow hampering our progress at every turn, until I was so tired I felt drunk.

I trudged the whole way to the station, which took me a good three hours, and checked there. Apparently there had been some talk amongst the guests of getting a train back to London.

'One of the guests has gone missing,' I told the station master, Alec. He's a hulk of a man with a saturnine face: low eyebrows. 'We're looking all over the estate.' I gave him a description of the missing guest.

'They couldn't have got on a train?' I knew it was ridiculous, but felt it had to be asked.

He laughed in my face. 'A train? In this? Are you mad, lass? Even if it weren't like this, there's no trains on New Year's Day.'

'But perhaps you saw something—'

'Haven't seen anyone,' he told me. 'Not since I saw that lot arrive a couple a days ago. No. Woulda noticed if there were a stranger pokin' about.'

'Well,' I said, 'perhaps I could have a look around?'

He spread his hands wide, a sarcastic invitation. 'Be ma guest.'

There wasn't much to search: the waiting room, a single caretaker's closet that appeared at one point to have been a toilet. And the ticket office I could see into through the window: a small, paper-strewn cubicle from which, through the money and ticket gap, came the scent of something sweetish, slightly rotten. Three crushed cans of soda decorated one corner of the desk. I saw Iain in there once with Alec, having a smoke. Iain often takes the train to collect supplies; they must have struck up something of a friendship, even if only of convenience.

Just beyond the office was a door. I opened it to discover a flight of stairs. 'That,' Alec said, 'leads up to ma flat. Ma private *residence*' – with a little flourish on 'residence'.

28

'I don't suppose—' I began. He cut me off.

'Two rooms,' he said. 'And a lavvy. Ah think Ah'd know if someone were hidin' themselves away in there.' His voice had got a little louder, and he'd moved between me and the doorway. He was too close; I could smell stale sweat.

'Yes,' I said, suddenly eager to leave. 'Of course.'

As I began my tortuous journey back towards the Lodge I turned, once, and saw him standing there, watching me leave.

Doug and I found nothing, in all the hours of searching. Not a footprint, not a strand of hair. The only tracks we came across were the small sharp impressions left by the hooves of the deer herd. The guest, it seemed, had not been active since the snow started coming down.

There's CCTV in one place on the estate: the front gate, where the long track from the Lodge heads towards the road. The boss had it put up to both deter and catch poachers. Sometimes, frustratingly, the feed cuts out. But the whole lot was there to watch this time: from the evening before – New Year's Eve – to yesterday, New Year's Day, when the guest was reported missing. I fast-forwarded through the grainy footage, looking for any sign of a vehicle. If the guest had somehow left by taxi – or even on foot – the evidence would be here. There was nothing. All it showed me was a documentation of the beginning of this heavy snowfall, as on the screen the track became obliterated by a sea of white.

Perhaps a body had begun to seem like a possibility. But the confirmation of that is something so much worse.

Doug pushes a hand through his hair, which has fallen,

snow-wet, into his eyes. As he does, I see that his hand – his arm, the whole of him – is trembling. It is a strange thing to see a man as tough-looking as Doug, built like a rugby player, in such a state. He used to be in the Marines, so he must have seen his fair share of death. But then so did I, in my old line of work. I know that it never quite leaves you, the existential horror of it. Besides, being the one to find a dead person – that is something else completely.

'I think you should come and take a look too,' he says. 'At the body.'

'Do you think that's necessary?' I don't want it to be necessary. I don't want to see. I have come all this way to escape death. 'Shouldn't we just wait for the police to get here?'

'No,' he says, 'They're not going to be able to make it for a while, are they? And I think you need to see this now.'

'Why?' I ask. I can hear how it sounds: plaintive, squeamish.

'Because,' he draws a hand over his face; the gesture tugs his eye sockets down in a ghoulish mask. 'Because . . . of the body. How it looks. I don't think it was an accident.'

I feel my skin go cold in a way that has absolutely nothing to do with the weather.

When we step outside, the snow is still coming down so thickly that you can only see a few feet from the door. The loch is almost invisible. I have shrugged on the clothes that are my de facto outdoor uniform in this place: the big, down Michelin-man jacket, my hiking boots, my red hat. I tramp after Doug, trying to keep up with his long stride, which isn't easy, because he's well over six foot, and I'm only a whisker over five. At one point I stumble; Doug shoots out a big, gloved hand to catch my arm, and hefts me back onto my feet as easily as if I were a child. Even through the down of my sleeve I can feel the strength of his fingers, like iron bands.

I'm thinking of the guests, stuck in their cabins. The inactivity must be horrible, the waiting. We had to forbid them from joining us in the search, or risk having another missing person on our hands. No one should be out in these conditions. It is the sort of weather that people die in: 'danger to life', the warnings say. But the problem is that to most of the guests, a place like this is as alien as another planet. These are people who live charmed exist-ences. Life has helped them to feel untouchable. They're so used to having that invisible safety net around them in their normal lives – connectivity, rapid emergency services, health and safety guidelines – that they assume they carry it around with them everywhere. They sign the waiver happily, because they don't really think about it. They don't believe in it. They do not expect the worst to happen to them. If they really stopped to consider it, to *understand* it, they probably wouldn't stay here at all. They'd be too scared. When you learn how isolated an environment this really is, you realise that only freaks would choose to live in a place like this. People running from something, or with nothing left to lose. People like me.

Now Doug is leading me around to the left shore of the loch, towards the trees.

'Doug?' I realise that I am whispering. It's the silence here, made more profound by the snow. It makes your voice very loud. It makes you feel as though you are under observation. That just behind that thick wall of trees,

31

perhaps, or this pervasive curtain of white, there might be someone listening. 'What makes you think it wasn't an accident?'

'You'll see when we get there,' he says. He does not bother turning back to look at me, nor does he break his stride. And then he says, over his shoulder, 'I don't "think", Heather. I know.'

Three days earlier
30th December 2018

MIRANDA

Of course, I didn't bother looking at the email Emma sent, with that brochure attached. I can never get excited about a trip in advance – just seeing photos of turquoise seas or snow-capped mountains doesn't interest me. I have to actually *be* there to feel anything, for it to be *real*. When Emma mentioned this place, the Lodge, I'd vaguely imagined something old-timey, wooden beams and flagstones. So the building itself comes as a bit of a surprise. Fucking hell. It's all modernist glass and chrome, like something out of *The Wizard of Oz*. Light spills from it. It's like a giant lantern against the darkness.

'Christ!' Julien says, when the blokes finally arrive in the Land Rover. 'It's a bit hideous, isn't it?' He would say that.

For all his intelligence, Julien has zero artistic sensibility. He's the sort of person who'll walk around a Cy Twombly exhibition saying, 'I could have drawn that when I was five,' just a *bit* too loudly. He likes to claim it's because he's a 'bit of rough': his background too grim for anything like the development of aesthetic tastes. I used to find it charming. He was different: I liked that roughness, beside all those clean-behind-the-ears public schoolboys.

'I like it,' I say. I do. It's like a spaceship has just touched down on the bank of the loch.

'So do I,' Emma says. She would say that – even if she really thinks it's hideous. Sometimes I find myself testing her, saying the *most* outrageous things, almost goading her to challenge me. She never does – she's so keen just to be accepted. All the same, she's reliable – and Katie and Samira have been AWOL of late. Emma's always up for going to the cinema, or a trip shopping, or drinks. I always suggest the venue, or the activity, she always agrees. To be honest, it's quite refreshing: Katie's so bloody busy with work it's always been me going to her, to some lousy identikit city slicker bar, just to grab three minutes of her time.

With Emma it's a bit what I imagine having a little sister would be like. I feel almost as though she is looking up to me. It gives me a rather *delicious* sense of power. Last time we went shopping I took her into Myla. 'Let's pick out something that will really make Mark's jaw fall open,' I told her. We found exactly the right set – a sweetly slutty bra, open knickers and suspender combo. I suddenly had an image of her telling Mark that it was me who helped to pick it out, and I felt an unexpected prickle of desire at the thought of him knowing that it was all my work. It's not Mark, of course, never has been. I've always found his unspoken attraction nicely ego-stroking, yes. But never a turn-on.

With Katie absent and Samira busy all the time with Priya – she is a bit obsessed with that child, it can't be healthy to share *quite* so many photos on social media – I have found myself falling back on Emma's company instead. A definite third choice.

I have been looking forward to this, to catching up with everyone. There's a security to it, how when we're together we fall back into our old roles. We can have been apart for months, and then when we're in each other's company everything is back to how it always was, almost like it was when we were at Oxford, our glory days. The person I most want to catch up with is Katie, of course. Seeing her this morning at the train station with her new hair, in clothes I didn't recognise, I realised quite how long it's been since I last saw her . . . and how much I have missed her.

Inside the Lodge, it's beautiful – but I'm glad we're only going to be having meals in here, not sleeping. The glass emphasises the contrast between the bright space in here and the dark outside. I'm suddenly aware of how visible we would be from outside, lit up like insects in a jar . . . or actors on a stage, blinded by the floodlights to the watching audience. Anyone could be out there, hidden in the blackness, looking in without our knowing.

For a moment the old dark feeling threatens to surface, that sense of being watched. The feeling I have carried with me for a decade, now, since it all began. I remind myself that the whole point is that there *is* no one out there. That we are pretty much completely alone; save for the gamekeeper and the manager – Heather – who's come in to welcome us.

Heather is early-thirties, short, prettyish – though a decent haircut and some make-up would make a vast improvement. I wonder what on earth someone like her is doing living alone in a place like this; because she does actually *live* here – she tells us that her cottage is 'just over there, a little nearer to the trees'. To be here permanently must be pretty bloody lonely. I would go completely mental with only my thoughts for company. Sometimes, on days at home, I turn on the TV *and* the radio, just to drown out the silence.

'And you,' she says to us, 'have all of the cabins nearest to the Lodge. The other guests are staying in the bunkhouse at the other end of the loch.'

'The other guests?' Emma asks. There is a taut silence. 'What other guests?'

Heather nods. 'Yes. An Icelandic couple – they arrived yesterday.'

Emma frowns. 'But I don't understand. I was certain we had the place to ourselves. That was what you told me, when we spoke. "You should have the whole place to yourselves", you said.'

Heather coughs. 'I'm afraid there has been a . . . slight misunderstanding. I did understand that to be the case, when we spoke. We don't always rent out the bunkhouse. But I'm afraid I was unaware that my colleague had booked them in and – ah – hadn't yet got around to filling it out in the register.'

The mood has definitely been killed. Just the phrase 'the other guests' has an unpleasant ring to it, a sense of infil- tration, of trespass. If we were in a hotel, that would be one thing, you'd expect to be surrounded by strangers. But the idea of these other people here in the middle of nowhere with us suddenly makes all this wilderness seem a little overcrowded.

'They'll be at the Highland Dinner tonight,' Heather says, apologetically, 'but the bunkhouse has its own kitchen, so otherwise they won't be using the Lodge at all.'

'Thank God,' Giles says.

Emma looks as cross as I have ever seen her, her hands are clenched into tight fists at her sides, the knucklebones white through the skin.

There's a sudden *Bang!* behind us. Everyone turns, to see Julien, holding a just-opened bottle of champagne, vapour rising from the neck like smoke.

'Thought this would liven up the gloom a bit,' he says. The liquid foams out of the top of the bottle and splashes onto the carpet by his feet: Bo holds out a glass to rescue some. 'Hey, who knows . . . maybe the other guests will be fun. Maybe they'll want to come and celebrate New Year's Eve with us tomorrow.'

I can't think of anything worse than some randoms coming and spoiling our party; I'm sure Julien can't, either. But this is his Mr-Nice-Guy act. He always wants so badly to be liked, to seem fun, for other people to think well of him. I suppose that is one of the things I fell in love with.

Heather has helped Emma bring glasses from the kitchen. The others take them, smiling again, drawn by the sense of occasion that has just been created by the champagne. I feel a rush of warmth. It's so good to see them again. It has been too long. It's so special, these days, all being together like this. Samira and Katie are either side of me. I hug them to me. 'The three musketeers,' I whisper. The innermost ring of the inner circle. I don't even mind when

I hear Samira swear, softly – my hug has jolted her into spilling a little champagne on her shirt.

I see that Julien's offering Heather a glass, even though you can tell she doesn't want one. For goodness' sake. We had a tiny bit of a disagreement over the champagne yesterday, in the vintner's. Twelve bottles of Dom Pérignon: over a grand's worth of champagne. 'Why couldn't you just have got Moët,' I asked him, 'like a normal person?'

'Because you would have complained. Last time you told me it gave you a headache, because of "all the sugar" added in the standard brands. Only the finest stuff for Miranda Adams.'

Talk about pot calling bloody kettle black. It always has to be a bit extra with him, that's the thing. A bit more extravagance, a bit more cash. A hunger to have more than his fair share . . . and his job hasn't helped with that. If in doubt, throw money at it: that is Julien's go-to solution. Fine . . . mine too, if I'm being completely honest. I often like to joke that we bring out the worst in each other. But it's probably truer than I let on.

I let him buy the bloody champagne. I know how much he wants to forget the stress of this year.

As I expected, the woman, Heather, isn't drinking it. She's taken one tiny sip, to be polite, and put it back down on the tray. I imagine she thinks it's unprofessional to have more than that, and she's right. So, thanks to Julien's 'generosity' we're going to be left with a wasted glass, tainted by this stranger's spit.

Heather runs us through arrangements for the weekend. We're going deer-stalking tomorrow: 'Doug will be taking you, he'll come and collect you early in the morning.'

Doug. I'm rather fascinated by him. I could tell he didn't

like us much. I could also tell that I made him uncomfortable. That knowledge is a kind of power.

Giles is asking Heather something about walking routes now. She takes out an OS map and spreads it across the coffee table.

'You have lots of options,' she's saying. 'It really depends on what you're looking for – and what sort of equipment you've brought. Some people have arrived with all the gear: ice picks, crampons and carabiners.'

'Er, I'm not sure that's really us,' Bo says, grinning. Too bloody right.

'Well, if you want something very sedate, there's the path around the loch, of course' – she traces it on the map with a finger – 'it's a few miles, completely flat. There are a few waterfalls – but they have sturdy bridges over them, so there's nothing to tax you too much. You could practically do it in the dark. At the other end of the scale you've got the Munro, which you may be interested in if you're planning on "bagging" one.'

'What do you mean?' Julien asks.

'Oh,' she says, 'like a trophy, I suppose. That's what it's called when you climb one. You claim it.'

'Oh yes,' he says, with a quick grin. 'Of course – maybe I did know that.' No, he didn't. But Julien doesn't like to be shown up. Even if he has no artistic sensibilities to speak of, appearances are important to my husband. The face you present to the world. What other people think of you. I know that better than anyone.

'Or,' she says, 'you could do something in the middle. There's the hike up to the Old Lodge, for example.'

'The *Old* Lodge?' Bo asks.

'Yes. The original lodge burned down just under a century ago. Almost everything went. So not a *great* deal to see, but it makes a good point to aim for, and there are fantastic views over the estate.'

'Can't imagine anyone survived that?' Giles says.

'No,' she says. 'Twenty-four people died. No one survived apart from a couple of the stable hands, who slept in the stable block with the animals. One of the old stable blocks is still there, but it's probably not structurally sound: you shouldn't go too near it.'

'And no one knows what started it?' Bo asks. We're all ghoulishly interested – you could hear a pin drop in here – but he looks genuinely alarmed, his glance flitting to the roaring log fire in the grate. He's such a city boy. I bet the nearest Bo normally gets to a real fire is a flaming sambuca shot.

'No,' Heather says. 'We don't know. Perhaps a fire left unattended in one of the grates. But there is a theory . . .' Heather pauses, as if not sure she should continue, then goes on. 'There's a theory that one of the staff, a game-keeper, was so damaged by his experiences in the war that he set fire to the building on purpose. A kind of murder–suicide. They say the fire could be seen as far away as Fort William. It took more than a day for help to come . . . by which time it was too late.'

'That's fucked-up,' Mark says, and grins.

I notice that Heather does not look impressed by Mark's grin. She's probably wondering how on earth someone could be amused by the idea of two dozen people burning to death. You have to know Mark pretty well to understand that he has a fairly dark – but on the whole harmless – sense of humour. You learn to forgive him for it. Just like we've all learned that Giles – while he likes to seem like Mr Easy-going – can be a bit tight when it comes to buying the next round . . . and not to speak to Bo until he's had at least two cups of coffee in the morning. Or how Samira, all sweetness and light on the surface, can hold a grudge like no one else. That's the thing about old friends. You just know these things about them. You have learned to love them. This is the glue that binds us together. It's like family, I suppose. All that history. We know everything there is to know about one another.

Heather pulls a clipboard from under her arm, all business, suddenly. 'Which one of you is Emma Taylor? I've got your credit card down as the one that paid the deposit.'

'That's me.' Emma raises a hand.

'Great. You should find all the ingredients you've asked for in the fridge. I have the list here. Beef fillet, unshucked oysters – Iain got them from Mallaig this morning – smoked salmon, smoked mackerel, caviar, endive, Roquefort, walnuts, one hundred per cent chocolate, eighty five per cent chocolate, quails' eggs'– she pauses to take a breath 'double cream, potatoes, on-vine tomatoes . . .'

Christ. My own secret contribution to proceedings suddenly looks rather meagre. I try to catch Katie's eye to share an amused look. But I haven't seen her for so long that I suppose we're a bit out of sync. She's just staring out of the big windows, apparently lost in thought.

EMMA

I check the list. I don't think they've got the right tomatoes – they're not baby ones – but I can probably make do. It could be worse. I suppose I'm a bit particular about my cooking: I got into it at university, and it's been a passion of mine ever since.

'Thank you,' Heather says, as I hand the list back.

'Where'd you get all this stuff?' Bo asks. 'Can't be many shops around here?'

'No. Iain went and got most of it from Inverness and brought it back on the train – it was easier.'

'But why bother having a train station?' Giles asks. 'I know we got off there, but there can't be many people using it otherwise?'

'No,' she says. 'Nor have there ever. It's a funny story, that one. The laird, in the nineteenth century, insisted that the rail company build the station, when they came to him with a proposal to put a track through his land.'

'It must have been almost like his own private platform,' Nick says.

The woman smiles. 'Yes, and no. Because there were some . . . unintended consequences. This is whisky country. And there was a great deal of illegal distilling going on back in the day – and robbery from the big distilleries. The old Glencorrin plant, for example, is pretty nearby. Before the railway, the smugglers around here had to rely on wagons, which were very slow, and very likely to be stopped on the long journey down south by the authorities. But the train was another matter. Suddenly, they could get their product down to London in a day. Legend has it that some of the train guards were in their pay, ready to turn a blind eye when necessary. And some' – she stops, poised for the *coup de grâce* – 'say that the old laird himself was in on it, that he had planned it from the day he asked for his railway station.' She sits forward. 'If you're interested, there are whisky bothies all over the estate. They're marked on the map. Discovering them is something of a hobby of mine.'

Over the top of her head, I see Julien roll his eyes. But Nick is intrigued. 'What do you mean?' he asks. 'They haven't all been found? How many are there?'

'Oh, we're not sure. Every time I think I must have discovered the last one, I come across another. Fifteen in total at the last count. They're very cleverly made, small cairns really, built out of the rocks, covered with gorse and heather. Unless you're right on top of them they're practically invisible. They disappear into the hillside. I could show you a couple if you like.'

'Yes please,' Katie says – at the same time as Julien says, 'No thanks.' There is a slightly awkward pause.

'Well,' Heather gives a small, polite smile, but there's a flash of steel in the look she gives Julien. 'It's not compulsory, of course.'

I have the impression that she may not be quite as sweet and retiring as she looks. Good on her. Julien gets away with a little too much, as far as I'm concerned. People seem prepared to let him act as he likes, partly because he's so good-looking, and partly because he can turn on the charm like throwing a switch. Often he does the latter after he's just said something particularly controversial, or cruel – so that he can immediately take the sting out of it . . . make you think that he can't really mean it.

This might sound like sour grapes. After all, Mark is always blundering around offending people just by being himself: laughing inappropriately, or making jokes in bad taste. I know who most people would prefer to have dinner with. But at least Mark is, in his way, authentic – even if that sometimes means authentically dull (I am not blind to his faults). Julien is so much *surface*. It has made me wonder what's going on beneath.

My thoughts are interrupted by Bo. 'This is incredible,' he says, staring about. It *is*. It's better than any of the places anyone else has picked in the last few years, no question. I feel myself relax properly for the first time all day, and allow myself just to enjoy being here, to be proud of my work in finding it.

The room we're standing in is the living room: two huge, squashy sofas and a selection of armchairs, beautiful old rugs on the floor, a vast fireplace with a stack of freshly-chopped wood next to it – 'We use peat with the wood,' Heather says, 'to give it a nice smokiness.' The upper bookshelves are stuffed with antiquarian books, emerald and red spines embossed with gold, and the lower with all the old board-game classics: Monopoly, Scrabble, Twister, Cluedo.

On the inner wall – the outer wall being made entirely of glass – are mounted several stags' heads. The shadows thrown by their antlers are huge, as though cast by old dead trees. The glass eyes have the effect some paintings have; they seem to follow you wherever you go, staring balefully down. I see Katie look at them and shiver.

You'd think that the modernist style of the building wouldn't work with the homey interior, but, somehow, it does. In fact, the exterior glass seems to melt away so that it's as though there is no barrier between us and the land-scape outside. It's as though you could simply walk from the rug straight into the loch, huge and silver in the evening light, framed by that black staccato of trees. It's all perfect.

'Right,' Heather says, 'I'm going to leave you now, to get settled in. I'll let you decide which of the cottages suits each of you best.'

As she begins to walk away she stops dead, and turns on her heel. She smacks a palm against her head, a panto-mime of forgetfulness. 'It must be the champagne,' she says, though I hardly think so; she has only had a couple of sips. 'There are a couple of very important safety things I should say to you. We ask that if you are planning on going for a hike beyond our immediate surroundings – the loch, say – you let us know. It may look benign out there, but at this time of year the state of play can change within hours, sometimes minutes.'

'In what way?' Bo asks. This all must be very alien for him: I once heard him say he lived in New York for five years with only one trip out of the city, because he 'didn't want to miss anything'. I don't think he's one for the great outdoors.

'Snowstorms, sudden fogs, a rapid drop in temperature. It's what makes this landscape so exciting . . . but also lethal, if it chooses to be. If a storm should come in, say, we want to know whether you are out hiking, or whether you are safe in your cottages. And,' she grimaces slightly, 'we've had a *little* trouble with poachers in the past—'

'That sounds pretty Victorian,' Julien says.

Heather raises an eyebrow. 'Well, these people unfortunately *aren't*. These aren't your old romantic folk heroes taking one home for the pot. They carry stalking equipment and hunting rifles. Sometimes they work in the day, wearing the best camouflage gear money can buy. Sometimes they work at night. They're not doing it for fun. They sell the meat on the black market to restauranteurs, or the antlers on eBay, or abroad. There's a big market in Germany. We have CCTV on the main gate to the property now, so that's helped, but it hasn't prevented them getting in.'

'Should we be worried?' Samira asks.

'Oh, no,' Heather says quickly, perhaps realising for the first time how all of this might sound to guests who have come for the unthreatening peace and quiet of the Scottish Highlands. 'No, not at all. We haven't actually had any proper poaching incidents for . . . a while, now. Doug is very much on the case. I just wanted you to be aware. If you see anyone you do not recognise on the estate, let either of us know. Do not approach them.'

I can feel how all this talk of peril has dampened the atmosphere slightly. 'We haven't toasted being here,' I say, quickly, seizing my champagne glass. 'Cheers!' I clash it against Giles's, with slightly too much force, and he jumps back to avoid the spillage. Then he gets the idea, turns to Miranda, and does the same. It seems to work: a little chain reaction is set off around the room, the familiarity of the ritual raising smiles. Reminding us of the fact that we are celebrating. That it is good – no, wonderful – to be here.

KATIE

There's no point in my expressing any preference over which cabin I get. I am the singleton of the group, and it's been tacitly agreed by all that my cabin should be the smallest of the lot. There's a bit of good-natured wrangling over who is going to get which of the others. One is slightly bigger than the rest, and Samira – probably rightly – thinks that she and Giles should have it, because of Priya. And then both Nick and Miranda clearly want the one with the best view of the loch – I suspect for a moment that Nick is saying so just to rile Miranda, but then he defers, graciously. Everyone is on best behaviour.

'Let's go for a walk now,' Miranda says, once it's all decided. 'Explore a bit.'

'But it's completely dark,' Samira says.

'Well, that will make it even better. We can take some of the champagne down to the loch.'

This is classic Miranda. Anyone else would be content simply to lounge in the Lodge until dinner, but she's always looking for adventure. When she first came into my life, some twenty years ago, everything instantly became more exciting.

'I have to put Priya to bed,' Samira says, glancing over to where the baby has fallen asleep in her carrier. 'It's late for her already.'

'Fine,' Miranda says, offhandedly, with barely a glance in Samira's direction.

I don't know if she sees Samira's wounded look. For most of today Miranda has acted as though Priya is a piece of excess baggage. I remember, a couple of years ago, her talk of 'when Julien and I have kids'. I haven't seen her enough lately, so I'm not sure whether her indifference is genuine or masking some real personal suffering. Miranda has always been a champion bluffer.

The rest of us – including Giles – traipse outside into the dark. Samira gives him a look as she stalks off towards their cabin – presumably he, too, was meant to go and help with Priya's bedtime. It's probably the closest I've ever seen them come to a disagreement. They're such a perfect couple, those two – so respectful, so in sync, so loving – it's almost sickening.

We walk, stumbling over the uneven ground, down the path towards the water, Bo, Julien and Emma using the torches provided in the Lodge to light the way. In the warmth indoors I'd forgotten how brutal it is outside. It's so cold it feels as though the skin on my face is shrinking against my skull, in protest against the raw air. Someone grabs my arm and I jump, then realise it's Miranda.

'Hello, stranger,' she says. 'It's so good to see you. God I've missed you.' It's so unusual for her to make that sort of admission – and there is something in the way she says it, too. I glance at her, but it's too dark to make out her expression.

'You too,' I say.

'And you've had your hair cut differently, haven't you?' I feel her hand come up to play with the strands framing my face. It is all I can do not to prickle away from her. Miranda has always been touchy-feely – I have always been whatever the opposite of that is.

'Yes,' I say, 'I went to Daniel Galvin, like you told me to.'

'Without me?'

'Oh – I didn't think. I suddenly had a spare couple of hours . . . we'd closed on something earlier than expected.'

'Well,' she says, 'next time you go, let me know, OK? We'll make a date of it. It's like you've fallen off the planet lately.' She lowers her voice. 'I've had to resort to Emma . . . God, Katie, she's so nice it does my nut in.'

'Sorry,' I say, 'it's just that I've been so busy at work. You know, trying for partnership.'

'But it won't always be like that, will it?'

'No,' I say, 'I don't think so.'

'Because I've been thinking, recently . . . remember how it used to be? In our twenties? We'd see each other every week, you and I, without fail. Even if it was just to go out and get drunk on Friday night.'

I nod. I'm not sure she can see though. 'Yes,' I say – my voice comes out a little hoarse.

'Oh God, and the night bus? Both of us falling asleep and going to the end of the line . . . Kingston, wasn't it? And that time we went to that twenty-four-hour Tesco and you suddenly decided you had to make an omelette when you got home and you dropped that carton of eggs and it went everywhere – I mean *everywhere* – and we just decided to run off, in our

51

big stupid heels . . .' She laughs, and then she stops. 'I miss all of that . . . that *messiness*.' There's so much wistfulness in her tone. I'm glad I can't see her expression now.

'So do I,' I say.

'Look at you two,' Julien turns back to us. 'Thick as thieves. What are you gossiping about?'

'Come on,' Giles says, 'share with the rest of us!'

'Well,' Miranda says quickly, leaning into me, 'I'm glad we have this – to catch up. I've really missed you, K.' She gives my arm a little squeeze and, again, I think I hear the tiniest catch in her voice. A pins-and-needles prickling of guilt; I've been a bad friend.

And then she transforms, producing a new bottle of champagne from under her arm and yelling to the others, 'Look what I've got!'

There are whoops and cheers. Giles does a silly dance of delight; he's like a little boy, letting off pent-up energy. And it seems to be infectious . . . suddenly everyone is making a lot of noise, talking excitedly, voices echoing in the empty landscape.

Then Emma stops short in front of us, with a quiet exclamation. 'Oh!'

I see what's halted her. There's a figure standing on the jetty that we're heading for, silhouetted by moonlight. He is quite tall, and standing surprisingly, almost inhumanly, still. The gamekeeper, I think. He's about the right height. Or maybe one of the other guests we've just heard about?

Bo casts his torch up at the figure, and we wait for the man to turn, or at least move. And then Bo begins to laugh. Now we see what he has. It isn't a man at all. It's a statue of a man, staring out contemplatively, Antony Gormley-esque.

* * *

We all sit down on the jetty and look out across the loch. Every so often there's a tiny disturbance in the surface, despite there being very little wind. The ripples must be caused by something underneath, the glassy surface withholding these secrets.

Despite the champagne, everyone suddenly seems a bit subdued. Perhaps it's just the enormity of our surroundings – the vast black peaks rising in the distance, the huge stretch of night sky above, the pervasive quiet – that has awed us into silence.

The quiet isn't *quite* all-pervasive, though. Sitting here for long enough you begin to hear other sounds: rustles and scufflings in the undergrowth, mysterious liquid echoes from the loch. Heather told us about the giant pike that live in it – their existence confirmed by the monstrous one mounted on the wall of the Lodge. Huge jaws, sharp teeth, like leftover Jurassic monsters.

I hear the *shush-shush* of the tall Scots pines above us, swaying in the breeze, and every so often a soft thud: a gust strong enough to disturb a cargo of old snow. Somewhere, quite near, there is the mournful call of an owl. It's such a recognisable yet strange sound that it's hard to believe it's real, not some sort of special effect.

Giles tries to echo the sound: '*Ter-wit, ter-woo!*'

We all laugh, dutifully, but it strikes me that there's something uneasy in the sound. The call of the owl, such an unusual noise for city dwellers like us, has just emphasised quite how unfamiliar this place is.

'I didn't even know there were places like this in the UK,' Bo says, as if he can read my thoughts.

'Ah Bo,' Miranda says, 'you're such a Yank. It's not all London and little chocolate box villages here.'

'I didn't realise you got outside the M25 much yourself, Miranda,' Nick says.

'Oi!' She punches his arm. 'I do, occasionally. We went to Soho Farmhouse before Christmas, didn't we Julien?' We all laugh – including Miranda. People think she can't laugh at herself, but she can . . . just as long as she doesn't come out of it looking *too* bad.

'Come on, open that bottle, Manda,' Bo says.

'Yes . . . open it, open it—' Giles begins to shout, and everyone joins in . . . it's almost impossible not to. It becomes a chant, something oddly tribal in it. I'm put in mind of some pagan sect; the effect of the landscape, probably – mysterious and ancient.

Miranda stands up and fires the cork into the loch, where it makes its own series of ripples, widening out in shining rings across the water. We drink straight from the bottle, passing it around like Girl Guides, the cold, densely fizzing liquid stinging our throats.

'It's like Oxford,' Mark says. 'Sitting down by the river, getting pissed after finals at three p.m.'

'Except then it was cava,' Miranda says. 'Christ – we drank gallons of that stuff. How did we not notice that it tastes like vomit?'

'And there was that party you held down by the river,' Mark says. 'You two' – he gestures to Miranda and me – 'and Samira.'

'Oh yes,' Giles says. 'What was the theme again?'

'*The Beautiful and Damned*,' I say. Everyone had to come in twenties' gear, so we could all pretend we were Bright Young Things, like Evelyn Waugh and friends. God, we were pretentious. The thought of it is like reading an old diary entry, cringeworthy . . . but fond, too. Because it *was* a wonderful evening, even magical. We'd lit candles and put them in lanterns, all along the bank. Everyone had gone to so much effort with their costumes, and they were universally flattering: the girls in spangled flappers and the boys in black tie. Miranda looked the most stunning, of course, in a long metallic sheath. I remember a drunken moment of complete euphoria, looking about the party. How had little old me ended up at a place like this? With all these people as my friends? And most particularly with that girl – so glamorous, so *radiant* – as my best friend?

As we walk back towards the lights of the Lodge and the cabins, I spot another statue, a little way to our left, silhouetted in the light thrown from the sauna building. This one is facing away from the loch, towards us. It gives me the same uncanny little shock that the other did; I suppose this is exactly the effect they are meant to achieve.

The privacy of my cabin is a welcome respite. We've spent close to eight hours in each other's company now. Mine is the furthest away from the Lodge on this side, just beyond the moss-roofed sauna. It's also the smallest. Neither of these things particularly bothers me. I linger over my unpacking, though I've brought very little with me. The aftertaste of the champagne is sour on my tongue now, I can feel what little I drank listing in my stomach. I have a drink of water. Then I take a long, hot bath in the freestanding metal tub in the bathroom using the organic bath oil provided, which creates a thick aromatherapeutic fug of rosemary and geranium. There's a high window facing towards the loch, though the view out is half-obscured by a wild growth of ivy, like something from a pre-Raphaelite painting. It's also high enough that someone could look in and watch me in the bath for a while before I noticed them – if I ever did. I'm not sure why that has occurred to me – especially as there's hardly anyone here to look – but once the thought is in my mind I can't seem to get rid of it. I draw the little square of linen across the view. As I do I catch sight of my reflection in the mirror above the sink. The light isn't good, but I think I look terrible: pale and ill, my eyes dark pits.

I'll admit, I half-wondered about not coming this year. Just pretending I hadn't seen the email from Emma in my inbox until it was 'too late' to do anything about it. A sudden, rebellious thought: Perhaps I've done my part? I could just stay hidden here for the three days, and the others would make enough noise and drama without actually noticing that I had disappeared. Nick and Bo and Samira are loud enough when they get going, but Miranda can make enough noise and drama for an entire party on her *own*.

Of course, it would help that I'm known as the quiet one. The observer, melting into the background. That was the dynamic when we lived together, Miranda, Samira and me. They were the performers, I their audience.

If you told all this to the people I work with I reckon they'd be surprised. I'm one of the more senior associates at the firm now. I'm hopefully not far off making partner. People listen to what I say. I give presentations, I'm pretty comfortable with the sound of my own voice, ringing out in a silent meeting room. I like the feeling, in fact . . . seeing the faces upturned towards me, listening carefully to what I have to say. I command respect. I run a whole team. And I have found that I like being in charge. I suppose we all carry around different versions of ourselves.

With this group I have always been an also-ran. People

have often wondered, I'm sure, what someone like me is doing with a friend like Miranda. But in friendship, as in love, opposites often attract. Extrovert and introvert, yin and yang.

It would be very easy to dislike Miranda. She has been blessed by the Gods of beauty and fortune. She has the sort of absurd figure you see held up as a 'bad, unrealistic example to young girls' – as though she has been personally Photoshopped. It doesn't really seem fair that someone so thin should have breasts that size; aren't they made up largely of fat? And the thick, infuriatingly shiny blonde hair, and green eyes . . . no one in real life seems to have properly green eyes, except Miranda. She is the sort of person you would immediately assume was probably a bitch. Which she can be, absolutely.

The thing is, beneath her occasionally despotic ways, Miranda can be very kind. There was the time my parents' marriage was falling apart, for example – when I had a standing invitation to stay at her house whenever I felt like it, to escape the shouting matches at home. Or when my sixth-form boyfriend, Matt, dumped me unceremoniously for the prettier, more popular Freya, and Miranda not only lent me a shoulder to cry on, but put about the rumour that he had chlamydia. Or when I couldn't afford a dress for the college Summer Ball and, without making a thing of it at all, she gave me one of hers: a column of silver silk.

When I opened my eyes at one point on the train journey up here I caught Miranda watching me. Those green eyes of hers. So sharp, so assessing. A slight frown, as though she was trying to work something out. I pretended to sleep again, quickly. Sometimes I genuinely believe that Miranda has known me for so long that somewhere along the way she might have acquired the ability to read my mind, if she looks hard enough.

We go back even further than the rest of the group, she and I. All the way back to a little school in Sussex. The two new girls. One already golden, the sheen of money on her – she'd been moved from a private school nearby as her parents wanted her 'to strive' (and they thought a comprehensive education would help her chances of getting into Oxford). The other girl mousey-haired, too thin in her large uniform bought from the school's second-hand collection. The golden girl (already popular, within the first morning) taking pity on her, insisting they sit next to each other at assembly. Making her her project, making her feel accepted, less alone.

I never knew why it was that she chose me to be her best friend. Because she *did* choose me: I had very little to do with it. But then she has always liked to do the unexpected thing, has Miranda, has always liked to challenge other people's expectations of her. The other girls were lining up to be her friend, I still remember that. All that hair – so blonde and shiny it didn't look quite real. Eyelashes so long she was once told off by a teacher for wearing mascara: the injustice! Real breasts – at twelve. She was good at sport, clever but not *too* clever (though at an all-girls' school, academic prowess is not quite the handicap it is at a mixed one).

The other girls couldn't understand it. Why would she be friends with me when she could have them, any of them? There had to be something weird about her, if her taste in people was so 'off'. She could have ruled that school like a queen. But because of this, her friendship with me, she was probably never quite as popular as she might have been. But that didn't matter to the boys at the parties we began to go to in our teens. *I* never got the invites to houses of pupils from the boys' grammar up the road, or parties on the beach. Miranda could have left me behind then. But she took me with her.

When I think of this, I feel all the more ashamed. This feeling is the same one I used to get when I stayed over at her beautiful Edwardian house and was tempted to take some little trophy home for myself. Something small, something she'd hardly notice: a hairclip, or a pair of lace-trimmed socks. Just so I'd have something pretty to look at in my little beige bedroom in my dingy two-up two-down with stains on the walls and broken blinds.

There's a knock on the front door at about eight: Nick and Bo, thank God. For a moment I had thought it might be Miranda. Nick and I met in freshers' week, and have been friends ever since. He was there through all the ups and downs of uni.

The two of them come in, checking out the place. 'Your cabin is just like ours,' Nick says, when I let them in, 'except a bit smaller. And a *lot* tidier . . . Bo has already covered the whole place with his stuff.'

'Hey,' Bo says. 'Just because I don't travel with only three versions of the same outfit.'

It's not even an exaggeration. Nick's one of those people who have a self-imposed uniform: a crisp white shirt, those dark selvedge jeans, and chukka boots. Maybe a smart blazer, and always, of course, his signature tortoiseshell Cutler and Gross glasses. Somehow he makes it work. On him it's stylish, authoritative – whereas on a lesser mortal it might seem a bit plain.

We sit down together on the collection of squashy armchairs in front of the bed.

Bo sniffs the air. 'Smells amazing in here, too. What is that?'

'I had a bath.'

'Oh, I thought that oil looked nice. Don't do things by halves here, do they? Emma's really knocked it out of the park. It's awesome.'

'Yes,' I say, 'it is.' But it doesn't come out quite as enthusiastically as I'd meant it to.

'Are you all right?' Nick jostles me with his shoulder. 'I hope you don't mind my saying this, but you seem a bit . . . off. Ever since this morning. You know, that thing on the train earlier, with you being put in the other carriage, I'm sure it wasn't intentional. If it had been Miranda, that would be a different story . . .' He raises his eyebrows at Bo, and Bo nods in agreement. 'I wouldn't necessarily make the same assumption. But it was Emma. I just don't think she's like that.'

'I'm not sure she's my biggest fan, though.' Emma's so decent, and I've wondered in the past if it's that she's seen something she doesn't like in me and recoiled from it.

Bo frowns. 'What makes you say that?'

'I suppose it's just a feeling . . .'

'I really wouldn't take it so personally,' Nick says.

'No,' I say. 'Maybe it's just that I haven't seen everyone in such a long time. And I shouldn't drink in the day – it always makes me feel weird. Especially when I haven't had enough to eat.'

'Totally,' Bo nods. But Nick doesn't say anything. He's just looking at me.

Then he asks, 'Is there something else?'

'No,' I say. 'No, there isn't.'

'You sure?'

I nod my head.

'Well, come on then,' Nick says, 'let's go fuel you up at this dinner. There better be at least some combination of bagpipes, venison, and kilts, otherwise I'm going to ask for my money back.'

Nick, Bo and I walk over to the Lodge for the dinner, arm in arm. Nick smells, as ever, of citrus and perhaps a hint of incense. It's such a familiar, comforting scent that I want to bury my face in his shoulder and tell him what's on my mind.

I was a bit in love with Nick Manson at Oxford, at first. I think most of my seminar group was. He was beautiful, but in a new, grown-up way entirely different from every other first-year male – so many of them still acne-plagued and gawky, or completely unable to talk to girls. His was a much more sophisticated beauty to, say, Julien's gym-honed handsomeness. Nick might have been beamed in from another planet, which in a way he had. He'd taken the baccalaureate in Paris (his parents were diplomats) where he had also learned fluent French and a fondness for Gitanes cigarettes. Nick laughs now at how pretentious he was – but most undergraduates were pretentious back then . . . only his version seemed authentic, justified.

He came out to a select few friends in the middle of our second year. It wasn't exactly a surprise. He hadn't gone out with any of the girls who threw themselves at him with embarrassing eagerness, so there had perhaps been a bit of a question mark there. I had chosen not to see it, as I had my own explanation for his apparent celibacy: he was saving himself for the right woman.

It was a bit of a blow, his coming out, I'm not going to pretend otherwise. My crush on him had had all the intensity that one at that age often does. But over time I learned to love him as a friend.

When he met Bo he fell off the radar. Suddenly I saw and heard a lot less of him. It was hard not to feel resentful. Of Nick, for dropping me – because that's how it felt at the time. Of Bo, as the usurper. And then Bo had his issues. He was an addict, or still is, as he puts it, just one who never takes drugs any more. Nick became pretty much his full-time carer for a few years. I suspect Bo resented me in turn, as a close friend of Nick's. I think now he's more secure of himself and their relationship these days . . . or perhaps we've all just grown up a bit. Even so, with Bo, I sometimes feel as though I'm overdoing things a bit. Being a little too ingratiating. Because if I'm totally honest I still feel that with his neediness – because he *is* needy, even now – he's the reason Nick and I aren't such good friends any more. We're close, yes. But nothing like we once were.

It's even cooler now; our mingled breath clouds the air. There are ribbons of mist hanging over the loch, but around us the air is very clear, and when I look up it's as though the cold has somehow sharpened the light of the stars. As we stumble along the path to the Lodge, I happen to look over towards the sauna, where I saw the second statue, earlier, the one that had been facing towards us. But, funny thing, though I search for it in the light thrown from the building, assuming it must be hidden in shadow, I can't see it. The statue is gone.

NOW
2nd January 2019

HEATHER

As I tramp through the snow, trying to step in Doug's big footprints, I'm thinking of the guests, sitting about in their cabins and wondering: not knowing yet.

Unless . . . I push the thought away. I can't let my mind race to conclusions. But if Doug is right, there's something more sinister at play. And something had gone wrong between them all, that was clear. There had been a 'disagreement', that was how they all put it when they came to tell me about the disappearance.

It would be easy to say, with hindsight, that I had a sense of foreboding three days ago, when they all arrived. I didn't see this coming. But I did feel *something*.

My Jamie was fascinated by the idea of the 'lizard brain'.

Maybe it was something to do with his job. He saw people on the edge, acting purely on instinct: the father who ran from a burning house before saving his children, or, conversely, the one who shielded his wife and baby from a blaze and suffered third-degree burns over half of his body. It's all down to the amygdala – a tiny nodule, hidden amongst the little grey cells, the root of our most instinctive actions. It's behind the selfish urge to grab for the biggest cookie, the comfiest seat. It's what alerts you to danger, before you even consciously know of a threat. Without it, a laboratory mouse will run straight into the jaws of a cat.

Jamie believed that people are basically civilised animals. That the essential urges are hidden beneath a layer of social gloss; stifled, controlled. But at times of even fairly minor stress, the animal within has a go at breaking through. Once he was stuck just outside Edinburgh on a train for four hours, because of an electrical fault. 'You saw straight away which people would eat you,' he told me, 'without any hesitation, if you were stuck on a lifeboat together. There was a man who was hammering on the driver's cabin after only a few minutes, bright red in the face. He was like a caged animal. He looked at the rest of us like he was just waiting for one of us to tell him to shut up . . . then he'd have an excuse to lose it completely.'

That's the thing, you see. Some people, given just the right amount of pressure, taken out of their usual, comfortable environments, don't need much encouragement at all to become monsters. And sometimes you just get a strong sense about people, and you can't explain it; you simply know it, in some deeper part of yourself. That's the lizard brain, too.

So I find myself, now, returning to three days ago, the evening they all arrived. My first, animal impressions.

The Highland Dinner on the first night of the stay is one of the promises made by the brochure. But every time we host it, I think the guests would be quite happy to do without. It always seems to take on the atmosphere of an enforced occasion, like a state dinner. I'm sure it's just another means of extracting money from them. The mark-up on the food, even accounting for the fact that the 'best local ingredients' are used, is huge. I've also wondered if it's a way of keeping the community onside, because local lads and lasses are employed as the waiting staff, and all the ingredients are bought from nearby suppliers; save the venison, which comes from here.

I have read the headlines from when the boss first bought the place – from the family who had owned it for genera-tions – articles complaining about the 'elitist prices', the 'barring of local people from their own land' – there's a right to roam in the Highlands, which the old laird had always upheld, but the boss had fences and threatening signs put up. He claims they are to deter poachers but, funny thing, apparently that wasn't so much of a problem under the previous owner. Maybe the poachers hadn't got themselves organised, weaponised, hadn't realised the healthy demand for venison and mounted stags' heads. But I think there might be another angle to the deer killings that happen now. In the vein of a lesson taught, something taken back.

Once, in our nearest shop in Kinlochlaggan (still over an hour away), I happened to tell the shopkeeper where it was that I worked. 'You seem nice enough, lass,' she said, 'but it's a nasty place. Foreign money.' (By which she meant, I presume, the boss's Englishness, and the fact that the guests often come up from England, or from further afield.) 'One of these days,' she told me, 'they'll pay the proper price for keeping people from what's theirs.' I remembered then the theory I'd heard about the Old Lodge, the one I don't tell guests: that the fire hadn't been started by the game-keeper, but by a disgruntled local, slighted by the laird.

If the Highland Dinner is meant to stem this ill will towards the place, I'm not sure it has worked. If anything, the waiting staff probably return home with tales of the guests' bad behaviour. I remember a stag party where a drunk – but not that drunk – best man groped a very young waitress as she bent to retrieve a dropped napkin. Guests have passed out in their plates, succumbing to too much of the Glencorrin single malt. Some have vomited at the table, in full view of the staff.

The London group of guests would be better behaved than the stag party, I was sure. There was a baby among them, so surely that meant something, even if the parents weren't joining us (the mother had asked for their food to be brought to them in their cabin). That left seven of them. The dark-haired man, the tall blonde. Julien and Miranda. A perfectly matched pair, the most beautiful, even the poshest names of the lot. Then there was the thin, sleek, auburn-haired man with the architect's glasses – Nick – and his American boyfriend, Bo. The third couple: Mark, and Emma. He might almost have been good-looking, but his eyes were too close together, like a small predator's, and his top half was disproportionately heavy, lending him the unnatural appearance of an action figure. I found myself thinking she was like a budget version of the taller blonde; dark hair at the roots, a roll of flesh showing at the top of her jeans where her top had ridden up. I was surprised at myself. I'm not, as a rule, a judgemental person. But even if you don't have much interaction with other human beings – as I do not – it turns out that the instinct to judge one another, that basic human trait, does not leave us. And the resemblance was un-ignorable. Her hair was dyed the same shade, the clothes were of a type, and she'd even made up her eyes in the same way, little flecks of black at the corners. While they made her friend's eyes look large and catlike, they only served to emphasise the smallness of her own.

Then there was the last one, Katie. The odd one out. I almost missed her at first. She was standing so still, so quiet, in the shadows at the corner of the room – almost as though she wanted to disappear into them. She didn't match the others, somehow. Her skin was sallow, and there were large purple shadows beneath her eyes. Her clothes were too formal, as though she were going on a business trip and had turned up here by mistake.

Normally, though I have to learn the names, I prefer to *think* of the people who stay here as simply the 'guests': guest 1, guest 2, et cetera. I'd prefer not to think of them as individual people with lives outside this place. Perhaps this sounds odd. I suppose I could argue it's a survival tactic. Don't get involved in their lives. Don't let their happiness – or otherwise – touch you. Don't compare yourself to their wholeness, those couples who come for a romantic retreat, the happy families.

The last twenty-four hours has meant a closer acquaintance with this group – a forced intimacy that I could well have done without.

But I suppose, if I'm honest, even from the beginning I was curious about them. Perhaps because they were roughly the same age as me: early-to mid-thirties, at a guess. I could have been like them, if I had found a high-paying job in the city, like some friends did after university. This is what you could have had, it felt like the universe was saying to me. This is where you could have been, what you could have been doing, at the loneliest time of the year (because New Year's Eve is, isn't it?).

I might have been envious. And yet I didn't feel it. Because I couldn't put my finger on it, but there was an unease, a discontent, that seemed to surround them. Even as they laughed and jostled and teased one another, I could sense something underneath it – something off. They seemed almost at times like actors, I thought, making a great show of what a wonderful time they were having. They laughed a little *too* hard. They drank a great deal too much. And at the same time, despite all this evidence of merriment, they seemed to watch each other. Perhaps it's hindsight, making this impression seem like more than it was. I suppose there are probably tensions in most groups of friends. But I was struck by the thought that they did not seem completely comfortable in one another's company. Which was odd, as they'd told me right at the beginning that they were very old friends. But that's the thing about old friends, isn't it? Sometimes they don't even realise that they no longer have anything in common. That maybe they don't even like each other any more.

The other guests, the Icelandic couple, walked in just as the starter was being served – 'locally-caught salmon with wild herbs' – to a frisson of hostility from the others.

Iain had booked them in. I'd been on one of my rare trips to the local shop, so he'd had to take the call. He could see that the bunkhouse was free on the system, he said, and he'd checked with the boss, who'd okayed it all. I was annoyed he hadn't written their names down in the book: if I had known, I wouldn't have promised the other group they'd have the run of the place.

I wasn't sure what sort of behaviour to expect from these two. They weren't the usual, well-heeled sort. Both had wind burned complexions, the roughened look of people who spend a lot of time in harsher elements. The man had very pale blue eyes, like a wolf's, and stringy blond hair tied back with a leather thong. The woman had a double-ended stud passing through the septum of her nose and a tangled dark ponytail.

They arrived at the station with huge backpacks, half the size of themselves. They explained that they had caught a passage on a fishing trawler from Iceland to Mallaig further up the coast – I saw the beautiful blonde wrinkle her nose at this – where Iain collected them and brought them to the estate in his truck. They came with proper gear – Gore-Tex jackets and heavy boots – making the Barbours and Hunter wellies the other lot wore look slightly ridiculous. They hadn't changed out of their outdoor gear for dinner, so that even Doug and Iain, in their special Loch Corrin kilts, looked rather tarted up next to them, as did the serving staff, the two girls and the boy in their white shirts and plaid aprons. The beautiful blonde looked at the two new arrivals as though they were creatures that had just emerged from the bottom of the loch. Luckily, they were either side of me; she was seated opposite, next to Doug, and fairly quickly seemed to decide that she would waste no more of her attention on them, and give it whole-heartedly to Doug instead. I looked at her, with all that gloss: the fine silk shirt, the earrings set with sparkling –

diamond? – studs. She watched him as though whatever he was saying was the most fascinating thing she had heard all evening, her lips curved in a half smile, her chin in her palm. Doug wouldn't go for someone like her – would he? She wouldn't be his type, surely? Then I remembered that I had absolutely no idea what his type would be, because I didn't really know anything about him.

I focused my attention back on the Icelandic guests either side of me. They spoke almost perfect English, with just a slight musicality that betrayed their foreignness.

'You've worked here long?' the woman – Kristin – asked me.

'Just under a year.'

'And you live here all by yourself?' This was from the man, Ingvar.

'Well, not quite. Doug . . . over there, lives here too. Iain lives in town, Fort William, with his family.'

'He's the one who collected us?'

'Yes.'

'Ah,' he said, 'he seems like a nice man.'

'Yes.' Though I thought: really? Iain's so taciturn. He arrives, does his work – upon orders received from the boss – and leaves. He keeps very much to himself. Of course, he could say exactly the same of me.

Ingvar said, almost thoughtfully, 'What makes someone like you come to live in a place like this?' The way he asked it – so knowing – almost as though he had guessed at something.

'I like it here,' I told him. Even to my own ears it sounded defensive. 'The natural beauty, the peace . . .'

'But it must get lonely for you here, no?'

'Not particularly,' I said.

'Not frightening?' He smiled when he said this, and I felt a slight chill run through me.

'No,' I said, curtly.

'I suppose you get used to it,' he said, either not noticing or ignoring my rudeness. 'Where we come from, one understands what it is to be alone, you see. Though, if you're not careful, it can send you a little crazy.' He made a boring motion with a finger at his temple. 'All that darkness in the winter, all the solitude.'

Not quite true, I thought. Sometimes solitude is the only way to regain your sanity. But it also got me thinking. If you lived in Iceland – with its long winter nights – wouldn't you go a little further from the cold and dark than Scotland? For the price of the cabins at this place you could get all the way to the relative warmth of Southern Europe. And for that matter, I wondered how two people who got here by hitch-hiking on a fishing trawler could have afforded our rates. But perhaps they did it simply for the adventure. We get all sorts, here.

'Should we be worried?' Ingvar asked, next. 'About the news?'

'What do you mean?'

'You don't know? The Highland Ripper.'

Of course I knew. I'd been hoping the guests didn't. I'd seen the pictures in the paper the day before: the faces of the six victims. All youngish, pretty. You might bump into a hundred girls like that walking down Princes Street in Edinburgh – and yet the images had the ominous look of all victim photos, as though there was something about each innocuous smiling snap that would have foretold their fate, if you had known what to search for. They looked, somehow, as though they had been marked for death.

'Yes,' I said, carefully. 'I've seen the papers. But Scotland is a pretty big place, you know, I don't think you've got anything—'

'I thought it was the Western Highlands, where they found the victims?'

'Still,' I said, 'It's a pretty large area. You'd be as likely to bump into the Loch Ness monster.'

I sounded a little more blasé than I felt. That morning, Iain had said, 'You should tell the guests to stay indoors at night, Heather. On account of the news.' It rather put me on edge that Iain – who hardly ever mentioned the guests – had expressed concern for their welfare.

I didn't think this man, Ingvar, was really scared of anything. I sensed, instead, that he was having a bit of fun with the whole thing; a smile still seemed to be playing around the corners of his mouth. It was a relief when he asked about hunting, and I could escape the scrutiny of those pale blue eyes. I remember thinking that there was something unnerving about them: they didn't seem quite human.

'Oh, you're better off asking Doug about hunting,' I said. 'That's definitely his side of things. Doug?'

Doug glanced over. The blonde looked up too, clearly annoyed at the interruption.

'Do you ever shoot the animals at night,' Ingvar asked, 'using lamps and dogs?'

'No,' Doug said, very quickly and surprisingly loudly.

'Why not?' Ingvar asked, with that odd smile again. 'I know it's very effective.'

Doug's reply was bald. 'Because it's dangerous and cruel. I'd never use lamping.'

'Lamping?' the blonde guest asked.

'Spotlights,' he said, barely glancing in her direction, 'shining them at the deer, so they freeze. It confuses them – and it terrifies them. Often it means you shoot the wrong deer: females with young calves, for example. Sometimes they use dogs, which tear the animal apart. It's barbaric.'

There was a rather taut silence, afterwards. I reflected that it might have been the most I had ever heard Doug say in one go.

The two Icelandic guests have been very eager to help with the search. They're probably the only two that I'd trust in these conditions: they must see similar weather all the time. But they are still guests, and I am still responsible for their well-being. Besides, I know nothing about them. They are an unknown quantity. All of the guests are. So my lizard brain is saying, loud and clear: *Trust no one.*

I wonder what the guests all make of me. Perhaps they see someone organised, slightly dull, absolutely in charge of everything. At least, that is what they will have seen if I have pulled it off, this clever disguise I have built for myself, like a tough outer shell. Inside this shell, the reality is very different. Here is a person held together by tape and glue and prescription-strength sleeping pills – the only thing I can be persuaded to make a foray into civilisation for, these days. Washed down sometimes, often, with a *little* too much wine. I'm not saying that I have a drinking problem; I don't. But I don't ever drink for pleasure. I do it out of necessity. I use it as another painkiller: to blunt the edge of things, to alleviate the chronic, aching torment of memory.

Three days earlier
30th December 2018

MIRANDA

Dinner is served in the big dining room in the Lodge, off the living room, which has been lit with what appear to be hundreds of candles, and staffed by a few spotty teenagers in plaid aprons. We're two short: Samira and Giles are having supper in their cabin. Samira said she's heard too many stories about parents 'just leaving their kids for an hour or so' when everything goes horribly wrong. Yes, I told her, patiently – but not in the middle of nowhere. Besides, Priya's hardly going to be wandering off on her own at six months, for God's sake. Still, Samira wasn't having any of it.

I almost can't believe this woman is Samira, who at one party in our early twenties decided to jump the two-foot gap

75

between the house building and the building next to it, just for a laugh. She was always one of the wild ones, the party girl, the one you could rely on to raise the tempo of things on a night out. If Katie's the one who I go way back with, Samira's probably much more like me: the one I've always felt most akin to. Now I feel I hardly recognise her. Perhaps that's just because she's been so busy with Priya. I'm sure the real Samira is in there somewhere. I'm hoping this will be our chance to catch up, to remember that we're partners in crime. But honestly, when some people have kids it's like they've had a personality transplant. Or a lobotomy. Maybe I should count myself lucky that I don't seem to be able to get pregnant. At least I'll remain myself for Christ's Sake.

I've got the gamekeeper, Doug, on one side of me and the other guy, Iain, on the other. Both of them are wearing identikit green kilts and sporrans. Neither looks particularly happy about it. As you might imagine, the gamekeeper wears his outfit best. He really *is* quite attractive. I am reminded of the fact that, before Julien, I was sometimes drawn to men like this. The reticent, brooding sort: the challenge of drawing them out, making them care.

I turn to him and ask: 'Have you always been a game-keeper?'

He frowns. 'No.'

'Oh, and what did you do before?'

'The Marines.'

I picture him with a short back and sides, in uniform. It's an appealing image. He looks good scrubbed-up, even if I'm sure his hair hasn't seen a brush any time in the last five years. I'm glad I made an effort: my silk shirt, undone perhaps one button lower than strictly necessary, my new jeans.

'Did you have to kill anyone?' I ask, leaning forward, putting my chin in my hand.

'Yes.' As he says it his expression is neutral, betraying no emotion whatsoever. I experience a small shiver of what might be disquiet . . . or desire.

Julien is sitting directly opposite us, with a front and centre view of things. There is nothing like stirring a bit of jealousy to fire things up in a relationship – especially ours. It could be an over-familiar waiter in a restaurant, or the guy on the next sunlounger who Julien's convinced has been checking me out (he's probably right). 'Would you want him to do this to you?' he'd pant in my ear later, 'or this?'

If I'm honest, sex has become, lately, a mechanism for a specific end rather than pleasure. I've got this app that Samira told me about, which identifies your most fertile days. And then, of course, there are certain positions that work best. I've explained this to Julien so many times, but he doesn't seem to get it. I suppose he's stopped trying, recently. So yes, we could do with things being spiced up a little.

I turn back to Doug, keeping Julien in my peripheral vision. He's talking to the Icelandic woman, so I touch a hand against Doug's, just for fun. I've had a couple of glasses too many, maybe. I feel his fingers flinch against mine.

'Sorry,' I say, all innocence. 'Would you mind passing me the *jus*?' I think it's working. Certainly Julien's looking pretty pissed off about something. To all intents and purposes he might be having a whale of a time – always so important to present the right face to the world – but I know him too well. It's that particular tension in the side of the neck, the gritting of the teeth.

I glance over to where poor Katie, across the table from me, is seated next to the Icelandic man with the strange eyes, who seems to have taken a bit of a shine to her. It's a bloody nightmare, them being here too. Are we going to have to share the sauna with them? Judging by the state of the clothes they're wearing I'd have to disinfect myself afterwards.

The man, now, is leaning towards Katie as though he has never seen anything so fascinating or beautiful in his life. Clearly – judging by his partner – he has *unconventional* taste.

Though . . . there is definitely something different about Katie. She looks tired and pale, as per, but there's that new haircut for a start. At the place she normally goes to, they style her hair *à la* Mrs Williams, our old school hockey teacher. You would have thought that with her corporate lawyer's salary, she might try a bit harder sometimes. I've been telling her to go to Daniel Galvin for ages – I go for highlights every six weeks – so I don't know why I feel so put out about her finally having listened to me. Perhaps because she hasn't given me any credit for it, and I feel I deserve some. And perhaps because I had sort of imagined we might go together. Make a morning of it, the two of us.

I still remember the girl she was back then: flat-chested when everyone else was starting to develop. Lank-haired, knock-kneed, the maroon of the school uniform emphasising the sallowness of her complexion.

I have always liked a project.

Look at her now. It's difficult to be objective, as I've known her so long that she's practically a sister, but I can see how some men might find her attractive. Sure: she'll never be pretty, but she has learned to make the best of herself. That new hair. Her teeth have been straightened and whitened. Her clothes are beautifully cut to make the most of her slight frame (I could never wear a shirt like that without my boobs creating the kind of shelf that makes you look bigger than you really are). She had her ears pinned back as a present to herself when she qualified at her law firm. She looks almost . . . chic. You might think she was French: the way she's made the best of those difficult features. What's that expression the French have for it? *Jolie laide*: ugly beautiful.

Katie would never be wolf-whistled at by builders or white-van men. I never understand why some people think you might be flattered by that. Look, OK, I *know* I'm attractive. Very attractive. There, I've said it. Do you hate me now? Anyway, I don't need it confirmed by some pot-bellied construction workers who would catcall anyone with a short skirt or tight top. If anything, they cheapen it.

They wouldn't shout at Katie, though. Well, they might shout at her to 'Smile love!' But they wouldn't fancy her. They wouldn't understand her. I'm *almost* envious of it. It's something that I'll never have, that look-twice subtlety.

Anyway. Maybe now we're finally together, I can find out what's been going on in her life – what it is that has prompted this mysterious change in her.

EMMA

It's hard not to spend the whole of the meal looking around the table, checking that everyone's enjoying themselves. I really wish I'd opted us out of this dinner when I'd booked – it seemed like a great idea at the time, but with the Icelandic couple here as well there's an odd dynamic. And this close proximity to the other guests just emphasises the mess-up over our not having the place to ourselves. I know I should be able to let it go: *que sera sera*, and all that, but I so wanted it to be perfect for everyone. It doesn't help that the other guests are so weird-looking and unkempt: I can see how unimpressed Miranda, in particular, is by them. Katie's sitting next to the man, Ingvar – who is looking at her as though he wishes she were on the plate in front of him, not the over-scented meat.

I, meanwhile, am sitting next to Iain. He doesn't say very much, and when he does his accent is so thick it's hard to understand everything.

'Do you live here too?' I ask him.

'No,' he says. 'Fort William – with my wife and kids.'

'Ah,' I say. 'Have you worked here long?'

He nods. 'Since the current owner first bought the place.'

'What do you do?'

'Whatever needs doing. Odd jobs, here and there: working on the pumphouse, at the moment, down by the loch. I bring the supplies in too: food, the bits for the cabins.'

'What's the owner like?' I ask, intrigued. I imagine a whiskery old Scottish laird, so I'm a bit surprised when Iain says, 'He's all right, for an Englishman.' I wait for him to say more, but he either doesn't have anything to add, or is reluctant to do so.

I seem to have run out of questions, so it's a relief when the Icelandic man asks about the deer-stalking, and the whole table's attention is turned to that. It's as if the idea of a hunt, a kill, has exerted a magnetic pull upon everyone's attention.

'We don't hunt the deer just for the sake of it,' the game-keeper says. 'We do it to keep the numbers down – otherwise they'd get out of control. So it's necessary.'

'But I think it's necessary for another reason,' the man – Ingvar – says. 'Humans are hunters, it's in our very DNA. We need to find an outlet for those needs. The *blood lust*.' He says the last two words as though they have a particularly delicious flavour to them, and there's a pause in which no one quite seems to know what to say, a heightening of the awkward tension that's plagued this meal. I see Miranda raise her eyebrows. Perhaps we can all laugh about this later – it'll become a funny anecdote. Every holiday has these moments, doesn't it? 'Well, I don't know about all that,' says Bo, spearing a piece of venison, 'but it's delicious. Amazing to think it came from right here.'

I'm not so sure. It's not terrible, exactly, but I could have done so much better. The venison is overly flavoured with juniper, you can hardly taste the meat, and there isn't nearly enough jus. The vegetables are limp: the cavolo nero a slimy over-steamed mush.

I'll make up for it tomorrow evening. I have my wonderful feast planned: smoked salmon blinis to go with the first couple of bottles of champagne, then beef Wellington with foie gras, followed by a perfect chocolate soufflé. Soufflés, as everyone knows, are not easy. You have to be a bit obsessive about them. The separation of the eggs, the perfect beating of the whites – the timings at the end, making sure you serve them before the beautiful risen crest falls. Most people don't have the patience for it. But that's exactly the sort of cooking I like.

It's a relief, to be honest, when the dessert (a rather limp raspberry pavlova) is finally cleared away.

As everyone is readying to leave, Julien motions us all to sit back down. He's had a bit too much to drink; he sways slightly as he stands.

'Darling,' Miranda says, in her most silken tones, 'what are you doing?' I wonder if she's remembering last New Year – in the exclusive environs of Fera at Claridge's restaurant – when he stood up out of his seat without looking, only to send a waiter's entire tray of food crashing to the ground.

'I want to say a few words,' he says. 'I want to thank Emma . . .' he raises his glass at me, 'for picking such a fantastic place —'

'Oh,' I say, 'I haven't really done anything . . .'

'And I want to say how special it is to have everyone here, together. It's nice to know that some things never change, that some friends are always there for you. It hasn't been the easiest year—'

'Darling,' Miranda says again, with a laugh, 'I think everyone gets the idea. But I absolutely agree. Here's to old friends—' she raises her glass. Then she remembers, and turns to me. 'And new, of course. Cheers!'

Everyone echoes her, including Ingvar – though of course she did not mean him. But even his interjection doesn't spoil it. The toast has rescued the atmosphere, somehow – it's brought a sense of occasion to the meal. And I feel, again, that special little glow of pride.

DOUG

About an hour after the dinner there's a knock on his door. The dogs, Griffin and Volley, go crazy at this unexpected excitement: no one *ever* comes to his cottage. He checks his watch: midnight.

'What the—'

It's the beautiful one, the tall blonde who sat next to him at the meal. Who touched her hand to his, which was, as it happens, the first time anyone has touched his skin in a long time. She smiles, her hand lifted, as though ready to knock again. He can smell trouble coming off her.

Griffin barrels past him and leaps up at her even as Doug roars, 'Down!' She throws her arms up, and as she does her sweater lifts, exposing a taut sliver of stomach, the tight-furled bud of her navel. The dog's nose leaves a wet slick across the skin.

She seems embarrassed by her reaction of fear; she bends to caress Griffin's head, a show of bravado. 'Pretty girl,' she says, sounding less than completely convinced. She grins up at him, all her white teeth. *Look at me*, the grin says, *look how relaxed I am*. 'Hi. Hope you don't mind my interrupting you like this.'

'What is it?'

Her smile falters. Too late, he remembers that this is a guest, that he owes her a service, even if it is ridiculously late for her to be asking anything of him. He attempts some damage limitation with the next question. 'How can I help?'

'I was wondering if you could help us make a fire,' she says, 'in the Lodge.'

He stares at her. He cannot imagine how nine people might not have the skills between them to set a fire.

'We've been trying to make one,' she says, 'but without much luck.' She leans one arm against the doorpost, slouching her hip. Her jumper has ridden up again. 'We're Londoners, you see. I know you'd make it *much* better than we ever could.'

'Fine,' he says, curtly, and then remembers again that she is a customer. A *guest*. 'Of course.'

He senses that she is the sort of woman who is used to getting her way. He can feel her trying to peer into the interior of the cottage. He is not used to this: he blocks her view with his body and closes the door behind him so quickly that he only just avoids Griffin's eager nose.

She crooks her finger at him, inviting him to follow. Just toward the Lodge, to light the bloody fire . . . but still. He knows what she is offering up to him. Not the act itself, perhaps, but the whisper, the hint, the wink of it.

How long has it been? A long time. More than a year – maybe a lot more.

As he follows he catches that scent of her perfume again, the church-like smokiness of it. It smells to him like trouble.

He follows her back to the Lodge. As he kneels in the grate, the big guy – Mark? – comes over and says in a man-to-man way, 'Waste of your time, mate. She insisted on going and getting you. But I practically had it going. The wood's just a bit damp, that's all.'

He looks at the haphazard arrangement of logs in the grate, the twenty or so burned matches scattered around, and says nothing.

'Want some help?' the man asks.

'No, thanks.'

'Suit yourself, *mate*.' The man's face has reddened in a matter of seconds with either embarrassment, or, Doug suspects, anger. Short fuse on that one, he thinks. Takes one to know one.

NOW

2nd January 2019

HEATHER

Normally the water of the loch reflects the landscape as perfectly as if the mountains and trees and lodge were peering into a mirror. Sometimes in this reflection they look somehow more crisp, more perfect than they do in reality. But today the surface is clouded, blind, scarred by ice. Please, I think, following Doug around the bend of the path beside the water, don't let it be the loch. Don't let him have found the body there.

The loch is my sanctuary, my church.

The first time I wandered into those freezing depths I didn't intend on coming back out. It was in the early days here, when I realised that I hadn't been able to outrun everything. But something happened, as my clothes became weighed down, and the cold surrounded me in its terrible grip. Some essential urge, beyond my control, to kick, to fight. Here was life, suddenly: inside me, powerful, insuperable. The feeling was – is – addictive. It is one of the few times that I do not feel that I am drowning.

I have my routine down pat now. I get myself up and get straight into my swimming costume, a chaste one-piece like those we used to wear for swimming lessons at school. I'm not trying to impress anyone, and it's the most coverage I can get for warmth without resorting to a full wetsuit. I go every morning of the year. I do it especially when it is below freezing – like now – and when I have to break the ice on the surface of the loch. When the water is so cold that it grips you like a vice and squeezes all thoughts from your mind, and your heart seems to be beating so hard it might explode. That's when I am most myself, without the weight of everything upon me. The one time these days when I really feel alive.

Afterwards I dry off and go back to my cottage. By then every nerve ending in my body is tingling pleasantly. I suppose you could say it's the next best thing to sex.

I saw Doug swimming in the loch, just once. I have an uninterrupted view of the water from my cottage. He went right to the edge and stripped off down to his boxers, revealing powerful shoulders, skin pale as milk. When he swam – not a moment's hesitation at the cold – it looked as though his body was a machine specifically designed to cut through the water with the greatest possible speed. When he stepped out his face was grim.

As I watched I felt a powerful sense of shame, as though I had intruded upon some private moment of his, even though all it took was a glance from the window. And shame too, because it felt like a disloyalty. Because I had looked, and kept on looking, and had not been immune to the sight of my co-worker's body. Because I had held the image of it in my mind when I took a bath, later, and gave myself the first orgasm I had had in more than a year.

Now Doug turns around, to check I'm following, and I feel the heat rise instantly to my cheeks. Hopefully the sting of the cold will be enough to justify it.

We are about to plunge into the thicket of trees that ring the loch on this side. A fringe of dark pines. Some of them aren't native; they're Norwegian imposters, planted after the war. They're much denser than the local Scots pine, and when you're among them all sound from the outside world seems to be muffled. Not that there are many sounds here, beyond the occasional cawing of the birds.

On my good days, I persuade myself that I love these trees: their glossy needles, the cones that I collect to keep in bowls around the house, the warm, green Christmas scent of the resin when you walk among them. On my bad days I decide they look funereal, like sinister black-cloaked sentinels.

We are out of sight of the Lodge now. Completely alone. I am suddenly reminded that though I've worked alongside this man for a year I know almost nothing about him. This is definitely the most time I have ever spent in his company – and quite possibly the most we have ever spoken to one another.

I'm not sure he speaks to *anyone*. Early on, I kept expecting him to ask me if he could use the Internet: to send an email, perhaps, or check up on friends and family on Facebook. But he never did. Even I check in with friends and family every so often. 'Your mam worries about you,' my dad said, at the beginning. 'Stuck in a place like that all on your own, after everything you've been through. It's not right.' So I try and go back every few months or so to put her mind at rest, though the experience of re-entering the outside world is not one I particularly relish.

But Doug *never* seems to leave the estate unless he has to: taking guests into town to visit the shops, for example. I made the mistake of mentioning him to my mum, the lonely existence he leads. Of course, in true parental style, she was worried for me.

'He could be anyone,' she told me. 'What's his background? Where does he come from?'

I told her the one thing I did know, that he'd been in the Marines. This did not reassure her in the slightest. 'You need to goggle him, Heather,' she told me.

'Google, Ma.'

'Whatever it is. Just promise me you'll do it. You need to know who this man is . . . I can't sleep for worrying about you, Heather. Running off and leaving us all behind just when you need your family about you most. Not letting us help you like we want to. No word for days, weeks. I need to know that you're safe at least. Who you're working with. It's not fair, Heaths.' And then she seemed to check herself. 'Of course – I know it must sound awful, me saying that. What happened to you . . . that was the most unfair thing that could happen—'

'All right, Ma,' I said, not wanting to hear any more. 'I'll do it, I'll google him.' But I didn't, not then. Truthfully, the thought of it felt like a betrayal.

Of course, when my mum asked me what I had found – I could tell it was one of those things that she wouldn't give up on, a terrier with a bone – I reassured her. 'It's fine,' I said. 'I looked. There's nothing there. You can stop worrying about me now.'

There was a pause. 'I never stop worrying about you, pet.' I put the phone down.

The truth is, she's right. I don't know anything about Doug. Just what the boss hinted at during my interview, that his background made him well suited to the job – particularly seeing off any poachers. When he was asked to take his pick of the cottages he chose the one furthest from anything – at the bottom of the flank of the Munro, with no sheltering trees, with no view of the loch. It's unquestionably the worst of all of them, which would suggest he chose it purely for its position. I understand the need to be alone. But the need for even further isolation within this remote wilderness makes me wonder exactly what it is he is trying to distance himself from.

'Where are we going, Doug?'

'Just a little way now,' he says, and I feel a leap of trepidation, a powerful urge to turn and start in the other direction again, back towards the Lodge. Instead I follow Doug as we tramp further into the trees, the only sound the squeak of our boots in the snow.

Up ahead of us I see the first of the waterfalls, the small wooden bridge that spans it, the pumphouse building a little way further up. Normally it would take us only ten minutes to get here. But in these conditions it has taken the best part of half an hour.

I see the big impressions of Doug's boots in the snow on the bridge, where he apparently stood the first time, looking down. There are no other footprints, I notice. But then there wouldn't be. This snow has been falling for hours. Any other tracks – including those of the dead guest – will have long ago been obscured.

'There,' he says, pointing.

I step warily onto the bridge. At first I can't see anything. It's a long way down to the bottom, and I'm very aware of Doug standing just behind me. It would only take a little push, I find myself thinking, to send me over. I grip the chain rail hard, though it suddenly seems very flimsy in my grasp.

There is a moment of incomprehension as I stare into the void. All I can make out is a lot of snow and ice gathered in the ravine.

'Doug,' I say, 'I can't see anything. There's nothing there.'

He frowns, and points again. I follow his finger.

Suddenly, peering down among the rocks, the great pillows of fallen snow, it appears below me like the slow emergence of a magic eye image.

'Oh God.' It's more an exhalation of air, like a punch to the gut, than a word. I have seen dead bodies before in my time, in my old line of work. A greater number than the average person, definitely. But the horror of the experience never leaves you. It is always a shock – a profound, existential shock – to be confronted with the inanimate object that was once a person. A person so recently thinking, feeling, seeing, reduced to so much cold flesh. I feel the long-ago familiar swoop of nausea. At medical school they told us it would go away, after our first few. 'You get used to it.' But I'm not sure I ever really did. And I am unprepared, despite knowing what I have come to see. I have been ambushed, here in this place, by death. I thought that I could outrun it.

It almost looks like part of the landscape now: I think that is partly what helped it to blend in. But now I can see it, I can't believe I missed it before. The corpse has a kind of dark power, drawing the eye. The lower half of it is covered modestly by fallen snow, though the shield of the bridge has protected the top half of the body. The skin is a greyish blue, leached of all blood and human colour. That hair too, spilling behind the head, might just be more dead weed, such as those that poke obstinately through the snow in places.

There seems to be a great deal of skin, in fact. This is not the corpse of a person who came out dressed for the elements. The cold would have killed in an hour – less – if nothing else had. Or *someone* else had.

I see now, looking harder, the halo of blood about the head: rust-coloured, covering the rocks beneath like a peculiar species of lichen. There is a lot of it. A fall onto rock. That could have been the thing that did the killing, in itself.

But I can see that it is more complicated than that. There is an unmistakable necklace of darkness about the neck. The skin there, even from this distance away, looks particularly blue and bruised-looking. I know very little about forensics – barely more than someone with no background in medicine. My old vocation was in saving life, not examining the evidence left after its loss. But you would not need to be an expert in the field to see that something has compressed the skin there, injured it.

The face . . . no, I don't want to think about the face.

I turn back to Doug. His gaze is a blank; as though there is no one behind his eyes. I take a step back, involuntarily. Then I get a grip of myself.

'I see it,' I say. 'I see what you mean. Yes.'

We must wait for the police to arrive, to make their judgements, of course. But I know now why Doug wanted me to come and take a look. This does not look like an accident.

Three days earlier
30th December 2018

EMMA

We're back in the living room of the Lodge, all a bit tipsy. Tired from the day, too – but no one wants to go to bed, because it's a novelty to be together like this. Samira and Giles have joined us now – Priya's finally fallen asleep apparently, though Samira keeps holding the baby monitor up to her ear as though worried it has stopped working. There's a lot of laughter and hilarity, the booze loosening us.

'So what did we miss?' Giles asks.

'Not a lot,' Nick says. 'Though clearly I should have brought a kilt. *De rigueur* here, it seems.'

'I think it's a good look,' Miranda says, with a glance in the direction of the gamekeeper, who's kneeling in the grate to make our fire. 'Oh,' she says, mysteriously, 'and we met the other guests . . .'

'What are they like?' Samira asks.

Bo does a heavily accented impression of the man, Ingvar.

'Ze blood lust,' he says, gesticulating, 'don't you feel it stirring in you in a place like zis, ze urge to keeeeeell?'

Miranda snorts with laughter, 'Yes, yes – that's it exactly!'

He's a good mimic – he would be, being an actor. But he's also slurring a bit, drunker than everyone else. He had some problems with drugs in the past, apparently, but alcohol doesn't seem to be off limits. At the dinner he was knocking back the glasses of wine like water.

'God,' Samira says, 'he sounds like a bit of a freak. But presumably . . . you know, a harmless one?'

'He liked you, Katie!' Miranda says.

'*Did* he, Katie?' Giles asks, grinning.

Katie colours. She's curled up on one of the sofas next to Nick, feet tucked under her, as though she's attempting to take up as little room as possible. 'I don't think so,' she says.

'Oh yes he did,' Mark says, 'I think he wanted to drag you off into the woods and have his way with you.'

Again, I'm aware of the gamekeeper's presence. But he's hardly going to tell the other guests what he's overheard, is he? I watch as he makes a teepee of the wood and kindling: there's something satisfying about his efficiency. Giles and Mark were peeved that Miranda thought it necessary to go and get him, but their first few attempts fizzled out within minutes. He doesn't look particularly impressed about being asked, either – I suppose it is pretty late. I wonder if anyone other than Miranda would have been able to summon him at this time of night.

Miranda, speaking of, is now at the cocktail cabinet

making us 'boulevardiers', her speciality: a negroni, with the gin swapped out for bourbon. She had them served at her wedding.

'Want one?' she asks the gamekeeper.

'No,' he says, looking at the floor. 'I've got to be getting back.'

'Suit yourself.'

He stands up, wipes the soot from his hands on his jacket, and makes for the door. 'Goodnight!' Miranda calls, as it closes.

'Good riddance,' Mark says, 'he's hardly a barrel of laughs, is he?'

'Not everyone has your wit and charm, Marky-Mark,' Miranda says, as she brings the cocktails over to us, then huffs down onto the sofa, kicking off her pumps in one fluid motion. Her toenails are painted a perfect dark blood red. I love that colour, really chic. I'll have to remember to ask her what shade it is.

'I want a smoke,' she announces. 'I always want a smoke with one of these.' She takes out her packet. They're Vogue lights. I know, because I smoke the same ones – I haven't smoked anything else since I took up the habit, at nineteen.

'I don't think you can smoke in here,' Nick says.

'Of course I can. Fuck that. We've paid enough for the privilege, haven't we? Besides,' she points at the giant fire in the grate, which is sending up clouds of peat-scented smoke, 'that thing stinks enough to mask the smell.'

But someone could look in and see you, I think. Heather, or the gamekeeper, Doug. When you look at the windows now you can mainly just see the reflection of us, the room, the fire. And then just beyond, the very faint outline of the night-time landscape: the darker black of the trees and the gleam of the loch. But we're pretty blind to anything else out there.

It said it on the form, I remember. Quite clearly: no smoking indoors, please. If someone sees her, we'll be charged the damage deposit. But I won't say anything, not now at least. The last thing I want to be is a killjoy. I just want everyone to have a good time.

'For fuck's sake,' Miranda says, 'where's my lighter? I thought I'd left it right there on the coffee table. It's a special one: it was my grandfather's. It has our crest on it.'

Miranda always finds little ways to remind people of the grand stock she comes from. But I don't think she does it in a mean way, really. It's just how she is.

Mark fumbles in a pocket, finds his lighter. Miranda leans forward into the flame, so far that we can all see the raspberry lace of her bra.

'Perhaps your stalker took it?' Nick says teasingly, leaning back and taking a sip of his whisky – he refused a cocktail.

'Oh God,' Miranda says, widening her eyes. 'I swear . . . every time I lose something, I half find myself blaming it on him first. It's rather convenient.'

'What stalker?' I ask.

'Oh,' Miranda says, 'I always forget how new you are, Emma.'

No she doesn't. She's always reminding me how new I am to the group. But I suppose I don't mind.

'Manda had this stalker,' Samira says. 'It started in Oxford, but it carried on in London for several years, didn't it, Manda?'

'You know,' Miranda says, airily, 'sometimes I could almost believe that there never really was one. That it was someone playing a joke on me, instead.'

'Funny sort of joke,' Julien says. 'And I don't remember you being that blasé about it at the time. It was fucking creepy – you must remember how much it frightened you?'

Miranda frowns. I suspect she doesn't like the implication that it had worried her. Playing the victim is not her style. 'Anyway,' she says, 'he used to take stuff from me. Weird things, little things – but often with some sentimental value. To be honest, it took me a while to work it out. I'm so disorganised that I'm always losing things and never finding them again.'

'He'd return them, too,' Katie says, over the top of the magazine she's reading. She's been so quiet for the last hour or so – while everyone else has been making so much noise – that I'd almost forgotten she was there. 'Later on, he'd return them.'

'Oh yes,' Miranda says. For a moment I think I see a shadow of something in her expression – some fear or disquiet – but if the memory unnerves her, she conceals it quickly. 'At Oxford he used to leave the things he'd taken in my locker at college, with a little typed note. And then when we were in London, I'd get stuff posted to me – also with a note. Little things: an earring, a jumper, a shoe. It was like he was just keeping them for a while.'

'It was horrible,' Samira says. 'Especially when we lived in that gloomy little house in second year next to the railway tracks – do you remember? I always thought you must have been so scared. *I* was scared, just thinking that he was lurking around.'

'I think I actually found it quite funny, more than anything,' Miranda says.

'I'm not sure you did at the time,' Katie says. 'I remember, in college, you coming to my room in the middle of the night with your duvet over your shoulder, saying you felt like someone had been in your room, watching you. You used to come and sleep on my floor.'

Miranda frowns. I suppose that's the problem with old friends; they have long memories. It's as if Katie's not playing by the rules – her comment has cut through the fun.

'You know,' Julien says. 'I always thought it was someone you knew. It had to have been someone who was always there, near you – close enough to take those things.'

I see Katie dart a look at Mark, and then quickly glance away again. I'm sure I know what she's thinking. I bet her pet theory is that he was the stalker. He has always had a crush on Miranda. Yes, I know about it. No, it doesn't bother me. It's harmless, I know it is. Mark is, at heart, a fairly simple soul. He has a temper, yes, but he lacks the calculating nature needed for such behaviour.

I see the pity in the way Katie looks at me sometimes. It irks me. I do not need her pity. I wish I could tell her that, without sounding like I am protesting too much.

MIRANDA

People have always been entertained by tales of my stalker. I know how to dress them up to give that little ghost-story shiver down the spine. And it's such a *bizarre* thing, isn't it? A real-life stalker. Everyone seems to think it only happens to celebrities: actresses, singers, breakfast TV hosts. Sometimes I'll catch the person I'm telling looking at me: squinting, head on one side, as though they're assessing me. Do I really deserve to be stalked? Am I really *that* interesting?

I often bring up my stalker as a piece of dinner party conversation. At times it feels like he's an exotic and fascinating pet, or a particularly gifted child. It starts conversations. It can stop them too: the idea of someone watching you, knowing everything about you. And then I'll segue neatly into my whole routine – about how, when you think about it, in the times we live in we are *all* stalkers. All of us knowing so much about one another's lives. Even people we haven't seen in years. Old childhood friends, old school mates. I'll talk about how we all submit to being stalked. How we think that we're in control, sharing what we think we choose to share, but really putting a lot more out there than we're aware of.

'So really,' I'll say, at this point in my performance, 'my stalker was just a bit ahead of the game! A trend-setter, of sorts. He was just analogue. Although having probably been a student at Oxford too' – little pause to let that settle, let it glimmer and impress for a moment – 'for all I know he's probably behind some social media app anyway. Sharing his expertise with the world!'

Cue: wry laughter. Cue: an ongoing discussion about privacy, and what we should submit ourselves to and where we should draw the line . . . and how privacy is the true battleground of the twenty-first century. Cue: an exchange of various weird experiences people have had: private messages from strangers on Instagram, trolling on Twitter, a creepy friend request on Facebook from someone they've never met. None of it, however, nearly as strange and *special* as my own experience.

I will sit back, feeling a little glow. As though I've just performed some well-practised routine, and pulled it off with even more sparkle than before. My own little social gymnastics display. Julien will probably be rolling his eyes at this point. He's heard the whole thing – what, maybe fifty, a hundred, a thousand times before? And he's never been able to see the interesting, or amusing side of it. He was the one who thought, all those years ago, that I should get the police involved. He used to look annoyed when I brought up the subject, because he thought I shouldn't make light of something 'so fucking creepy', as he put it. Now I think he's mainly just a bit bored of hearing it.

But the truth I don't tell anyone, is that I was – am – frightened of my stalker. There are things the stalker knows about me, secret, shameful things, that I have told no one. Not even Katie, not even back then when we were thick as thieves, not Julien.

The stalker knew, for example, that every so often I liked to dabble in a bit of recreational shoplifting at Oxford. Only at times of high stress: exam season, or before a big paper had to be in. My therapist (the only one I've told about this little habit) thinks it was a control thing, a bit like my dieting and exercising: something I had power over, and was good at. She thinks it's in the past, though – she doesn't know that sometimes I'll still snaffle the odd lipstick, a pair of cashmere gloves, a magazine. There's the thrill of getting away with it, too; my therapist hasn't worked that part out.

I stole a pair of earrings from the Oxford Topshop. Gold hoops with a little painted parrot sitting on each one. A few days after I'd lifted them they disappeared from my room. They were returned a few weeks later in my cubbyhole, with a note: '*Miranda Adams: I'd have expected better from you. Sincerely, a concerned friend. xxx*' The kisses were the worst fucking part of it.

He must have been *right* next to me in the shop when I did it. It had been crowded, I remembered: and there had been men in there as well as women, trailing after girlfriends, or making their way down to Topman. No particular face stood out, though. I had no memory of anyone looking at me – more than normal – or acting weirdly.

While the earrings were missing I remember seeing a bespectacled girl in the Bodleian in that exact pair – and almost chased after her into Short Term Loans. Until I realised that anyone could have bought them. They were from Topshop, for Christ's sake. There might have been twenty – fifty – girls in the city with them. This was how paranoid my stalker had made me, bringing me to the point of chasing down a complete stranger.

Then there was the essay that I bought from a student in the year above, with the intention of plagiarising it for my own. Both had been sitting on the desk in my room – the original, and my poorly disguised copy. I'd gone out for a drink at the pub and returned to find them both gone. I'd had to cobble something together, drunk, in the hours before the deadline, and ended up getting a bare pass, my worst mark yet – though not ever. A week later they were returned to me. The note: '*I don't think you want to go down that path, Miranda.*' And yet, a week later, when a few students got held up for their own acts of plagiarism, I was almost oddly grateful.

And there was the time, very early on with Julien, when I cheated on him. A drunken shag with a guy in my tutor group. As luck would have it, my period didn't arrive that month. I took a pregnancy test – thankfully negative – which was returned a week later with a note that read, '*Naughty, naughty, Manda. What would Julien say?*'

The casual use of Manda, which is what only my closest friends call me.

I didn't tell anyone of these particular communications. Not even Katie, or Samira. They revealed aspects of myself that I would have preferred no one know anything about. And I feared that if I did something to displease my stalker he would use all my secrets to destroy me.

Nevertheless, I did go to the police – though, again, I didn't tell anyone. I took along a couple of the notes: the ones I could bring myself to show. I wasn't taken very seriously. 'Have there been any threats made in the notes, miss?' the officer I spoke to asked.

'Well, no.'

'And you haven't noticed anyone behaving in a threatening manner?'

'. . . No.'

'No signs of forced entry?'

'No.'

'It seems to me,' he picked up one of the notes again and read it, 'that one of your mates might be playing a prank on you, my dear.' Patronising arse.

That was that. I regretted ever having gone – and not just because the police were no help. In doing so I had made myself into the victim I refused to be.

But it carried on in London for several years. He worked out where I was living. It's one thing to access a student room on a relatively accessible corridor. It's quite another to gain entry to a London property with three high-security locks on the door. And then we moved, and it *kept* happening. The items that went missing were always of a similar kind. On the surface, valueless, but all with some inner significance. The tiniest doll from the very inside of the beautiful painted matryoshka I was given by my beloved godmother, before she died from cancer. The batik scarf I bought in a Greek village on my first holiday with Julien – the summer of our second year. The woven friendship bracelet that Katie gave me in our first year of knowing each other.

I thought I'd always have my stalker. He had begun to feel like a part of my life, a part of me, even. But then, out of the blue, it stopped. A couple of years ago now. At least,

I think it stopped. I've received no packages, no notes. But sometimes, when I misplace something, I have that old frisson of fear. There was that silver baby rattle I bought from Tiffany's recently, on a whim as I was walking down Bond Street. I'm sure it will show up somewhere. I'm not the most organised person, after all. I tell myself that it's just paranoia. But I haven't ever shaken that feeling of being watched.

I haven't told anyone – not even Julien, or Katie or Samira, say – of the feeling of creeping horror I get, sometimes. Moments when I am in the middle of a crowd and suddenly convinced that someone is standing right behind me, breathing on my neck . . . only to turn around and see that there is no one there. Or a sudden certainty that someone is watching me with an intensity that isn't normal. You know . . . that prickling feeling you have when you know you are being looked at? It's happened at music festivals and on shopping trips, in supermarkets and night-clubs. On the tube platform I sometimes find myself staggering back away from the edge, convinced that someone is standing right behind me, about to give me a shove.

No, I don't tell anyone these fears. Not Katie, not Julien, certainly not my amused dinner party guests.

I have bad dreams, too. It's worst when Julien is away on business trips. I have to double-check all the locks on the doors, and even then I'll wake in pitch blackness convinced that someone is in the room with me. Similar to the sort of tricks your mind plays on you, if you've just watched a horror film. Suddenly you'll see sinister shadows in every corner. Only this is a hundred times worse. Because some of those shadows might be real.

KATIE

Miranda's finally coming to the end of her little repertoire. Just at this moment the wind chooses to do a long, melodramatic howl down the chimney. The fire seems to billow out, a scatter of sparks landing just inside the grate. It is perfect, horror-movie timing. Everyone laughs.

'Reminds me of that house we stayed in in Wales,' Giles says.

'The one where we kept having blackouts?' Nick asks. 'And the heating kept going off at random intervals?'

'It was haunted,' Miranda says, 'that's what the owner told us – remember. It was Jacobean.' That place had been Miranda's choice.

'It was definitely old,' says Mark, 'but I'm not sure ghosts are an excuse for dodgy plumbing and electrical faults.'

'But there had been plenty of sightings,' Emma says, loyally. 'The woman said they'd had people from *Most Haunted* come to visit them.'

'Yes,' Miranda says, pleased by this. 'There was that

story about a girl being thrown out of a window by her stepbrothers, because they'd realised she was going to inherit the property. And people had heard her, screaming at night.'

'I certainly heard someone screaming at night,' Giles says, grinning at her. There had been a lot of hilarity over the thinness of the walls, and certain 'noises' keeping everyone up at night. Miranda and Julien had been singled out as the main culprits.

'Oh stop it,' Miranda says, hitting Giles with a cushion. She's laughing, but as the conversation moves on she stops and I see a new expression – wistful? – cross her features. I look away.

Giles's mention of Wales has opened a conversation about other years past. It is a favourite hobby, raking over our shared history together. These are the experiences that have always bound us, that have given us a tribal sense of affiliation. For as long as we have known each other, we have always spent New Year's Eve together. It's a regathering of threads that have become a little looser over the years, as our jobs and lives take us in different directions. I wonder if the others experience the same thing that I do, on these occasions. That however much I think I have changed, however different I feel as a person at work, or with the few non-university friends I have, at times like this I somehow return to exactly the same person I was more than a decade ago.

'I can't believe I drank so much last year . . . while I was pregnant with Priya,' says Samira, looking horrified.

'You didn't know at the time,' Emma says.

'No, but still – all those shots. I can't even imagine drinking like that now. It just seems so . . . excessive. I feel like an old lady these days.'

She certainly doesn't look like one. With her shining black hair and dewy, unlined skin, Samira looks like the same girl we knew at Oxford. Giles, on the other hand, who once sported a full head of hair, looks like a completely different person. But at the same time Samira has changed, perhaps more dramatically than Giles has. She used to be spiky, slightly intimidating, with that razor-sharp intellect and impeccable style. She was involved in everything at Oxford. The Union, several sports, theatre, the college orchestra – as well as being a notorious party girl. Somehow she seemed to fit ten times the normal amount of activity into her four years and still emerge with a high First.

She seems softer now, gentler. Perhaps it's motherhood. Or things going so well with her career – apparently the consultancy firm where she works is desperate for her to return from maternity early; it's not hard to imagine the place being on its knees without her. Perhaps it's simply growing older. A sense that she doesn't need to prove herself any longer, that she knows exactly who she is. I envy that.

Julien's talking about a place we visited in Oxfordshire a couple of years ago – Emma's first New Year's Eve with us, I believe.

'Ha!' Mark takes a sip of his drink. 'That was the one where I had to show those local oiks who was boss. Do you remember? One of them actually tried to beat me up?'

Not quite how I remember it.

This is what I recall. I remember the group was exactly the wrong size. Fifteen people – not big enough for a party, not small enough for intimacy. The plan was to go to the races on the afternoon of New Year's Eve. I had been expecting something a bit more glamorous, scenes borrowed from *My Fair Lady* and *Pretty Woman*. Not so much. There were girls wearing skirts so short you could see their Ann Summers' thongs, and boys in cheap shiny suits and bad haircuts and sun-bed tans, strutting around and getting more and more raucous as the evening went on. The food was less champagne and caviar, more steak and ale pies and bottles of WKD. And yet it was all a bit of fun. They were all just kids, really, those mini-skirted girls and those shiny-suited lads, preening and swaggering and hiding their self-consciousness beneath the haze of booze, just as we had all done before them.

And then Mark decided to make some comment about the place being 'overrun with pikeys'.

Admittedly we were in a deserted bit of the stadium, drinking our alcopops – most people were down at the racetrack, cheering on their horses. But there were still a few people around. A group of *youths*, as the *Daily Mail* might label them. And Mark hadn't made any effort to be quiet. He's like that. Sometimes I think that if Emma weren't so unobjectionable, so ready to muck in, people would tolerate him a lot less.

Two of the booze-fuelled teenagers heard him. Suddenly they were squaring up to him. But you could see that they didn't really mean it. It was just something they felt they should do, to protect their slighted honour, like in a nature documentary when the smaller males of the pack can't afford to show any fear, or risk being eaten. Quite understandable, really.

The foremost one was a short, thin guy, with the faintest whisper of teenagerish stubble about his chin, a particularly garish pinstripe number. 'Say that again, mate.' His voice had an unmistakable adolescent reediness to it; he couldn't have been more than nineteen.

I waited for Mark to apologise, defuse the situation – make light of it somehow. Because that would have been the only sensible, adult thing to do. We were the grown-ups, after all. Mark stood a couple of heads taller than his pinstripe-suited aggressor.

But Mark punched him. Took two steps forwards, and punched him full in the face, with one of those meaty hands. So hard that the boy's head snapped back. So hard that he fell like a toppled statue. There was a noise, a crack, a simulacrum of the racecourse starting gun; the way I had thought only really happened in films.

We all just stood there, stunned, including his little gaggle of mates. You might have thought his friends would fight back, try to avenge him. Not so. That was the quality of the violence. It was too sudden, too brutal. You could see: they were terrified.

They bent down to him, and, as he came round, asked if he was all right. He moaned like an animal in pain. There was a trail of bright red blood coming from his nose, and another – more worryingly, somehow – coming from his mouth. I'd never seen anyone bleed from their mouth before, either, apart from in films. It turned out that he had bitten off the tip of his tongue when his head hit the ground. I read that in an article online, in the local rag, a couple of weeks' later. I read, too, that the police were looking for the perpetrator. But there was also some mention of the fact that the guy was a bit of a troublemaker – so perhaps it wasn't a very serious hunt.

What was so odd, I thought, was that Emma didn't even seem particularly shocked. I remember thinking that she must have seen this side of Mark before. She had a clear, immediate idea of what to do – as though she had been waiting for something like this to happen. All practicality. 'We need to leave,' she said, 'now. Before anyone gets wind of this.'

'But what if he's not OK?' I asked.

'They're just a load of drunk chavs,' Emma said. 'And they started it.' She turned around to face us all. 'Didn't they? Didn't they start it? He was just defending himself.'

She was so earnestly convincing – so convinced – that I think we all rather started to believe it. And no one mentioned it again, not for the whole duration of the three-day break. On New Year's Eve, when Mark danced on the table wearing a silly wig and a big, goofy grin, it was even easier to believe that it had never happened. It's almost impossible to imagine it now, looking at him pulling Emma onto his lap, ruffling her hair tenderly as he smiles down at her – the image of the caring boyfriend. Almost, but not quite. Because the truth is I have never quite been able to forget what I saw, and sometimes when I look at Mark I am jolted back to the memory of it, with a little shock of horror.

DOUG

Two a.m. When he lifts the curtain he can see light blazing from the Lodge, which seems brighter now, almost, a defiance against the darkness surrounding it. He has been lying awake for hours now, like an animal whose territory has been encroached upon, who cannot rest until the threat is gone. He can hear the guests even from here, the music thumping out, the occasional staccato of their laughter. He can even hear the low vibration of their voices. Or is he imagining that part? Difficult to be certain. For someone who was once told at school that he had 'an unfortunate lack of imagination' his brain seems to conjure a fair amount from thin air these days.

He chose this cottage specifically because it was the furthest from all the other buildings. The windows predominantly face the bleak greyish flank of the Munro; the loch can only be glimpsed through the window of the toilet, which is almost entirely overgrown with ivy. He can almost imagine himself completely alone here, most of the time. It would be best if he were completely alone. For his own sake, for that of others.

He vaguely recalls a man who was sociable, who enjoyed the company of others – who had (whisper it) *friends*. Who could hold court over pints, who had a bit of a rep as a comic, a raconteur. That man had a life before: a home, a girlfriend – who had waited for him through three long tours in Afghanistan. She stuck by him even when he came back from the last tour, broken. But then the thing happened – or rather he did the thing. And after that she left him.

'I don't know you any more,' she had said, as she piled her things haphazardly into bin liners, like someone fleeing from a natural disaster. Her sister was waiting in the car, she said, as though he might try to do something unspeakable to stop her. 'The man I loved—' and there had been tears in her eyes as though she was grieving someone who had died, 'wouldn't do something like that.'

More than that, she was frightened of him. He could see it as he moved towards her, to try to comfort her – because he hated to see her cry. She had backed away, thrust the bag she was holding in front of her like a shield. She moved away; changed her number. His family, too, retreated. The idea that the man he remembers was, in fact, himself, seems too absurd to be real. Better to imagine him as some distant relative.

He saw how they looked at him, the guests, as though he were a curiosity, a freak show. When he has – rarely – caught a glimpse of his appearance in a mirror he has some idea of why. He looks like a wild man, someone on the very margins of society. This is probably the only profession in which looking the way he does, the unbrushed hair and battered old clothes, might actually be considered a kind of prerequisite. Sometimes he wonders whether he should drop this pretence of living like an almost-normal person, and live fully wild. He could do it, he thinks. He's definitely tough enough: those first few months of training with the Marines quickly sloughed off any softness, and the years since have only toughened him further, like the tempering of steel. The only weak thing about him, the thing he seems unable to control, is his mind.

He has a particular set of skills, knowledge of how to survive in the wild indefinitely. He could take a gun, a rod: shoot and catch his own food. Everything else he could steal, if he needed. He has no qualms about taking a little back. He has given everything, hasn't he? And most people don't realise how much more they have than they need. They are lazy, and greedy, and blind to how easy their lives are. Perhaps it isn't their fault. Perhaps they merely haven't had the opportunity to see how fragile their grip on happiness is. But sometimes he thinks he hates them all.

Except for Heather. He doesn't hate her. But she's different. She doesn't move around in a cloud of blithe obliviousness. He doesn't know her well, true, but he senses that she has seen the dark side of things.

He climbs out of bed. No point in pretending he's ever going to sleep. As he opens the door to the living room he rouses the dogs, who look at him from their bed in sleepy confusion at first, then dawning excitement, leaping up at him, tails wagging furiously. Maybe he will take them for a walk, he thinks. He likes the more profound silence of this place at night. He knows the paths nearest to the Lodge just as well by darkness as he does by day.

Lucy Foley

'Not yet girls,' he says, reaching for the bottle of single malt and sloshing some – and a bit more – into a glass. Perhaps this will take the edge off things.

NOW
2nd January 2019

HEATHER

I call the police, to tell them about the body.

The operator (who can't be older than nineteen or so) sounds ghoulishly animated.

'It doesn't look accidental,' I say.

'And how did you work that out, ma'am?' There's a faint but definite note of facetiousness to his tone – I'm half-tempted to tell him who I used to be, what I used to do.

'Because,' I say, as patiently as I can, 'there is a ring of bruising around the neck. I'm . . . no expert, but that would suggest to me a sign of something, some force.' *Such as strangulation*, I think, and do not say. I do not want to give him another chance to think I'm getting ahead of myself.

There's a longish pause on the other end of the line, which I imagine is the sound of him working out that this is something above his pay grade. Then he comes back on. His tone has lost all of its former levity. 'If you'd wait a few moments, madam, I'm going to go and get someone else to speak to you.'

I wait, and then a woman comes on the line. 'Hello, Heather. This is DCI Alison Querry.' She sounds somehow too assured for a little local station. Her accent isn't local, either: a light Edinburgh burr. 'I've been seconded to the station to assist in the investigation of another case.' Ah, I think. That explains it. 'I understand that what we have is a missing person situation that has now, unfortunately, turned out to be a death.'

'Yes.'

'Could you describe to me the state of the deceased?'

I give the same description I did to her junior, with a little more detail. I mention the odd angle of the body, the spray of gore across the rocks.

'Right,' she says. 'OK. I understand that access is currently proving impossible, due to the conditions and the remoteness of the estate. But we're going to be working hard on a way to get to you; probably via helicopter.'

Please, I want to beg her, this Alison Querry with her calm, measured tones, *get out here as quickly as you can. I can't do this on my own.*

'When,' I ask, instead, 'do you think that will be?'

'I'm afraid we're still not sure. As long as it keeps snowing like this, it's rather out of our hands. But soon, I'm sure of that. And in the meantime, I'd like you to keep all of the guests indoors. Tell them what you need to, obviously, but please keep any of the details you gave to me out of the picture. We don't want to alarm anyone unduly. Who's there at the moment?'

I struggle to count past the tide of tiredness – I haven't slept now for twenty-four hours. I have spent that time veering between exhaustion and surges of adrenaline. Now my thoughts feel treacle-slow. 'There are . . . eleven guests,' I say, finally, 'nine in one group from London, and a couple from Iceland. And the gamekeeper, Doug, and myself.'

'Just the two of you, to manage that big place? That must be a bit of a strain, mustn't it?'

She says it sympathetically, but it feels as though there's something behind the enquiry – something sharp and probing. Or maybe it's just my sleep-deprived mind, playing tricks on me.

'Well,' I say, 'we manage. And, there's one other employee, Iain, but he left on New Year's Eve after finishing his work for the day. He doesn't live here, you see – it's just Doug and me.'

'OK. So as far as you know the only people on the estate that night were you, your colleague the gamekeeper, and the eleven guests? So: thirteen.'

Unlucky for some . . . I seem to hear.

'Well, that keeps it simple, I suppose.'

Simple how? I wonder. Simple, I realise, because if it really was a murder, the culprit is probably among us. Twelve suspects. Of which presumably, undoubtedly, I must be one. The realisation shouldn't surprise me. But it does, because of DCI Querry's easy manner, the sense she has given – the pretence, I realise now – of putting me in charge in her absence.

'So,' she says, 'to summarise: keep everyone where they are. In the meantime, it would be a great help to me if you could have a good hard think about anything you might have noticed over the last forty-eight hours. Anything that struck you as odd. Maybe you saw something, maybe you heard something – maybe you even noticed someone about the place that you didn't recognise? Any detail could be significant.'

'OK,' I say. 'I'll think.'

'Anything that comes to mind now?'

'No.'

'Please. Just take a moment. You might surprise yourself.'

'I can't think of anything.' But as I say it, I do remember something. Perhaps it's because of where I am standing while I speak to her: at the office window, looking out across the loch to the dark peak of the Munro and the Old Lodge, crouched there like some malignant creature. I get a sudden mental image, almost the same scene I see before me but in blackness, viewed from my window at some ungodly hour in the morning – if you could call it that – of New Year's Day. I shut my eyes, try to clarify the image. Something had woken me: I couldn't work out what at first. Then I heard the guests' baby wail. That might have been it. I staggered to the loo, to splash some water on my face. As I looked out of the little bathroom window there was the towering shape of the Munro like a cut-out against the night sky, blotting out the starlight. And then something odd. A light, moving around like a solitary firefly – a wayward star. It was moving in the direction, I thought, of the Old Lodge. Traversing its way slowly across the side of the dark slope.

But I can't tell her this. I'm not even sure it was real. It's all so nebulous, so uncertain. I can't even be sure exactly *when* I saw it, just that it was at some point in the early morning. As I try to sharpen the memory in my mind, interrogate it for anything else I might have forgotten, it fades from me until I'm almost certain it was nothing more than my imagination.

'And one more thing. Just informally, for my picture of things so far. It would be so helpful. Do you remember what you were doing, the night the guest went missing?'

'I was – well, I was in bed.' *Not quite true, Heather. It isn't a lie, exactly – but it's not the whole truth, either. But as you've just remembered, you were stumbling around at God knows what time of night.*

New Year's Eve. The loneliest night of the year, even if you're with people. Even before my life fell apart I remember that. There's always that worry that you're maybe not having quite as much of a good time as you could be. As you should be. And this year, the sound of all the fun the Londoners were having – even if I had told myself I didn't envy any of them – didn't help. So I'd had quite a lot more to drink than usual: forgetting that trying to get drunk to assuage loneliness only ever makes you feel lonelier than before.

When I'd staggered into the bathroom at whatever time it was – five, six? – I was in no fit state to be sure of what I had seen, or even whether I really witnessed anything at all. And I can't tell her any of this. Because then I'd have to admit just how drunk I really was. *And then what?* a little voice asks. *You'd have to admit you aren't the capable, forthright person you're pretending to be? You'd lose her trust?* I am reminded once again that for all her questions about what I might have noticed, her pretence of putting me in a position of responsibility until she arrives, I am one of the thirteen who were here that night. I, too, am a suspect.

'You've gone quiet on me there, Heather,' DCI Alison Querry says. 'Are you still there?'

'Yes,' I say. My voice sounds small, uncertain. 'I'm still here.'

'Good. Well, let's keep in touch. Any questions, I'm here. Anything that occurs to you, don't hesitate to pick up the phone.'

'Of course.'

'I will be there as soon as possible. In the meantime, it sounds like you have a very capable grip on things.'

'Thank you.' Ha. I remember my sister, Fi: 'Sometimes it's OK not to put a brave face on things, Heaths. It can do more harm than good, in the end, keeping everything bottled up.'

'And I'll be in touch very shortly with an estimate of timings,' DCI Querry says, 'when we think we'll be able to get the chopper out. We just need this snow to ease off enough for safe flying conditions.'

What do we do until then? I wonder. Just wait here in the falling snow with the spectre of death just outside the door?

And then I ask it, even though I know I probably won't get an answer. 'The case you've been seconded to,' I say, 'which one is it?'

A short pause. When she next speaks her tone is less friendly, more official. 'I'll let you know that information if and when it becomes necessary to do so.'

But she doesn't need to tell me. I'm fairly certain I know. The body, the way it looked. I've read about it in the papers. It would have been impossible not to. He has his own chokehold over the nation's imagination. His own title, even. The Highland Ripper.

Three days earlier
30th December 2018

KATIE

It's nearly two-thirty in the morning. I'm just wondering if it's late enough that I could slink away to my cabin without being called a buzz kill, when Miranda flops down next to me on the sofa. 'Feel like I've hardly had a chance to talk to you this evening,' she says. Then she lowers her voice. 'I've just managed to escape Samira. Honestly, I love her dearly, but all she can talk about these days is that baby. It's actually a bit – well, it's a bit bloody insensitive, to be honest.'

'What do you mean?'

She frowns. 'I can't even remember if I told you last time I saw you – it's been ages. But . . .' she lowers her voice even further, to a whisper, 'we've been trying, you know . . .'

'To get—'

'Pregnant, yes. I mean, it's early days and everything. Everyone says it takes a while.' She rolls her eyes. 'Except Samira, apparently – she says she got magically knocked up the *second* she came off the pill.'

'I suppose it's different for everyone.'

'Yes. I mean, maybe it's a blessing in disguise, to be honest. It's the end of everything, isn't it? Life as we know it. Look at those two. But it's like . . . I don't know, suddenly it's a rite of passage. Every single person I know on Facebook seems to have a kid, or has one in the oven . . . it's like this sudden *epidemic* of fertility. Do you know what I mean?'

I nod. 'I stopped checking Facebook a while ago, to be honest. It's toxic.'

'Yes, toxic!' she says, eagerly. 'That's it, exactly. God, it's so refreshing talking to you, K. You're out of all of it – single, doing your own thing . . . so far away from even thinking of kids.'

'Yup,' I say, swallowing past something that seems to be stuck in my throat. 'That's me.'

'Sorry,' she says, with sudden sensitivity, 'I meant that as a compliment.'

'It's OK,' I say – the lump in my throat's still there. 'I understand.'

'Look – I've got something that will cheer us up.' She winks at me, and fishes something from the pocket of her jeans. Then she calls out to the others: 'Does anyone want any pudding?'

'You baked?' Nick asks, in mock surprise. 'Never remember you being much into your cooking, Miranda.' This is an understatement – which I'm sure is his point.

Miranda is a *terrible* cook. I remember a particularly awful risotto where half the rice had stuck to the bottom of the pan and burned black.

'But we've had some,' Giles says, quickly. 'That meringue and raspberry thing at the dinner.'

Miranda grins, wickedly. Now she is the Miranda of university days, the undisputed chief party queen. She has that gleam to her eyes: something between excitement and mania. It sends a jolt of adrenaline through me, just as it did so many years ago. When Miranda is like this she is fun, but also dangerous.

'This is a *bit* different,' she says, holding aloft a little plastic Ziploc bag, a rattle of small white pills inside. 'Let's call them our "after dinner mints". Like a palate cleanser. And for old time's sake . . . in the spirit of our all being here together.'

I know immediately that I can't take one – I can't handle the loss of control. The one time I did it went horribly wrong.

Ibiza. Our early twenties. A big group. I hadn't actually been invited, the organiser was someone I'd never known very well at Oxford (read: he didn't consider me cool enough to invite along to any of the famously debauched parties he held). But the week before the holiday, Miranda's granny had died, and she sold her place to me, for a discount. Julien was going, and Samira and Mark, and lots of others who have long since fallen away. I'm not sure I could remember many of their names even if I particularly wanted to try.

I liked the long, lazy lunches by the pool. The evenings drinking rosé, getting a tan, reading my book. What I wasn't so keen on was the part of the evening when the pills came out, and everyone looked at me – when I refused – like I was a parent who'd come along to spoil everyone's fun. And then they would descend into lesser versions of themselves – hysterical, uninhibited, huge-pupiled: like animals. If only they could have seen themselves, I thought. At the same time, I felt uptight, boring: a poor replacement for Miranda. Samira – always with the 'in' crowd – took me to one side and told me: 'You just need to loosen up a bit.'

By the end of the week, they would hardly get up at all during the day. The house had become disgusting. Everywhere you stood there seemed to be dirty clothes, beer cans, used condoms, even puddles of vomit half-heartedly cleaned up. I was on the point of booking a flight home. This was meant to be a holiday, for God's sake. A respite from the job where I was working eighty-hour weeks. I knew that I would be going back feeling tired, sullied, and angry. But I stuck it out. I found a bit of terrace just out of sight of the main house. I dragged a sunbed there and I spent the last few days reading. At least I'd get a proper tan, finish my book: a simulacrum of what you were meant to do on holiday. At least I'd *look* – to all my colleagues, my family – like I'd had a good time.

On the last night, by some miracle, everyone mastered the energy to put together a barbecue like the ones we'd had at the beginning of the week, before they all ruined themselves. I drank quite a lot of cava, and then some more. In the candlelight, looking at everyone's faces, and the dark turquoise glimmer of the sea, I wondered how I could possibly have decided I wasn't having a good time. This was what it meant to be young, wasn't it?

So when the pills inevitably came out, I took one. The euphoria hit me shortly after, I felt invincible. Freed from the prison of being me: Miranda's less fun, less cool friend.

A lot of what happened after seemed to take place in a liberated, not-quite-real place. I remember the swimming pool, jumping into it fully clothed; someone eventually pulling me out, telling me I'd get cold, even though I kept insisting I just wanted to 'stay in the water *for ever*'. I remember loving all of it, all of them. How had I not realised how much I loved them?

Later I remember a man, and I remember the sex in the dark poolhouse, long after everyone else seemed to have disappeared to bed. Almost total blackness, which made all the sensations only the more intense. I was driving it, I was in charge of it. When I came, I felt for a moment as though my whole body had shattered into stars. I was at once the most myself I had ever felt . . . and like someone else completely.

The next morning I couldn't believe it. That daring, sexual person couldn't have been me, could it? If Miranda had been there I might have asked her: how much of what I thought I remembered had been real? Had she seen me go off with the man to the poolhouse? Had that actually happened? Or had it, in fact, just been a particularly lurid hallucination? I couldn't bring myself to ask Samira, for fear that she'd laugh at me and tell me to grow up.

It must have happened, I decided: there was a telltale ache between my legs that said it had. I was convinced I could smell him on me. But no one said anything the next day. I checked for any signs of joking or bravado among the boys, but there was nothing.

Luckily, there are several of us abstaining this evening. Bo – of course, Samira, Nick in support of Bo. I could see how unimpressed Nick was by this addition to the evening in his glare when Miranda proffered the bag to him, practically reaching across Bo to do so. She seemed utterly oblivious, but then she's always given a good impression of shrugging off things, as though nothing can touch her. As her oldest friend, I know that this isn't necessarily the case. Sometimes it takes no small effort to appear so carefree.

Now she's over by the record player in the corner of the Lodge's living room, flicking through a shelf full of old records. Eventually, with a cry of victory, she finds the one she wants – HITS: STUDIO 54 – and places it on the turntable. As the music spills out, some husky-voiced songstress, Miranda goes to the middle of the room and begins to dance. She is completely at ease, dancing like this with the rest of us watching, sitting still. She's so in tune with her body. I have always longed for that lack of inhibition. Because, really, isn't that what dancing is? It isn't about being particularly talented: not unless it's something you do professionally. It's more an ability to shake off your own self-consciousness. I have never been able to do that. It's not really something you can learn to do. You either have it, or you don't.

I remember our teenage years, blagging our way into nightclubs. Though Miranda didn't have to blag. They always let her in on first sight: she was fifteen going on twenty-five, and already gorgeous. In hindsight, when I think about the looks men would give her, the comments they made to her, it turns the stomach. I'd creep in behind her, hoping no one would notice me. I remember dancing beside her, warmed by the vodka stolen from my mum's limitless supplies. Copying Miranda's moves as faithfully as her own shadow; because I have always been that: her shadow. The darkness to her flaming torch. Feeling almost as though I had shaken off my awkwardness.

Miranda is the sort of friend who makes you bold. Who can make you feel six foot tall, almost as radiant as she is, as though you are borrowing a little of her light. Or she can make you feel like shit. Depending on her whim. Sometimes on those nights out she would compliment me on how I looked – always in something borrowed from her already extensive wardrobe, baggy in the bust and hip region, a bit like a girl playing woman in her mother's clothes. Other times she would say something like: 'Oh God, Katie, do you know how serious you look when you're dancing?' then an impression – squint-eyed, grim-mouthed, stiff-hipped – 'You look like you have the *worst* case of constipation. I'm pretty sure that isn't how Sean Paul intended people to dance to this.' I would feel all my newfound confidence desert me – I would feel worse than ever. I would take a big long swig of whatever vodka-and-something drink I was holding, until I felt the slide, the shift. And I'd understand then why my mother seemed to use alcohol like medicine.

As ever, it is almost impossible not to watch Miranda dance. She is so graceful, so fluid, you could assume that she has had some kind of special training. The only one of us who is not watching her, actually, is Julien. He's looking out of the window at the blackness, frowning, apparently lost in thought.

Miranda gestures to us all to join her. She grabs Mark's hand, pulls him to his feet. At first he looks lumpish and awkward in the middle of the carpet. But as she fits her body to his they begin to move together, and with her he acquires a rhythm, sinuous, even sensual, that he would never find on his own. It seems to be infectious, the thrum of the music exerting a pull over everyone. Samira gets up – she's always been a fantastic dancer. She has that looseness, that sense of ease in her own skin. Giles grabs Emma's hand, pulls her to her feet and dances her around the room. Giles has no rhythm at all, but he clearly doesn't care – he's like an overgrown, drunken schoolboy. They cannon into one of the deer heads on the wall, knocking it askew. Emma tries to right it, with an anxious grin, but as she does Giles seizes her around the waist and turns her upside down.

'Giles!' Samira shouts, but she's laughing, and she turns away from them with her eyes closed, lost to the music. Emma's laughing, too – though she's perhaps the only self-conscious one of all of them, tugging her top down as Giles sets her back on her feet. Now Nick's standing, too, putting his hand out for Bo, and they're arguably even better dancers than Miranda, they move so well together.

As ever, though, it is Miranda the eye is drawn back to: the sun around which all the others are orbiting planets. Mark is in his element, leaning into the grooves of her body as they dance. Never has his crush on her been more blatant. If you can call it a crush. Sometimes I have wondered if it might be something more.

When Miranda and Julien started going out, I remember thinking it was a bit odd that his mate seemed to be acting as a kind of courier between them, ferrying messages back and forth. Mark would arrive at our college, asking to speak with her. He had something to tell her from Julien. Julien, like a king, sending out an envoy, wanted to invite her to his rugby game that weekend. Or to accompany him to some party. It was pathetic, I thought. It couldn't really be a friendship at all, more like a form of hero worship, or slavery. Who did Julien think he was? And why did Mark put up with it? True, like Miranda, Julien has the sort of looks – and the kind of charisma – that are prone to attracting acolytes. But Mark wasn't unattractive, or awkward and shy. He didn't need to stoop so low. And it was bizarre. We all had mobiles by then. Julien could simply have sent a text.

But then I started to notice how Mark looked at her, I began to suspect that those visits weren't at Julien's instigation, after all. Mark had volunteered. He began turning up not just outside, on the quad below our block, but actually in our very corridor. Someone had let him in, he'd say, when I asked how he'd got past the door code.

Once I ran into him sitting just outside Miranda's room.

'She's out,' I said. 'She has a meeting with her tutor until four.' It would be an hour and a half until she came back.

'It's fine,' he said. 'I don't have anything else to do.' And I realised that he wanted to be there, waiting around for her.

There was one other time that sticks in my mind. Julien and Miranda were properly together by then, the hot new couple. We went for a barbecue at Julien's house on a boiling day after exams – we'd moved into private housing by then – the huge, ramshackle townhouse where he lived with eight other rugby lads, including Mark. I was the invisible plus one. Admittedly a couple of Julien's friends had tried, half-heartedly, to flirt, but I'd been cold and stand-offish with them. I didn't want to be known as Miranda's worse-looking but easy friend.

Julien was at the grill, holding court, his shirt off to show the expanse of his muscled back, tapering into that surprisingly neat waist. Despite the fact that it was only the beginning of the summer, he had somehow managed to acquire an even, golden tan. I couldn't help comparing myself: the angry flare of heat rash across my chest and upper arms, the rest of me pale as milk. Miranda was looking at him too, in a not dissimilar way to how she'd looked at her glossy new pony, Bert, at sixteen. Then she turned to me, and caught me looking.

So I glanced away, towards Mark. He was wearing try-hard Ray-Bans that didn't particularly suit his broad face. If you glanced quickly at him he might have appeared to be daydreaming, staring into space. But as I continued to look I saw that his sunglasses weren't as opaque as I had thought. And I could see that his eyes were fixed in one prolonged sidelong look at Miranda. He did not look away once. Every time I glanced that way he was looking at her. And when she pulled off her vest to expose her bikini top, I saw his look intensify, indefinably. I saw him shift in his seat.

Later I told Miranda what I had seen. 'Seriously Manda,' I told her, 'it was weird. He wasn't just looking, he was staring. He looked like he wanted to eat you alive.'

She laughed. 'Oh Katie, you're so paranoid. He's harmless. You were like this about Julien, too.'

It was almost enough to make me doubt what I had seen. Even to ask myself: was I just jealous? I was fairly certain it wasn't that. But I *was* humiliated, cross with her for not taking me seriously.

'And you two!' I'm jolted back to the present. Miranda's looking at Julien and me – the two outside the bubble, the only ones not dancing with abandon around the room.

'Julien,' she says, 'dance with Katie for God's sake. She won't do it on her own.' There is the faintest edge of steel to her tone.

There is nothing I feel less like doing, but Julien gets up, takes my hands in his. I am suddenly reminded of watching them dancing at their wedding. Five, six years ago? Miranda made him take dancing lessons, beforehand, so they could foxtrot their way around in front of us. It was all quite typically Miranda, the wedding. She wanted to do something tiny, she claimed, different. She wanted to elope!

In the end it was at her parents' manor house in Sussex. Two hundred guests. Those spindly gold chairs you only ever see at weddings, the round tables, the 'starry night' LED ceiling above the dance floor. And then, the cherry on the tiered, sugar-flowered cake: the couple's dance.

Julien, who up until then looked very much the part of the dashing, handsome groom, had shrunk into himself. He had missed steps, tripped on Miranda's train (almost as long as Kate Middleton's), and generally looked as though he wished himself anywhere but there. He wears the same expression now.

MIRANDA

I watch Katie as she dances – or makes some half-hearted attempt to do so. She looks as if she's actively trying *not* to have a good time. She's been off since we got here, now I think about it. Fine, she's always been a bit quiet, but never such a sullen, monosyllabic presence. I have the sudden uncanny feeling that I'm looking at a stranger.

I've always known exactly what's going on in Katie's life. She has always known exactly what I've chosen to share of mine. But lately, I don't have a clue about her. She's made all these excuses over the last couple of months not to see me. I've told myself they're genuine: she is always so busy, busy, *busy* with her fucking work. Busy being a proper grown-up, unlike me. Or having to go down to Sussex to see her mum, who's been ill (read: all that drinking has finally caught up with her). I've even offered to go with her to see Sally; I have known the woman for going on twenty years, for God's sake. Even if she never liked me – she used to call me Miss Hoity Toity to my face, her

137

breath wine-sour – it seemed like the right thing to do. But Katie shrugged off the suggestion so quickly it was as if the idea appalled her.

The thing is, I've needed her recently. I know I've always given the impression of being self-sufficient, of not wanting anyone to poke their nose in. But, lately, it's all become a bit much. Katie's the only one I can talk to about the problems we've been having. I can't tell her everything about Julien's issues, because it is so important that no one else finds out about that, but still.

I've told her about the fertility problems now. Or rather, I told her *something*. The truth is that we haven't only just started trying. It's been over a year now – a year and a half, in fact. Two years is enough for the NHS to offer you IVF, isn't it?

I could also have told her about the lack of sex – which isn't exactly conducive to getting pregnant. The sense of distance that seems to have been growing between Julien and I over the last year . . . maybe even longer.

If I'm completely honest with myself, I know the reason I haven't shared is that I enjoy the idea of being the one with the perfect life; the friend who has it all. Always ready to step in and offer advice when needed, from her lofty position. It would take more than a few arguments, a few months of infrequent sex, for me to want to give that up.

Maybe this distance between Katie and me is inevitable, a part of growing up, becoming adults with our own lives. Responsibilities, family, coming in the way of friendship. It is only going to get worse, surely, not better. I suppose I can't blame her. I know that friends grow apart, grow out of enjoying each other's company. I look at Facebook sometimes, those decade-old photos from our time at Oxford, and there are photos of me with people – faces that recur in many of the snaps – who I hardly recognise . . . let alone remember names for. It's slightly unnerving. I'll scroll through the images: parties upon parties, in houses and bars and Junior Common Rooms, my arms draped around people who might as well be complete strangers. The photos from the first year are the most obscure. They say you spend your first year at university trying to shake off all the 'friends' you make in your first week, and that was true for me: I made the mistake of chatting with an overly-intense girl at interviews; of drunkenly talking to a guy at a freshers' welcome do who then used to 'bump into' me in various spots around college so he could suggest we go for coffee.

After uni you spend the next few years winnowing those remaining friends down, realising that you don't have the time and energy to trek across London or indeed the country to see people who have barely anything in common with you any more.

I never thought it would happen to Katie and me, though. We've known each other since we were children. It's different. Those friends are always there, aren't they? If you've already stuck together this long?

Still, if I didn't know better, I would say it's like Katie has outgrown me. And at the back of my mind is an insistent little voice. An unpleasant voice, the worst version of myself – saying: 'I made you who you are, Katie. You would be nothing without me.'

Anyway. I'm not going to let her spoil my mood. I take a long gulp of my drink, and wait to feel the pill start its work.

In the next hour there's a general loosening. Giles begins tearing through the pile of board games stacked near the fire. He unearths a box of Twister with a cry of triumph.

'Oh fuck off!' Julien shouts, but he does so with a grin. It's a long time since I've seen him smile, properly. It's probably just the pill, but it makes a bubble of something like happiness expand inside me. Maybe it's time to let him out of the doghouse, after all. It's been a year, now. And it's exhausting: him acting so guilty all the time, me feeling disappointed in him.

It takes several attempts and lots of giggling for us to even get the plastic mat laid out. Everyone is suddenly pretty high.

'I'll be caller,' Katie says, quickly. She didn't have a pill – neither did Samira, but she at least has a good reason: the baby monitor clipped to her chest like a policewoman with a radio. In this moment Katie's face – the expression she wears, of adult exasperation in the face of childish silliness – almost pierces through the bubble of joy inside me. I want to say something, call her out on it, but I can't find the words to do it. Before I can, Mark has grabbed my arm and launched me forward to land: left hand, red. Julien goes next: right foot, green. Then Emma, Giles, Mark. Bo, then Nick: even Nick isn't above Twister, for God's sake. Soon Julien is half straddling me, and through the fuzz in my head I think how curiously intimate it feels. Probably the most intimate we have been for a while, that's for certain. We'll have sex tonight, I think, in that big, draped four-poster bed. Not baby-making sex. Just for the sheer fun of it.

Emma topples and puts herself out of the game. She staggers to her feet, laughing.

A few more moves. Nick staggers a foot outside the mat and goes out, then Giles collapses trying to cross his left leg over his right. It's just Bo, Mark, Julien and me in the game now.

I become aware of a hand on the side of my torso, just below my right breast, and moving upwards. It's on the side that's out of sight of the others. I smile and look around, expecting to see Julien. Instead I find myself following the hand to Mark's arm. We are faced away from Emma, and because Julien is above me I'm fairly certain no one else can see. There is a moment while Mark and I look at each other. His eyes are glazed like a sleepwalker's. My head suddenly feels the sharpest it has since I took the pill, since even before I started drinking. Wrong, is all I can think. This is wrong.

It's like he has forgotten the rules. We flirt, yes, and he fancies me, and I quite enjoy it, and he does things for me, and his reward is looking. But he can't touch. That's different.

I shrug myself out of his grip. As I do I must unbalance him – he sways and crashes to the mat.

'Mark's out!' Emma cries, in glee.

I feel a bit sick, all that rich food and the booze and then the pill. I roll out of my position, amid catcalls of 'spoilsport!' and summons back to the mat, and stumble down the corridor to the bathroom. I want to wash my face – this is the mantra in my head – I want to wash my face with cold water.

I look at myself for a while in the mirror. In the bright light, despite all my efforts, I look older than thirty-three. It's not lines – I've made sure there are as few of those as possible – it's something intangible, something strained and tired about my face. I feel a strange sense of disconnection between the person looking back at me and my internal self. This isn't me, is it? This woman in the mirror? What was I thinking, getting that stuff? I forgot how after the hilarity and the ease it can quickly make me feel so off. But then who am I kidding? I've been feeling like this more and more recently, pills or not.

It used to be enough. Just to be me. To look the way I do, and to be a bloody Oxbridge graduate, and to be able to talk with fluency about current affairs or the state of the economy and the new trend for body con or slip dresses.

But I woke up one morning and realised I was supposed to have something more: to be something more. To have, specifically, 'A Career'. 'What do you do?': that's the first question at any drinks gathering or wedding or supper. It used to sound so pretentious when someone asked this – in our early twenties, when we were all just playing at being adults. But suddenly it wasn't enough to be Miranda Adams. People expected you to be 'Miranda Adams: *insert space for something high powered*'. An editor, say, or a lawyer, or a banker or an app designer. I tried for a while to say casually that I was writing a novel. But that only led to the inevitable questions: 'Have you got an agent? A publisher? A book deal?' Then, 'Oh.' (Silently) So, you're not really a writer, are you?

I stopped bothering.

Sometimes, for shock-value, I'll say, 'Oh, you know, I'm a housewife. I just like to keep things nice at home for Julien, and look after him, make sure he's comfortable.' And I'll pretend to myself that I am very amused by the appalled silence that follows.

That was why you flirted with Mark. To prove you've

*still got it. To prove you're not a . . . whisper it . . .
has-been.*

It was stupid. I mean, I flirt with pretty much everyone:
something Katie pointed out when we were first at university. But I know it's different with Mark – that I shouldn't
lead him on.

I hear footsteps in the corridor. Perhaps it's Julien, come
to check I'm all right. Or Katie, like in the olden days. But
when the door opens, slowly, it is the last person I want
to see.

He's so tall; I always forget this. He's blocking the
doorway with his frame.

'What the fuck, Mark?' I hiss. 'What was that? You
groping me out there?'

I wait for him to plead with me not to tell Emma, claim
he was too out of it to realise what he was doing.

Instead, he says, 'He doesn't deserve you, Manda.'

'What?' I glare at him. 'And you do, I suppose?' I feel
filled with righteous anger and shove out at him. 'Let me
past.'

He moves aside. But as he does he reaches out, quick as
a flash, to grab my upper arm. I try to twist away from
him, but his fingers only tighten, gripping me so hard it
stings like a Chinese burn. I feel a shot of adrenaline and
pure fear. He wouldn't try anything, would he? Not here,
with the others only in the next room?

'Get the fuck off me, Mark,' I say, my voice low and
dangerous. He's never been like this before – not with me,
anyway. I try to tug my arm away, but his grip is vice-like.
I think of all those useless body combat sessions I've done
in the gym: I am so weak compared to him.

He bends down to my ear. 'All this time, I've been there

for him. Since Oxford. Looking out for him, covering for him if necessary. And does he look out for me? Does he help me out when I ask him to? To have something of my own, for once? No. I'm sick of it. I'm not lying for him any longer.'

He sounds completely sober, his words clear-cut. It's as if the pill hasn't affected him at all. In comparison I feel fuggy and confused. Except for the pain in my arm, anchoring me.

'What do you mean?' I ask him. I feel as if I'm several minutes behind.

'I know about him. I know his little secret. Shall I tell you what he's been up to?'

I'm shaking, with a mixture of fear and anger. It's important, here, to pretend I don't know anything – don't *want* to know anything.

'Whatever it is,' I say, 'I don't want to hear it. I don't want anything to do with it.'

He looks momentarily taken aback. His grip slackens, and I wrench my arm away. 'I . . .' he fumbles, 'you mean – you really don't want to know?'

Does he really imagine that my own husband wouldn't have let me in on his shameful little secret? Still, definitely best to play dumb. Just in case there comes a time when I need to distance myself from it all, to insist on my own innocence.

'No,' I say. 'I don't want to know.'

'Fine,' he says, looking genuinely astonished, all the bluster gone out of him. He steps back. 'If that's really what you want.'

I stumble on unsteady legs back into the dining room, sure that someone will notice the expression on my face and ask me what the matter is – I'm not sure whether I want their attention right now, or not.

No one sees me at first. There's another game of Twister going on, and they're all cackling with laughter as Giles tries to straddle Bo. The atmosphere is exactly the same as it was before – everyone joyful, riding the high of booze and pills. But suddenly I'm on the outside looking in, and it all seems ridiculous . . . false even, like they're all trying too hard to show what a good time they're having.

Emma turns and sees me standing in the doorway. 'Are you OK, Manda?' she asks.

'We thought you'd got stuck in there,' Giles says, with a stupid, goofy grin. 'So Mark went to check you were all right.'

'Oh God,' Emma says, 'Manda – do remember that time someone had a house party and you got stuck in the loo?'

'No,' I say. But even as I do I realise that I do remember it, vaguely. The feeling of humiliation when someone had to crowbar me out. God – mortifying. I could swear it happened at least a decade ago. But if Emma remembers it, it must have been much more recently. 'When was that?'

'Hmm,' Emma says, 'it must have been in London at some point. The days when everyone actually had house parties – when we were fun, you remember? So recent, and yet it feels like centuries ago.'

I nod, but something about the mention of it has given me an odd, uneasy feeling. But I cannot work out why.

'*Are* you all right?' Emma asks again.

Her tone's so maternal, so caring . . . so fucking patronising. 'Yes,' I say, 'why wouldn't I be?'

Perhaps it comes out as sharply as I meant it: she looks stung.

I sit it out for an hour or so. I've done better than Katie – she must have gone back to her cabin while I was in the bathroom. And yet she's the one I want to talk to about what just happened – more so than my own husband, somehow. I could go and find her . . . she might still be awake. But if I leave I might show Mark that he has me rattled, and I don't want that. The effects of the pill have completely worn off for me, and I look enviously at the others, blissed out, beaming at each other.

Finally, when I decide I've stuck it out long enough, I turn to Julien. 'I'm tired,' I say. He nods, vaguely, but I think he has barely registered the fact that I've spoken. Pills have always affected him strongly. I'd half meant it as an invitation to walk me back to the cabin, but I'm not going to embarrass myself in front of the others by making that clear now.

When I step outside, the moon shines full and the loch is lit up silver. It's a clear night, except for a band of cloud on the horizon where the light of the stars disappears, as though a shroud has been pulled over them.

I think about Mark, and what just happened. The top of my arm still aches where he grabbed me. I'm sure there will be bruises in the morning: the reminders of his fingers.

I fish the iPhone from my pocket and turn on the torch. It casts a weak stream of light in front of me; a small comfort, a lantern against the dark. Several times I have to turn around and look behind me to check that no one is following. It's silly, probably – but I'm on edge, and the silence out here feels watchful, somehow. I am reminded of dark, drunken walks home in London in the early clubbing days, keys between my knuckles. Just in case. But here I'm in the middle of nowhere, with no one except my closest friends. The silence here, the expanses, seem suddenly hostile. That's a ridiculous thought, isn't it? In the morning, it will all seem different, I tell myself.

Or we could leave in the morning. I could tell Julien, and we could leave. He wouldn't like it – I'm sure he's been looking forward to this trip. We both have, actually – perhaps me even more so. I think he would agree, if I explained everything. We could go back to the house and have champagne and maybe order something in and watch the Westminster fireworks over the rooftops. I realise that when I think of this I'm not imagining our current home: the grown-up, stuccoed house. I'm actually thinking of our first flat in London: before I failed to do anything interesting with my life, became an also-ran. Before Julien got so busy with making money.

It might be fun.

But it would also be giving up. It should be Mark who is ashamed, who has to leave. Not me. The thought fills me with rage. Then I think of that moment, looking at myself in the mirror – seeing more than I wanted to, beyond the effects of the pill. Even before that, even before Mark groped me during Twister, I'd been feeling like I wasn't enjoying myself quite as much as I should have done. There was Samira, talking my ear off about sleep schedules and breast pumps, showing me the stains on her baggy old T-shirt. This, from the girl whose nickname at Oxford was Princess Samira, because she was always so perfectly coiffed, glamorously tailored, even at nineteen. I loved what a stir we'd cause going into a pub or bar together, or even just the Junior Common Room; the two of us roughly the same height, one dark, one blonde, dressed in the best clothes. Birds of a feather.

147

Then there's Katie – so distant since we got here, probably thinking of something much more important, something at work. Acting like she is better than all of us: the successful lawyer. I'd had this sudden, rushing sense of being left behind. That was why I'd got everyone dancing. It was why I'd brought the pills out when I did. I'd been saving them for tomorrow, in fact, for New Year's Eve. But suddenly I needed to be the one in control again, dictating the order of things.

As I round the corner I see in the distance three rectangles of bright light, blazing out into the dark. It's the gamekeeper's cottage, of course. When I walked there earlier I didn't realise quite how far away it is from the other buildings, almost at the foot of the mountain. As I continue to look, a dark figure appears in the central window, haloed in light. It must be the gamekeeper, Doug, still up. But from this distance he is featureless and spectral. I take a step back, which is ridiculous: even if he can see the tiny pinprick of light from my phone, he can't see me. But it feels as though he is looking straight at me. And it's nothing like earlier, when I went and knocked on his door. Right now, with what just happened, I feel vulnerable, displaced, the landscape so vast and alien and silent around me. I long for the noise and lights and bustle of the city.

I half run the rest of the way along the path. Inside the cabin I feel safe for a moment. But only briefly, because when I go to bolt the door I realise that there is no lock.

I get ready for bed, and when I next look out of the windows I can see that lights have gone on now in the other cabins. Everyone must have chosen to go to bed shortly after me.

So where is Julien? Presumably on his way back along the path – but he's taking his time about it.

Half an hour passes, then an hour. My arm aches where Mark grabbed it. I pull on a jumper, some big silly fluffy slippers that Julien hates because they make me look 'like a suburban sixties housewife' and yet I have never got rid of because they're too bloody comfortable. My teeth are chattering, I realise – even though I'm not really cold.

I wake at 4 a.m. I don't know where I am. The first thing I see are the numbers blinking on the little alarm beside the bed. At first I think I'm at home, but then I realise it's too quiet for that: in the city there'd be that background music of sirens and car engines, however late at night. I'm not sure what has woken me. I don't actually remember falling asleep. I'm still in the jumper and slippers, I realise, lying on top of the coverlet. The light is on, in the hallway. Did I leave it on? I can't remember.

Then I see a figure standing in the dark by the doorway. I scrabble backwards, away from him. Then he steps forward and I see that it's Julien. His cheeks are red from the cold. His eyes are oddly blank.

I sit up. 'Julien?' My voice comes out small and reedy; it does not sound like my own. I see him start at the sound of my voice. 'Where have you been?'

'Sorry,' he says. 'I went for a walk.'

'In the middle of the night?'

'Well yes – to clear my head. Those fucking pills – and then I got the come-down, started worrying about everything. I walked the whole way around the loch.' He runs a hand through his hair. 'Oh, and I saw that weirdo, the game-keeper.'

'You did?' I remember now how unnerved I was by his silhouette in the lit-up window on my walk back.

'He was creeping around the edge of the loch – coming out of the really dense bit of forest. He had dogs with him. What on earth could he have been doing? Honestly, I think he might be a bit of a nut job. I think you should stay away from him.'

I am both touched and irritated by this chauvinistic display of protection. At least it shows he cares, I think, then I catch myself. Have I become so uncertain of his affection recently that I have become that needy?

'He's not the one to worry about,' I say.

'What do you mean?'

'Mark. He came on to me in the loo. He grabbed my arm. Here.' I pull up the sleeve of the jumper to show him. 'He said he knew your *dirty little secret*. Yes, that's how he put it.'

I see him flinch.

'Does he mean what I think he does?' I ask. 'Did you tell him? We've gone over this before, Julien, you can't tell anyone. It would destroy everything. And don't tell me I'm being paranoid. The moment you decided to use me you made *me* part of it, like it or not.'

There is a longish pause. Then, 'Look, Manda,' Julien says, pushing his hand through his hair and sighing, 'we all had a lot to drink . . . and then the pills—'

I feel a flush of anger. 'Are you saying I'm making this up? That you don't believe me?'

'No – no. What I'm saying is that he might not have really meant it, to hurt you, that is. He's a big guy, sometimes he just throws his weight around a bit too much. I mean, how long have we known him?'

'Hang on a second,' I say, 'it sounds to me like you're defending him.'

'I'm not, I promise I'm not. But . . . look, is it really worth spoiling everything for ourselves because of his stupidity? He's one of my oldest friends. Don't you think we should give him the benefit of the doubt?'

I suddenly see what he's doing. He isn't protecting Mark. He's protecting himself. Because if Mark really does know his – our – secret, and Julien challenges him, Mark might use it against him.

I should be outraged. But suddenly I just feel very tired.

He's undressed now. He takes out his pyjamas. They're very chic ones, a present from my mother, who likes to be up on any new style trend: a Christmas purchase from Mr Porter. Nevertheless, there was a time – not so long ago – when he wouldn't have worn anything in bed, not even boxers. We liked to lie skin to skin.

'Don't,' I say, as he goes to shrug the trousers on. He stands for a minute looking particularly naked and confused. 'It's cold,' he says.

'Yes,' I say. 'But you can put them on . . . afterwards.' I suddenly want the comfort of his arms around me, his weight on top of me, his mouth on mine: I want to obliterate that odd, creeping feeling I've had since this evening.

For emphasis I pull the jumper over my head. I'm naked underneath. I lie back and let my legs fall open, so he can be in no doubt about what I have in mind. 'Come here,' I say, beckoning him.

But he makes a kind of grimace, his mouth pulling down at the edges. 'I'm really tired, Manda.'

I feel my skin prickle with the chill of his rejection.

In the first few years of knowing each other, of being

together, it was always me who turned him down. Perhaps just twice in eight years it was the other way around: the exception that proved the rule, when he had the flu, say, or an interview the next day. But lately I've been keeping count. The last ten times, perhaps more, it has been him.

I have two separate underwear drawers at home. One is for everyday: my M&S undies and bras, made exclusively for comfort. Julien used to cringe in horror at my beige T-shirt bras as they came out of the wash. Then another drawer: froths of Agent Provocateur and Kiki de Montparnasse, Myla, and Coco de Mer. Hundreds, perhaps even thousands of pounds' worth of silk and lace. The sort of lingerie that is not meant to be worn under clothes, that is meant only to grace your flesh for a few minutes before it is whipped off. I realised, packing for this trip, that I had not worn any of those pieces for as long as I could remember. I was half-tempted to chuck them out: they seemed to be mocking me. Instead, I gathered the whole lot into my arms and dumped them into the suitcase. Armour, for a desperate – last ditch? – offensive.

I suppose it makes a kind of sense that Julien's gone off sex. He has a lot on his plate – though most of it's his own fault – and there's been my insistence on getting pregnant. But here, in this beautiful wilderness, fuelled by champagne and pills, I thought it would be different. I feel a tiny tremor of fear as he lies down next to me and rolls away to face the wall.

I move towards him, to borrow some of his warmth. I reach out a hand to touch the back of his head. My palm comes away damp. 'Your hair,' I say.

'What?' His voice doesn't even sound sleepy. I wonder if he's been pretending, lying there awake, like me.

'It's damp, here, at the back.'

'Oh, well – it started raining on the way over.'

As I lie there I think of the clear sky and my walk to the cabin, and think the clouds must have come over very quickly for it to have started raining. It's too cold to rain anyway, surely. It would have been snow. I'm suddenly sure he's lying. Though what about, and why, I have no idea. I tell myself that there's no point in worrying. I already know his worst secret, after all.

It was about a year ago that Julien said, very casually, one evening, 'I've got a friend. He'd love you to design a website for him. He's left the City and he's trying to set up a business. What do you reckon?'

Did I know, even then, that there was something off about it? It's only with hindsight that I can see the way he asked it was a little too casual. That he was drumming his fingers against the kitchen counter: a direct contrast to his tone. That he would hardly look at me as he spoke. There was also the fact that he had never up to that point seemed to think much of my skills in website design, or my little business idea: to set it up as a company, seek out commissions. He had called it my 'project', as though I were making a quilt.

It would only be my second commission to date – the first had been for a friend's baby shower. But I decided to overlook my misgivings. I assumed that the reason for his shiftiness was that this was clearly a bit of a pity project, whatever else he claimed. He earned enough money for the two of us put together, more than we needed, but I think he knew that my pride had been hurt by my own lack of success. So, to tell the honest truth, I didn't look too closely into it. Not then. And it would be a useful showcase, I thought. It would be helpful simply to have another happy client under my belt: to share on my website, via my social media. You have to have a bit of a body of work to entice others. A bit chicken and egg, but there it is.

'Should I send him a quote?' I asked Julien. 'Because I hope he knows I'm not going to work gratis.' I didn't want this guy to think that just because I was his mate's wife I would do him a freebie. I might give mates' rates, certainly, but I was a professional. My time was valuable. It had been a long time since I had felt really useful to anyone professionally, if ever, and I was going to savour the feeling. That was my biggest worry at the time. That I might be humiliated by working for free.

'Don't worry about the money,' Julien said. 'He's already reassured me that he'll pay you handsomely.' He grinned. 'Some in cash, some in a bank transfer – so you don't have to declare it all to HMRC if you don't want to.' Well, that wasn't exactly a concern. The company hadn't made any money yet – it was unlikely it would be in profit by the end of the tax year. Surely Julien knew that?

Even then I didn't feel any particular suspicion. Should I have done? He was my husband, for God's sake.

It was only when a payment of £50,000 arrived in my bank account, and when Julien returned home from 'watching rugby at the pub', with the same amount in fifties, that I became suspicious. 'Julien,' I asked him, 'what the fuck is going on?' He grinned awkwardly, spread his hands wide. 'This is just what he wants to pay you,' he said. 'He was so pleased with the work. He has absolutely pots of money, so this is just like loose change to him.'

I might even have believed him, if I hadn't seen his eyes.

'Julien,' I said, sharply, so he knew there was no bullshitting me, 'this money is in my account. So whatever else, I am now involved in whatever the fuck is happening here. And I am your wife. So I think you need to tell me everything, right now.'

'It will be good for us, in the end,' he said, blusteringly. 'I . . . I suppose you could say I saw an opportunity.'

'What sort of opportunity? Outside work?'

'Well,' he gripped the back of the chair in front of him, hard. 'I suppose you could say it is connected to work. Loosely . . .' He seemed to gather himself. 'Look, it was just – sitting there, right in front of me. There was some information that I was aware of, and it would have been completely stupid not to use it.'

It was then, finally, that it struck me. 'Oh my God, Julien. Oh my God. Do you mean insider trading? Is that what you're saying to me? Is that where this money comes from?'

I knew the truth less from anything he said then than from the way his face drained immediately of all colour. 'I wouldn't call it anything as formal as that,' he said. 'No, it's nothing like that. I've just given a couple of people a bit of a nudge. Friends. Nothing really big. This sort of thing happens all the time.'

I couldn't believe what he was telling me. 'I think what you mean, Julien, is that people get arrested all the time.'

Only the other week I had been reading about Ray Yorke, a partner at one of the big investment banks who was serving time for trading secrets with his golf buddy. As they made their way around the course he'd casually dropped in titbits of information – supposedly not realising that his mate was trading on the information, and making millions in the process. He claimed he didn't realise even when he

155

started accepting the gifts his friend pressed on him: a Rolex watch, jewellery for his wife, parcels of cash. When he was caught, his life had ended. He'd lost his job, he'd gone to prison, his wife had divorced him, he'd never work in finance again. CNN had shown an interview of him outside the courthouse practically weeping: offering himself up as a cautionary tale. And of course, in the process, he'd had to give it all back – and then some.

I'd had zero sympathy for the guy. Who, I had thought, could be that fucking stupid? It had seemed so obvious to me. Of course you get found out for something like that, in the end.

As it turned out, my husband could be exactly that fucking stupid. 'What on earth is wrong with you, Julien?' I said. 'You're like a gambler, always in for one more hand.'

'I'm sorry, Manda, I don't know what to—' And then suddenly his face had changed, hardened. He stopped the expansive innocent guy routine, he called off the cringing, hand-wringing *mea culpa*. 'Well, I suppose it's easy for you to say, Miranda,' he said. 'But you seem to forget quite how much you enjoy this life. The holidays – Tulum, the Maldives, St Anton – they don't come for free, you know. Half the time you seem to be sitting around reading some kind of brochure for holidays that cost more than some people earn in a year. Or the boxes that turn up from Net-a-Porter every season, or the five hundred pounds you pay every month to your fucking nutritionist. Yes, I earn a lot. But we have practically no savings. And now you're talking talking talking about having children – do you know how much private school costs these days? Because of course the children of Miranda Adams couldn't go anywhere so lowly as a *free* school, like I did. And university, now they've hiked the fees? And with only one of us working . . .' He looked me straight in the eye. 'My job isn't as secure as you think it is, Miranda. The financial crisis wasn't all that long ago. And then we'd have been screwed.'

I couldn't believe it. 'You can't put this on me, Julien. This is your fuck-up.'

Perhaps I should have seen it coming. Because this is how he has always been. He didn't grow up in a well-off household, like me, with a solid family unit. His mum was a single parent. It cost her everything to put him through university. Though you would never know it, from the way he acted there. He has a profound shame of the fact that he used to be – not even poor – from a lower income family. He has a fear of looking bad – which is what poor is, in his mind. It's like he has always felt the deficit. Perhaps if it weren't this, it would be something else. It would be an affair, for instance, or a gambling addiction. Maybe I should even be grateful that it isn't something more, something worse: though it's difficult to imagine what that would be, right now.

DOUG

It is dark, late. This is his favourite time. He has the whole place to himself – finally. Or at least he thought he did, until he came across that idiot guest, the one who had pestered him about the Wi-Fi, the one with the handsome, punchable face. Julien. When the torch beam passed over him he was walking along the track that led from the Lodge to the cottage where he and his wife were staying. But it was about an hour after all that awful noise from the Lodge had stopped – and after the lights had gone off.

The man had started in surprise when he caught him with the torch. He had looked like an animal, like one of the herd, fixed in the Land Rover's beam. His face had worked, as though he were wrestling with himself as to whether he should explain what he was doing out so late. But in the end he had settled for a grimace and a nod, and continued on his way without turning back. He looked as guilty as a man could look. He had the hunched shoulders, the stiff, mincing walk, of someone who had been up to

159

no good. Doug would bet that the man had not expected to see anyone else on his way. And in whatever he was doing, he had been caught out.

That, at least, had made up for the interruption to his peace. Thinking about it now, he smiles.

He has taken the dogs out with him. Griffin and Volley: Griffin a beautiful flat coated retriever with a mouth as soft as velvet, and Volley an Australian Shepherd, beautiful too, but also strange-looking, with one milky blue eye and a marbled coat like ink dropped into water. They actually seem to like him, seem not to sense the darkness in him in the same way that people do.

Both of the dogs are skittish, excited, this evening. It's the promise of the snow in the air, he's sure – the scent sharpening, metallic, strange. There has been nothing in the forecast, but in a place like this you learn to trust what you can see and smell over any supposed science.

He'll have to go and warn the bloody guests about it tomorrow. There could be a lot of it coming. If they need any groceries for the next few days they'll have to let him know by this evening. If it's a bona fide dump, the track will be impossible to navigate, even in the Land Rover – even with the snow tyres on. No one will be able to get back in here. Or out.

He picks up a stick from the path and throws it. It disappears outside the beam of his head-torch beyond his vision. Both dogs hurtle after it, their sight keener than his. They are almost a match for speed, though Griffin is getting old, and slackens her pace first. Volley bounds ahead, true to his name, and takes the prize, tail wagging furiously, an unmistakable air of triumph in the proud way he holds his head.

The Hunting Party

At times like this Doug breathes easier.

Now, Volley has dropped the stick, and begun to whine. 'What is it boy? Hey, what is it?'

Griffin has caught the scent too. They begin to follow it, muzzles down. A rabbit, perhaps, or a fox. Maybe even a deer, though they don't tend to come around the side of the loch as regularly. Then Doug hears something a little way off: the noise of a large animal passing through the undergrowth beside the path. 'Who's there?' he calls.

No answer, but the unmistakable noise of snapping and tearing continues, at a greater pace. Something – or someone – is running from them.

The dogs tear ahead, after the sound. He calls them back. They turn and trot back to him; reluctant, but obedient. If it's another of the guests, the dogs could terrify them.

Doug flashes the beam of his torch on the earth around him and illuminates a man's footprint a few feet ahead. Just one; apparently this is the only part of the path soft enough to take an impression. A large foot. He places his own inside it: roughly the same size. Might be one of the guests of course, though he would be very surprised if they'd got this far from the Lodge in their evening explorations. He'd heard them down by the lake before supper, but he doubts they would have ventured much further in the dark. And this boot has a good tread on it. The London guests all turned up wearing city people's idea of rugged outdoor wear – Dubarry boots and Timberlands.

The Icelanders then, perhaps, with their proper boots. But the question remains: why would any of the guests have run away, when he called?

* * *

161

He often comes out at this time to check for anything untoward. Some of his night-time forays, however, are not so intentional.

Once he woke up and discovered himself lying in the damp heather a little way from the other end of the loch, near the deserted Scout camp. It was the middle of the night, but luckily there was enough of a moon for him to see where he was. He had no memory of how he had got there, but his legs ached as though he had been running. His hands stung. Later, in the light of the cottage, he would discover that they were lacerated by cuts and grazes, in a couple of places very deeply.

He could not remember anything that had happened before this point. Once, as a boy, he had a general anaesthetic. It had been a black curtain coming down upon his consciousness, a light switched off, the time lost like the blink of an eye. These were like that. Great mouthfuls of time swallowed, leaving voids in their place. He could have been anywhere. He could have done anything.

It had happened to him in the city, too. That was worse: then he had ended up on the other side of town, had come around wandering in unknown streets, or lying in a children's playground, or stumbling his way down a railway siding.

There is a word for it, a word that sounds like a piece of music: fugue. A beautiful word for something so terrifying. They were brought on by the trauma, the psychiatrist said. They were a symptom, not a condition in and of themselves. The first thing he had to do was start talking about what had happened to him. He understood that, didn't he? Because this problem, while so far it hasn't caused any great harm other than a few confusing nights – well, it could be dangerous. For himself. For others around him. After all, there was already the incident in question: the very reason he was having the sessions.

'Yes,' he had said, looking the psychiatrist right in the eye. 'But that didn't happen in a *fugue* state. I knew exactly what I was doing then.'

The psychiatrist had coughed, looked uncomfortable. 'Still: I think we have established that both the incident and these episodes, directly or less so, stem from the same trauma.'

There had been an enforced number of sessions, though the psychiatrist wrote in her report that she believed they needed more. He double-checked: this was only advisory, not mandated. He was free to ignore her advice. He couldn't quite believe that he had got off so easily, and he suspected that she couldn't, either. It had stuck with him though, the idea that he could hurt someone: not intentionally, as the other thing had been, but without even knowing what he was doing. So instead of getting to the bottom of the issue – because he didn't think he could ever talk about that day, even if it were to save his life – he has come somewhere where there are very few people that he could hurt.

He waits for a while longer at the edge of the trees, his ears prickling for any further movement. But there's nothing, and the dogs seem to have lost interest too. He turns and tramps back along the path in the direction he has come.

When he returns to the cottage he lies back on his bed, fully clothed. Allows himself, finally, to hope for the possibility of sleep.

The room is spartan. Here there are no pictures upon the walls, no knick-knacks on the shelves, which hold only a couple of slim volumes: a book of short stories, a collection of poems. He never reads these days, but they are clues, tethers to the person he used to be. There is nothing here to tell you about the man who inhabits the room, unless the nothing is in itself a clue to something. It has the anonymity of a prison cell. This, if one knew him, which no one does well, is no coincidence.

He turns onto his side, and closes his eyes. It is a mimicry of sleep. If he is lucky he will get perhaps an hour – maybe even two – of rest. He has learned to exist on this, to drink enough coffee to combat the dizziness, to take enough painkillers to mask, as much as possible, the migraines. There was a time when he used to sleep the deep, untroubled sleep of an animal. He cannot imagine it now. That life belonged to a different man. Now every time he closes his eyes he sees their faces. With pleading eyes they ask him: *Why us? What did we do to deserve it?* Their hands grope for him, catch at his hair, his clothes. He can feel them on him – he has to fight them off. Even when he opens his eyes he can feel the ghost traces of their fingertips upon his skin: cobweb memories.

NOW
2nd January 2019

HEATHER

After I call the police, I dial the boss's number, in London. I don't get through to him first, of course: it's a silken-voiced PA. 'How can I help?'

I tell her everything. There's a stunned silence on the line, then: 'I'll put you through to him,' she says, in a much more ordinary voice, as though she has quickly decided that the husky purr isn't appropriate here.

He comes on the line quickly. 'Hello Heather,' he says, as familiarly as if we talk every day on the phone like this. From the one time I met him, I remember him being quite handsome (though difficult to say whether that was just the effect of good grooming, and all that charm), with the smile of a politician.

'It's bad,' I say. 'We found a body.'

'Oh,' he says. 'Oh, God.' But he doesn't sound particularly shocked. Instead, I am certain I can hear him thinking – just like the politician he resembles – of how to manage this, of how to protect the estate.

'And I'm afraid it doesn't look like an accident.'

'Hmm,' he says. 'You've called the police, of course?'

'Yes,' I say, 'just before I called you.'

'I'd come up,' he says, 'but I'm not sure that would help matters.'

'It's likely you wouldn't be able to get here anyway.' I explain the situation with the weather, the fact that we're essentially snowbound here.

'It was Doug who found the body, you say?'

'Yes.'

'Where?' He asks it with a new sharpness in his tone. Maybe he's wondering if there's any way he could be sued for this.

'In the waterfall near the old watermill.'

'OK. And did you see anything? Did Doug?'

'No – nothing in particular.'

'Does Iain know, too?'

'Er . . . no, not yet. He would have left on New Year's Eve, once he'd finished his work for the day.'

'Well, he'll still need to know, of course. Important that you put him in the loop too.'

'Yes,' I say. 'Of course. I'll try him now.'

'Do. And keep me posted with any updates please.'

'Of course.' I tried for something assertive, but it came out as little more than a whisper. He sounds so businesslike, so removed. Perhaps it's possible to be so where he is, far away in London . . . untouched by the atmosphere of death that has permeated every inch of this place.

I try Iain next. I only have a mobile for him, no home number. It goes straight to voicemail. The problem with only being contactable by mobile in this part of the world is that most of the time you don't have enough signal to be reached. I'll leave him a voicemail. I'm sure he'd be touched by the boss's concern, but frankly he's the least of my worries at the moment.

I'm about to leave a quick message when there's a knock on the door.

It's Doug. 'They're here,' he says. 'The guests.' While I've been on the phone, he's gone and rounded up the others from their cabins, shepherded them into the Lodge.

Doug looks awful – I'd noticed it earlier, but not really *seen* it, being too distracted by the immediate disaster. His eye sockets are a dark, bruised purple, as though he hasn't slept for a week. It looks almost as though the guest's death has affected him personally. His hand, I notice, is bandaged, a thick gauze covering most of the skin. I hadn't seen it when we were outside, of course, because he had been wearing gloves.

'What happened to your hand?' I ask.

'Oh,' he says. He holds it up and looks at it as though he's never seen it before. 'I suppose I injured it.'

'When? It looks bad.'

'Don't know,' he says. He scratches the back of his head with his other hand. 'A few days ago, I suppose.' But that's not true – it can't be. He hadn't been wearing a bandage at the Highland Dinner . . . I'm sure of that; I would have noticed it. And the injury beneath must be bad for him to have used the bandage: I've seen Doug with terrible cuts and bruises before, and he hasn't even bothered with a plaster.

'Shall I tell them you're coming out to talk to them?' he asks. I notice that he has hidden the bandaged hand in the pocket of his jacket.

Somehow the role of telling the guests has fallen to me: we seem to have agreed upon that without even discussing it. Trying to swallow down my mounting dread, I nod, and follow him out of the office.

The guests are assembled just down the corridor in the living room, waiting for the news. Just the London guests: the Icelandic pair are back at their bunkhouse. Doug and I decided to tell the group of friends first: the death, after all, will be a much more devastating revelation for them.

When I go into the living room they all look up at me. I have been on this side before, in my old job. All those anxious families waiting for news, me having to tell them the very last thing they want to hear. *It was not successful. There was an unforeseen complication. We did everything we could.*

I dig my nails into the skin of my palms. I have also been on the other side of this. I know exactly how it feels. Their faces swim before me, upturned, expectant, utterly intent on what I am about to say. I feel a lurch of nausea in the pit of my stomach. What I am about to tell them is going to change their lives for ever.

'We have found her,' I say. The questions begin almost at once; I put up a hand for silence. The important thing is to get the terrible news to them as quickly as possible now, to extinguish any lingering hope. Hope is a great thing, when there is still a chance of everything being OK. But in cases that are quite literally hopeless it can do much more damage than good. Though: I don't think any of them really have hope any more. They know already. But the confirmation of that knowledge is something else.

'I'm afraid it's very bad news,' I say. You could suddenly cut the atmosphere with a knife. The horrible power of being in this situation hits me with full force. I hold all of the cards, ready to lay them down in front of the guests – they will make of them what they will.

'I'm very sorry to tell you that she's dead.'

There's the shock at first: they are united in that. They stare at me as though they are waiting for me to deliver the punchline. And then each begins to process the information and their grief in different ways: hysterics, mute incomprehension, anger.

I know that none of these reactions are any more or less valid. I saw all of these on the ward, whenever I had to inform next-of-kin. And as any paramedic will tell you, it's often the quiet ones you need to worry about after a disaster: not those who wail and scream about their pain. But those who wail and scream are still in pain. Grief can be as different in the way it displays itself as the people who experience it. I know this all too well.

But the thought goes through me, all the same: is it possible that one of these displays is just that? A display? A performance? As they ask me questions about the body, how I found it, how it looked when I found it, I wonder: does one of them know all of this already? Does someone know more than he or she is letting on?

Back in the sanctuary of the office my phone rings. I seize it, expecting the boss again, or the police – perhaps with an update on when they expect to be able to get here. It's not the police.

169

'I can't talk right now, Mum.'

'Something bad's happened. I can tell.'

How can she tell from six words? I clench my jaw. Then unclench. 'I can't talk now. I'm fine, that's all you need to know at the moment. I'll tell you about it later. OK?'

'You didn't call yesterday, like we agreed you would. So I knew something had happened.' Her voice is ragged, frayed at the edges with worry. 'Oh Heather, I knew I shouldn't have let you go and live in that place.'

She has never understood it. Why, having suddenly found myself all alone in the world for the first time in fifteen years, I would choose to compound that loneliness by moving to such a place. But what she couldn't understand – because it wasn't really something I could explain, only something I felt – was that I felt much more alone surrounded by people. All our friends, however much they were trying to help, and sympathise, reminded me of him. And the city we had lived in together. Around every corner was a café where we had eaten brunch, or a bookshop we had browsed, or even a branch of Sainsbury's where we had picked up a ready meal curry and a bottle of wine. Our apartment was worst of all, of course. I could hardly bring myself to be inside it before it was sold. Here were all the memories of a life together, of growing up together: the place we had lived in practically since we left university. My whole adult life.

And being around people – people carrying on with their lives, busy and messy, settling down, having children, getting married – just emphasises how much my own has stalled, indefinitely. Perhaps for ever.

So yes, sometimes, I get lonely here. But at least this

landscape has always seemed suited to loneliness, and I am not confronted, every day, by all that I have lost, by the echoes of my old life, whole and happy and filled with love. And yes, sometimes as I had in the city, I have found myself almost unable to get out of bed, and have had to force myself to get dressed, eat my breakfast, make the short walk to the office in the Lodge. But it is a lot easier to face the day when you know you won't have to face other people and their happiness.

Here, I have been able to go and howl my misery and my anger – yes, there's a lot of that – at the mountains and the loch, and feel the vast landscape soak up something of my grief. Here, loneliness is the natural state of things.

When it happened, part of me wondered if I had been simply waiting for it, that I had always known it would come. I had always felt, ever since Jamie and I got together, that it was too good, that we were too lucky. That happiness like this couldn't possibly last: we were using up more than our allotted quota of the stuff, and at some point someone had to notice. Fate decided to prove me right. The expression that Jamie's boss, Keith, wore when he came to tell me. I knew before he opened his mouth. Smoke inhalation. No one realised, in the chaos, that Jamie hadn't reappeared. He'd been trapped, in the burning house. The other firemen had done everything they could. Had been hunkered down there with the paramedics.

Keith had done CPR on Jamie for a full forty-five minutes before they could get there. When he began to cry I had had to look away, because it was such a terrible, unexpected sight. Seeing a man like Keith cry. And because that, more than anything, made it all real.

Jamie was a fireman. He could have been many things,

with that brain of his: a scientist, a lawyer, a professor. But he wanted to do something that he really felt mattered, he told me – like I did. The thing that made him one of the best was that he always went the extra mile. As Keith said, at the service, when others had given up on a lost cause, Jamie would try that little bit harder, risk that little bit more. He had seemed, at times, almost invincible. But he wasn't. He was just a man. A big-hearted, brave, self-sacrificing man – but definitely mortal.

What they don't tell you is that when someone you love dies you might be angry with him. And that was true, I was so angry with Jamie. Before, life had meaning. Everything about us was meant to be. The way we met – him deciding at the last minute to come to a house party thrown by a friend of a friend. The beautiful light-filled apartment we found in Edinburgh's Old Town, which the owner decided to rent for a song to anyone who would also dog-sit for him when he went away travelling. Even just the way we fitted together, he and I – two pieces of a very simple jigsaw that, when combined, made the picture complete.

When he died, nothing made sense any more. A world in which he could be taken from me had to be a cruel, chaotic place. And I thought – briefly, but definitely – about ending it all. In the end it wasn't any desire to survive that stopped me from doing it; it was the knowledge of what it would do to my family.

Coming here was the next best thing, you see. It was a way of escaping from life as I had known it, from everything that tied me to the past. Sometimes I think it's a little like dying – a slightly more palatable option than the pills and the jump from the Forth Bridge that I had contemplated in the weeks after Jamie's death. So in an odd way this landscape has been a sanctuary. But now, with this new horror and the falling snow trapping us in and keeping help out, it has become, in the space of twenty-four hours, a prison.

Two days earlier
New Year's Eve 2018

EMMA

Last night, Mark and I had some pretty great sex. He threw me onto the bed. There was an intensity to his features, a dark cast to them. He looks quite similar when he is turned on to when he's really angry.

I don't know what got into him. It might have been the stuff we all took (which I shouldn't have had, looking back, because I say stupid things – things I don't mean to say aloud). But his intensity might also have had something to do with the thing he's just told me, too – the thing he's found out – that strange, almost erotic delight we sometimes take in someone else's messing up.

I know people wonder about Mark and me. 'How did you two meet?' they ask. Or 'What drew you to him?' and

'When did you know he was "the one"?' Sometimes I'll tell them it was his dance moves to Chesney Hawkes in the middle of Inferno's dance floor that got me, and that will normally get a laugh. But that's only a temporary measure to stall the questions that will undoubtedly follow, the deeper, more probing enquiries.

They're looking for the romance, the chemistry, the vital spark that drew us together, that keeps us together. Normally, I think they probably end up disappointed in their search. Because, the truth is, there is no great romance between us. There was no grand passion. There wasn't ever that – even in the first place. I don't mind admitting it. It wasn't the thing I was looking for.

There are people who hold out for love, capital letters LOVE, and don't stop until they've found it. There are those who give up because they don't find it. Boom or bust – all or nothing. And then, perhaps in the majority, there are those who settle. And I think we're the sensible ones. Because love doesn't always mean longevity.

I'm happy with what we've got. Mark too, I think. People seem to comment a lot on the fact that we're not that similar. 'Opposites attract,' they say with a knowing look. 'Isn't that right?' The important thing is for a couple to have certain interests or hobbies in common, that's how I see it. A few areas – or even just one area – for which you share the same degree of interest. Which we do. There's one thing in particular. And no, it's not that, though we do have good, even great sex.

So no, we don't have the huge chemistry of a couple like Miranda and Julien . . . though something, now I come to think of it, seems to be off between them – I wonder if I'm the only one to notice it. And yes, I do know Mark has a whopping crush on Miranda, in case you were wondering. I'm not an idiot. In fact, I see quite a bit more than most people give me credit for. I don't mind. I really don't. I can almost *hear* the incredulity. But I promise it's the case. You're just going to have to take my word for it, I'm afraid.

So no, when I saw Mark in that sweaty nightclub just off Clapham High Street, I didn't necessarily think: Here is the man of my dreams, this must be the thing great literature and film is made of; true love, love at first sight. It wasn't like that.

What I saw was at once more and less than that. I saw a life. A new way of being. I saw the thing I had always wanted.

Mark and I both had difficult childhoods. I was moved from school to school every few years and never managed to find any proper friends. This pales in comparison to Mark's experience. His dad beat him. Not a couple of ill-advised slaps for being naughty. Proper, old-fashioned, barbaric beating. Once, he told me, his mother put concealer on him to go into school, to cover the bruising around his eye. She didn't stop his father. She couldn't. Not as frequently – but every so often – she was the victim of one of his fits of temper herself. When he was younger, Mark was small for his age, and used to get pummelled on the rugby pitch, to his dad's disdain. Then he began to grow. He drank protein powder shakes and hit the gym. The beatings finally stopped; as though his father had suddenly come to the realisation that his son might be able to fight back: and win.

Mark has inherited something of his dad's temper. He throws his weight around. He has never been violent with me . . . though there have been just a couple of times in the midst of a particularly explosive argument when I have felt he's on the edge. A door slammed with such force that the wood fractured, a picture we'd disagreed about, smashed against a wall. But he's not the unfeeling bonehead that people might assume. Last night he may have joked about that incident at the races, but I remember the remorse afterwards, his horror at what he had done . . . how he was almost in tears hearing that boy had been taken to hospital. I had to stop him from going and turning himself in.

Mark desperately does not want to turn out like his father. But I also know that, at times, he is frightened that he is becoming him.

MIRANDA

I wake early. Julien is curled away from me beneath the sheet. Immediately memories of last night arrive, all looped together and unclear, like a tangled ball of wool. Mark – in the bathroom. The way he had towered over me, the threat of his grip upon my upper arm.

I get up and dress. I'll go for a run, try to breathe the weirdness of last night from my lungs. I like running now. I've come to like it – it hasn't always been the case. I didn't like it at fourteen, when I suddenly went up a couple of sizes and my darling mother got me a gym membership for my birthday.

I sprint past the other cabins and the Lodge as quickly as I can. I really don't want to see any of the others yet. I haven't got my face on – and I don't mean make-up. I mean tough, fun, up for anything Miranda. When I reach the dark shelter of the trees that edge the loch and there has been no call of 'Where are you off to?' I breathe a sigh of relief.

Mark: how *dare* he? I'm tempted to tell Emma, today. But I can tell how hard she's worked to bring this all together, how much pride she takes in having found such an awesome place – I'm not *quite* so insensitive to that sort of thing as people think. So maybe I should wait until afterwards, broach it over drinks with her in London. She must have seen that side of him, mustn't she? If he was like that with me, how does he behave with her? She seems so capable, so in charge of her life, but – as I well know – the face we present to the world can be misleading.

The air is noticeably colder today. Some of the puddles of rainwater seem to have frozen overnight. There's an edge, a rawness, to this cold that is unfamiliar. A chilly day in London is always offset by the warm blasts from overheated shops, the stickiness of the tube, the press of other bodies. But here the cold has a chance to get you properly in its grip. It feels a little like I'm trying to outrun it.

I've taken my phone with me so I can listen to music – I find it always helps to relax me, drowns out all the other noise in my head. Much better than the 'mindful silence' my therapist is so bloody keen on. As promised, the little signal indicator is empty. Funny, that we live in a world now where a lack of connectivity might be advertised as a feature in itself.

A few yards ahead, the path forks off towards another jetty. It's a perfectly beautiful, melancholy spot. I jog down towards it. There are canoes stacked here, presumably from the summer season – one is on its bottom, and has filled with a winter's worth of rainwater, now frozen solid. I stand over it, and as I look inside it's as if my reflection is trapped beneath the surface of ice – as though I am trapped in there. I shiver, though I'm well wrapped up against the cold. I head back to the path.

I've run perhaps two hundred yards along the rutted track we drove along last night, the forest on one side of me, the loch on the other, when I come to a bridge spanning one of the waterfalls that feeds the loch. The waterfall itself is overlooked by a small, derelict-looking building. I wonder what on earth it is. I hang over the edge of the bridge – there's just three lines of chain between myself and the void – and look down at the waterfall itself, now mainly frozen into icicles, and the black, moss-covered rocks.

Beyond this, the path is uneventful for a stretch. But at one point I come to a small patch of burned ground, a circle, as though someone has lit a fire here. Nearby are a couple of burned, rusted beer cans. I remember what Heather told us about poachers.

I step off the pass onto the bank that shears down to the water, ducking my way through the branches of the trees at the lochside, stumbling and slipping over ancient moss-covered roots, twigs snagging at my hair, face and jacket. At one point I almost lose my footing entirely and begin slithering towards a small inlet of water to my right, only just regaining my balance at the last minute. As I do I catch sight of something gleaming beneath the surface. Shocking white, so much brighter than the brownish rocks surrounding it. I peer closer, and realise what it is. A bone. Quite a large one, half concealed by rotted leaves. As I look about me I see another – and another, scattered about the grassy bank. Some are even larger than the one in the water, as long as my own femur. They are animal bones, I know this. I tell myself this, as I search for the skull that will confirm it. An animal killed by another animal, or dead from old age. But some of them, I see, have scorch marks. And there is no skull to be seen. Again, I remember the warning about poachers trespassing; perhaps they've taken the heads away for mounting. I shudder. The killing of something this size must have involved a certain amount of violence, and intent.

I need to put some space between myself and this place. The grisly discovery sits queasily on my empty stomach. So I push myself going up the slight incline until I can focus only on the burn in my lungs and legs. I remind myself what a beautiful place this is. The bones have sent a chill through me, put a dark cast on things. But there is nothing sinister here. It is just different, I remind myself. Remote, wild.

Now I'm almost at the opposite end of the loch from the Lodge: it glitters strange and magnificent on the other bank. There's a gap in the trees that ring the loch here, leaving a bald-looking stretch with a lot of rocks and some dead-looking heather. There's a building here, too, low-slung and timbered like the cabins. This must be the bunkhouse where the Icelanders are staying. All the windows are dark, no sign of life within. Perhaps they're still asleep.

I carry on my way, picking up the pace for the second half of the lap as I always do when I run. As I plunge back into the trees again I hear a sound, high and keening, like an animal in pain. I think inevitably of the bones on the other bank. It's difficult to tell exactly where the sound is coming from, but I peer in the vague direction of the noise into the dark thicket. And now I see them – I can't believe I didn't originally. Jesus. So much naked skin. The woman crouches on the mossy ground on her hands and knees, the man mounting her from behind, hips flexing powerfully, his hand tangled in her black hair. Her head is thrown back, or possibly pulled back by the force of his grip. Both of them are making a lot of noise, and the noises are bestial, uninhibited. There is something horrifyingly compelling about the sight. My feet are rooted to the spot, I'm unable to glance away.

And then the man turns his head and looks straight at me. With two fingers he makes a kind of beckoning motion with his hand. 'Come,' he calls, 'join us.' Then he laughs, a kind of cackle. He's mocking me. The woman looks up, to see who he's speaking to. She, too, grins at me: the half-drugged expression of someone in the throes of lust. Their exposed skin is very white in the stark light. Her knees are almost black with dirt.

And though I have always liked to think of myself as *very* open-minded, sexually liberated, once my limbs decide to work again I find myself stumbling backwards, then turning and running away as fast as my legs will carry me, branches snagging at my ankles and whipping my cheeks. I feel as though I can still hear his laughter ringing out, though worryingly I'm not absolutely sure that it isn't in my head.

Back at the Lodge, I go to make myself a coffee from the Nespresso machine. My fingers don't seem to work properly. They're trembling. I'm sure it's just the cold, but it would be a lie to say that scene in the woods didn't rattle me. It was the animal nature of it, the *violence* of it, in the middle of all that wildness. I hear the door open behind me. I do not turn around. I'm already certain – from the lack of greeting – that it's Mark. Oh, for God's sake. I could really do without seeing him now.

Finally, I wrestle the little gold capsule into the slot and clunk the lever down. Press the button, and wait for something to happen. I hear the capsule fall into the cavity at the back. 'Fuck!' I seem to have become completely uncoordinated.

Suddenly Mark is next to me. 'Here,' he says, 'you have to turn it on before you put the capsule in.' He shows me, and a perfect stream of velvet brown pours into the cup.

'Thanks,' I say, without looking at him.

'Miranda,' he says. 'Manda . . . I want to apologise for last night. I don't know what came over me. I'd had too much to drink, and then those pills – what even were they?'

'That's no excuse,' I say.

'No,' he says, quickly. 'No excuse, I know that. I behaved unforgivably. Did I hurt you?'

I push up my sleeve to show him the bruise, which has turned a rather impressive purple.

He hangs his head. 'I'm sorry. I can't believe I did that. Sometimes – I don't know, I let my anger get the better of me. It's like something takes over . . . again, it's unforgivable. And it wasn't even you I was angry at – of course it wasn't. It was Julien. That's one thing I won't, can't, take back. He doesn't deserve you, Miranda. He never has. But especially recently—'

'No,' I put up a palm, 'whatever you think you know about his "little secret", or whatever you call it, I want you to keep it to yourself. For my sake, if you won't do it for his. Do you understand?'

'I think so, but . . .' he looks dumbfounded. 'I just— I'm thinking of you, Miranda. I feel like you have a right to know what he's been up to. You're sure?'

'Yes,' I say, nodding my head for emphasis. 'Absolutely sure.'

I sip my coffee. It's too hot, and scalds my tongue, but I won't wince in front of him. 'Oh, and Mark?'

'Yes?'

'Touch me again like that – either like you did on the Twister mat, or in the bathroom – and I'll *fucking* kill you. Have you got that?'

KATIE

I didn't sleep well last night. I don't think I've slept properly for months. It feels like years.

When I come in for breakfast, Emma is standing in the kitchen of the Lodge, making preparations for tonight's supper. Her hair is scraped off her face, no make-up. I'm not sure when I've ever seen her without make-up, actually. It's odd, sometimes, seeing someone bare-faced for the first time. Especially someone fair, like Emma, who is usually equipped with the punctuation of mascara, eyeliner; she looks almost featureless.

She has planned a big feast for this evening, she tells me. The fridge is packed with smoked salmon and the finest beef fillet, and she's whipping up a batter for blinis. She makes her own blinis, for God's sake. 'The shop-bought ones taste like rubber,' she says. 'And it's so easy to do them.' She is in her element, humming away to herself. She has me cutting tiny triangles of salmon with much more care than I normally would. It's actually nice to have something to focus on.

Though try as I might, my thoughts keep wandering. I carry on until Emma cries out, 'Katie, oh my God! You're bleeding! Didn't you notice?' And in a slightly irritated tone, 'Oh, you've got blood all over the salmon.'

'Have I?' I look down at my hand. 'Oh.' She's right, I've cut quite far into the flesh of my forefinger. A bright red gash. The fish is slick with it, made suddenly gory.

Emma stares at me. 'How did you not notice?' She takes my hand, a little roughly. 'Oh, you poor thing. That must have hurt. It's quite deep.'

She is trying to sound sympathetic, but it doesn't quite conceal a note of irritation.

All at once the pain arrives. Sharp, bringing tears to my eyes. But I find myself almost enjoying the sting of it. It feels right, like what I deserve.

Later, we eat brunch in the dining room at the Lodge, all of us around the big table in the centre, apart from Samira and Giles, who haven't arrived yet. They're awake though – when I passed their cabin I heard raised voices and a shriek of infant rage.

The atmosphere is subdued this morning – the conversation around the table stilted, everyone picking listlessly at their fry-ups. There are the hangovers from last night, of course, but maybe there's something else, too. Something slightly strained . . . as though everyone's somewhat exhausted their quota of niceness on yesterday's reunion. Only Emma is all brightness and bustle, checking everyone has enough bacon, enough coffee.

'For Christ's sake,' Julien says, 'sit down Emma! We're all *fine*.' I'm sure he was going for a light, teasing tone, but he doesn't quite manage it.

Emma sits, a flush stealing up the side of her neck.

'Katie,' Miranda pulls out the seat next to her, 'sit by me.'

I take the seat and reach for a cold piece of toast to butter. Miranda's wearing a lot of perfume this morning, and, as I chew, it's like the toast has taken on the heavy, fragrant flavour of it. My stomach churns. I take a swig of coffee, but this, too, tastes off.

When I finally look up, I realise Miranda has turned in her seat to look directly at me, her head on one side. I see rather than feel the piece of toast tremble in my hand. Those X-ray eyes of hers. 'You've got a new man, haven't you?' she asks. She's grinning at me . . . but it occurs to me that it's more a grimace than a smile. I know her too well not to guess when something is off. If I were a good friend I'd ask her about it . . . but I can't quite bring myself to. Besides, I reason, it's too public a forum here, with everyone around us. 'What makes you say that?' I ask.

'I can tell. You look different. The hair, the clothes.' I move an inch or so away; her breath is a little stale, which is unlike her. She once told me that she brushes before *and* after breakfast in accordance with some fascist rule of her mother's. She must have forgotten. 'And,' she says, 'you've been so elusive recently. Even more so than normal. You've always done this when there's a new guy on the scene. Ever since I've known you.' Everyone else suddenly seems to be listening. I feel the eyes of the room upon me. Nick's eyebrows are raised. Because if I am seeing someone, I know he's thinking, I would have told him, wouldn't I?

I take a bite of toast, but it sticks in my gullet and it takes several attempts to swallow it. My throat feels raw, wounded.

'No,' I say, hoarsely. 'I don't have time at the moment – I'm far too busy with work.'

'God,' she says. 'All work and no play, Katie – have you ever heard that one? You're completely obsessed. I don't understand it.'

But then she wouldn't. Miranda has tried and failed to make a go at several different careers, with no real success. She crashed out of Oxford with a Third, in the end. She didn't care, she told me. But I know better. She had been arrogant enough to think that she could just breeze through as she had always done. The thing is, Miranda is clever, but she isn't necessarily Oxford clever. Her mum hired a tutor to help her get those four As at A level, and I'm sure she dazzled them in the interview. But still. Once in, she was in a different league entirely. She somehow managed to blag the first and second years of university, and she ignored the warning signs in our third year that she wasn't on the right track, even though I tried to point them out. I swear I wasn't pleased when she opened that envelope and saw her result. But I must confess that perhaps I did feel a little – a tiny *tiny* bit – as though justice had been done.

That Third was an insult. It smarted. It stung her pride. If you look at all of us, now, she's the odd one out. All of us have good jobs. Samira's a management consultant, I'm a lawyer, Julien works for the hedge fund, Nick's an architect, Giles is a doctor, Bo works for the BBC, Mark for an advertising firm. Emma works for a literary agency – I remember when Miranda learned that one. 'I don't understand,' she said. 'How did you get that job in the first place? I thought that agency *only* picked from redbrick, and usually Oxbridge.'

Emma was unfazed. 'I don't know,' she said, with a shrug. 'I suppose I must just give good interview.'

Miranda herself had had a crack at getting into the publishing industry. Then a go at advertising. Mark gave her a much bigger leg up than he probably should have done, persuading one of his colleagues to interview her for an assistant position. She got it, but left after only two months. She was bored of it, she said. But I met a girl who used to work there at a wedding and she told me that it was a little more complicated.

'They let her go,' she told me. 'She was unbelievably lazy. She seemed to think she was above things. Once, stuffing envelopes, she actually refused to lick them to seal them shut. She said she hated the taste and it was below her pay grade to do it. Said she hadn't been to Oxford just to do that. Can you imagine?'

Yes, bad friend that I am, of course I could.

Giles and Samira have arrived now. They look several degrees more shattered than everyone else. Samira flops into a chair and puts her head in her hands with a groan, as Giles tries to lift Priya into the highchair. She grizzles, fighting this restraint. As the pitch rises to a shrill whine I see Nick sneak his fingers into his ears. 'Oh God,' Samira groans. 'Priya woke us up at five, and then again at six.'

'I can't even imagine,' Bo says. 'I couldn't dress myself this morning, let alone a little person. Nick had to point out my T-shirt was on backwards, didn't you?' Nick smiles, wanly.

'Well I suppose it's a life choice, isn't it?' Miranda says, breezily, pouring herself an orange juice. 'It's not like you're forced to have kids, is it?'

Even for Miranda – who miraculously often manages to get away with such comments – this is a cattiness too far.

But then there's definitely something about her this morning. Her brightness has a brittle edge.

I haven't seen Samira angry for a long time, but now I remember that it's a terrifying spectacle. There's a proper temper hidden under that calm, groomed exterior. She has gone absolutely rigid in her chair. We all watch her, silently, waiting to see what she will do next. Then she seems to give a sort of shiver, and reaches for the cafetière. Her hand shakes only a little as she pours. She does not look at Miranda once. For the sake of group harmony, perhaps, she has evidently decided to rise above it.

With a bit of a stutter, the conversation around the table moves on. We're going stalking today, because apparently this is a 'must-do' if you're staying on an estate in Scotland.

'I suppose you two won't be coming stalking, will you?' Mark asks, indicating Nick and Bo.

'Why not?' Nick asks.

'Well,' Mark's mouth curls a little at the corner. 'Because – you know.'

'No. I don't know.'

'Just didn't think you'd be into that sort of thing.'

'Hang on a sec, Mark,' Nick says. 'If I've got this correct, it sounds as though you've decided we won't be coming because we're gay. Is that really what you're saying?'

Spoken aloud it sounds so ridiculous that even Mark must be able to see it.

'It's not a disability, Mark. Just want to make that clear.'

Mark makes a noncommittal noise at the back of his throat. Nick's knuckles are white about his coffee mug. For all Mark's muscle, I'm not sure that I would back him in a fight between the two.

'It's true,' Nick goes on, 'that like most sensible people, I don't particularly like the idea of killing animals for pure sport' – Mark assumes an *aha!* expression – 'but, from what I hear, the deer numbers get out of control if they aren't managed. So I'm at peace with the idea. I'm also a pretty good shot: the last time I went to shoot clays I hit eighteen out of twenty. Thanks, though, for your concern.'

After this, no one, not even Miranda, seems to be able to think of anything to say.

NOW
2nd January 2019

HEATHER

I have made endless cups of tea, so much so that I have begun to feel like an extension of the kettle. No one seems to actually be drinking them, but every time I ask, they all nod, vaguely, and then sit holding the cups as the hot tea slowly cools, untasted. Beyond the windows the snow shows no sign of stopping. It is difficult to imagine a time when it was not there, this moving curtain of white.

Normally, after a body has been found, I am sure it is all flashing lights, men in white hazmat suits, and commotion. But this is no ordinary place. And in this case the landscape has had its own ideas. The weather has forced us to bend to its own whims. I realise, for one of the first times since I moved here, quite how alien this place is, how little I really know of it. It might as well be another planet. I am certain that there are secrets here beyond the whisky bothies, beyond the monster pike deep in the loch. Those are just the small things the landscape chooses to reveal.

There is a loud wail from the next room, cacophonous in the silence, startling me so much that I spill water from the kettle onto the floor. It's just the baby, of course. I remember the sound of the baby crying on New Year's Eve when I woke to go to the toilet, and when I saw – or thought I saw – that strange light, up on the flank of the Munro. And I wonder now whether it's possible that the sound could have concealed any other noises out there.

I think of all the sounds in this place that have come to seem normal, that I choose not to question. As I wait for the kettle to boil I'm remembering one of my very first nights at the Lodge. I'd moved into the cottage, and was focusing on not thinking too much about anything. It was the week of the terrible anniversary. I'd had quite a lot of wine – a medicinal quantity, a bottle and a half, perhaps. I remember sinking into the bed and pulling the duvet up over me. One thing I have learned about 'silence' – at least this sort of silence, that of the wilderness – is that it is surprisingly loud. The building is old, it creaked around me. Outside in the night were the sounds of animals; two owls conversed in long mournful calls. The wind was moving through the tops of the great Scots pines just beyond my window. It sounded like a moan. It could be soothing, I remember telling myself. Perhaps I would get used to it. (I have never quite got used to it.)

Then there was a sound that ripped through everything

else. A scream, high-pitched, desperate: horrible, the sound of a person in terrible pain. The air rang with the echo of it for several seconds afterwards. I sat up in bed, all the drowsiness from the wine leaving me. My ears felt sensitive as an animal's, the whole of me prickling, waiting for another scream. None came.

I waited for a response: surely someone else must have heard it? Then I remembered that it was just me and the gamekeeper: no one else for miles around . . . apart from, presumably, whoever it was that had screamed. I imagined Doug pulling on those big boots of his, taking one of the rifles from the barn. He would be the right person to go, I told myself. Not five-foot-two drunk me. But the night seemed even quieter now than before.

I pulled the shutter open a little way and looked out. I couldn't see any lights. I checked my watch. Two a.m. The hours had blurred; I had not realised how much time had passed. Wine does that, I suppose. It began to occur to me that Doug might be sleeping. That I might be the only one of the two of us awake to have heard the scream.

I started to believe that I had imagined it. Perhaps I had dropped off to sleep for those two minutes, without realising. I couldn't even quite remember how it sounded, though there was still the reverberation of it in my ears.

Then, as if to remind me, it came again, and this time it was more terrible than the last. It was the sound of purest agony, something almost animal in it. I climbed out of bed, felt for my slippers. I had to go and see – I could not pretend now. Someone out there was in trouble.

I crept downstairs, shrugged on my coat and boots, took the cast-iron poker from the fireplace and the torch from the windowsill.

The night outside was black and still. I remember noticing that above me the sky had a depth I had never seen before, how at that moment it looked sinister, like a void.

I peered into the shadows, trying to discern any sign of movement. 'Hello?' I called. My hands were shaking so much that the light from my torch bounced everywhere, illuminating indifferent patches of earth. The silence around me felt like a held breath. 'Hello?'

Perhaps it was inevitable that I felt I was being watched, haloed as I was by light from the door. I realised that in calling out I had exposed myself, made myself visible and audible. I might just have put myself in danger.

I took a few steps. And somewhere in the direction of the loch I caught a movement. Not with the torch beam, rather with some animal sense I didn't know I had: a mixture of sight and sound. 'Who's there?' Fear had stifled my voice – it came out as a tiny, strangled squeak. I directed the torch beam towards where I thought I had caught the movement. Nothing. Then another flicker, much closer at hand.

'Heather?'

I swung my arm and illuminated a face. In the torchlight the figure was ghoulish, and I almost shrieked; was glad as realisation dawned that I did not. It was Doug.

'Are you all right?' he asked. There was no urgency in his voice, just the deep, unhurried tone he always spoke in.

'I heard someone scream. Did you hear it?'

But he frowned. 'A scream?'

'Yes. Very high-pitched. Whoever it was sounded terrified. I came out to see . . .' In the face of his evident incredulity I faltered. 'You didn't hear it?'

'Was it,' he asked, 'like this?' And then, to my amazement,

he mimicked the sound almost perfectly. I felt the same cold flood of dread down the backs of my legs.

'Yes. That's it exactly.'

'Ah. In that case, you heard a fox. A vixen, to be precise.'

'I don't understand. It sounded like a woman.'

'It's a terrible sound – and an easy mistake to make. You certainly aren't the first to have done so. There was a story, quite recently, about a man killing himself on a train track outside Edinburgh trying to help what he thought was a woman in distress.' He raised his eyebrows. 'You didn't hear that story, living in the city?'

'No,' I said. I was beginning to be embarrassed by the tremor in my voice, and wished I could bring it under my control.

'It's when they're —' he grimaced. '—the male's . . . you-know-what, is barbed. So it's not exactly a pleasant experience for the female.'

I couldn't prevent my wince.

'Exactly. So not pleasant. But not someone being murdered, either.' He paused. 'You're sure you're OK?'

'Yes.' Even to my own ears it didn't sound quite convincing. I tried to bolster it by saying, 'Honestly, I'm fine.'

'In that case, I'll let you get back to bed.'

I remember that his eyes swept over me then, so quickly that I might almost have imagined it. But not quite. I was wearing pyjamas. But I felt more exposed, suddenly, than if I had been standing there completely naked.

'Thank you,' I said.

He doffed an imaginary cap. 'You're welcome.'

I closed the door, stepped inside, and pressed a hand to my chest. My brain did not seem to have told my heart that the danger had passed. It was beating so hard and fast it seemed to be trying to leap out of my ribcage. It was only when I finally climbed back into bed, and pulled the duvet over myself, that it occurred to me to think properly about what had just happened. If it wasn't the scream that had woken Doug, as it had me, then what on earth was he doing wandering the grounds in the dead of night?

I think of his hand; how he's been so vague about the way in which he injured it. I think of the boss's mention of how good he would be at fighting off any poachers, the intimation of violence. It isn't enough that I don't want him to have had anything to do with any of this. *And that's just because you fancy him*, a little voice says. *Just because you made yourself come thinking about him*. With some effort, I mute this train of thought.

I remember my mother's words about googling him. It suddenly seems important, necessary.

With a quick step I move to the door of the office and lock it. If Doug tries to come in I'll pretend I've done it accidentally, 'force of habit'. Still, I don't have long, unless I want to raise suspicion. I open the doors to the cabinet where I keep all the filing. The two personnel files: my own, Doug's. Iain's only a contractor, and I think he worked for the boss before, didn't need to apply for his job the way Doug and I did ours.

I open Doug's file. There's a short CV, detailing a period in the Marines: six years. Nothing more. What exactly am I looking for? I move to the computer, plug Doug's full name into the search engine, and wait for the results to load via the creakingly slow Internet connection. It is only when my chest starts to burn that I realise I have been holding my breath. There won't be anything, I think. There won't . . . and I'll feel terrible for doing it, because I'll have breached his trust without him ever knowing, but it will stop there. He will never know. And I will be able to lay any suspicions – if that is even what they are – to rest.

Finally, the page blinks into life.

I can see immediately that there are a lot of hits. For a normal person, someone who isn't a celebrity or notorious in some other way, you'd expect to get, what? Three hits, at most? A few social media profiles, including those of anyone sharing the same name, perhaps the odd mention of a sporting achievement or a part in the college play. But Doug's unusual name takes up the entire first page of hits. And none of it is very nice. In fact, it's all pretty horrible.

I wish I hadn't looked. I wish I had never seen any of this.

Two days earlier
New Year's Eve 2018

MIRANDA

We traipse after Doug to the yard behind the Lodge, where his Land Rover sits parked next to a big old red truck – maybe that's what Heather gets around in. The thought of her, all five-foot-nothing, behind the wheel of that big old vehicle makes me laugh.

Doug opens the barn for us with a state-of-the-art keypad that looks completely bizarre against the old wood. I suppose they need it, if there are guns in here. As he yanks the heavy wooden door back I enjoy watching his muscles move beneath the old shirt he wears (just a shirt – in this weather!). He would make, I think, an excellent candidate for Lady Chatterley's lover, so tall and broad and tousled. Bit of an unflattering contrast for Julien, I can't help

203

thinking, whose various ointments and tinctures jostle for space on the bathroom shelf beside my own.

He kits us up in the barn: over-trousers and jackets, even walking boots for Katie, who has failed to bring anything remotely sensible. Mark asks for one of the hats, which are ridiculous Sherlock-Holmes affairs.

'If you want one, mate,' Doug says, with something that might be mistaken for a sneer.

Beside the jackets and the trousers hang ten rifles. There is something lethal-looking about just the shape of the weapons, as though they could somehow kill you without ever being fired.

Then there's a long talk on safety, and on where we're going today: up the steep hillside past the Old Lodge, because apparently that's where the deer have been congregating lately: though we're only looking for the hinds, the females, because it's the wrong time of year for shooting stags. At the end, I say, 'So, let me get this right. We might well not actually get a deer today. And even if we do shoot a deer it won't have antlers, because it's not the right season. But we're paying hundreds of pounds for the privilege.'

'Yep,' Doug nods. 'That's pretty much the size of it.' His tone is direct, but I notice he can't quite make eye-contact. I feel a little thrill of triumph. I recognise *that* particular symptom, you see. I have always been faithful to Julien – well, with that one exception, right at the beginning. But it would be a lie to say I do not enjoy flexing my power, dropping a lure. My own sort of hunting, I suppose. Much more fun than freezing wet heather and hideous waterproof over-trousers.

Doug locks the door behind him with a seamless click of metal. Now he has us lie on the ground to shoot at a box with a target. Julien, Giles, Bo and Mark are terrible, laughably so. With the exception of Bo, who is always so light-hearted (though surely, with that druggie past, he can't always have been?) they aren't finding it at all funny. Mark – I can just about bring myself to watch him – wears his mouth in a snarl as he shoots. When Julien has his sixth attempt, I see that muscle in the side of his jaw draw tight in the way that it does when he's angry about something, and with each report his eye twitches. He cares, I realise. They all care. Even mild-mannered Giles seems to have undergone a personality transplant. Perhaps they're imagining themselves in some action film or video game. I'm sure that's it: men reverting to little boys. All the same, it's a bit weird.

Katie is *awful* too, but I'm not sure she's even bothering to try – just as she seems to have stopped bothering to pretend she's having a good time. Samira – who, after much persuading left Priya with the manager, Heather, for a couple of hours – is not great, but she makes up for it with lots of intensity. I'm reminded of her rowing blue past. Give her a week with this and she'd probably be Olympian standard. It's a glimmer of the old Samira, the girl I knew before, and I'm glad of it. This, after all, is the woman who once set fire to the dining table in our house, in imitation of a bar in Ibiza, and had a formal reprimand from the college dean for her behaviour.

I'm not bad, but I'm not quite as good as I had thought I would be: I've always had a knack for sports. Doug tells me I'm being too 'vigorous' with the trigger. 'You just need to coax it with your finger,' he says. He's straight-faced – but . . . is it just me, or does that sound a bit filthy?

Nick is pretty good, as he'd told us he would be. No

surprise there, funnily enough. He was always good at sport, and he's so precise about things, so intense, sometimes. But it's Emma, of all people, who excels. Doug says she is a 'natural', and she smiles and shakes her head, typically modest. 'Women are often better,' he says. 'They're more accurate, more deadly. This sport isn't about testosterone or brute strength.'

I wish I didn't mind so much that it's not me earning his praise.

We begin our ascent up the hillside. We're walking towards the Old Lodge, the building Heather pointed out to us yesterday afternoon. I hate walking. It's so boring, and purposeless. Give me a run any day, something that burns double the number of calories in half the time. Mark, Julien and Nick jostle for position at the front, as though each is determined that they will be the one to take the shot. Katie, meanwhile, is a few feet ahead of me, talking to Bo. I feel slighted that she hasn't chosen to walk with me. I could go and join them, but I'm not going to grovel for her to pay me attention. It seems like I offended her at breakfast, asking if she had a new man. Fine, I could have been a little more subtle about it – she's intensely private about that sort of thing – but I was only trying to show an interest. And, frankly, after all this time apart it wouldn't fucking kill her to ask me about my life. That's not like her: in the past she's always been such a good listener. Julien once – not too kindly – joked it was a lucky thing that I'd found a friend who likes to listen as much as I like to talk. But he wasn't totally wrong. I've always thought of her as my opposite, my complementary part.

The path has melted away now, so we're just trekking upwards through the heather, and it's hard, hard work.

Every so often it tangles around an ankle, yanking me back as though reminding me who's in charge. Because this landscape is definitely in charge. It's brutal. The temperature has dropped even more, and the air is raw, stinging any exposed flesh. Even my teeth hurt when I open my mouth to speak. It feels like the cold has got inside the jacket I've been lent, and the beautiful – and I'd thought very warm – cashmere jumper I'm wearing under it, and is pressing against my skin.

The ground is boggy in places too, there must be streams under the soil. Every so often I step into a particularly soft patch, and freezing water comes up over my boots, soaking my socks. They'll be ruined. They're cashmere too – a present in the autumn from Julien. There was a period when every week he seemed to come home with some sort of gift – guilt over what he'd made me a part of, I'm sure, though he claimed he just wanted to spoil me.

Nick, Mark and Julien can't go fast enough. They're almost elbowing each other in their haste to get ahead, to be first up the hill. That can't be very safe while carrying loaded rifles, can it? At one point Mark turns and seems to shove Julien. Lightly, but unmistakably. He makes a joke of it, and I see Julien force a laugh . . . but I can see he's not really amused.

It's a relief when we pause at the Old Lodge: a sad, fire-blackened old ruin. Doug gets out a hip flask and passes it around. When he hands it to me I let my fingertips touch his, for just a moment too long. His eyes are such a dark brown that you can hardly make out the pupils. I want Julien to see this, to register this man desiring me.

I'm not a big fan of whisky but somehow it feels right here, in this wild place. And the warmth of it helps, too, seems to soothe this weird mood I seem to have found myself in since last night. I take another swig, and when I pass it back to Doug I see that my mouth has left a pleasing stain of lipstick around the neck.

It looks as though someone might have been up here before us. It's just the remains of a few cigarettes, scattered here and there. But Doug picks up one of the stubs and looks at it, intently, as though there might be a secret message written on the side. I notice that he pockets it. Bizarre. Why would you pick up someone's old cigarette butt? Then I look at his battered jacket, his worn boots, and feel an unexpected tug of pity. Perhaps, I realise, he's going to keep it and smoke it later.

KATIE

The Old Lodge, when we get to it, is a horrible place. It's probably the only ugly thing in this landscape, a burned shell, with just one blackened block still standing. It's somehow colder here than anywhere else, perhaps because it's so exposed to the elements. Why on earth would you build something here? So far from shelter, and from help. I think of the fire. It must have been seen for miles around – like the beacons they lit for the millennium up and down the country.

There is a silence here that is different to the silence on the rest of the estate. It's like a held breath. It feels – as clichéd as this might sound – as though we are not alone. As though something, someone, is watching us. The stones are like old bones: a skeleton of someone who has died and been left out in the open, denied the dignity of a burial. When we get near enough I am sure the air smells of burning. That's impossible, isn't it? Or could there be some way in which the smoke has gone deep within the stone, remained locked in there? It wouldn't be hard to believe that the fire happened a few years ago, not nearly a century in the past.

The stable block – the bit that survived because the flames couldn't make the leap – is almost obscene in its wholeness. They've put a keypad lock on it too, I realise – like the one on the barn – presumably to stop guests just wandering in, if it's not safe. The sky is a very pale violet. Doesn't that mean snow? What would we even do if it did start to snow, properly, while we're stuck out here? We're completely exposed here, on the flank of a mountain. The Lodge – the New Lodge, I suppose – looks like a small shard of glass from here, beside the loch, which looks grey and opaque as lead in the strange light, the trees ringing it a charcoal bristle. The station, roughly the same distance from us here as the Lodge is on the other side, looks like a toy town model.

'I don't know why we're doing this,' Miranda says, suddenly, 'when we could be back at the Lodge getting stuck into the champagne.' She complained on the climb up here, too: about the boggy ground and the icy water seeping over the top of her boots. It's because she wasn't any good at the target practice – I'm sure of it. If she had turned out to be a crack shot, it would be a different story – she'd be leading the charge. Miranda hates being bad at anything. I could practically see her lip curl as Doug praised Emma, as though she didn't believe someone like Emma had any right to be a good shot.

'It's so fucking cold,' she adds, 'I'm sure the deer will be hiding somewhere out of sight, if they have any sense. Surely we're not going to catch anything now?'

Nick wheels suddenly on his heel to face her. 'Hey!' the

gamekeeper shouts. 'Careful man, you're carrying a loaded weapon.'

'Sorry,' Nick looks slightly abashed. 'But to be honest, I'm pretty tired of hearing about how bored you are, Miranda. Why don't you go back to the Lodge, if you're so keen for that? We're never going to surprise anything if you keep moaning about what a terrible time you're having.'

There's a resounding silence in the aftermath, the freezing air seems to drop another few degrees. Miranda looks as if she has just been slapped. Everyone has been a little more tense on this excursion, but this is the first openly hostile thing that anyone has actually said. Perhaps it's no surprise that it's between Nick and Miranda. Nick, after all, has never been Miranda's greatest fan. I don't think he's ever really forgiven her.

When Nick came out to a few of us, in our first year at Oxford, he hadn't yet told his parents, who were then serving an ambassadorship in Oman. It wasn't that he was afraid of doing so, he told me. 'They're pretty liberal, and they might have guessed already – there were a couple of guys, when we were in Paris, who I got close to.'

But he wanted to choose the right moment, because it was an important milestone, an affirmation of who he was.

Miranda claimed that she knew none of this when Nick's parents came up for reading week, and Nick introduced them to everyone in the JCR. There was some discussion about end-of-year exams, and Miranda said – in a nudge-nudge wink-wink tone – 'Don't worry, Mr and Mrs . . . M, we'll make sure Nick has his nose to the grindstone and doesn't just go off chasing after all the prettiest boys.'

She wasn't even supposed to know, that was the worst

of it. The select group Nick had confided in had not included Miranda. I had not been proud of myself for telling her. I was very good, normally, at keeping secrets. But I had been drunk, and Miranda had been teasing me about my crush on Nick, and it had just come out. Of course, I had begged her not to say that she knew. And yet she claimed to have no memory of this at all. She claimed, too, afterwards, that she assumed Nick's parents 'just knew'.

I was sure that Nick would never forgive me. So I was relieved by his reaction. He was furious, that was true. But not, thankfully, with me. He told me that he had thought of several unpleasant ways in which to exact his revenge on Miranda, but couldn't find anything that matched the scale of what she'd done to him.

'I know it shouldn't really matter,' he told me, 'I was going to tell them this week anyway . . . over a nice lunch or something. But it was the principle of it. I *know* it wasn't an accident. I think she did it because she liked having that power. And to cause trouble between the two of us, of course.'

'What do you mean?' I asked, surprised.

'I'm pretty sure she resents your being friends with me.'

'That's rubbish,' I told him. 'Miranda has loads of other friends, and I have . . . a few.'

'Yes, but she doesn't have any other *close* friends – have you noticed that, Katie? She's only got you – and Samira at a pinch. And I don't think she likes sharing her toys.'

Now, of course, that's all water under the bridge. Or, at least, Nick has done a good job of suggesting as much. I wonder, though, whether he still thinks of it. Wounds inflicted at that sort of raw, unformed time in our lives tend to cut the deepest – and leave the worst scars.

* * *

'Hey,' Samira says, sharply. 'Let's all just chill out, OK? We're here on holiday.'

Funny, I don't remember Samira being quite so sanguine in the past about things. And I recall her struggle with herself at brunch, how she managed to bite back whatever rejoinder she might have made to Miranda then.

Miranda mutters something under her breath, defiantly. But I can see that she's really stung. She can give it out, you see, Miranda – but she can't always take it. Underneath that tough, glossy exterior she's softer than she looks. And I think she's always secretly admired Nick, sees him as an equal.

I see her glance at Julien. I wonder if she's waiting for him to stick up for her. If so, she's disappointed, but perhaps not surprised. She has always said that he hates confrontation, likes to try to please everybody – never wanting to be seen as the bad guy.

I don't want to take sides, either. I can't afford to. I have enough of my own issues to deal with. I feel as though I've been catapulted into the past: Miranda causing drama, me having to mediate between her and the unlucky opponent – feeling that each of them is asking me to choose. I'm not going to do it now. I walk away from the group, around to the other side of the ruin, and stand in the full force of the wind for a few minutes, my eyes closed.

I clench my fingernails into my palms until they sting. I have to stop. I have to stop this thing, this compulsion, once and for all. But every time I have tried I find that I can't bring myself to. When it really comes to doing it, I'm never strong enough. I can't believe I've got myself into the mess that I have. I take a few deep breaths, open my eyes, and try to distract myself with the view.

I have been to some beautiful places in my life, but
nowhere quite like this. It's the wildness of the landscape,
perhaps: raw, untouched by human hand other than the
small cluster of dwellings below us, the tiny station on the
other side, and the old ruin behind us. It is bleak and brutal,
and its charm, if it can be called that, lies in this. The
colours are all muted: slate-blue, the old bruise yellow of
the sky, the rust red of the heather. And yet they are just
as mesmerising as any turquoise sea, any white sandy beach.

As I watch, a huge clump of the heather seems to lift up
and move, and I realise that it is deer, running as one, their
sleekness only offset by the comedy flashes of their white
tails. Perhaps it's this movement that draws my eye to
another flash of movement, lower down the slope. I don't
think I would have seen it otherwise. Seen him, that is. He
is some fifty yards away, wearing camouflage gear, a large
backpack on his back. I can't make out his face, or even
his height – because he's up to his waist in heather. He
appears to be making an effort not to be seen, keeping low
down, close to the heather as he moves. It must have been
him that scared the deer and set them sprinting off.

I don't think he's seen me yet. I can feel my heartbeat
somewhere up near my throat. There's something menacing
about the way he moves, like an animal. Then, like a predator catching my scent on the breeze, he looks up and sees
me. He stops short.

I can't make sense of what happens next. It defies all
logic. In the next couple of seconds he seems to sink from
view; to disappear into the heather itself. I blink, in case
something has actually happened to my vision. But when
I open my eyes there is still no sign of him.

I think of the manager's instructions. 'Tell the gamekeeper

or me if you see anyone you don't recognise on the estate.'
So should I tell them? But I'm not even completely sure of
what I have seen. A person doesn't just dissolve in plain
sight, do they? It's true that my eyes are full of tears from
the rawness of the wind, and I'm still a bit groggy from
the sleeping pills I took last night. The others will think
I'm simply making it up, or imagining things. I'm too weary
to try to explain what I saw. If I were Miranda, I'd make
this into a big drama, a ghost-story anecdote. But I'm not.
I'm Katie: the quiet one, the watcher. Besides, there can't
be any real harm in not saying anything. Can there?

DOUG

There's a change in the group. He noticed it even before the argument between the man with the glasses and the beautiful blonde. He has seen it happen before, this shift. It starts with the rifles. Each of them is suddenly invested with a new, terrible power. At first, during the target practice, they flinched with each report, at the jump of the device as it punched bruises into the flesh beneath their shoulders. But quickly – too quickly, perhaps – it became natural, and they were leaning into each shot: focused, intent. They began enjoying themselves. But something else crept in too. A sense of competition. More than that . . . something primeval has been summoned. The 'buck fever' felt by all novice hunters before their first trophy. The blood lust. Each of them wants to be the one that makes the kill. And yet they don't even know what it is they're yearning for. Because they have never killed before – not beyond the odd swatted fly, or trapped mouse. This is something completely different. They will be changed by

217

it. An innocence they did not know they possessed will be forsaken.

There is the landscape, too. It has made them edgy. Up here the harsh, skeletal lines of the land are revealed, granite peeking like old bone through the rust red fuzz of heather. Up here they become aware of quite how alone they are in this place – not another human soul for a very long way indeed.

Except . . . his fingers now find the cigarette stub in his pocket. He doesn't like it. It shows that someone has been up here, recently. Heather doesn't smoke, as far as he knows – and she certainly doesn't go anywhere near the Old Lodge if she can help it. Iain smokes, he thinks, but he has no need to come up here: he's been working down by the loch, on the pumphouse. It could also have been the Icelandic couple – but he saw them smoking rollies the other evening, after the dinner.

He'll mention it to Heather, later. Just to check whether she's noticed anything.

Poachers? But there would have been some other evidence of them, surely? In the past he has found blood-smeared grass where they have dragged their illegal bounty, or the cartridge shells with which they killed it. He has found the remains of fires they've made to attempt to burn the rest of the body (it's the heads they're after, in general) and the blackened bones that remain. Sometimes he's even found the kill before they've come back to claim it – they'll take the head, the most valuable part, and leave the headless corpse hidden in the grass until there's an opportune time to come and collect it.

It could merely have been dropped by a hiker – there's still a right to roam, though they're no doubt discouraged by the (probably illegal) 'private property' signs. He can't remember the last time he saw a walker. Besides, hikers are all bright cagoules and cling-filmed lunches and earnestness, not the sort to callously litter the landscape they've come to enjoy.

No, he doesn't like it one bit.

He's pleased to put the Old Lodge behind him. Its story parallels his own ghosts. The gamekeeper haunted by his own war, burning the place down. He knows the sorts of forces that might drive a man to such an act.

They find the hinds in the stretch of land beyond the Lodge. There is a stain of darkness in the sky already – the sun, invisible behind cloud, must be readying to set. They need to be quick. He has the guests lie in the heather and crawl towards the deer, so as not to alarm them.

One has got separated from the others, an old doe, with a hobble to her walk. Perfect. You only shoot the old, the limp. Despite what the poachers might think, this is not about magnificent trophies.

When they are close enough, he turns to the shorter, not-beautiful blonde. 'You,' he says. 'Want to try her?'

She nods, solemnly. 'All right.'

He helps her sight it. 'The largest part of the chest,' he says, 'not the head. Too much room for error with the head. And not too low, or you'll shatter her leg. And *squeeze* the trigger, remember, gently does it.'

She does as he says. The gun discharges, a flat thunder-clap of noise, ringing in the ears. The other deer scatter in fright, fleeing at astonishing speed. There are exclamations from the other guests behind him, sharp intakes of breath.

There is a beat, as always, when it seems that the bullet

must have misfired, or disappeared completely. Then the doe jerks as though passed through with an electric current. There is the belated thud of the bullet's impact, the metal entering flesh. A bellow, the sound as much like rage as pain. She staggers a couple of steps, swaying on her feet. And then finally, down she goes – quite gently, as though she is being careful with herself, her legs folding underneath her. Her chest is, suddenly, a mass of red. A perfect shot.

He walks the hundred yards or so to the dying beast. She's still there, just: her breath mists in the cold. There is a moment when her eyes seem to meet his. Then he takes his knife and shoves it in, clean, to that place at the base of the skull. Now she is gone. He feels little remorse, other than for the grace that once was, now stilled. Unlike other deaths for which he has been responsible, he knows this one is right, necessary. Unchecked, the population would get out of control; resources would be so thin that the whole herd would begin to starve.

He bends, and dips a hand into the wound, coating his fingers with gore. Then he walks back to the woman, Emma, and – in time-honoured tradition – anoints her forehead and cheeks with the blood.

EMMA

The gamekeeper told me I'd have to wait for the fillet from the deer I shot. It needs to be hung for a few days – apparently in the first twenty-four hours rigor mortis really sets in and it would be inedible until the tissues start to soften again. But they've got some properly aged meat that I can use if I want. I was going to do a beef Wellington tonight, but I've realised I could make it with venison instead. That would be perfect, wouldn't it – a reminder of our day?

I've come over to the barn to collect it. I've washed my face first, of course. Apparently there's some old wives' tale about not cleaning it off until midnight or bad luck will befall you, but that's just nonsense and superstition. Besides, it had dried and crusted into a very unsightly mess.

When I get to the barn there's no sign of anyone, but the door is slightly ajar. I give it a push with one hand and it swings open.

I can hear the murmur of voices, low and urgent. At the sound of my footsteps, they cease. It's gloomy inside, and

I have to squint to adjust my eyes. When I do I take a step back. At one end of the room hang two huge, grisly, bloody pendants of meat next to the carcass of the deer I shot, skinned, its eyes still glassy black and staring. There's a distinctive smell, impossible to mistake: heavy, metallic.

Behind the carcasses I make out the odd-job man I sat next to at the dinner, Iain, wielding a large cleaver in one hand, and wearing a butcher's apron soaked in blood. He raises his other hand in greeting; his palm is stained red. Next to him are the two Icelandic guests.

I wonder what these three strangers could have been talking about so fervently.

'Got your venison ready for you,' Iain says. He reaches towards the counter behind him and lifts up a parcel wrapped in stained greaseproof paper.

'Thank you,' I say, taking it from him gingerly. It's heavy, cold.

'These two,' he points to the two other guests, 'were just asking me if they could have the heart from your kill, as that's best fresh. I hope you don't mind them taking that?'

'No . . .' I say, trying to conceal my distaste, as a good chef should. 'Not at all.'

The man, Ingvar, grins at me. 'Thank you. You know, you should try it sometime. It's the tastiest part.'

NOW
2nd January 2019

HEATHER

I stare at the computer screen. I sit with my hand over my mouth like a pantomime of shock. But I am genuinely stunned by what a simple search of Doug's full name has brought up. It's bad. Really bad. It's far worse than probably even my mother could have guessed in her most lurid imaginings.

I can see that even from the brief precis of each article on the Google results page. He almost killed someone. I've been living in this place alone with a man who has served time in jail. Who was convicted of, as the official line has it: 'causing grievous bodily harm with intent'.

The *Daily Mail* article is the first hit. I click it open. There is a photo of Doug, hollow-eyed, mouth a grim line, hair shorn to the scalp. Another of him in an ill-fitting suit, being shepherded out of a car into the courthouse, his teeth bared at the photographers in a snarl. He *looks* like a criminal; he looks violent, dangerous. The article that follows is a lurid attack on every aspect of his character. Educated at a private school; university dropout; time in the Marines, the only one to survive an attack by the Taliban in 'murky circumstances'. Strongly insinuating, if not stating outright, that some foul play or cowardice was involved on his part.

And then a 'brawl in a bar'.

As I read on, it only gets worse. The form of 'bodily harm'? *Attempted strangulation.* I look for anything in the article that might exonerate Doug's behaviour in some way: something I could latch onto. I want him to be exonerated. Not just because the idea of having lived with someone capable of cold-blooded murder (or at least the attempt of it) is horrifying, but because, despite his taciturn ways, I have come to rather like Doug. I genuinely believed what I said when I told my mum he was 'harmless'.

There is nothing to excuse him though. I discard the *Daily Mail*, click on the BBC News link, which should give me an account without bias or sensationalism. That article contains a quote from an eyewitness: 'It just happened out of nowhere. One moment they were talking, I think – just two blokes having a quiet chat in the corner of the pub, the next that man was trying to strangle him. People tried to pull him off, and he fought them all, until finally there were enough of them to overpower him. It was terrifying.'

My skin prickles with cold, even though the heating in the Lodge is turned right up. Attempted *strangulation.* I remember the bruising around the guest's neck, the black and blue collar.

And yet what possible reason could Doug have had to kill the guest? She had only been here for two days. She was a complete stranger.

Maybe, a little voice says, he didn't need a reason. The man in the pub, according to these articles, was also believed to be a complete stranger.

There is at least one thing that doesn't fit, I tell myself. Doug's discovery of the body. Why show me the whereabouts of the body, rather than conceal it somehow? In order to control the situation? Maybe . . . but then it would only make sense to do that if it were still possible to make it look like an accident. It is fairly obvious, even to someone who is not a doctor, that she was strangled.

There's a knock on the door. I freeze, then slam the laptop closed. With a few swift steps I'm at the door, have unlocked it. When I open it, on the other side – as I had somehow known he would be – is Doug.

Two days earlier
New Year's Eve 2018

KATIE

Everyone is heading to their own cabins to get ready for the evening. Miranda wants us all to dress up. 'It's ridiculous,' Samira muttered to Emma and me, 'we're in the middle of nowhere, in the countryside. Funnily enough, I have other priorities besides tarting myself up – I thought we all came here to relax?'

'Oh, but I suppose it'll give it all a sense of occasion,' Emma said, loyally.

Besides, in matters like this there is no point in putting up any resistance. Miranda *will* get what she wants.

I don't spend the time before supper getting ready, however. I spend it in my bathroom, crouched over a little plastic stick, and then pacing the length of my cabin, wondering what I am going to do. I want to scream. But this place is so bloody quiet they'd all hear me.

Maybe, I tell myself, trying to breathe, the test was faulty somehow. I wish I had got a spare. I was too flustered in the Boots at King's Cross, though, too afraid that one of the others would see me buying it. Besides, the little sheet of instructions suggests that while it's possible for the test *not* to pick up on a positive result, the reverse pretty much never happens.

It's eight o'clock before I know it, and I pull on a black dress I just remembered to throw in the case, an old office-to-cocktails affair, and pull a brush through my hair, so hard I hurt myself.

I am not sure whether it is my imagination or not, but the dress feels tighter than it was at the office Christmas party, and when I study my reflection sideways in the mirror, I am certain that I can see a tiny protuberance where I have had nothing before. Oh God. I turn, this way and that. It's definitely there. Dread rises in me.

Now that I have noticed it, it seems unmistakable; I'm amazed that Miranda hasn't commented on it. Add this to the fact that I've noticed a little more tenderness in my breasts – and that my appetite has been up and down. And yet: how the hell did this happen? I thought I'd been so careful. Clearly not careful enough. And I don't know what I am going to do about it.

I sit back on the bed. I don't want to go. I can't do this – I can't go out there and face them all. I sit for maybe half an hour. Wondering . . . hoping . . . maybe they've forgotten all about me?

There's a knock on the door. For a moment I can almost pretend I imagined it.

'Katie? What are you doing in there? I can see you sitting on the bed!'

I go to the door and open it – what choice do I have? I feel like an animal, routed in its den. Miranda stands there, a hand on one hip. She looks incredible, of course: she's gone for a skin-tight gold sheath dress; the sort of thing you can only get away with if you look like Miranda, and even then probably only on New Year's Eve.

'Well,' she looks me up and down. *Can she see it? I'm standing front on, so probably not.* 'Not very festive,' she says. Then she opens the little evening bag she has slung over one arm. 'Here, this will help.' In a kind of daze I feel her press the lipstick onto my lips; the waxy scent of it almost overpowering.

She stands back. 'There. That's better. Come on, then.' She grasps my wrist, her nails grazing my skin – half drags me through the open doorway, forces my arm through hers.

I can't take this close contact right now. I extract my arm from hers. 'I'm fine, thanks,' I say – it comes out sharper than I had intended. 'I think I can just about manage to walk there on my own.'

Miranda stares at me, as shocked as if I'd just yelled at her. You see, I never answer back. She likes to tell people that, as friends, 'we just don't fight'. But that's not down to her, for God's sake. It's because I've never, in the past, put up any resistance.

'Look,' she says, her voice low, dangerous, 'I don't know what's up with you, Katie. You've been a total misery ever since we got here. It's like you're too *good* for us suddenly. Like you can't be bothered to take part. But, well, tonight you're going to. You're bloody well going to have a good time.' She turns on her heel. And I find myself following her as meekly as if she had a rope around my neck, as I have done so many times before. What other choice do I have?

There's different feeling this evening. Last night it was high spirits, a sense of camaraderie, togetherness. Tonight, the atmosphere carries a dangerous edge. It's as though that time out there, in all that wilderness, has put us on our guard. I wonder if the others can still see the deer, like me: buckling to her knees. It has become a dark thing between us, with the freighted quality of a guilty secret. We killed something together. We were all complicit, even if Emma was the one who took the shot. We did it for 'fun'.

Everyone – apart from me – seems to have fractured into their proper pairs, drawing back into their primary alle-giances: Nick and Bo, Emma and Mark, Miranda snaking an arm around Julien's waist. At a little remove, Giles and Samira stand talking to each other in a low murmur. Miranda has persuaded them to leave Priya in the cabin tonight so we could 'all be grown-ups' this evening, but judging by Samira's mutinous expression she isn't exactly happy about it.

There's some enforced jollity as Julien carries a bottle of champagne around, pouring liberally, but everyone seems to be gulping it down, hardly tasting it, as though they are trying to drink themselves into the spirit of things. Of course, perhaps I'm imagining this: projecting onto them a tension that really exists only in my own mind. But I'm not so sure. Because I see the quick, animal, darting looks they are all giving one another – I am not alone in that. We are looking for something in each other's faces. But what is it? Familiarity? A reassuring reminder of all that holds us close? Or are we fearfully searching for some new element, glimpsed out there on that bleak mountainside? Something new and strange and violent.

'Dinner is served!' Emma calls from the kitchen. It's a relief to have a new focus, not to have to stand around making small talk – that suddenly feels as strained and difficult as it might with complete strangers.

It's venison Wellington: although not made with the deer from earlier, I'm relieved to hear. Emma is a wonderful cook. It goes hand in hand with her incredible organisation, I suppose. She has planned this whole trip, down to the very last detail. And she at least seems unchanged by whatever strange spirit has possessed everyone else: brisk and energetic as she carries the dish to the table with a flourish.

'God,' Miranda says, 'I'm in awe of you, Emma. Half the time, if you look in our fridge, you'll just find a bottle of champagne and half a jar of olives. It's like you're a proper adult.'

Emma flushes with pleasure. Except . . . I don't think it was a compliment. It makes her look homey, sort of dull. Whereas Miranda comes out of it looking glamorous, in an unpredictable, rock 'n' roll way.

It's not even true. Yes, she's not a good cook, but she does *do* it. But she'll never let an opportunity slip to look superior to Emma in some way.

What a bitch. I catch myself, stifle the thought. What has got into me? And, after all, *I* am a fine one to talk.

We all applaud and exclaim over the venison: the golden sheen of the pastry, the neatness of the compact parcel of meat.

I cut a morsel. It's perfectly cooked: the pastry flaky, the venison miraculously pink in the middle. But, as I prod it with my fork, a little bloody stream seeps out. I think of that deer today, staggering to her knees, the terrible groan that seemed to echo from the surrounding peaks as she went down, and I feel my stomach turn over. I take a bite, anyway, and sit there struggling to swallow. For a brief, panicked moment the food seems to catch at the back of my throat, and I think I might really choke. It takes a big gulp of my water to send it on its way, and I find myself coughing hoarsely in the aftermath.

Samira, next to me, gives me a nudge. 'Are you all right?'

I nod. Emma, I see, has turned to look at me. 'I hope it's OK?' she asks.

'Yes,' I say, my throat raw, 'it's absolutely delicious.'

She gives a very small nod of her head. But she doesn't smile. I wonder if she saw the difficulty I had forcing it down: worse, my grimace of slight disgust at the sight of the bloodied meat. But I think it's more than that. Emma has never really seemed to like me much. I've tried so hard with her – perversely I've tried much harder than I might have done if she had seemed to like me. And, it should be the other way around, shouldn't it? She should make the effort with me. She should be the one looking for some kind of acceptance with Mark's oldest friends. She's certainly made the effort with Miranda, despite Miranda being an absolute bitch to her, at times.

I definitely felt a bit sorry for Emma, when she joined our group. There was so much to catch up on, so many in-jokes, so much history. It was different for Bo. His Americanness, somehow, set him apart. He was exotic – a New Yorker – and besides, he studied at Stanford, so there wasn't exactly going to be an inferiority complex there. Whereas Emma went to Bath, and Miranda has always seemed determined to find little ways to lord Oxford over her, to show her up as not being quite as good as the rest of us. I don't think she wants Emma to feel bad, per se, she just wants a kind of serf-like acknowledgement of her superiority.

To her credit, Emma barely seems to notice when Miranda has a go at her. She has a robustness about her, a self-containment. I feel like she's one of those people it's easy to be friends with, because she has no baggage . . . but she's not the kind of person who would be my *best* friend. She doesn't seem to have a deeper layer; or if she does, she hides it well. Refreshing, yes, but also perhaps just a tiny bit dull. God, I'm starting to sound like Miranda.

'You know,' I'd told Emma, two New Years ago, when she was very new to the group, 'you really shouldn't put up with Miranda's crap.'

'What do you mean?' she asked, wide-eyed.

'The way she talks to you. She's like it with all of us, to be honest. I sometimes think she has this idea that everyone was put on earth to serve her.' I knew how that felt, well enough. 'I love her dearly, because she has her many good qualities too – but it's definitely one of her less admirable ones. You don't want to play up to her idea of her own superiority.'

Emma frowned. 'I really don't mind, Katie.' There was a sharpness to her tone that I had never heard before.

'Oh,' I said, 'I only thought—'

'You don't need to worry about me,' she repeated, 'I really don't mind.'

And she genuinely doesn't seem to. I watch her now, grinning away at everyone, asking Miranda where she bought her dress. Maybe I'm being oversensitive, but I have

sometimes got the impression that she is just barely toler-
ating me, for the sake of group harmony. That under the
surface, there might be real dislike. Or as close as someone
like Emma comes to dislike.

It's quite upsetting, to feel yourself disliked by someone
as straightforward and good – 'good', yes that's exactly the
word – as Emma. Sometimes, in my more paranoid moods,
I have wondered if she recognises that there is something
'off' about me. That she saw the destructiveness and the
selfishness in me even before I recognised them myself.

Miranda is picking through her meal, carefully separating
the fillet from the pastry, and then only eating half of that.
She has always been very careful about her weight. Which
is ridiculous, because she has pretty much the perfect figure,
at least according to the glossies and the *Daily Mail*. But
I remember meals at her house, and her mother taking
away her plate before she had finished. 'A lady,' she would
say, 'leaves her plate unfinished and keeps her waist under
twenty-five inches.' And I thought I came from a dysfunctional
family. For a couple of years Miranda went vegan, then she
did the 5:2 for a while. And on top of that every Pilates,
ballet barre and soul cycle class offered at her upscale gym.
She's obviously gorgeous, but if you ask me she'd look
better with a little more weight, more softness. Already, in
her thirties, she's starting to get that brittle ageing Hollywood
starlet look. Oh, and I'm certain she's had Botox. You
would imagine, as her best friend, I might know this for
a fact either way. But she's oddly private about such things.
The fact that she gets regular fake tans, for example: she'll
turn up to a wedding looking as though she's spent three
weeks in St Barts. But when I comment on it she'll say

something like, 'Oh yes, I spent a lot of time in the sun recently – I tan so easily' and abruptly change the subject.

'He's so hot, isn't he,' she's saying now, 'that game-keeper? The strong and silent type . . . Like something from a Mills & Boon novel. So skilled. I didn't realise stalking a deer was so difficult. And so *tall*. Couldn't you just climb that?'

'God yes,' Samira says, to a wounded 'Oi!' from Giles.

But Miranda hardly seems to notice that she's spoken. She is looking at Julien. The 'tall' part seems a particularly pointed barb. Julien is many things; the one thing he is not, and never will be, is tall. 'Such a *masculine* sort of man,' Miranda adds. 'There's something almost dangerous about him . . . But that makes him all the more attractive. You just know he'd be able to fix anything, or build you a shelter in the middle of a wood. No one has those sorts of skills any more.'

'You know what you two sound like?' Giles says. His tone is light, but I think he's a bit pissed off too.

'What?' Miranda says, playfully.

'A couple of desperate old spinsters.'

I do not miss the glances at me – even Nick, for God's sake. Because if anyone is a desperate old spinster here then it is, well: yours truly. I concentrate on getting a perfect morsel of venison and pastry onto the end of my fork.

'I think,' Miranda says, undeterred, 'on behalf of women everywhere, that you should try and seduce him, Katie.' She says it playfully, but there's an edge to it, and I wonder what it means. She seems slightly *too much* this evening: the gold dress, her hair piled into a kind of warrior's head-dress, the gleam in her eyes, her laugh just a fraction too loud.

'And get herself murdered?' Giles says, laughing. 'Well, you've got to wonder, haven't you? What's a chap like that doing all alone somewhere like this? I mean, it's beautiful and tranquil and everything for a few days, but it would be pretty creepy living here all the time on your own. You'd go mad even if you weren't already.'

'He's not on his own,' I say. 'There's that woman in the office, Heather.'

'Yes,' Miranda says, 'but they're not together, are they? And she's probably a bit cuckoo too. If you've chosen this life you're obviously a bit of a weirdo, or you have something to run away from.'

'I think she seems perfectly normal,' I say. I don't know why I'm defending them. It isn't a good idea to disagree with Miranda when she's in this sort of mood. 'And he seemed perfectly harmless. And yes, I suppose he is good-looking.'

'I see,' Julien says, in the unconvincing manner of a kindly uncle. 'That's your type is it, Katie?'

I can feel them all peering at me, as though I am a specimen at the bottom of a jar. I swallow the morsel of Wellington, take a long draught of my water, though I long for the wine. 'Maybe it is.'

After we've eaten supper it's still quite early. Emma is doing her best to keep everyone well-lubricated. She keeps insisting on getting up and topping up glasses – which is faintly embarrassing, as though she's our waitress for the evening. In spite of her efforts, conversation around the table seems to have run dry. There's a strange pause. What to do, what to fill the time with? With the ease of last night mysteriously vanished, it doesn't seem enough to sit around and reminisce together. I remind myself it always feels like this on New Year's Eve, because of all the enforced celebration. Midnight – not particularly late on any given night – suddenly seems like a faraway milestone.

'I was wondering,' Samira says, 'and I know it's a bit teenage . . . But we could play Truth or Dare?'

There are mingled groans.

'We're in our thirties, Samira,' Nick says, raising an eyebrow. 'I think we're a bit beyond Truth or Dare.'

'Oh come on,' Miranda says, 'some of us here like to consider ourselves as young.'

'And it could be fun?' Emma says. She's the only one whose mood doesn't seem to have changed from yesterday morning: she's all enthusiasm, flushed with pleasure from the meal's success. She's made a proper effort this evening – she can't match Miranda's glamour, but her off-the-shoulder gunmetal dress has a bit of a shimmer to it, and she's coloured her lips in bright red. It's almost a perfect match for the tiny smear of blood that she's missed, up above her ear next to the hairline, a leftover from this afternoon's hunt.

In the absence of another suggestion, everyone seems to accept that this is what we are doing now: playing Truth or Dare. There's a palpable relief, in fact, that we have a structure for the next part of our evening, something to keep us occupied.

We sit down around the table. Emma grabs an empty wine bottle and spins it. It lands on Bo. 'Dare,' he says.

'Kiss Mark,' Miranda says.

Bo wrinkles his nose. 'Do I have to?'

Mark looks, frankly, terrified. But Bo leans over, matter-of-factly, and plants his mouth on Mark's. And for a moment

– blink-and-you'd-miss-it – I think Mark responds, his mouth moving sensually under Bo's. It's kind of hot. I see Nick frown. He's noticed it too.

Everyone's laughing. But there is a new tension in the air, now, a frisson of sex.

Bo spins the bottle. It lands on Miranda. 'Truth,' she says, with a slightly vacant smile. Between this, and the lazy, sleepy look of her eyes, I can tell she's already had quite a lot to drink.

'OK,' Nick says, 'I've got one. Have you ever slept with anyone else around this table?'

Miranda giggles. 'Have I ever slept with anyone else?' she says – and there's a slight slur on the 'slept'. 'I suppose you mean apart from my *husband*?'

'Yes,' Nick says. There's an intensity in the way he's looking at her: it reminds me of a cat watching a bird.

'Um,' she puts a finger up to her lips – though the first time she misses and catches her chin – in a pantomime of thought. 'I suppose in that case I would have to say . . . yes.'

There's a stunned silence. That can't be true, can it? If so, I've never heard anything about it. How do *I* not know? I glance at Julien, but he doesn't look particularly surprised. Does he know? Who can it have been? I study all the faces around the table, but no one's expression seems to give anything away. Mark? He's the most likely, I suppose, but I feel that would have come out, somehow, before now. Still, I think of him spending all that time hanging around college, waiting to give Miranda some message from Julien. There would have been opportunity.

Miranda shrugs at us all. 'I'm not going to tell you anything else, so you might as well spin again.'

'Come on,' Samira says, 'you *have* to tell us.'

'Yes,' Bo says, 'you can't tell us that and not say any more.'

'Yes I can,' Miranda says, with a sly smile. 'I've answered the question. I've told my Truth.'

Giles hands Miranda the bottle. 'Right. Next.'

The gleam in Miranda's eye has grown brighter. After her revelation, the stakes feel higher, the air charged. She spins, and it lands on Mark.

'Dare,' he says, almost before it has even fully stopped.

'OK,' Miranda thinks for a moment. 'Drink this.' She holds out a bottle of Dom Pérignon.

'The whole thing?' Emma stares. 'You can't do that.'

'It used to be my party trick,' Mark says. 'Have I never told you? A whole bottle in ten minutes.'

I remember. I also remember the mess afterwards. Mark is one of those people who shouldn't drink. It makes some people emotional, some belligerent, others angry – you can guess which group Mark falls into.

'I'll do it,' Miranda says, getting to her feet. She pops the cork with an air of ceremony, making sure to do it carefully so that none spills. Then she walks towards Mark. 'Kneel down,' she says, half seductress, half sergeant major. 'Open wide.' He does what she says, and she upends the bottle, with no warning and very little gentleness, shoving the neck between his parted lips. He makes a kind of gagging sound, but she doesn't relent. If anything, I think I see her give the base a further thrust with one manicured hand.

Mark gulps the liquid, his throat working hard and his eyes streaming, red, almost bloodied looking. Julien and Giles are egging him on: 'Get it down you!' and 'Chug,

chug, chug . . .' – remnants of chants from rugby socials, no doubt. The rest of us just watch.

His nose is running with snot, like a crying child's. He makes more of those gagging sounds, and beneath them there is a kind of low, animal whine that makes the hairs on my arms stand to attention. For all that, most of the booze is frothing over his chin and soaking into his smart shirt, the crotch of his suit trousers.

'Oh God,' Samira says, 'he's probably had enough.'

'For fuck's sake,' Miranda barks, completely ignoring her. 'Drink it. You're not drinking it.'

I think of how dense the bubbles are in champagne, how painful it is to down even a glass of the stuff.

It's horrible to watch, a grotesque imitation of a sexual act. But for some reason it is both impossible to look away and to do anything to stop it. The guys have stopped cheering him on now, their chants dwindling to an uneasy silence. Even Emma doesn't move, doesn't make a sound to help her boyfriend. We sit watching as though stunned, mesmerised by this obscene spectacle.

Finally, it's drained. Slowly, almost reluctantly, Miranda withdraws the bottle. She gives it a slap with the flat of one hand, and a few more drops fall out, one of them splashing into Mark's eye in a final indignity, the punctuation to the insult.

Mark is wheezing, retching, doubled over, his hands on his knees for support. For a horrible moment it looks as if he's going to vomit. Samira, nearest to him, puts a reassuring hand on his back. He shrugs her off with a violent jerk of his shoulders. We wait, silent, no one saying a word, to see how this will play out. Finally, after what feels like a long time, Mark raises his head. He gives us a weak, unconvincing grin, and puts one hand into the air like a victor. He must know, surely, that whatever we just witnessed was in no way *his* victory. Still, there's a collective sigh of relief. The others cheer. It was a game! Ha, ha – Miranda, you're so brutal. Mark – well done, chap!

When Mark goes to spin the bottle, his hand shakes.

It lands, as I had somehow known it would, on me.

'Dare,' I say. I don't want to do one: Miranda's dares have always been notoriously horrible. But I'd take pretty much any dare over a truth right now.

'Mark?' Samira asks, turning to him. 'Got any ideas?'

Mark puts a hand to his throat, and tries to speak, but only a hoarse kind of wheeze comes out. He shakes his head, and defers his choice.

'Fine,' Miranda says, matter-of-fact, apparently unconcerned by the fact that she's the cause of this indignity. She steeples her fingers, then goes to Emma, whispers in her ear. Jesus Christ, it's like something from school. How can Emma be so friendly with Miranda, after what she just inflicted on her boyfriend? But perhaps we really are pretending it was just fun and games, no harm meant or done.

Emma is nodding. 'Or,' she says, and whispers something in Miranda's ear in return.

Bo laughs. 'Going to share with us?'

Emma shakes her head at him, playfully. Miranda doesn't even bother glancing in his direction. She is looking straight at me. I feel a chill go through me.

'Into the loch,' she says. 'Ten seconds, fully submerged. Then out.'

I stare at her. She can't be serious. 'Miranda, it's below freezing out there. There's ice on the surface.'

'Yes,' Nick cuts in. 'Miranda – she'll freeze to death.'

I expect Samira to have my back, too. But she's frowning into space as though her mind is somewhere else completely.

Miranda smiles, blithely, and shakes her head. 'The manager told me she swims in there most days, even in winter. Besides, we'll be ready for you with a towel. You'll be fine, Katie.'

I stare at her. I can't believe she's actually going to make me do this. But her eyes are blank, expressionless. 'Go on,' she says, with a little nod of encouragement. 'Strip.'

So often, at school, Miranda was my vanquisher: belittling the girls who tried to have a go at me. But there was another side, too. Miranda, the bully. When she wanted to be she could be far crueller than any of the classroom bitches. It was rare, but it did happen. The flicking of a switch, the flexing of her muscles. Just to remind me who was in charge.

I have one particular memory – one of those you just can't shake, however much you try. Year 9. In the changing room before hockey. One of the girls – Sarah – was complaining about the fact that Miss wouldn't let her sit it out, despite it being the first day of her period. 'She says it's supposedly "good for" me. Says it will make it better. But I know it won't. It's not fair.' The others: nodding and murmuring in sympathy.

I remembered the packet of paracetamol in my rucksack: dug it out and offered it to her. Sarah was one of the less terrible ones. Sometimes we sat together in class: the ones I didn't have with Miranda, of course. She looked up at me and smiled as she took the pills. 'Thanks, Katie.' I felt a little warmth, spreading through my chest.

And then Miranda's voice, clear as a bell. 'But I suppose Katie wouldn't understand. Seeing as she hasn't even got hers yet.' All the other girls turned to me in shock, in fascination. Looking at me as though I were exactly what I felt: a freak show. It had been a sign, I was sure of it – that there was something definitely, definitively wrong with me. Fourteen and no period to speak of. I had confided in Miranda in the strictest confidence. At the time she had reassured me, said she was certain fourteen wasn't that late, in the grand scheme of things.

And then she had used it to humiliate me. As a way of keeping me in check.

She's doing this now.

This is absurd. I'm thirty-three years old. I have people who respect and depend on me at work. I have responsibilities. I'm a brilliant lawyer, in fact – I know that – I never let the other side win. I will not allow myself to be humiliated like this.

Fine, I think, looking at Miranda. I see you. I raise you. As though it is nothing at all in the world, I wriggle out of my dress, so I'm standing in front of them all in my underwear. I've somehow managed to wear good underwear, in fact: yellow silk, lace trimmed. New. I see Miranda's eyebrows rise a fraction. She was expecting some greige over-washed horrors, I suspect, in order to compound my humiliation. I wonder if they have noticed my belly. Perhaps it can be explained away by post-dinner bloat. I hunch over, all the same, as I walk across the room without a single look at any of them, open the front door.

Fuck. It is even colder than earlier, if that is possible. It's so cold that it actually hurts. I can feel my skin shrinking. I can't think about it, or I won't be able to do it. I have to be steely, my best, strongest self. The water is only a few yards away, down the path. It looks black as ink. But

I can see small pale fragments of ice, gossamer thin, on its surface. I walk towards it and simply keep going as the water covers my ankles, my calves, my stomach, then I plunge downwards, up to my neck. Unbelievable cold. It feels as if I'm drowning, though my head is above the surface. The cold is forcing all the air from my lungs; I'm breathing too quickly, but I can't seem to draw any breath in. And then, finally, I get myself under control. I turn and look at them all, watching me now, from the bank. All of them cheering and whooping, except Miranda. She's just watching me.

I look straight back at her, as I tread water. I hate you, I think. I hate you. I don't feel bad any more. You deserve everything that is coming to you.

EMMA

I find Katie a towel from the loo in the Lodge. She's so cold that her teeth are chattering with a sound like someone shaking dice. In the light of the living room her lips are bluish. But it's her eyes that are most disturbing. I know this look, it is that of someone on the edge. I've seen it in Mark. I saw it that day at the racecourse.

'I hate her,' she says, in a hiss. 'I actually hate her. I can't believe she just made me do that. You don't know her properly, Emma – so perhaps you can't understand. You don't know what she's capable of.'

Actually, I think, I know her a lot better than you're always trying to make out. Who has been there for her recently, when you've dropped off the planet? And I certainly know what *you're* capable of, Katie Lewis.

I don't say this, of course. Instead I grit my teeth and say, 'How about a glass of champagne? That will warm you up, won't it?'

'No. I don't want a glass of champagne. Besides, hasn't

your boyfriend drunk it all?' She's spitting the words out. I stare at her. I've never seen her like this. I'm not sure I've ever actually seen Katie angry.

'Look, Katie, I'm sure she didn't mean it. She's just had a lot to drink, and she thought it would be funny.'

'It was fucking dangerous,' she growls. 'Do you have any idea how cold that water is?'

'Come on, Katie. It's about to be a new year. 2019. A *whole new year*. Try and forget about it? I'm sure we've all done things we aren't proud of, recently.' I fix her with a look, just enough to give her pause. She swallows, and then bows her head, as though she is conceding something.

'I just really want everyone to have a good time,' I say. 'I've been planning this for so long.'

'Yes,' she says, chastened. 'I know. Sorry, Emma.'

I usher her into the loo, persuade her to change back into her clothes. Suddenly, she is obedient as a child.

I find a record at random and put it on the player, cranking it up to full volume. It's Candi Staton, 'You've Got the Love'. My favourite song. It's like it was meant to be.

And it has the required effect. Everyone starts dancing. Even Katie – albeit somewhat half-heartedly.

Miranda is pretty drunk now. But she's still a better dancer than anyone else here, swaying in the middle of the room, her gold dress incandescent with light. I stand up to dance with her, mirroring her moves, and she gives me a big grin. Then her smile wavers, falters.

'What is it?'

'Sho weird . . .' (She's slurring her words now, using Sean Connery 'S's.) She squints at me, 'but I feel like this has all happened before. Do you ever get that? When you could swear that you remember this exact moment happening in the past?'

Typical of Miranda, bless her, to think déjà vu is an experience unique to herself. 'Yes,' I say, 'sometimes.'

'It's this song . . .' She frowns. 'I really mean it. I know we've danced to it somewhere before. Don't you feel like this has all already happened?' She's looking at me, questioningly. I don't know what to say, so I laugh. If I'm honest, she's scaring me a little bit. I'm relieved when she spots Julien over my shoulder.

'Julien,' she says. 'Dance with me.' She reaches for him, her hands groping at his shoulders.

He humours her for a few minutes, swaying obediently to the music, his hands on her hips, but there is a curious lack of intimacy about the pose. He looks bored, if anything. But it all makes sense now, of course.

Everyone suddenly seems very drunk. I feel like the only one still in control of my faculties – apart from Katie, perhaps. Mark has seized the deer's head from the wall and is parading around with it, wearing it like a mask, pretending to charge at people. I can see how drunk he is after downing that bottle, his movements uncoordinated. Samira shrieks – something between laughter and real terror – and ducks away from him, falling back onto one of the sofas.

'Mark,' I shout, 'put that back.' But he doesn't hear me – or he ignores me. There is no reasoning with him when he's like this.

Giles, meanwhile, is strolling around the room, drinking straight from an open bottle of champagne. As though struck by sudden inspiration, he puts his thumb in the end and begins to shake it, furiously – like a Formula One driver. Then he lets go, aiming for Julien. Julien cowers beneath the spray – a fountain of champagne – as it soaks the front of his shirt, his groin. A good deal of it missed him, though. I see it flooding onto the sheepskin rug, the rich fabric of the sofa . . .

'Stop—' I shout, running towards them. 'Stop!' But they're completely oblivious to me. In their drunkenness they seem somehow outsized, their actions bigger, more dramatic. Now Julien leaps at Giles, catching him by the front of his shirt and yanking down, the shirt ripping open, buttons spraying everywhere, landing with little pinging sounds. Mark turns and sees them. He drops the deer's head, like a child who has caught sight of others playing with better toys. He cannons towards them as though not wanting to be left out, tackling both of them about the necks. The three of them lurch, struggle, and then topple. There's a crash as they come down, straight into the glass coffee table in the middle of the room. The dancers – Miranda, Nick, Bo and Samira – stop what they're doing and look over. I watch as the glass cracks down the middle, slowly, almost ponderously, and then shatters into fragments, which skid everywhere. The three of them surface, blearily.

'Oh, fuck,' Giles says. Then he giggles.

'Doesn't matter,' Julien slurs. 'Don't worry Emma—' he looks about for me, 'I'll pay for it.' He stretches out both his arms. 'I'll pay for all of it.' He puts out a hand to Mark, who has somehow managed to clamber to his feet. 'Help me up, mate.'

Mark takes it. He begins to pull Julien to his feet. Then, just as he's almost lifted him to full height, he lets go, so that he crashes back to the floor. I wonder if I'm the only one who saw that it wasn't an accident.

'Sorry, mate,' he says.

Julien is looking up at him, and he's trying to laugh. But his eyes, I see, are intense, almost black.

It's all going horribly wrong. I look about me at the wreckage of the room, to the beautifully dressed dining table beyond – which seems to be mocking me. This is not anything like what I had planned. Then, on the wall clock, I see the time. I could weep with relief.

'Hey,' I shout, making a funnel of my hands over my mouth, knowing this might just catch their attention like nothing else, 'it's nearly midnight!'

MIRANDA

We stumble outside to the edge of the loch. Julien is hunched over himself – I think he might have hurt himself a bit when he was messing around with Giles and Mark just now. They broke a table, for Christ's sake – they're like children. Katie is still wrapped in one of the big woollen blankets, over the top of her clothes. She can't *still* be cold, can she? She's always been so bloody fragile. Still, I feel quite bad about my behaviour. Not for Mark – he had that coming, ever since last night. But Katie hasn't done anything to me, really, beyond being a bit distant and not much fun. Sometimes these impulses over-take me – the urge to push things a bit further . . . even the urge to wound. I can't stop myself, it's like a compulsion.

I'd like to say something to Katie, to apologise, maybe, but I can't find the words. The champagne has hit me really hard. My breath is misting in the air, but I can't actually feel the cold, wrapped as I am in my own little blanket of booze. I feel numb. I'd forgotten I had so much wine before the champagne. My thoughts are jumbled, my mind fuggy. Maybe it would be better if I were sick.

The countdown to midnight begins. 'A minute!' Emma shouts, looking at her watch.

I stare up at the stars. The new year. What is it going to bring for me?

'Thirty seconds!'

I look around at the others. They're all grinning, but their faces, in the light thrown from the Lodge, look strange, spectral, and their smiles look like snarls.

Mark stands poised with a new bottle of champagne. He hasn't glanced in my direction once, since the game. I'm used to having his eyes on me. I don't miss it, of course I don't. But at the same time, as I stand here in the dark, I have this feeling of being invisible . . . untethered . . . like a balloon that might suddenly float up into that starlit sky.

'Twenty seconds . . .' The others are chanting now. 'Nineteen, eighteen . . .'

I don't like it, all of a sudden. It feels like the countdown to something terrible . . . the explosion of a bomb. I imagine the little red lights blinking down.

'Five, four, three, two . . .'

'Happy New Year!' The rest of us parrot it in response. Giles is fumbling with a lighter at the shoreline.

'Be careful!' Samira calls, her voice high and shrill.

'Come on!' I shout, trying to shake off the bad feeling. 'We're all waiting!'

Finally, Giles seems to manage to light the thing. He staggers backwards. Then there's a promising fizz, and then a whoosh, and a big red rocket erupts from the ground with a sound like a scream and explodes over the loch. The water reflects it: a thousand tiny fragments of fire. It's beautiful. I try to focus on it, but everything is spinning. The silence afterwards is so . . . heavy. The dark around us is so thick, like I could reach out . . . touch it. If we were in London – or anywhere near civilisation for that matter – we would be able to see all the other firework displays going off around us. Reminding us of other people, other life. But here we are absolutely alone.

I can still hear the scream of the firework inside my head. But it no longer sounds the same, it sounds like a person. And I have this thought . . . that it wasn't like a firework at all. More like one of those safety flares. SOS. Fired from the deck of a sinking ship.

Julien comes back over to us. 'It's not quite Westminster fireworks,' he says.

'But who wants Westminster – all those sweaty bodies pressed together – when you can have this?' Emma asks. 'This place,' she spreads her arms wide, 'and best friends.' She links her arm with mine, and smiles at me, a proper, warm smile. I want to hug her. Thank fuck for Emma.

And then she begins to sing – her voice is surprisingly good. I try and join in:

Should old acquaintance be forgot,
and never brought to mind?
Should old acquaintance be forgot,
and days of old lang syne?

Ok, I know I've had a lot to drink but together, out here in the dark and silence, our voices sound beautiful, and there's something vulnerable about the noise. The trees around us are so thick and black. Anyone could be watching us, going through this little ritual together.

It must be all the booze, I think, that is making me feel so . . . strange. There's a loud bang, and I jump with shock. But it's just Nick opening another bottle of Dom. He pours it into glasses. As he passes one to Katie, I see her face, and it makes me shiver. What's wrong with her? It can't all be due to her dunk in the loch, can it? She doesn't even look at the glass of champagne being passed to her, and it slips from her grasp. 'Whoops!' Bo says, catching it. 'That was nearly a goner!'

Nick raises his glass. 'To old friends!' he says. He looks straight at me while he says it. I don't know why, but I have to look away. I down my glass.

There's a strange pause, now. No one seems to know what to do next. The landscape around is so quiet in the lapse. I feel my stomach do an unpleasant somersault; the ground beneath me seems to shift under my feet. Wow. I'm *definitely* drunk.

'We should kiss,' Samira says. 'Where's the kissing?' She reaches up and smacks a kiss on Julien's cheek. 'Happy New Year!'

Mark turns to me. I don't want him to kiss me. When he leans in, I duck so that his lips barely graze my ear. I catch the flash of annoyance, even anger, in his expression. I think of his eyes last night, the menace of his tone.

I turn to Julien. His face is completely in shadow from this angle. I cannot make out his features, or his expression: just the dark gleam of his eyes. When I lean in to kiss him – on the mouth, of course – I have this . . . feeling that he, too, is a stranger. This man with whom I have spent so much of my life, with whom I have shared a house and a bed, beside whom I have slept most nights. How little it takes, I think, just some shadows, really, to make ourselves unknown to each other. Wow. Alcohol always makes me think deep thoughts.

'Happy New Year,' I say.

'Happy New Year,' he says. And I'm not sure, but I think he turns slightly as I reach up to him, so that my lips land on the very corner of his mouth. Just like I did, with Mark.

Nick is on my other side. 'Nick!' I say, with forced jollity. 'Happy New Year again! Come here.' I put out my arms; he lets me hug him. He smells amazing, like the Byredo counter at Liberty. 'Why have we never been better friends, Nick?' I ask. It comes out sounding pretty fucking needy. I didn't quite mean to say it out loud.

He steps back, his hands on either side of my shoulders: to everyone else he might be holding me in an affectionate embrace. He looks straight into my eyes as he says, 'Oh, Miranda, I think you know the answer to that.'

It's the way he says it: so quiet, under his breath, so that no one else can hear. I suddenly feel cold in a way that I don't think has anything to do with the freezing air. I take a step back.

I drink a bit more. Then *much* more, as the others go on partying around me. I want to get back into the swing of things. I want to get rid of this feeling. A kind of fear, deep in my belly, deeper, somehow, than anything I felt last night, in the bathroom. I feel I am clinging to a cliff edge and slowly, slowly, my fingers are loosening their grip. That beneath me is . . . nothing, the loss of everything . . . everything important.

Bo slides up to me. 'You all right?' He's always been the one to notice when someone isn't OK. It's because he's quiet – he observes, while the rest of us are busy making lots of noise. And he's kind. He's so unlike Nick, with all his sharpness.

'Yes,' I say.

'Want to go have a drink of water?'

I know he's saying I need it because I'm drunk, but, actually, I *do* feel a bit weird. 'All right.' I follow him into the kitchen and watch dumbly while he runs me a glass from the tap. When he hands it to me I say, 'Thanks. I might just sit by myself for a bit, if that's OK.'

'OK . . .' he says, hovering.

'Go!' I shoo him away.

'All right,' he says, and then, with a teacher-like waggle of his finger. 'But I'm coming back in a little while if you haven't reappeared.'

'Fine.' And then I remember to say, 'Thank you, Bo.'

'Forget it, darling. The number of times someone helped me out like this – I owe the universe a great deal.'

'But Bo,' I say, before I can stop myself, 'I'm not a junkie. I've just had a bit too much champagne.' Oops. I didn't quite mean to say that.

Something in his face changes, his eyes going all narrow. I've never seen Bo look like this before. I've always thought there must be someone else in there: someone darker. And from what Katie told me once, someone capable of some fairly out-there behaviour. It's like he's been wearing this . . . mask, and I've just seen behind it. I suddenly feel a bit more sober.

'I'm sorry, Bo,' I say. 'I didn't mean it – I don't know what's wrong with me. I've had too much to drink. Please . . .' I reach out a hand to him.

'It's OK,' he says, his tone light. But he doesn't take my outstretched hand.

I wait until he's gone, and then I click off the light and let my legs collapse under me like a folding chair, so I'm sitting on the floor. I'll just rest here a bit, until I sober up . . . What the fuck is wrong with me? How could I have said that to *Bo* of all people, when he was trying to help me?

Katie once told me I was 'careless'. 'You say things off the cuff,' she said, 'without thinking. The only problem is people who don't know you might think you mean them.'

She knows me so well. But I'm not sure even she knows how I hate myself, later on, after making one of these so-called careless remarks. The way, at Oxford, I'd lie in my bed the morning after a night out and think, think, think about how I'd behaved: everything I'd said and done.

'Everyone falls in love with you,' Samira told me, once. 'They can't bloody help it.'

But, I have often wondered, do they actually like me?

I'll just let my eyes close here, just for a little bit . . .

I'm woken by the sound of a voice: low, urgent.

'Miranda?' It's a man's voice, little more than a hoarse whisper, as though he doesn't want to be heard. Who is it? 'Julien?' I squint through the gloom. I'm confused by the dark. In the distance I can hear the rumble of voices . . . the others, I realise. My head's swimming.

He steps forward, and finally, I see who it is. I've never seen him like this. There's a strange, almost threatening, expression on his face.

DOUG

He's sitting in the one armchair in his cottage. Every so often he reaches over and pours a little more from the bottle of single malt. His aim is to get so drunk that he simply passes out, or anaesthetises himself, but his mind is still obstinately clear.

New Year's Eve. Another year clicking over. They say that time is the greatest healer, but it hasn't done much good in his own experience. Events from six months ago are a blur – the days run into one another here, with little to differentiate them other than the slowly changing seasons. But that day in his past – three years now – is as clear as if it happened yesterday, an hour ago.

Beyond the window there is an explosion. He feels his whole body go rigid with shock; he almost drops to the floor, his heart feels like it's going to punch its way out through his chest. Then he realises what it is. A firework. He fucking hates fireworks. Still, after all these years, they have this effect on him.

* * *

259

The day your life changes for ever. Does anyone see it coming? He definitely didn't. It had been an uneventful few weeks. Things had settled into a pattern, had started to feel as normal as you can get in a place like Helmand Province. All the men had relaxed, perhaps got a bit sloppy. It's impossible not to, even though you're trained in how to keep yourself alert. But when you have to be more 'on' than the human body is ever meant to be, for four days in a row, it's impossible not to switch off when the threat level lessens.

It was a routine excursion. As usual as a police officer's beat. Just to check that everything was as it should be. The men making a patrol of the street, him up above as cover. Doug was one of two snipers; they had to take turns, shifts, to make sure that they were really focused, and this one was his watch.

The men were just below him, coming around the corner in the armoured trucks, when the spotter shouted out to him. A small child – a little boy – running from the other end of the street. Everything froze, apart from the small running figure. Doug realised the boy looked bulky. He was wearing a jacket several sizes too big for him. And he was running straight towards the men. He was only about five years old. Hardly even a proper little boy yet, hardly older than a toddler. But immediately Doug was thinking: bomb. He knew what he had to do. He took aim through the viewfinder. Tracked the boy. His finger was on the trigger. He was ready. But he wanted to get a better visual. He couldn't see any proper evidence of a device, other than that bulky jacket.

He had perhaps ten seconds. Then nine, then five, then three. The spotter was screaming at him, but it was as if he was underwater: his brain and body seemed to have slowed. He could not shoot.

And then everything exploded. The men. The trucks. Half the street. All in the same second that he finally managed to exert the required pressure on the trigger.

The therapist he saw told him that his reaction had been completely understandable – that the situation had been an impossible one. And yet this didn't help him explain it to himself, or to the families of the dead men who visited him at night. This is why he does not sleep: because as long as he is awake, he does not have to see their faces, and answer to their silent interrogation. Though lately, they have begun arriving even in his waking hours. He sees them approaching in the middle of the landscape. So real that he swears he could reach out and touch them.

This is why he is lucky to have this job. In any other, he might not be able to hide it. Someone would notice that he was acting oddly, and report it, and that would be it. But here there is no one to notice. There's Heather, in the office, but she gives him a wide berth. And perhaps she has some hiding of her own to do. Why else would a young, thirty-something, attractive woman come and live in a place like this on her own? He doesn't ask her her reasons, and she in turn doesn't ask him his. It's an unspoken, mutual agreement.

He was lucky that the boss didn't care about the other thing, even though he had to declare it on his application. 'The boss,' said the suit who interviewed him, 'doesn't mind about all that. He wants you to feel you have a clean slate here.' A clean slate. If only.

He switches on the TV and immediately regrets it. All it shows, of course, are thousands of happy faces: families snug together on the bank of the Thames, eyes lit with red and gold flames as they watch the display. He wonders what Heather is doing, over in her cabin. He has seen her lights on, late at night. He knows she does not sleep well either.

He could go around, with the bottle of whisky, as he has thought of doing on more nights than he would care to admit. He recalls that night, when she opened her door to him – when she had heard the sound. He remembers everything about it, a picture clear in his mind: the flush of her cheeks, her dark hair mussed about her head, the giant pyjamas swamping her. She had invited him in – and then she had blushed, as she realised how it sounded. He had refused, of course. But he has imagined following her in. He has imagined a lot more too, in the lurid, sleepless small hours of the night, when he has glimpsed the light on in her cottage. He has imagined pushing her up against the wall, her wrapping her legs around his waist, how her mouth might taste on his . . . He will not go around there. Not tonight, not any night. Someone like him has a duty to stay away from someone like her. She does not deserve the catastrophe that he represents.

That sort of life is closed to him, now. He leans over, towards the fire. He raises a hand, and, with the dispassionate regard of a scientist, holds it in the flames, so that the skin sears like steak.

NOW
2nd January 2019

HEATHER

Doug stands in the doorway, frowning at me.

'Come in, Doug,' I say. 'Close the door.' He comes to stand in front of the desk, towering over me.

'Doug,' I say. 'I shouldn't have done this. But I have something to confess. I googled your name. I found out about the court case.'

He says nothing. His eyes are on the floor.

'What happened?' *Explain it to me*, I think. *What you did. The violence. Make me understand.* Although I'm not sure that he can. I can't see how there can be any way he could explain it.

He takes a breath, and begins.

He had been in a bar in Glasgow, he says, with friends,

about three months after returning home from his tour. 'Tour of Afghanistan, six months.' He'd had one too many, or rather several too many, but he was feeling loose and relaxed for the first time in as long as he could remember. And then this bloke swaggered over to him. 'Hey,' he said. 'I recognise your face. I know you from somewhere.'

'I doubt it.' He'd barely glanced at the guy.

'No,' the man said, 'I do.' He took out his phone, did something on it. He held the screen up. Facebook, a photograph, it was him. It was in Helmand. 'My best mate, Glen Wilson. I knew it. This is you, isn't it? In the photo with him. I know it's you.'

He could hardly bring himself to look at the photograph. 'Then I'm sure you're right,' he'd said, feeling the beer sour in his stomach, still just trying to brush the guy off. Maybe this would placate him. 'It must be me.'

'So you were there?' The man was standing too close.

'Yes, I was there. I knew Glen. He was a great guy.' He wasn't, actually. Not one of the best – always picking fights – but you didn't speak ill of the dead. And he knew so very many dead.

'You were in his regiment?' The man's face, beer-stale, was squared up to his own. He was speaking too loudly. There was a pugnacious twist to his face, his shoulders set. Doug could sense the interest of those surrounding them quickening in the background, the irresistible lure of confrontation. *Something's going on.*

'Yes,' he said, trying to stay measured, to speak calmly, to counteract the man's tone. The therapist had taught him some breathing exercises – he could try those. 'I was.'

'But I don't understand,' the bloke said, smiling, except it wasn't a smile at all, it was more like a snarl. 'I thought everyone in that regiment was killed. I thought they were all surrounded, and blown up by the Taliban.'

Doug closed his eyes. *It was al-Qaeda, actually.* 'They were. Most of us . . .'

'Then how did you manage to get away, eh, mate? Look at me, I'm talking to you. How are you standing here, alive and well, drinking a fucking beer, *mate*? While my best friend is lying dead in Durka Durkistan? Can you explain that to me?'

He could feel something rising inside him. Something dangerous, rapidly growing outside his control. 'I don't have to explain it to you. Mate.' He tried breathing in through his nose, out through his mouth. It didn't seem to be working.

The man took another step forward. 'I think you do, actually. And we've got all night. I'm not going anywhere until you explain it all to me, piece by fucking piece. Because I loved that guy like a brother. And from where I'm standing, shall I tell you what it looks like?'

'What?' he managed – he was still fighting it, the thing rising in him. 'What does it look like?'

The bloke prodded him, hard, in the centre of his chest. 'It looks like you're a fucking coward.'

That was when the mist had come up over him: the red mist they talk about – though it was more like a flood. If anything, he was most purely himself in that moment – more than he had been in months. More so than he had been since the good days at the beginning of the tour.

He had lunged forward and grabbed the man by the front of his shirt. 'What's your name?'

The man gulped, but didn't speak.

'What's your name, *laddie*? Forgotten how to speak?'

The man had made a kind of garbled noise in his throat, and Doug had realised then he was actually holding his collar too tightly for him to get any words out. He relaxed his grip infinitesimally, and roared in the bloke's face: 'What's your fucking name?'

The man's friends, it seemed, weren't interested in helping him out. 'Some mates you've got, eh?' He looked at them. He felt as though he could take all of them on, if necessary, and he wondered if they knew it, too.

'It's – it's Adrian.'

'Well. Let me tell you, *Adrian*. I don't think you should go meddling in things you don't understand, got it? I don't have to explain myself to anyone – especially not a little dipshit like you. What do you do for a living?'

'I'm – ah – ah – an accountant.'

'Right. An accountant.' He gave the bloke a shake, and he whimpered. He couldn't be bothered, he realised; suddenly he just felt tired, and very sober. The flood was ebbing away. This man wasn't worth his energy. He let him go. 'Do yourself – do everyone – the favour, and stop meddling in things you can't possibly understand. Yeah?'

There was no answer. The man was massaging his throat. But he nodded, twice.

Doug's hand ached. He flexed it. He wasn't proud of what he had done, but at least he had stopped himself. Then he heard, sotto voce, 'Fucking coward.'

That was when he had lost it properly, according to the eyewitnesses, of which there were many: it was a crowded bar, after all. They said they thought he was trying to kill the bloke. The police had to drag him off him. Adrian Campbell. That was his full name. There had been extenuating circumstances, to a degree. Campbell had a history of involving himself in brawls, and generally disrupting the peace. There was the nature of the insult – put in context with his own, previously undiagnosed condition: Post Traumatic Stress Disorder, making him not fully in charge of his own actions.

He knew otherwise. Unsurprisingly, his lawyer advised him not to mention this in court. The sentence was two hundred and fifty hours' community service, and the sessions with the psychiatrist. He thought, when it came to the latter, that he probably would have preferred to stay in prison.

'OK,' I say, when Doug finishes. But it's not really OK. I'm not OK. I don't know what to feel about it. On the one hand there is the fact that, for all its violence, the story has a strange kind of logic to it. He was suffering from PTSD, and he was viciously provoked. From what he says, that man was trying to get a rise out of him, pushing all his buttons. I suppose it at least provides some context for the horror I read on the Internet. But there's a small voice that's also saying: *You are drawn to this man, in spite of yourself – therefore you are trying to excuse the inexcusable.* Because his blunt, even dispassionate, account of the incident has illustrated exactly what he is capable of. Far more graphically, somehow, than any of those lurid column inches could.

What exactly the boss thought he was doing employing me here with a man who had done such a thing as my sole other co-worker, I don't know, but that's another matter. The important question is, does it make him capable of killing that guest? No, of course it doesn't. At least . . . probably not. Hopefully not.

Unless, of course, she provoked him.

One day earlier
New Year's Day 2019

EMMA

The party by the loch has suddenly diminished. Giles told us he was going to check on Priya, Katie has gone to get another jumper. It's too cold to sit out here much longer.

'Crap,' Bo says, 'Miranda still hasn't come back. I bet she's passed out. She told me to leave her . . . and to be honest she isn't her best self right now.'

'Leave her,' says Nick. 'She could do with sleeping a bit of it off.'

'I don't know,' Bo says, 'she was in a pretty bad way—'

'I'll go,' I say.

It's dark and very quiet when I step into the Lodge, so much so that I assume Miranda can't be here at first. Then I hear the voices. Something makes me stop; there's an intimacy to the darkened room that makes me feel I shouldn't disturb them. One voice is low, hoarse, almost a whisper. The other drunken, belligerent. 'I had to tell the truth. Duh. It was Truth or Dare.'

'No you didn't. You know you didn't. You were doing it to wind me up.'

A laugh, sharp and mean. 'Believe it or not, Giles, I didn't think of you *once*.'

'Fine – exactly. You didn't think. You don't. And what about Julien?'

'Oh . . . he won't think anything of it. I told him I slept with Katie once, to turn him on. He has this whole little fantasy about us – slutty schoolgirls. Chill out. She's *never* going to guess it was you, Giles.'

'If you hadn't noticed, there aren't that many candidates here. It wouldn't take a genius. Samira knows we were in the same tutor group together.'

'Oh for fuck's sake. I don't know why you're getting your knickers in such a twist. It happened a million fucking years ago.'

'Except not so much so that you could helpfully forget about it for one stupid bloody game. If Samira found out about us – even though it happened a long time ago – it would be really, really bad. She had a lot of trouble, after Priya was born, more than you know. And she's always had this suspicion, this idea that something might have happened. That I have a thing about you. Which is completely ridiculous, of course.'

'Is it?' Miranda says now. 'Is it Giles? What about that party—'

'For God's sake, yes. What are you trying to say? Don't look at me like that. Look . . . we've all had a lot to drink.

I think it's probably time we all went to bed. I *know* you're not going to say anything to her. I just got worried, for a second . . . when we were playing that stupid game.'

'No. I don't think so. Can't promise anything, though. Might be good for your marriage – a little test. Might be refreshing for us all. Show you aren't quite as bloody perfect as you think you are.'

'For God's sake Miranda.' He's practically hissing now. 'You know what? One of these days you're going to go too far.'

Then, suddenly, there's a groan: a deep, animal sound.

'Oh for God's sake,' Giles says again.

Miranda is hunkered over in her gold dress, on her hands and knees, vomiting onto the ground.

Giles watches her, impassive. He doesn't seem at all like the man I have come to know, the caring husband and father – the man who saves people's lives on a ward. I would have expected that man to kneel down, to hold back her hair. I've seen another side of him, this evening.

Then he turns, suddenly, before I have time to hide myself. His eyes meet mine.

MIRANDA

When I wake it's very dark, and quiet. For a moment I have absolutely no idea where I am. I grope about with one hand to get my bearings. My first impression is of feeling absolutely disgusting, like my insides and my throat have been scoured with wire wool. The taste in my mouth is sour, acrid. What's wrong with me? Am I ill? I grope for a switch, blink it on.

Oh. The light returns me to my surroundings. With a horrible inevitability the events of the evening come back to me. Drinking far too much. Having to prove myself as The Life and Soul of the Party. Giles accosting me with his paranoia. Well, maybe he's not *totally* paranoid. I know Samira's always had her suspicions. And I didn't feel good about it at the time . . . it was after a boozy night in the pub for our tutor group, and I already knew she liked him. But for God's sake – it was before they even started going out. If you let something like *that* upset you, you're frankly too bloody thin-skinned. If anyone needs to be worried, it's me. I *was* with Julien at the time, after all.

Oh God, and now I remember vomiting while Giles looked on, eyes on me the whole time, like he half wanted me to choke on it. When Julien appeared he just looked tired, vaguely disgusted. No: I wasn't so drunk that I don't remember that.

I glance in the mirror hanging above the dressing table. I thought I looked amazing in the gold dress. No, I *knew* I looked amazing. But it's like I've woken up in a parallel universe. Now the fabric is rumpled and stained, and my make-up (I was wearing quite a lot of it – I need to wear more of it these days) has sunk into the creases of skin about my eyes and mouth that I could swear weren't as deep yesterday. I move away from the light, thinking of Blanche DuBois, cringing away from lamps. Is that what I'm going to become? Is there anything sadder than a once-beautiful woman who has lost her looks?

For some reason there's a song going around and around in my head. Candi Staton's 'You've Got the Love'. And there's something about it that niggles at me, though I can't put my finger on it. It's like last night, when someone said that disconcerting thing. Who was it? And what did they say?

At least I'm feeling a bit less drunk now. I must have got rid of most of the booze from my system. I have no idea what time it is. But Julien isn't back yet – so the party must be continuing. I feel a sudden sense of FOMO, at the idea of them carrying on without me. I can't believe I managed to pass out. I've got to rally myself, get back out there. This is what is expected of me, after all. I stagger into the bathroom, drag a comb through my hair, splash some water on my face, and attempt to tidy the make-up smeared around my eyes, with little effect. I brush my teeth: that's something, at least. What time is it? I check the clock. Four in the morning. Wow, the others have really made a night of it, then. I feel that sting again, at the knowledge of the fun I must've missed. I have always been – prided myself on being – the life and soul of the party. That was what Julien said at our wedding: 'I love you', looking at me, looking into my eyes, 'because you are the life and soul of the party.' 'And a few other reasons, I hope,' I had laughed. He had grinned. 'Of course.' But it has stuck with me, that phrase. I remember the way he looked at me as he said it, and I can never let it go, that aspect of myself. Well, I'm going to show him now.

I open the door of the cabin. The cold hits me like a slap. I steel myself against it. There are lights on, coming not from the Lodge building, as I had first thought, but from the sauna. I feel a little sting of resentment – they could have come and got me, asked if I wanted to join them. I've been wanting to try out the sauna.

I slip and slide my way there along the frozen path, past the Lodge. All the lights in there are off bar a single lamp in the living room. I can just make out Mark, sleeping on one of the sofas. Another casualty of this evening, then. I feel a little better for knowing that I'm not the only one.

There is a smell in the air that I recognise from skiing trips: a freshness, almost metallic. I remember Doug's warning. Wouldn't it be wonderful if we were all sitting in the sauna, looking out towards the loch, and it started to snow? So picturesque. Give us a good memory of tonight, one that would erase my messiness.

As I get nearer, I hear a strange sound that literally stops me in my tracks. Something animal. Somewhere between a cry and a groan. It sounded as though it came from the direction of the sauna, the woods behind. I feel my skin wash with goosebumps as I hurry towards the sauna: it represents a haven now from the great, wild outdoors.

Only a couple of feet from the door I hear the sound again, and this time I hesitate. Because now I'm almost certain it came not from the trees behind the sauna, but from inside the sauna itself.

NOW

2nd January 2019

HEATHER

I go to the little toilet next to my office to splash some cold water on my face, in an attempt to try to clear my mind after everything I've just discovered about Doug.

I'm just drying my face when I hear something, a murmuring of voices. A man and a woman. It's two of the guests, I'm certain, but I can't work out which ones. Part of the problem is that they all have the same voices to my ear: Southern, middle-class, entitled.

The man, first: 'If they find out – I'm screwed.'

'Why would they find out?' The woman, answering.

'There's a note.'

I freeze, and move closer to the wall, as quietly as I can. Of course – the corridor to the back door wraps around beside my office. Someone could go there wanting to have a private conversation and never know that there's a room here, because the loo is only accessible through the office.

'The note?' the woman says, with a tremor of incredulity, 'You didn't destroy it?'

'No – I didn't think. I was too panicked, with everything else. I don't even know where it is now . . .'

There is a long silence, during which I am fairly sure the woman is trying to think of ways not to berate him. What sort of note? I wonder. A suicide note? That seems unlikely, the last time I checked it was pretty difficult to strangle yourself.

'The important thing,' the woman says, calmly, at last, 'is that you didn't have anything to do with her death. That's what counts. They'll be able to see that.'

'But will they, though?' he says. His voice rises to a shrill, panicked pitch. Then it sinks to a murmur again, quieter than before: I think she's shushed him. I press my head closer to the wall.

'When the other stuff comes out about me – when they decide what sort of person they think I am . . .'

There's a sudden crash. I jump back, confused, and realise that in my eagerness to hear I've managed to dislodge the little hunting scene on the wall next to me. It has fallen to the ground with an impressive explosion of broken glass.

The voices, of course, have gone quiet. I can almost feel them, standing there rigid with shock, on the other side of the wall – hardly breathing. As quietly as I can, I creep my way back into the office.

One day earlier

New Year's Day 2019

MIRANDA

The sight confronting me inside the sauna is absurd. I am so stunned that I feel a strange urge to laugh. I remember when our cat got run over when we were children, how when my mum told us, my brother's first reaction was, 'Ha!' I was so shocked I slapped him. But my mum explained that it was a simple reaction to the trauma. The brain short-circuiting, unable to make sense of something.

This is what I see: my husband, crouched on the floor of the sauna. Above him I see Katie. My best friend, my oldest friend. Completely nude. Her legs open, his head buried between them. My plain, flat-chested, thick-thighed friend. Her head thrown back in ecstasy. He grips her calves. She has her feet locked around his back. And as I watch, he reaches up and takes the nipple of one of her fried egg breasts in one hand. This, finally, is too much. It's torn out of me. 'Ugh.'

They freeze. Then both, slowly, turn to look at me. Julien – oh *Christ* – wipes his mouth with the back of his hand. Their expressions are blank at first, as they make sense of what they are seeing. I feel a tide of horror flooding through me, like a poison entering the bloodstream. I glance over at the scuttle of hot coals, and for a second I am tempted – really tempted – to pick up the shovel and chuck a load of the burning rocks at them.

It is all completely absurd. My husband and my best friend. It can't be possible. I almost expect them to both suddenly crack grins and congratulate themselves on pranking me, as they did at the surprise party for my thirtieth birthday. This would be rather difficult to explain away as a prank, though.

'Oh,' Katie says. 'Oh, God.'

'I thought you were asleep,' Julien says. 'I left you at the cabin. You were passed out . . .' And then, apparently, realising the ridiculousness of accusing his wife of not being where he thought she was while he cheated on her, he says, 'Oh God, Miranda. Oh fuck. I'm so sorry. It's not – it's not what it seems.'

And now I do laugh, a mad-witch cackle that only makes them look more afraid. Good. I want them to be afraid.

'Don't you dare come back to the cabin,' I say to Julien. 'I don't care where you stay, frankly. You can be with her, for all it matters to me now. But I don't want to see your face. So don't come anywhere near me.' I'm rather amazed by how calm I sound: at the contrast between my internal and external selves.

'We need to talk—'

'No, we don't. I don't want to speak or look at you for a long time. Perhaps never again.' As I say it, I realise I mean it. I was furious at him for the insider trading – at first I thought, briefly, about walking away. But I never *truly* considered it. Now this, this is different.

He nods, mutely. I can't bring myself to look at Katie. 'I can't believe I wasted so much time on you. Either of you.'

And then something occurs to me, something almost too horrible to vocalise. But I have to say it, have to know. I turn to Katie, still not looking at her, but in her vague direction. 'You didn't drink anything,' I say. 'On the train. I saw. You had a glass of wine, but you didn't drink it. You haven't been drinking at all, actually.'

Silence. She's going to make me say it out loud. I can see even now how she crouches over in her nakedness. Trying to hide it from me: what I saw earlier when she was in her underwear, but couldn't understand at the time, because I was too drunk, because it made no sense. It's no Christmas paunch. Katie isn't the sort of person to get a Christmas paunch.

'You're pregnant.' When she doesn't respond, I say it again, louder. 'You're pregnant. Say it, for fuck's sake. You're pregnant; it's his. Oh my God.'

I see Julien's mouth fall open. So he doesn't know yet. It's a small victory, at least, to see how appalled he looks.

'Manda,' Katie says, 'It was an accident . . . I'm s—'

I put up a hand to stop her. I will not cry in front of them. That's all I can think. Miranda Adams never cries.

'You're welcome to each other,' I say, while the grief and rage courses through me like acid. The pregnancy is so much worse than the affair, somehow. The sense of the theft is so much greater. It's like Katie has stolen it directly from me. That thing inside her should be *my* baby.

'I'm getting the early morning train back to London,' I say, and I'm proud that there's only the hint of a catch in my voice. 'There are some things I need to do. Something I need to set right – a secret I've kept for far too long. Julien, I think you know what I'm talking about?'

His eyes widen. 'You wouldn't, Miranda. You wouldn't do that.'

But I would. 'Oh wouldn't I?' I smile – I know it will unnerve him even more. 'You think you know me so well? Well, until just a few minutes ago I thought I knew you. But it would appear that I was wrong. What's to say you know me so well, in return? Want to find out how little you understand me?'

'It would destroy you, too.'

I put a hand to my lips, a pantomime of deliberation. I am almost enjoying this, making him squirm. It is a very tiny compensation. 'I don't think it will, actually. I'll explain it all to them, how you even tried to trick me, at first. It will be a bit embarrassing, yes, and I suppose there might be some small penalty for not doing it sooner. But I won't be the one losing my job. I won't be the one going to prison. That will be you, just in case you're unclear. You will be the one going to prison.'

His mouth is set, grim.

'It's a pretty big offence, isn't it? Especially in this post credit-crunch world. You think any jury would hesitate to convict you? You're a Fat Cat Wanker Banker. They'd take one glance at your smug face and tell the judge to throw away the key.'

I'm not even sure insider trading cases have a jury, but it is enough to see the look on Julien's face: the fear. Katie looks completely baffled. So this is one intimacy he has not shared with her. Lucky girl.

He comes towards me again, and this time I put my hands up, to stop his words landing on me, affecting me. To show him that I will not be swayed.

'It would ruin both of us, Manda.'

The short, affectionate version of my name – as though he thinks it might soften me.

'Don't you ever call me that again,' I say. 'And yes, when I divorce you, I suppose there will be less coming my way, once they finish with you. If that's what you're referring to. But at least I'll have a clear conscience.'

And I'll have got my revenge.

KATIE

So this is The Truth. The one I could never have told in that game.

It had been a really long week. I'd had two nights of sleeping in the office. They actually have these little rooms called 'sleeping pods' where you can grab a couple of hours' rest. No – in case you're wondering – that's not the company looking after its employees, it's simply in order to keep them close, to wring as much work out of them as possible. My mind felt numb. The case was over, I was going home – except that nothing was waiting for me there beyond a fridge with some curdled milk in it, if I was lucky, and a prime but utterly uninspiring view of the very square mile I slaved away in daily. And silence. The silence of a single woman with nothing for company but a bottle, or two, of wine.

It was ten o'clock. Too late to call anyone, scare up some plans. In my early twenties there would have been more of a chance of that. People might have been busy,

285

but invariably it would have been something I could join at late notice. A house party – Samira was always throwing them – or a night out clubbing with Miranda, a big dinner with the gang. Now everyone had plans that took place in smaller numbers, usually twos or fours, and were arranged in advance, didn't welcome a last-minute interloper. Maybe I could have called Miranda, but I wasn't sure I had the energy for her. For all that perfection. For her to make me her project, as she always did – has always done – and tell me what was wrong with my life.

So I could go home and sit with my bottle of wine in my empty flat, or I could do it in a bar, and perhaps pick someone up to bring home. This was my replacement strategy, you see, for the nights out and house parties and dinners of our twenties. I suppose in a way it was more efficient: at least you didn't have to make conversation.

Of the two options open to me, the second was infinitely more appealing. I could take someone home, and for a couple of hours the flat would have life and noise in it. So I walked into one of my regular spots in the shadow of St Paul's. The barman knows me so well that he started pouring me a large glass of Pouilly-Fumé before I'd even sat down – which is either thoughtful or depressing, depending on which way you look at it.

I sat down on the stool and waited for someone to approach me. It usually didn't take too long. I'll never be Miranda-beautiful, of course. This used to depress me. It's not easy growing up in the shadow of a friend like her. But of late, perhaps only really since I turned thirty, I have learned that I have something that seems to intrigue men – my own particular attraction for them.

There were a few people around the bar: groups of co-workers, probably, and a scattering of Tinder dates – but it wasn't packed. Only Tuesday evening, so not a proper night out. Perhaps I had been overly confident about my chances. There was only one man sitting along the other bar, perpendicular to me. I'd vaguely noticed him as I sat down, though he hadn't glanced up, and I hadn't actually looked properly at him. I could tell even from the hazy outline in my peripheral vision that he was 'youngish' in the way that I am 'youngish', and attractive. I don't know how I knew this without properly looking, it must have been some animal sense. And that same sense told me that there was something despondent about him, hunched-over.

And then both of us looked up at the same time, to get the barman's attention. I saw, with a shock, who it was.

'Julien?'

He looked surprised to see me, too. I suppose perhaps it shouldn't have been all that shocking, considering we both work in the City. But there are still thousands of bars and thousands of people, and I would have assumed Julien was at home with Miranda, anyway. This was one of the first things I mouthed to him. 'Where's Miranda?'

We had never had that much to do with each other, that was the thing, unless it was through Miranda.

'She's at home,' he mouthed back to me. And then he mimed: he was coming to sit next to me. I was half pleased, half put out. Now I definitely wouldn't be going home with anyone; by the time Julien and I had had our conversation and he'd headed off to Miranda I'd be too tired to start up anything with someone new.

He came to sit next to me. As he leaned down to pull

the stool towards him I caught the scent of his aftershave, a gin-and-tonic freshness, and I remembered how twenty minutes ago, when I thought him a stranger, I'd had the sense that he was probably good-looking. And he *was* good-looking. I had known this – I'd realised it when he and Miranda first started dating, of course – but at some point I had stopped noticing. Now it was as if I was seeing him clearly again. It was an odd feeling.

'What are you doing here?' I asked.

'I might ask the same of you,' he said. Which, of course, was not an answer.

I told him about finishing the case. 'So I suppose you could say I'm celebrating.'

'Where are the others? Your colleagues? Are they here?'

I couldn't exactly say, *They've gone to another bar, I never socialise with them if I can help it*. So I said, 'Home – all too knackered to think about going out.'

'So you decided to celebrate all on your own?'

'Something like that.'

'Isn't that a bit lonely?'

There was a strange tension between us. I think it was the knowledge of having known each other for ten years and yet suddenly being aware that we did not know each other at all. We were really little more than friendly strangers. We needed Miranda there to make sense of the connection between us. Both of us were drinking quite fast, in an attempt to dissipate this awkwardness. I hadn't even realised that I had finished my drink before he asked, 'Have another?'

'Oh, all right then.' I was rather flattered. He was enjoying my company.

'Where's Miranda?' I asked again.

'You've already asked me that.' The way he said it was a little teasing.

'Yes, but then why are you here all on your lonesome?' My reply was equally teasing. Oh my God, was I flirting with my best friend's husband?

'Just thought I'd have a quick one.'

The alcohol dared me to say it: 'So we're here, drinking – her best friend and her husband? We're like kids playing truant or something.' It was meant to be silly, off-the-cuff, but it had the inevitable effect of making what we were doing into a conspiracy from which Miranda was excluded. I drank a big slug of my wine.

'If she knew, she'd definitely be jealous,' he said. And then quickly, 'I know that she misses you.' He smiled, but there was something sad and tired about his eyes; they didn't participate in the smile. 'Look,' he said, more seriously, 'if I'm honest, I needed a bit of time to myself.'

'What's up?' I asked. I was worried – but with the very tiniest tinge of amusement that we sometimes get, hearing of our friends' problems. Everything about Miranda and Julien's life seemed flawless, golden.

I said as much to him. 'What could possibly be the problem? You guys are perfect.'

'Oh yes,' he said, with a smile that somehow went down at the corners rather than up. 'Perfect. That's exactly what we are. So bloody perfect.'

There was an awkward pause. I couldn't think what to say. 'You mean . . .' I looked for a way to put it. 'You mean – things aren't great between you guys? Miranda hasn't said anything.'

That was true enough. She hadn't said anything to me. But then we hadn't seen each other for quite a while. We'd chatted briefly a couple of times, but I am hopeless on the phone: something that always made my teenage years rather difficult. Besides, I hardly had any free time with work – and even if I did it was late at night, or early morning, times when I doubt Miranda would have relished a phone call. I felt a twist of guilt. She had asked me several times in the last month if I was free, and we had made a date, but I had to blow her off at the last minute because of a sudden crisis with the case.

'It isn't problems with us exactly,' he said. 'It's a bit more complicated. I suppose it would be more accurate to say it's a problem with me. Something like that. I have done something bad.' He saw my raised eyebrows. 'No . . . Not like that. I haven't cheated. I got myself involved in something bad. And now I can't get out of it.'

'And Miranda doesn't know?'

'No . . . She does know. I had to tell her, because it involved both of us. She's been' – he frowned – 'I suppose she's been quite good about it. Understanding. All things considered. Except sometimes I catch her looking at me, and she seems so disappointed. Like this isn't what she signed up for. It's just a bit of a mess.'

He pronounced mess as 'mesh', and I wondered quite how much he had been drinking before we started chatting.

'Do you want to talk about it?'

He shook his head. 'No. I mean – I'd like to, actually, but I can't.'

'Why not?' I caught myself. 'Sorry – I've had too much to drink. That was rude of me. Just tell me to shut up.'

'Please don't.' He gave me that funny downward smile again, so different from the expansive, charming gleam of his usual expression. I preferred this one; it was more real. 'I like talking to you,' he said. 'Isn't it funny – we've known each other all these years. What is it, ten?'

'Eleven,' I said. June 2007. That was when I had run into him coming out of our bathroom.

'And yet you and I have never really talked properly, have we?'

'I suppose not.'

'Well, have another drink, and let's talk. Properly.'

'Well – I . . .'

'Come on. Please. Otherwise I'm going to be here drinking on my own, and that's perhaps the saddest thing ever.' He caught himself, evidently remembering that was exactly what I had been doing. 'Sorry, I didn't mean—'

'It's OK,' I said. He was right. But drinking at home was worse. My empty flat, with the empty fridge, and the empty view: the sea of office blocks, the City – the place that ate all of my time, and meant that my life was empty, too.

The thought of going back there suddenly made my skin crawl. I'd prefer to have another drink with him, I thought. But there was something strange about it, being here in a bar with Miranda's husband, when she didn't know. And . . . strangely enjoyable, too, which was perhaps the worst thing about it.

'All right,' I said. *What the hell.*

'Good.' He grinned at me, and I felt something inside me somersault. 'What will you have?' And then, before I could answer: 'I know – let's have whisky. Do you like whisky?' Without waiting for my answer, he turned to the barman. 'We'll get the Hibiki.' He smiled. 'You'll like it. It's Japanese – twenty-one years old.'

I never drink whisky. I hardly ever drink spirits, to be

honest – I can sink a bottle of wine and hardly feel it, but spirits are another matter entirely.

The whisky went straight to my head. That is no excuse for what happened next.

Miranda was obviously a sore subject. So we ended up talking about everything else. I realised that Julien was a much better conversationalist than I had ever appreciated before. I had always thought of him as all charm, all surface, concealing some inner lack. We reminisced about Oxford, how easy life had been then, even though, back then, we thought we were working the hardest we would ever work in our lives.

We talked about my work – he'd read a little about the case I had been working on. For once, I didn't find myself second-guessing, assuming he was asking out of politeness, while he waited for Miranda to rescue him, or for someone more stimulating to come along. He was turned towards me on his stool, his knees pointing towards mine. A body language expert would have said that all the signs were very good. Or very bad, depending upon which way you looked at it. But I didn't think anything of it, still. Or, if I did, I pushed those thoughts away. They were ridiculous, weren't they?

We talked about the first time we'd met (he didn't remember the previous occasion, at the Summer Ball, and I was too proud to correct him), when he had come out of the bathroom clutching his towel.

'There I was,' he said, 'half naked, and there you were, looking so elegant.'

I was surprised by this; I had always just assumed he thought I was Miranda's uglier, more boring friend. Elegant. I realised that I would be turning that word over in my mind for a while.

'This is so nice,' he said to me at one point. 'Isn't it nice? Just chatting, like this? How have we never done this before?' His breath was laced with whisky, true, but I still felt his words warm me. And I realised he wasn't quite as arrogant as I had always thought – and also, clearly, not so perfect. Perhaps the years had rubbed some of the shine off him, and I hadn't stopped to notice. Or perhaps he had always been like this. Either way, he seemed much nicer, more humble, than I had ever appreciated. The sober me might have been able to point out that this was probably just Julien's famous charisma at work. But the drunk me liked it very much.

Because at some point I realised that we were both very drunk. 'I should go home,' I said. Though I realised that I didn't want to, and not just because of the depressing thought of the sterile single-person flat that awaited me. It was because I was actually having fun. I was enjoying his company. But I made a big show of finishing my glass, and getting down from my seat. As I slid from my seat and wobbled on my heels, I discovered that I was even drunker than I had thought. He got down from his stool, and I saw him sway on his feet, too.

'You can't go home on your own,' he said. 'I'll walk you back. It's not safe.'

For some reason I didn't bother to tell him that I walked home alone every night and that I'd been more drunk than this before when I did, sometimes with a complete stranger in tow. I think we both knew, even then, that it was mainly an excuse to keep the conversation going, to stay in one another's company.

I don't remember which of us made the first move. I just recall that suddenly we were standing in an empty alleyway, and all I could hear was the sound of our breathing. Just beyond that alleyway was the thoroughfare of Cheapside and cars and people, and beyond that the whole city, lit up, chaotic, with all its millions of inhabitants. But in that dark passage it was just the two of us, and we were both breathing very loudly. And neither of us was suddenly quite so drunk. That flash of desire had sobered us. And then there was the light pressure of his thumbs on my hipbones, and I could feel the greater pressure of him between my legs, how hard he was. And I took his hand and guided it up, beneath my skirt, and he groaned against my neck.

The sex was quick: it had to be, in that public place. Anyone could have come across us, at any moment. It was also very good. I came embarrassingly quickly. But he, despite the alcohol and the awkwardness of our position (he had to hold me up against the wall), followed soon after. It was the strangeness of it, I think, the illicitness of it, that made it incredibly exciting. Afterwards, we stayed glued together for several seconds, his face in my neck. I couldn't believe what we had done.

He said it out loud. 'I can't believe that just happened.'

'I know,' I said. 'Let's . . . Let's just pretend it didn't.' A small secret part of me was thinking: *Would anyone have done?* Was I just some girl in a bar, the right place, the right time. Or was it me?

These things should not have mattered, I knew. And yet they did. Because for so long I had assumed he saw me as the colourless, uninteresting counterpart, and that was why he had hardly bothered to speak to me. Now, here, was a new, thrilling possibility. That in fact he had desired me.

MIRANDA

I turn at the sound of footsteps behind me on the path. It's Julien, clutching a towel about his waist, his feet skidding on the mud.

'I've made a big mistake,' he says in a let's-all-be-adults tone. 'I know I've made a big mistake. But I've been under a lot of stress.'

'Sorry,' I say, 'you've been under a lot of stress?'

'Yes,' he says. 'It's – a deal went bad. And I'd cut Mark in on it. He wasn't happy.'

I think back to what Mark said on the first night, when he grabbed me. The reference to Julien's 'dirty little secret'. The choice of words had struck me as odd at the time. I'd thought he was talking about the insider trading, but now I understand. 'He knew,' I say, 'didn't he? About you and—' I can't bring myself to say her name, '—her.'

'I let something slip, when I was very drunk. I felt so guilty . . . I wanted his advice. He is – was – my best mate. And now he's threatening me, Manda.'

He looks ridiculously sorry for himself. I really, truly detest him, in this moment. Not just for what he has done, but for his cowardice, his pathetic self-pity. 'All of this,' I say, 'has been brought on by you, you fucking idiot. All of it because you always want a little bit more. You always think you're entitled to a bigger share. I should have seen this coming a mile off. Of course you were going to have an affair. Though I would never in a million years have thought of Katie. I thought you might have better taste than that.'

He grimaces then, a little quirk of the mouth, and for a surreal moment I actually think he might be about to defend her to me. Clearly, he thinks better of it. I know him too well; he's more worried about saving his own bacon.

'She seduced me, Manda.'

My skin crawls. 'Don't fucking call me that,' I hiss.

'Sorry. But I want to make that clear. It was all her. I think . . . I think she had a plan, from the moment she saw me sitting there in that bar. I think she knew, looking at me, at the state I was in – that I would have been incapable of resisting. I didn't have a chance. It was like that time in Ibiza.'

'What time in Ibiza?'

'Oh God.' He looks as though he immediately regrets having said anything. He rubs his face with a hand. 'You might as well know. That holiday we all went on. The last night. She came on to me. It was . . . crazy. I was a bit out of it, and I was missing you . . . She was like a woman possessed, Manda – sorry. She was all over me.'

I stare at him, bile rising in my throat. Ibiza. While I was at my grandmother's funeral . . . he was sleeping with my best friend. It wasn't that long after we'd first started going out, well before we were married – all of which makes it worse, means that that disgusting secret has been there between us for all that time. Julien is clearly regretting having revealed any of this to me. He makes a kind of desperate sweeping gesture with his hand, as though trying to brush it from view, and says, 'But . . . what I want to say is, I didn't mean any of it.'

It would almost be amusing, I think. To watch him falter, to continue to dig himself into this particular grave. Amusing if, that is, he weren't my husband, the man to whom I have given over a decade – all my youth – and if I weren't really the butt of this particular joke.

'Anyway,' Julien hurries on – he must see the disgust and utter incredulity on my face – 'when we bumped into each other in that bar . . . I think she saw I was at a low point. You'd been treating me like a second-class citizen. Barely speaking to me. I felt like an utter failure, a disappointment. She made me feel . . . desired, desirable. I tried to call a stop to it. I went around to her apartment the next day, to tell her to call it off. But she wouldn't let me do it. I was so weak, I see that. She was like a drug habit I couldn't shake—'

I hold up a hand. 'What script are you reading from, Julien? Do you have so little respect for me that you think I'm really going to buy any of this pathetic, clichéd crap?'

He makes a pleading, feeble gesture with his hands. 'I just wanted to try to explain.'

'Well. It's not going to do any good. Can't you see that? I'm not buying any more of your utter bullshit.' I think that if I had a weapon now I would kill him. If I knew the combination to that store with the rifles I think there would be very little stopping me from taking one, going back to

297

the sauna, and shooting both of them dead. Do people still get lighter sentences for crimes of passion? Any sentence, right now, seems worthwhile. No one screws Miranda Adams over like this.

I don't have a rifle. But perhaps the weapon I do have is more powerful than any gun.

The insider trading. I've been involved, of course. But I could get a good lawyer. My parents would help me out. And however bad it might be for me, it would be a tiny fraction of the shit that would descend on Julien. In this moment, it seems worth it.

'Actually,' I say, 'I do know what I'm going to do. I'll log on to your precious bloody Wi-Fi and send a sodding email right now. It will take a click of a button. Just one fucking click. I may not have a career, but I have friends, Julien – you know them too. Olivia, you know she's now at *The Times*? Or Henry, my ex from before uni? He's at the *Mail* now – I can just *imagine* the headline they'll dream up for you. And you know what? I reckon I could do pretty well from it myself.'

He takes a step back. His face is in shadow. I can hardly make out his features, let alone his expression. And, not for the first time – but with much better reason now – I think: *I do not know this person at all. I do not know what he is capable of.*

NOW
2nd January 2019

HEATHER

I walk back into the office. Doug's sitting there – and I'm about to tell him what I heard just now in the bathroom, when the phone rings. I pick it up. 'Yes?'

'Hello, Heather, it's DCI Alison Querry here.'

'Have you found a way to get here?' I can feel Doug's eyes on me.

'Well,' Querry says. 'We're still working hard on that, of course. The forecast suggests that the snow should be easing off in the next few hours, then we can make an attempt with a chopper. But there's something else. I just wanted to let you know that unfortunately I'm being called away: DCI John MacBride is going to take my place. He's extremely capable, I need not add. I'll put you on the phone to him now.'

My brain is racing. Alison Querry is the lead on the Highland Ripper investigation. If she's been called away from this one, that means . . .

As DCI John MacBride introduces himself I am hardly listening. I am googling with one hand, *Highland Ripper*, then the NEWS tab. The headlines triumph out at me from the screen: 'Suspect arrested in Glasgow hideaway', 'Raid on Glasgow Lair of the Ripper', 'Ripper Routed?' They've found someone. Glasgow is over two hours' drive from here, more in bad conditions. This can only mean one thing. If they have indeed found the man who killed those other women, he can have had nothing to do with this particular murder. It was someone else. It was someone here.

One day earlier
New Year's Day 2019

KATIE

Julien comes back into the sauna. Dimly, I register how absurd he looks: completely naked, his cock curled up from the cold, his feet covered in mud. And just for a moment, with perhaps the greatest force since we first started seeing each other, I ask myself, *What am I doing?*

Has it all been about Julien? The secret longing I have harboured for him for all these years? Or has it also been about Miranda? I could never have admitted this to myself, not before. But for all the remorse I felt, looking at her standing there, staring in horror, for all the shame . . . was there not something else? The tiniest hint of *Schadenfreude*? About, for once, having one up on her?

I'd like to point out that I originally went to the sauna

just to try and warm up from that horrible icy bath in the loch, not with an assignation in mind. I'd probably been in there for about ten minutes when there was a knock on the door.

I opened it, and saw Julien. He grinned at me, came in, quickly, furtively. Immediately, he began to shrug out of his clothes.

In spite myself I felt a shiver of excitement. Of anticipation.

'It's OK,' he said. 'I've put her to bed – she's completely out of it. And Mark's passed out in the Lodge, and Emma's back at her cabin. It's just us. I was actually on my way to your cabin when I saw the light on here and thought . . . well, what a good idea.'

'What if Miranda wakes up and finds you gone?'

'She's going nowhere. So it'll be like last night. I'll just tell her I've been for a walk.'

Sometimes it has made me uneasy, the speed at which the lies come to him. 'And you think she'd believe you? Julien, it's three in the morning.'

'Yes, I know. But you see . . . she knows I've had a lot on my mind recently.'

'The thing you'd like to share with me but can't possibly tell me about?'

'Yes. That.'

I don't know why it stung, that he had persistently refused to talk about it. 'We seem to have shared quite a bit recently,' I said. 'I suppose I just can't understand why you wouldn't talk about this particular thing.'

'I don't want to burden you with it,' he said. 'There's no need for you to know. Like I've said, if I told you, too, it would make you guilty by association – complicit.'

'But I am guilty,' I said.

'I know,' he said, and reached for me – but not without a backward glance, as though anyone could possibly see anything through the locked shutters. 'So deliciously guilty.'

'Julien,' I said. 'What are you . . . I thought we had agreed—'

He silenced my protest with his mouth. He ran his hands up and down my arms, then down my back, cupping my ass, lifting me up so that I had no choice other than to lock my legs around his back. All my resistance had melted, instantly.

'That was before,' he said. 'We agreed that before.'

'Before what?'

'Before I realised that I'm completely obsessed with you. These last few weeks, not seeing you – Christmas at Miranda's parents . . .'

'I've felt sick with guilt,' I said. 'Physically sick, Julien. I literally was – on the train, I had to go and throw up in the toilet.'

Although, actually, that might have been due to the thing I discovered this morning.

'Poor Katie did.'

'No, don't give me that. We can't go on like this. It isn't fair on Miranda.'

He nodded. 'It isn't fair on Miranda,' he said, 'and that's why I think we should tell her.' I opened my mouth to protest, but he shook his head. 'Hear me out. We were just kids when we got together. She seemed so certain of herself. She was dazzling. I wanted a bit of that. And yes, I fancied the pants off her. But then, over the years . . . all that drive seemed to go. Everything she wanted changed. She didn't want to do or be something amazing. She just wants *things* now, all the time: holidays and clothes and a new car and, well, a baby. But she hates kids. I'm not even sure she doesn't want a baby just because everyone else has one – because it's "Life Goals".

'And with you, Katie-did . . . it's different. It's more complex. It's deeper. It's so much . . . freer.'

I thought of that little plus on the stick. I'd wait, I thought. I'd find the right moment.

'You know who you are. You have a career, a life. You don't need me to validate who you are.'

I felt a strange, unexpected wave of sympathy for Miranda: over ten years, they have been together. In what world could that not be called deep? But beneath the sympathy, despite all the guilt . . . yes, I realised there was some dark, complex pleasure. All those years of playing the wing woman, the second fiddle, the understudy. Now, finally, I had bested her at something.

DOUG

Something has woken him. His body is alert, prickling with awareness – his mind struggling to catch up. He has been wrenched out of his whisky-soaked stupor agitated, his heart going double time. He looks about himself. He is surrounded by broken glass. But now he remembers . . . before he passed out he'd thrown his tumbler at the television, enjoyed the sound of it shattering the screen. Enjoyed how it briefly drowned out the sound of the guests partying over at the Lodge, the music turned up full blast. Making a mockery of his own 'celebrations' – a bottle of single malt and the depressing spectacle of others' happiness on the screen. Then he had drained the last drops straight from the bottle and sunk finally, gratefully, into unconsciousness.

But now something has roused him. A knock on the door. Loud as a rifle shot.

He stills, listening like an animal.

It comes again.

He didn't imagine it. He gropes for his watch. It's four

305

in the morning. Who could need him at four in the morning? Heather, he thinks, incoherently. She might need his help, somehow.

He opens the door, looks out with bleary eyes. It's her, the guest, the beautiful one. Except she looks . . . terrible. Still beautiful, in a long golden gown, but with a wrecked quality to everything: the fabric of her dress ripped, her face stained with make-up. Her lipstick is a long smear across one cheek.

'Hi,' she says, swaying slightly on her feet. 'Sorry, I hope it's not an imposition.' He is drunk, but she is drunker. The realisation sobers him.

She peers beyond him. 'Wow,' she says. 'It's really empty in here. Very . . . minimalist.'

'You can't come in here,' he says. He tries to block her entry with his body; she wriggles past.

'But I brought champagne!' She holds up an open bottle. Dom Pérignon, the really posh stuff. 'You wouldn't let me drink the rest on my own, would you?' As she steps nearer he realises that the now familiar smokiness of her perfume is tainted by something sour and rank.

He feels like an animal, routed out in its cave, its safe and private space. She takes a step forward and takes his head in her hands, and kisses him. Her mouth is a concentration of sourness, but also that perfumed smokiness, which seems to wrap itself around him. And her tongue is deft, and she has fitted her body to his. It has been so long. He feels desire rise up in him – mixing uncomfortably with the anger he still feels at the interruption. She is reaching for his fly, unzipping him, reaching her hand inside. Her fingers are tangling in his hair.

'No,' he says, his mind clearing.

She steps back from him. Her lip curls. 'Pardon?'

'No,' he says again.

'Fuck you! Don't tell me you don't want it. I can *see* that you do.'

'I can . . . make you a cup of tea,' he says, though he has no idea whether he currently has the wherewithal to complete this task.

She laughs, staggers on her glittery heels, and then scowls at him. 'I don't think so,' she says. And then she points at him. 'I know you want it. I've seen how you look at me. At that dinner . . . yesterday, on the shoot. You don't fool me.' She is furious, wrathful, her finger stabbing at his chest. 'But you're too scared. Do you know what you are? You're a *fucking coward*.'

Those words. He feels the rage and grief rising inside him, like that other time. He feels the red flood of his anger come down over everything, and something inside himself loosen, loosen . . . and break.

NOW
2nd January 2019

HEATHER

'That was the police,' I tell Doug. 'They've found the Highland Ripper. Miles away from here, so it doesn't look like he's anything to do with us. It must have been someone here.'

As I say it, I hear the truth of it for the first time. It becomes real. They are here. 'And I just heard something, while I was in the bathroom—' I stop, catching sight of the look on Doug's face.

'Doug?' I stare at him. 'Are you all right?' He's pacing in front of my desk, rubbing his jaw back and forth – so vigorously that the skin beneath his stubble is raw and red, though the rest of his face seems to have drained of all colour. His eyes are black and fathomless. It is as though he is taking all of this unusually personally. He has looked bad since the morning, I realise; I've noticed it, but I haven't really had a chance to properly consider it. It seemed natural, what with him finding the body, and everything.

'Doug?'

He turns towards me, but he hardly seems to have heard the question.

'Doug!' I snap my fingers in front of his face, force him to focus on me. 'What is it? What now?'

He shakes his head, for several seconds. And then he says, in a rush, 'There's something more. I didn't tell you all of it.'

Oh God. I brace myself. 'What is it?'

'That night, close to when you'd first got the job here,' he says, 'when you heard the scream . . . do you remember?'

'Yes,' I say. The sound is still imprinted upon my memory.

'Well, that wasn't a fox.' He grimaces. 'It was a scream. It was me.'

I think of my first impressions on hearing the noise – that it was a sound made by a person in profoundest agony. 'Oh, Doug.'

'I have these – episodes – I suppose, when I can't remember what I have been doing. I find myself in strange places, without knowing how I have got there. That night, for example . . . I wasn't aware of making any noise. I came round, in the trees beside the loch, and I realised it had to be me.'

I don't want to hear any more. But there is more – he keeps going, unstoppable. 'On New Year's Eve . . .' He runs his uninjured hand through his wild hair, in that nervous gesture I have seen him make so many times in the last few hours. 'I'd been drinking a lot . . . I remember that. And . . .' He blows out his cheeks. He doesn't meet my eyes. 'I was angry. So I drank some more. I think I passed out. And then there's a whole period of time that's just . . . a blank.'

A blank.

Finally, he meets my eyes. The expression in his is that of a drowning man.

One day earlier
New Year's Day 2019

KATIE

I've got to go and speak to Miranda. No, this isn't a late crisis of conscience. There's no point in apologising now, it is far too late for that. If I was really sorry, I would have stopped a long time ago. It's only now that I have seen Julien's reaction to all of this – his cowardice in scuttling straight after Miranda, and, I'm sure, pleading with her, then coming back here and pretending he hadn't – that I have properly regretted it for the first time. The scales, as they say, have fallen from my eyes.

But I want a chance to explain. I want her to understand that I didn't plan any of it, that I didn't do it on purpose, to hurt her . . . not consciously, at least. That the affair – because that's what it became – swept me along with it, strong as an undertow. This is not to excuse myself, as I know there is no excuse. Not for doing something this terrible to one of your oldest friends. But it seems important to say these things.

I'm also slightly worried for her. She seemed so wild, so drunk, standing there in her stained and ripped gold dress, like some vengeful fallen Goddess. It's so cold now – I hadn't realised it could get any colder, and she was wearing nothing more than a thin layer of silk, and her feet were practically bare, except for those ridiculous heels. She wouldn't do anything stupid, would she? No. I'm fairly certain that isn't Miranda's way. She would want to harm *us*, not herself.

I suddenly feel exposed out here. The dark surrounds me, fathomless, inscrutable. The only movement I can see is my breath leaving me in little huffs of vapour. It has just occurred to me that Miranda could be out here somewhere with me, watching from some hiding place. I think of that room from earlier, with the rifles. I must keep my wits about me. I wouldn't put that much past her at this point. As a friend she can be bad enough. The thought of having her as an enemy is frankly terrifying.

I knock on the door of her cabin. No answer. I look up at the dark windows, and imagine her looking out, seeing me, smiling to herself.

'Miranda,' I call, 'we need to talk.' The cabin looks back at me blankly, mocking me.

'I need to explain everything to you,' I call. My voice seems to echo in the silence, reverberations coming back at me from far away, from the encircling mountains. 'I'll be waiting, in my cabin, if you want to talk.'

There's no answer. Silence, like a held breath.

* * *

Back in my cabin Julien is sitting wrapped in a towel, huddled on the sofa, sipping neat from a bottle of Scotch. I think it might have been the complimentary one provided by the estate. I hadn't touched it at all, but it is now more than half empty.

'Julien.' I try to prise it out of his grasp. He clings onto it, like a child to a toy. 'Julien, you need to stop. You're going to kill yourself if you drink any more.'

He shakes his head. 'She'll kill me first. She'll take everything I've worked for. She'll destroy me . . . you don't understand.'

He looks completely pathetic, curled in the towel. Suddenly I'm almost repulsed by him. His broad, muscled chest looks ridiculous. Who has a body like that unless they're incredibly vain? Before it had seemed exotic, so different to the men I had been with. And the flattery of him wanting me – that had been perhaps the biggest turn-on of all. Over the last six months I have been able to overlook the little things that rankled with me: his selfishness after we'd had sex, always running to the shower first, or always demanding that we did things his way, or failing to respond to any of my messages for several days and then becoming irate if I left one of his unreplied to for more than an hour. The excitement of it all – the subterfuge, the illicit rendez-vous, and yes, the quality of the sex, had made them palatable.

Was that all it was? I ask myself, now. The real source of the excitement, beyond any chemistry, or physical attraction? The sheer disbelief that he wanted me, and not Miranda? Did I really envy her that much? *Yes*, a little voice says. Maybe I did.

NOW
2nd January 2019

HEATHER

Doug is right. It doesn't look good for him. It seems that he may have been the last person here to see the guest alive. But I now feel oddly invested in his innocence. I just don't think he did it.

It's funny, a couple of days ago I knew so little of him. I wouldn't have known whether I could trust him. Seeing those news results load, the horror of the headlines about him, had briefly seemed as good as a guilty sentence. But for some reason, since the vulnerability and honesty of his confessions about himself, I feel differently. He has bared his innermost, most shameful secrets to me, and yet, somehow, I find I can't judge him too harshly for it.

And then there was that conversation overheard in the

hallway. Two of the guests, at least, may not be as innocent in this as they appear. I only wish I hadn't dislodged that sodding picture, that I had been able to hear more.

I enter the living room, and they all look up.

'Are the police here yet?' the woman called Samira asks, jostling the baby on her lap. Could it have been her in the corridor, the woman's voice? I'm not sure. She was the one who alerted us to the disappearance in the first place. But that doesn't necessarily mean anything.

'No,' I say, 'though they're hoping it may be clearer by this afternoon.'

She nods, sullenly. They are all watching me, I know. I'd give a good deal to have the situation be reversed, so that I could observe them instead, watch them for any betraying anomalies, flickers of guilt. I go to the kettle, on autopilot, to make more tea, and I see we've run out already. At a rough calculation, that's some fifty teabags in a day. There are more in the store. I shrug on my down jacket, my red hat, my hiking boots, and tramp out into the world of white, the snow squeaking with each step.

I unlock the big doors of the barn, unleashing a scent of dust and wood shavings and turpentine. On one side are all of our supplies: bottled water in case of a supply fault (it has happened more than once), sugar and packs of Nespresso pods and loo rolls and crates of beer. Life's little necessities, even in this place.

Out here's also where we have the feed from the CCTV camera on the gate, humming away on an ancient TV screen. There's much better technology out there nowadays – I could get it all streamed to my computer in the office – but the boss is oddly stingy about some things. I glance at the display: the familiar image of the track. There's so much snow that there's barely any definition to the picture – everything it shows is white.

On the other side is all the stalking equipment: the camouflage gear, the walking boots, the binoculars. The neat row of hunting rifles. Doug's military precision.

Except . . .

I blink, look again. Recount.

. . . Except that one of the rifles seems to be missing. One of the brackets is empty. I think there are normally ten. And now there are only nine.

I turn on the radio, still in the pocket of my jacket. My hand hovers over the transmit button – I'm about to call Doug, to ask him if there's any reason for this absence. Has he, say, taken one of the rifles for something? Then I stop and think: *Can I trust him?* Should I really draw his attention to what I've noticed? *Because perhaps he already knows. Perhaps he was the one who took it.*

After all, whoever took the rifle must have had access to the store, which pretty much rules out one of the guests. There are only two other people who know the passcode. And the other left the estate on the afternoon of New Year's Eve to spend it with his family.

I'm trying to decide what to do with this new knowledge. It's not a reassuring thought, precisely, but it occurs to me that I'm not sure Doug would even need to take a rifle from here – I think he has his own. And maybe there have only ever been nine rifles. I rub my eyes, which are sore, gritty with tiredness. I'm so, so tired. Maybe I'm simply conjuring chimeras out of my own mind.

I grab the big box of tea. I won't say anything to Doug, I decide. But I'll keep it in mind, too. Just in case. As I pass the old CCTV monitor I glance at the screen displaying its unchanging snowy scene: the view from the gates. Our recordings might well be the most uneventful in the UK. It might as well be showing me a fixed image, if it weren't for the flakes of snow falling listlessly past the lens, the seconds ticking over in the top-right-hand corner. An identical scene to when I checked it for any sign of the missing guest, seeing nothing more than a time lapse of the snow. I remember fast-forwarding through the frames: nothing, nothing, nothing, dizzy with the sameness of it all. And yet . . . a sudden quickening of my heartbeat, my body seeming to understand something even before my mind does. *Nothing.* But shouldn't there have been . . . something? Shouldn't I have seen, for example, a red truck – Iain's truck – leaving the property on New Year's Eve? He left on New Year's Eve: this is what I've assumed the whole time. This is what I told the police.

But if I didn't see him leave . . .

. . . Then he must be here. Somewhere, on the estate. It's the only explanation.

My radio crackles. It's Doug. 'Where are you?' he asks.

I think of that light I saw on New Year's Eve, travelling up the flank of the Munro, towards the Old Lodge.

I think of the one other viable shelter on the estate, which Doug and I didn't even bother checking because no one goes in there, because it's locked. I suddenly know where I have to go. I think of how emphatically Iain has always told me *never to go near it* because of the danger. I think, too, of how he told me not to let the guests outside at night.

'Heather, are you there?' Doug's voice echoes in the silence of the barn. There is, I think, genuine concern in his voice. 'Are you all right?'

'Yes,' I say. 'I'll – I'll be back in a bit.' I slip the radio back into my pocket.

This is probably a very stupid idea. I know the sensible thing would be staying put, in the warmth and safety of the Lodge. But I'm sick of doing nothing. And I don't mean simply these last few days. Because, really, I've been doing nothing for so long, running away, hiding from everything. Here is a chance to prove something to myself.

I've kitted myself out from the storeroom. Even sturdier hiking boots, a pair of binoculars, a multi-tool. I have my mobile in my pocket, which is only really useful as a torch, unless I can get any signal up on the peak. I didn't bother with the camo gear, of course – it would be almost as visible as anything else against the white of the landscape. Oh, and I sling a rifle over my shoulder. I've only shot once, and I wouldn't say it exactly came easily to me. But it's better than nothing. It will act as a deterrent, if not a weapon.

As I walk, I summarise what I know of Iain. Not much, is the answer. I don't even know his surname. He's mentioned his 'missus' to me a couple of times, but I've never met her. I can't recall, trying to summon a mental image of him, whether he wears a wedding ring – but then I can't even precisely recall the features of his face. On the whole, when he has been here, he has seemed part of the landscape. He has gone about his work without any consultation with me, on – I have always assumed – instructions direct from the boss.

If anything, the snow is thicker still on the flank of the Munro. I slip and fall several times – the gradient is almost too much for my hiking boots, even this low down. This is exactly the sort of behaviour we would counsel the guests against. Do not go out without the proper equipment. At least I've got the radio in my pocket, if necessary.

I take a deep breath. I haven't come up here for a long time.

The ruins, and the standing stable block, look particularly dark against the fresh fallen snow. I hate this place. I can smell the burn on it, and it smells like death. It smells like everything that I have run away from. Well, I'm not running any more.

'Heather? Heather – where are you? It's been almost an hour.' My radio is crackling. It's Doug, of course.

It's the faint note of panic in his voice – something I've never heard, even when he was telling me about his past – that compels me to answer.

'I'm . . . outside.'

'Why? What are you doing?' He sounds angry.

'I just wanted to do a bit more exploring, that's all – I've had an idea about something.'

'For Christ's sake, Heather – are you mad? Tell me exactly where you are. I'm coming to find you.'

'No,' I tell him. 'You have to keep an eye on the guests.'

Before he can reply, I cut him off. I need to concentrate.

The door of the stable block is locked, just as it has always been, the little screen of the passcode panel blinking. It looks so incongruous against the old stone. Iain told me once, right at the beginning, that the building isn't structurally sound. It could fall down at any point. And then we'd end up with a horror of a lawsuit on our hands. 'The big man wants to make sure it's really secure,' he said. 'Don't go anywhere near it. We don't want any guests going in there and killing themselves when the roof falls in on them.'

I have always been very happy to give the place the widest berth possible. I have never come near the Old Lodge unless I can help it. When we were searching for the missing guest, we came up here. I tried the door, felt the unyielding resistance of the lock against my hand, and hurried away again. So now is the first time that it has occurred to me to wonder why I have never been given the passcode. At the time I had simply seen the locked door and assumed that meant that there was no way the guest could be within.

It feels, suddenly, like a secret that has been under my nose the whole time and which I've never stopped to see, so wrapped up have I been in my inner world, the long legacy of my grief. If I hadn't been, would that guest have died? I push the thought away. It is not worth thinking about now.

There is no way I can force the door: it's an ancient, heavy, oak affair, and there's no give against the lock when I push it. And if I shove too hard, I'm worried I really might bring the building down on my head. So I walk around to the back. All the windows are boarded up, impenetrable.

Ah, but now that I'm looking, I can see that one of the boards higher up is a little loose. There's a dark gap showing through a chink between it and the next one. If I stand on one of the rocks below I might just be able to reach it. I clamber onto one of the fallen stones, I take the multi-tool from my pocket, open up the pliers and use them to grip one end of the plank. The stone I'm standing on rocks beneath my weight ominously, and the rifle knocks against me. I take it off my shoulder. I'm sure the safety is on, but

I have a sudden vision of myself slipping and discharging the gun.

I work the pliers back and forth, using all my strength, until I feel the board begin to give. With a *pop!* a nail springs free, and the board swings downwards to expose a gap the length of my arm. After that it's easy to wrench the neighbouring boards away to expose a square foot of space. I peer inside, gripping the ledge of the plank below with my hands, feeling the rock tilt dangerously beneath me. There's a musty smell – and yes, just discernible – the century-old smell of burned things. Can that be possible, or is it just my imagination? I can make out very little – but what I can see is that the space is not empty. There is something in the middle of the room, a pile of something. I climb down and take out my phone, flip it onto the torch function. For a moment I have the strongest impression of being watched. I check in every direction, but see just the undisturbed sugar shell of snow – save the track of my own footprints. It is probably just the silence up here. The Old Lodge does that to you. It has a presence all of its own.

I cast the beam towards the object in the middle of the room. I can see it now, but can't quite work it out. It isn't one object, but a collection: a teetering stack of packages, tightly wrapped with clear film, each individual package roughly the size of a bag of sugar.

Actually, whatever is within, bulging through the clear wrapping, looks a little like sugar: some whitish substance. And then the penny drops. I'm suddenly fairly certain that whatever is inside those packages is something very different from and far more valuable than sugar.

As in a nightmare, I hear the footsteps behind me.

'What are you doing up there?' Almost polite, conversational.

I drop down in shock, my hands catching the rough wood on the way down, splinters tearing into my flesh. My legs hardly support me; they are suddenly weak with fear. I reach for the rifle and hear rather than feel the loud crack of something hitting the back of my skull. My sight is snuffed out like a blown candle.

When I come to it takes several seconds for my vision to clear. When it does, I make out a figure standing over me. At first I don't even recognise him, through the haze of pain in my head, and because of what he's wearing: a huge down jacket, even bigger than mine, that makes him look almost double his normal size. His face is pinched with cold, blue about the lips. He looks like someone who has been sleeping rough. But it is Iain.

'I don't understand,' I say, stupidly. 'I thought you were at home. Where have you—' I stop, because I see that he is carrying a gun. He holds it loosely, at the moment, but he hefts it in his hands. The gesture, I am sure, is to show his ease with it – and how simple it would be to lift it and aim it at me.

'I told you not to come up here,' he says. 'I told you to keep away.'

'Because you said it wasn't safe,' I say.

'Precisely. It isn't safe, as you see.'

'You told me it was because of the building, because it might fall down. Not because—' I don't know how to express it, whether it's safe to do so: *Not because there is something in here you don't want me to see.*

'Yes. You're either less stupid than I had banked on you being – or a lot *more* stupid. I'm trying to work out which. I think it's probably the latter.'

Why – why – did I not just wait for the police, voice my suspicions to them? I *am* stupid. More than that, I didn't even tell Doug where I was going. *Because you knew he would stop you.* I have been a complete idiot. This whole thing, suddenly, looks like a suicide mission. And the thought occurs to me . . . *was* it a suicide mission? I think of the oblivion I have contemplated in the past: the pills, the bridge. I have spent a long time thinking that perhaps dying wouldn't be such a bad thing after all. But now – and perhaps it's just some deep-rooted animal instinct – I suddenly discover I want to live.

'Look,' I say, trying to sound calm, reasonable. 'Let's pretend I didn't see any of this. I'll just go away, and it will be like it never happened.'

He actually laughs. 'No, I don't think we can do that.'

I stare at him. If it weren't so horrifying it might almost be fascinating, the change that has come over this man, who, from what I gleaned, seemed a simple, uncomplicated sort, if a bit taciturn. But then it isn't a change, I realise. This is the real him. He's just worn the other persona like a cloak.

He steps forward, reaching with his spare arm, and I flinch away. 'Fine,' he says. 'We'll do it like this.' He raises the rifle. I go rigid, my skin tightening, my throat closing up in terror. I think: *This is it. He's going to kill me.*

'Start walking,' he says. 'What are you waiting for?'

He directs me around the other side of the stable block. Keeping the rifle vaguely trained in my direction, he reaches for the keycode. This is my opportunity, I think. This is the bit where I could try and run. But run to where? There is just gaping whiteness, all around. He couldn't hope for a clearer target. So I can only wait while he opens the door and ushers me inside, into the darkness.

Immediately, I realise that it's much warmer in here than I expected. In the corner of the room, I see, he has set up a generator.

'How nice of you,' I say, trying to sound less afraid than I feel. 'To think of me.'

He sneers.

'And what have you got there?' I ask. 'Brown paper packages tied up with string?'

I am talking, because the talking – the effort of not screaming, of forming the words – seems to be keeping me calm.

'Exactly,' Iain says. 'And you definitely *don't* need to worry your little head about what's inside.'

But I need to keep him talking. I have to find a way to stay alive – and at the moment, distracting him from the business of killing me is the only card I have up my sleeve. There's no point in promising him I won't tell anyone about what I've seen. He won't believe me. He would probably be right.

So instead, I ask, 'Is this what you've been doing the whole time? The jobs about the estate – were they just a ruse? I can imagine this is probably a bit more lucrative.'

'Wouldn't you like to know?' he says. And then he gives a sort of 'why not?' shrug – which cannot be good. If he's deciding it's OK to tell me things, he has also decided that I won't have an opportunity to tell them to anyone else. No point in thinking like that. Just buy yourself time. Time is life.

'If you must know,' he says, 'I like to think of this as just another one of my jobs. I build a mean dry-stone wall. I can re-grout a windowpane in ten minutes. And I make a pretty good . . . delivery man.'

'I see,' I say, slowly, as though I am fascinated by his genius. 'You bring it in on your truck from—'

'Let's just say from *somewhere*,' he says, faux-patient.

'And then you keep it here and then—' I try to think beyond the wailing panic alarm in my head. What would be the point in bringing it here, one of the remotest places in the UK, with no way of getting it anywhere else?

And then I think of the history of the place. The old laird, insisting they build him his station. 'Then you put it on the train.'

He doffs an imaginary cap to me with his free hand. 'Straight down to London.' He smiles, and the expression makes him look all the more sinister. I wonder how I could ever have thought he was a normal, simple-living guy. He looks like a maniac. He looks more than capable of strangling that woman. I won't ask him about that yet, though. I'll keep him talking on this.

The radio, I think. If I could just get my hand to the transmit button, I might be able to get through to Doug. I could keep my finger on the button so there won't be any giveaway feedback. He'd hear everything. Perhaps I could even say something that would let him know exactly where I am.

'Straight down to London,' I say. 'How very clever. Like the whisky, in the old days. Of course – they think the laird himself was in on that, did you know?'

Iain doesn't say anything. But he does give me a look. *Duh.*

'Oh.' The realisation hits me like a punch to the gut. 'The boss is in on this too?'

Iain doesn't answer – he doesn't need to.

It's just like the old times: the laird taking a cut from

the smuggled whisky. And I've spent the last year blithely going about my business in the office – wondering, would the boss like to advertise the Lodge a bit more widely? Of course he didn't want to. The business must have been a nice blind for him – but too many visitors, and people might start noticing things.

I have been a complete fool. They must have been laughing at me, all this time. The idiot in the office, not seeing what was going on under her very nose.

'And how do you get it on the train?' I ask. 'Without anyone noticing?'

He gives me another look. Of course: that station guard, Alec. I think of how he behaved when I went to look around the station, the way he stood in front of the door up to his flat. Because he had something to hide.

Doug, I think. Does *he* know? Am I the only one here who has been kept in the dark? It might have been a kind of quid pro quo: turn a blind eye to the goings-on here, and we'll turn a blind eye to your criminal record.

If I radio him, now, will he simply ignore me? He wouldn't want me to die, though, would he? I think of how open, how vulnerable he was with me back at the Lodge. But that could all have been an act. Because the truth is, I realise, it was all a brief fantasy. I don't actually know him at all.

I have to try; it's my only chance. In incremental movements, so as not to draw attention, I inch a hand up my body, towards my pocket. Iain doesn't seem to notice. He's studying the gun as though it were a particularly fascinating pet.

I slide my hand into my pocket, slowly, slowly. My fingers brush the antenna of the radio, feeling for the hard body of it.

'What the fuck are you doing?'

His face is dark with anger. He strides over to me in a couple of steps. 'N-nothing.'

'Take your hand out of your fucking pocket.' He reaches roughly into my jacket and grabs hold of the radio. He looks at it for a couple of seconds, in mute rage, and then throws it at the wall with more force than I would have thought a man of his size capable of. It falls to the stone floor with a clatter, and in two pieces.

Now he comes at me with a roll of gaffer tape, and roughly binds my wrists, so hard that the bones bruise against one another, and my ankles. While he's down by my feet I test the bonds around my hands. I can't move them at all. He might as well have bound them together with a metal chain for all the give the gaffer tape has. I could try to kick him in the head, I think, while he's crouched there. But I'm not sure I could get enough force into my legs. He's not a big man, Iain, but he's strong enough: all the work he does on the estate. And if I just hurt him slightly, not enough to hinder him – which is the most likely outcome of this – he will only kill me quicker.

Iain stands up, looking proud of his work. Then there is a sudden, deafening bang. He pitches forward, with a look of slack-jawed surprise, and lands on top of me, the rifle clattering to the floor. I can't make sense of what has just happened. I can't see anything, either, because he's on top of me. And then I realise that the front of my grey jacket is wet with dark red blood.

One day earlier
New Year's Day 2019

MIRANDA

I can't believe the gamekeeper rejected me. The humiliation of it, when I had thought it might make me feel a bit better about myself.

The pain of it all winds me. I fold over on myself as if someone has actually punched me in the gut, and let myself sink to the ground. The sting of the sharp pebbles beneath my knees feels oddly right, so does the cold on my skin – though it doesn't feel cold, it feels like fire. I must look completely absurd, kneeling here in my gold dress and stiletto heels. And perhaps it's just because I'm aware of what a state I must appear . . . but I have the sudden strange, animal feeling that I'm not alone.

As I look about me I catch a shiver of movement in the

trees near the loch. I could have sworn I saw the dark shape of something – someone – in the darkness of the pines. I'm certain now. Someone else is out here with me. Oh, whatever. I don't care. Normally, I might be unnerved. But *nothing* can shock me as much as what I just saw, in that sauna.

No doubt my observer, in the trees, is very much enjoying my little display. I think of the Icelandic man's grin when I spotted them in the woods, his beckoning hand.

'Go on,' I shout, into the silence. 'Get a good long look. See if I fucking care.'

Emma, I think. I'll go and see Emma. I need to talk to someone. With any luck, Mark is still passed out on the couch in the sitting room of the Lodge. I check through the windows. Yes, he's there, spreadeagled on his back.

I knock on the door of their cabin. Silence. It's after four in the morning, after all. I try again. Finally, the door swings open. Emma stands there frowning, looking groggy. She's in pyjamas: silk, piped ones, not dissimilar to my own set.

'Oh,' she says. 'Hi, Manda.'

I normally flinch when she calls me that. It sounds too try-hard. Only Julien and Katie really use it, the two people closest to me. No, the irony of that is not lost on me.

'Can I come in?' I ask.

'Sure.' No questions, no hesitation. I feel a sharp stab of guilt for the way I've been with her. She has only ever been nice to me, while, at times, I've behaved like such a bitch – showing her up in front of the others, excluding her. Well, from now on everything is going to be different. I'm going to be different.

I follow her inside. It's almost the same design as ours:

the one large room, the armchairs and fireplace, the big four-poster, the dressing table – even the stag's head mounted on the wall. The major difference is that it's pin neat, like stepping into an alternative reality. Our belongings are scattered everywhere, we've always been such slobs. *Our*, I think, *we*. No more: it's all going to change. The house we bought together, all our plans. All that history. My legs suddenly don't feel capable of supporting me.

I stagger over to the nearest chair, which happens to be the little stool at the dressing table.

'Do you want a drink?' Emma gestures to the cocktail cabinet in the corner. She hasn't asked me what this is all about yet, but the gesture suggests that she knows something is wrong.

'Yes, please.'

She pours me a whisky. 'More please,' I say, and she raises an eyebrow a fraction, then slugs another inch into the glass. I thought I'd had a lot to drink last night, but suddenly I feel far too sober, my mind painfully clear, the images in it unforgettable, sharp-focused. I want to stop seeing them. I want to be numbed, anaesthetised.

Beyond the window the light in the sauna is still on. How could they have been so stupid? It's almost like they wanted to be found. Perhaps they genuinely hadn't appreciated how conspicuous it looks out there in the dark, like a lantern against the night. A beacon. I wonder – even though I know I shouldn't think about it – what they're doing, now. Are they discussing next steps, like co-conspirators? Have they even put their clothes back on? I can't get that image out of my head: her paleness against the tan of his skin, their dark heads together. I take a gulp of the whisky, letting it burn its path down my throat, focusing on the pain of it.

But I'm not sure all the whisky in the world will help me to forget how strangely, horribly beautiful they were together.

'Emma,' I say, 'do you have any paper?'

She raises her eyebrows only a fraction. 'Er . . . I think so.' She produces a pad from somewhere – Basildon Bond. It's so Emma, somehow, to have a pad of writing paper on hand.

Now my mind is oddly clear. As though some other power is guiding me, I go to the dressing table beside the bed, sit down, and write a note to Julien. I'll give it to Emma, make sure she passes it on.

All I want is to do as much damage as possible, to make him feel the sense of powerlessness that I do. My hand is shaking so much I have to press the pen to the paper to control my writing; twice it rips the whole way through. Good. He'll see that I mean business. With one fell stroke, he has just destroyed everything I thought I knew. Well, now I will destroy him.

NOW
2nd January 2019

HEATHER

Doug drags Iain off me, as though he were a sack of sand, and leaves him where he lies, moaning like an animal. Then he hunkers down in front of me, and grips my shoulders with both hands.

'Are you all right? Heather? What the fuck were you thinking? I followed your footsteps, through the snow—' and then, 'What did he do to you? Jesus Christ, Heather—' Something about the expression on his face, the concern in it – the care – is almost too much. So, too, is the feel of his hand – now cupping my jaw, his fingertips calloused but his touch light, brushing the hair back from my forehead, assessing for damage with infinite care. I would not have known such a big man could be so gentle.

'I'm fine,' I say. 'No – he didn't hurt me.'

'He did,' he takes his hand away from the side of my head and shows me his palm, slick with blood. 'That fucking—'

He gets up and lifts a foot, as if to kick Iain, who whimpers below him on the ground, his hand pressed to his shoulder, where the blood is seeping through his down jacket in a dark brown stain. He looks as though he might be about to pass out.

It's hard to watch. 'Don't, Doug.' It seems the old paramedic instinct is still in me: to preserve life.

'Why? Look what he did to you, Heather. I won't let him get away with it.'

'But . . . we don't want him to die.' That's a lot of blood. When Doug still doesn't look convinced I say, 'And he might know something – we have to find out.'

He wavers. 'Fine.'

He doesn't look convinced, but he lowers his foot. And at my insistence he makes a dressing, ripping a piece of fabric from the bottom of his own shirt, pressing it to Iain's shoulder beneath the jacket, to stop the bleeding.

Iain watches him with dull eyes, unresisting. His skin is greyish, his body is slumped. Doug keeps a foot on him, just above his groin, in case he were to try for an escape . . . though he hardly seems capable of that.

'You'll be all right,' Doug tells him, matter-of-factly, as if he can hear my thoughts. 'It's just torn your shoulder. I've seen worse. It'll sting like a bitch of course, but then . . . well, you deserve it, don't you, *mate*?'

'Why did you kill her?' I ask Iain.

'What?' He frowns, and then grimaces again, against the pain.

'The guest. Did you push her into that gully because she saw something? Because she was on to you?'

'I didn't kill her,' he moans.

'I don't believe you,' I say.

'I've never killed anyone,' he says, breathing heavily between each word, as though running up a hill. I hope Doug's right about the wound not being that bad. 'I've done some bad things in my time, but I've never *killed* a person.'

There seems to be a genuine repugnance about the way he says 'killed' – as though it really is something he sees as beyond the pale. But then he's done a fairly good job of acting the innocent up until now.

'I didn't kill that woman. Why would I?'

'If she saw something,' I say. 'Like I saw something – you were prepared to kill me. You were going to shoot me.'

'No,' he says, 'no – I wasn't. I hardly even know how to use that thing.' He gestures to the rifle, where it lies on the floor. Doug hefts his own rifle in his hand – a warning. *I do*, the movement says. I know how to use it. Iain sees this, swallows.

'But you took it from the storeroom,' I say, 'so you must have thought you might use it.'

He looks genuinely perplexed. 'No,' he says, weakly, 'no, I didn't.'

'What do you mean, you didn't? You've had it pointed at my head for the last hour.'

He looks at me as if I'm going mad. 'That's the rifle *you* had when you came up here. I pointed it at you to stop you from going anywhere.' He moves slightly, and winces against the pain. He is sweating horribly. 'Look, *I* was the one that saw something. That was why I moved the stash – from the pumphouse to up here.'

I'm caught by those words. *I saw something.* 'What do you mean?' I ask, urgently. 'What did you see?'

'I saw her get killed. The girl. And then I thought, Oh, fuck, the police are going to be all over this by the morning. They'll be searching the whole place. They'll find everything. I knew I had to move the stuff further away from the Lodge, and get it off the estate by the time they arrived. But I hadn't realised about the snow. They couldn't get here – but we couldn't get away, either. The train—' He stops, as though he knows he's given too much away. That *we* interests me, but there isn't time to ponder it now.

'You've been using the trains?' Doug asks at the same time as I say, 'How did she die? The woman. You said you saw it. I suppose you're going to say she fell?'

'No,' he shakes his head. 'Of course not. She was murdered. I saw it all. I was there, near the pumphouse. Early in the morning, about four a.m., checking on the stuff, like I told you. *She* killed her.'

'She?' I ask.

'Yes. The other woman. One of the guests. They had an argument, I think – I couldn't hear what about, exactly. But I did hear her saying, "You were never really my friend. Friends don't do that to each other." And I thought, oh, classic woman's tiff, about some love affair or something. Inconvenient, but no matter. I'll lie low, I thought, wait for it to blow over, wait for them to get out of the area. But then I saw the other one grab her by the neck, like she was trying to choke the words out of her. And then push her, right in the centre of the chest. Just watched as she fell. Cold as anything.'

One day earlier
New Year's Day 2019

MIRANDA

This is the only thing that brings me some relief: the thought of Julien's horror at the idea of me telling the world about him. He'll be thinking, *I won't try her yet. I'll try in an hour or so, when she's had a chance to calm down.* But he'll be too late. I'm going to hide out until I can get the first train down to London. I think of Julien going to the cabin, finding it empty, panic setting in properly. My note, left for him: *There is nothing you can say. I should never have kept your secret for you in the first place.*

'There.' I put the pen down, satisfied by my work. The dressing table is neatly ordered. A hairbrush, a small wooden box, a couple of lipsticks. One of them is Chanel. I turn it upside down, read the little label. *Pirate*: the same shade I wear. I thought I'd recognised it on Emma last night, but it's so difficult to tell: everyone wears colour differently.

'I have this one,' I say. 'It's my favourite.' Actually, I need to buy another. I've lost my old one somewhere, probably in the lining of one of my handbags.

'Oh yeah,' Emma says. 'I love it.' I open it up, and focus on applying it perfectly to my mouth in the mirror, a waxy crimson bow. I read somewhere once that sales of lipsticks go up when times are tough. I pout at myself in the mirror. Never has 'war paint' seemed like a more appropriate term. My face is pale, sunken-eyed, but the lipstick transforms it. It gives my face resolution, context, like a piece of punctuation. I try a smile, and quickly stop. I look deranged, like Heath Ledger's Joker.

'Lipstick looks so good on you,' Julien told me once. 'On other women it always looks like they're trying a bit too hard. But you're – what's that saying – you're born to wear it.'

I take a tissue from the dispenser, wipe it off. Now my mouth just appears raw-looking, bloody.

'Look,' Emma says now. 'Shall we go over to the Lodge? It's more comfortable there. Mark's passed out in the living room, but still . . .'

'Oh,' I say, 'no thanks. I don't want to see anyone else. I'm getting the first train in the morning, and that's going to be it. I don't ever want to see Julien or Katie again, if I don't have to.'

Her eyes go wide. 'Manda – oh my God . . . what's happened?'

I have an idea of myself delivering the news with the cool panache of a thirties movie star. But to my horror, I realise that the tears are coming; I can feel them rising within me, like an unstoppable tide. I haven't cried in so long – not since I got my Third, while just across from me Katie opened her envelope to reveal a big, shiny First.

I clench my hands into fists, dig my nails into the soft flesh of my palms. 'Julien and Katie have been sleeping together.' I still can't bring myself to say: *Having an affair.* Not yet. It sounds so intimate, so sordid.

'Oh my God.' She puts a hand to her mouth. But she's not quite meeting my eyes. The whole performance rings false.

I don't believe it. Emma, of all people, knew that my husband was screwing around while I didn't? What the fuck? 'You *knew*?'

'Only since yesterday night, I swear, Miranda. Mark told me.'

Mark, I think – the little secret of Julien's he'd warned me about. This was it. This is what he was trying to tell me. No wonder he looked confused when I told him I wasn't interested in hearing.

'I didn't want to just tell you, you know,' she says. 'I suppose I wanted to give Katie or Julien a chance to tell you themselves. I didn't want to presume I had any right.'

'What, to tell me my husband and my best friend are fucking?'

'I'm so sorry, Manda. I should have told you . . . I'll never forgive myself—'

She looks so tragic that I wave her away with a hand – I can't be bothered. 'You know what . . . whatever. It isn't about you. I know now. And I know what I'm going to do about it.' I hand her the note. 'Look,' I say, 'I want you to make sure Julien gets this. I can't bring myself to give it to him.'

'OK,' she says, taking it. 'But why—'

'Could I have another?' I say, at the same time, holding out my glass.

'Of course.' She smiles. 'It's medicinal, you know.'

She turns away and busies herself with pouring the measures, the ice.

For something to do, more than anything, I pick up the little box on the dressing table. It's a pretty, painted thing, one of those Chinese puzzle boxes. My granny used to have one. I turn it upside down. It's the same style, I think, as hers. I used to play with it – once she showed me the secret, the way to open it, I was obsessed. Can I still remember? I'm not sure. Tentatively, I push at one of the bottom panels; it doesn't budge. I turn it around and do the same on the other side. It moves. I feel a sense of simple satisfaction. What's the next bit? Oh yes, the panel on the shorter side. My fingers move of their own accord, pushing, twisting. Almost there – I just need to find that lever, pull it out. If it's the same, it will spring open. Aha! Here it is.

'Oh,' Emma says, in a strange voice. She's turned towards me, holding both whiskies. 'Oh, no – don't do that!'

It's too late. The box has sprung open, disgorging its contents onto the floor with a clatter. There's so much, it's amazing to think it's all been inside there, that little box.

I hear the crash of breaking glass and look up, confused. Emma has dropped both of the whiskies. Shards of broken glass scatter the floorboards, the liquid spilling around her feet.

'Oh shit,' I say, 'I'm such an idiot.'

But she hardly seems to hear. She hardly seems to notice the whisky. Instead she's on the ground, scrabbling at the fallen objects among the shards of glass, half-shielding the mess with her body.

'Careful,' I say, 'You'll—' and then the words leave me.

She does not want me to see. But I have seen. Several items I recognise. An earring, lost at the Summer Ball some eleven years ago: the evening I finally got together with Julien. I remember him reaching up to my earlobe, giving it a tug. 'Is this a new look? The single earring? Only you could pull it off.' It feels now as if it happened to someone else.

A pendant. A present from Katie for my twenty-first. It had given me such a pang to lose it, because it was the one she knew I really wanted from Tiffany's, and it must have cost her so much money.

A Parker fountain pen. I don't recognise that. Oh no, wait, I think I do. I'd lost it somewhere, in the first few weeks of university. I wasn't very good with my belongings, but I had been sure one morning it had been in my bag, and by the afternoon it was missing. I spent a few fruitless hours retracing my steps. Someone must have picked it up, I thought. Well: someone had.

Even my lighter – the one with the crest, lost only the other night.

'Emma,' I say. 'Why do you have all this stuff? It's all my stuff. Why is it here?' I'm thinking of the little notes left in my cubbyhole. The odd item being returned. But not these: these were clearly considered too precious for that.

'I don't know,' Emma says, not looking up at me. 'I don't know why all this is here. I had no idea what was in that box – it's Mark's.'

Set aside the fact that I can't for a moment imagine Mark owning such a thing. I'm looking at the way she's cradling the things to her chest – the pen, the earring, the necklace. I'm thinking of the look on her face – the sheer terror, that's what it was – when she saw me playing with the box, just before I pulled it open. Her shouted warning. The dropped whisky glasses.

I'm thinking, too, of the other night.

'Manda,' she says, 'It's so silly. I can explain.'

'No, Emma. I don't think you can.'

I'm just working out what it was that unsettled me so much, in what she said the other night. When she talked about that party – the one where I got stuck in the toilet. When she claimed it must've happened in London, when she was there, or that one of the others must have told her. But none of them could have. None of them were there. Because it didn't happen in London; it happened in Oxford.

It was the very first week. Now I remember it very clearly. That's why I was so mortified by it – I needed to make a good impression on everyone – and why I never told any of the others. But Emma, somehow, was in Oxford. At that party. There is no other explanation for it.

I take my phone out of my pocket.

'What are you doing?' she asks, looking up from where she's scrabbling on the floor.

'Finding proof.'

For a moment an expression flashes across her face – something violent and urgent – and I think she's about to lunge forward and knock the phone out of my hands. Then she seems to get herself under control.

'What proof?' she asks. She might be faking calm, but her voice is strange – high, shrill.

I don't answer. I'm briefly almost grateful to Julien for insisting that the Lodge's Wi-Fi be switched on. Still, it takes a while to open Facebook, and all the while I can see Emma, looking ready to lunge for my mobile. Eventually, when it loads, I click on 'photos of you'. I scroll through the photographs. I can't believe how many there are, and how many terrible ones, as I plumb the depths. After all this, when I'm starting afresh, I will have a cull. As I scroll, my face gets younger and younger – my cheeks are fuller, my eyes seem larger. I can't believe how much I've changed; I didn't realise. How much all of us have changed. There is Julien, the beautiful boy I fell in love with, the boy who became the man who has just ruined my life. But I don't have time for that. I'm looking for something else. I must have swiped through hundreds of photographs, half of them failing to load. It doesn't matter. It's further back than this. And then, finally, I'm in the right territory. First year freshers' week. A week of strangers, of trying to pick among them the people who might be your friends. Every face unknown, so that it would be difficult to remember any one face in particular. This is how she has hidden from me. I'm suddenly certain of what I'm going to find. And there, there it is: a photograph from that very party, I'm certain now, the one where I got stuck in the loo. A sea of milling almost-adults. Terrible quality, but it will do. Because there is a face among them, looking right at me, that I would never have noticed had Emma not given me her prompt. Mousey-haired, rounder-cheeked, the features less decided, the eyes obscured by Harry Potter glasses. Much younger looking, much dowdier looking. I look up and compare her to the woman in front of me. And despite all of the changes, it is her, it is unmistakably her.

'It wasn't Mark,' I say. 'It was you, Emma. You took these things.' I can't work out how, but this much is clear. 'My lighter,' I say, seeing it gleam in her fingers. 'Give me my fucking lighter, Emma.'

She hands it to me, wordlessly. Now she is looking at me – intently, as though trying to read my mind, work out what I'm going to do next.

Again, I think, I'd quite like to be cool in this moment. To light a fag with this very lighter, and sit back, and ask her to explain it all. How she, Emma, Mark's drippy little girlfriend, who I've only known for three years, came to be my stalker. But I can't. Two revelations in one night. It's too much. I feel, suddenly, like everything I thought I knew has been ripped from under me.

EMMA

So. Miranda and I do go back quite a way, after all. No, not as long as Miranda and Katie, her utterly false 'best' friend. But further than Julien or Mark, certainly. To explain, I have to take you back more than a decade.

Oxford interviews. Autumn. The Academic interview I'd be fine on, I knew. No worries there. I knew the slight concern, held by my parents, certainly, was the Personal interview. What if they had in some way got hold of my record: the trouble at my previous school? If so, I had been drilled. It had all been a terrible misunderstanding, you know how teenage girls can be – et cetera. No mention of the psychiatrist (it wasn't their right to ask about that, apparently), or his diagnosis.

Would they, essentially, see past the brilliance of my academic record, and see the real me (whoever that was)? And would that be a problem? Because, in actual fact, you don't get seven As at A level without having certain – one could say – obsessive qualities. The academic output was the positive manifestation of it. The other thing, with that stupid girl, was the negative.

When it came to the dreaded interview I got away with it. I got the 'interests' question, of course. As I answered – tennis, French cinema of the Nouvelle Vague period (all borrowed from interviews with various film directors and learned, rote), cooking – I wondered what they would make of it if I told them my real hobbies. Observation, close study, collection. The only issue was that the things I had liked to collect were rather unusual. I liked to collect personalities.

Here's the thing. I have never really felt like a real person. Not in the proper sense, the way other people seemed to feel it. From quite a young age I had discovered I was very good at certain things – particularly learning, academia. But a machine can learn. What I seemed to lack was a personality of my own. I lacked any sense of 'me'. But that's OK. What you don't have you can always borrow, or steal.

So I was always on the lookout for particularly colourful personalities, like a parasite searching for a host. There was the girl at the first school, which ended in a rather unfortunate way when she told her parents that I followed her home from school and sometimes sat in the treehouse opposite her window, watching her. This was rather unfair. I was only doing my homework, just like any other child. I could do all of my real homework on the short bus journey from school. The real swotting for me was in learning her habits, studying the way she was when she was on her own, what her bedroom looked like, what music she listened to. Then I would go home and emulate these tastes and habits: buy the same CDs, the same clothes.

I was moved to a different school, after the meeting with the headmistress. Then another, when the same thing happened at the next. 'Oh,' I said, blithely, in the interview, 'my father's job changed a lot, so we moved around the country following him.' She gave me an unconvinced look at this, but – as I suspected – my academic performance far outweighed any other concerns.

It was in the Junior Common Room of the college that I met Miranda. She seemed lit up from within. Had absolute confidence in who she was. She drank a beer with some of the guys, and played pool with them, and then seemed to get bored – perhaps it was the slavish adoration with which they were looking at her. Then her gaze landed, incredibly, on me.

She came and sat down next to me in the empty seat across the table. 'Hi. How did your interviews go?'

I was so stunned I couldn't speak for a second. Looking at her was like looking directly at the sun. It wasn't just that she was beautiful. It was that she was so very much herself – complex and contradictory and multi-layered, as I would learn – but absolutely, uniquely, triumphantly her own person.

'I have the same feeling,' she says. 'I mean, I think the first went *really* well, of course' – I remember the fabulous arrogance of that, even now – 'but I'm not at all sure about the second one. There were some horrible questions about the use of metaphors in Donne's Holy Sonnets and I totally froze up – I don't think they seemed very impressed. But maybe I winged it. That happens some-times, doesn't it?'

I nodded, though I wasn't even really sure of the question.

The question, really, was immaterial. Because I would have found it absolutely impossible not to agree with her.

'Look,' she said, 'I really need a drink. No more beer for me; I want something stronger. Do you want a drink?'

I nodded, still numb with blissful surprise. We had another Academic interview in the morning, but that seemed completely meaningless now.

She bought us two Jim Beam and Cokes, which at the time seemed the most sophisticated thing I had ever experienced: the sly, sticky warmth of the bourbon beneath all the sweetness of the soda. She drank hers with a straw, and somehow made it look cool. I kept waiting for her to really *see* me, or rather the lack of me, the thing that was missing; the void inside. She'd be appalled, she'd be disgusted – she'd realise her mistake and go off with any of the other bright young things who were so much more her type. But it never happened. What I hadn't come to appreciate then was that Miranda is – was – someone who spends so much time negotiating the various disparate parts of herself that she doesn't have very much time to properly see anyone else. To notice any discrepancy, or lack. And that has always suited me just fine. In addition to this, Miranda likes a project. She doesn't like to go for the expected thing. She has eclectic taste, is a collector in her own way. Before anything else we had that much in common.

It didn't seem to matter to her what I said – or indeed what I didn't say, as I sat there, dazzled. She was happy to have a mirror, a sounding board.

Already she made all the others, the ones before, the causes of so much heartache and shame, seem like paper cut-outs of people. Here, finally, was something to emulate. Here was a proper project, worthy of all my resources and attention. Or, as other people, normal people, might have put it: here was someone who could be my friend.

We went dancing in a club she'd learned about from a third year who was meant to be supervising us, but spent most of the evening trying to chat her up. As soon as we got in there, she shook him off with an 'as if' roll of her eyes, and grabbed my hand. We danced on a little retro multicoloured dance floor, sticky with spilled drinks. For once I wasn't aware of my fatness, or my weirdness, or – briefly, joyously – the absence inside, because I was borrowing from her light: I was like the moon to her sun, and it was meant to be.

I didn't believe I would see her again when I got accepted to Oxford. It would be too perfect, and I wasn't used to the things I wanted happening. Besides, for all her brilliance, I wasn't sure that she would have been bright enough – in the Oxford sense – to have got in. But there she was, at registration. My Best Friend To Be. My inspiration, my living mood board. The fount from which I might draw in the hopes of constructing a personality of my own.

I stood in line and waited for her to notice me. The moment would come, of course, I just had to be patient. It was impossible that she wouldn't notice me, we'd had that electric connection. Best friends at first sight. I imagined precisely how it would happen. She'd slouch along the row of freshers, all so raw and shufflingly awkward, already looking like she'd been there for years, like she owned the place. Her hair a gleaming sheet of gold, her leather bag of books pre-battered, her silk scarf trailing almost to the ground. Dazzling. And then she'd stop and do a double take when she saw me. 'It's you! Thank *God*, I haven't met anyone else I've wanted to chat to. Fancy going for a coffee?'

And all the others in the queue who had seen only a fat, bespectacled shell of a person would suddenly see something else – someone who was worthy of the attention of this Goddess. I waited for that moment as a priest might await the visitation of the divine presence, tingling with anticipation. She was turning, she was coming towards me – a lazy catch of the silk scarf, a toss of it over her right shoulder. And still I waited, almost trembling now. For a moment I was so overwhelmed I actually shut my eyes, one long blink. And when I opened them she was gone. I turned, in disbelief. She had walked past me. Straight by, without even stopping, let alone saying hello.

I saw that she was turning to talk to the girl behind her: dark-haired, too thin, dowdy. Her clothes almost conspicuously unfashionable – as unstylish as Miranda's were chic. And I understood: she already had a project, a hopeless case. This girl, whoever she was, had usurped me.

Still I had hope. I waited for her to notice me. I went to the Junior Common Room and sat at the same table and watched her at the bar, drinking her Jim Beam and Coke. I'd sit close enough that I could hear all the things she talked about. I heard once that she hated the food in the canteen – but couldn't cook herself, so supposed she was stuck with it. So that was when I learned to cook, of course. I'd spend hours in the kitchen on her hallway, making elaborate meals as good as any you could find in Oxford's restaurant scene. I'd wait for her to come past and loiter outside the door and say something like, 'Oh my God, that smells incredible.' Then I'd offer her some of it – because of course it was all for her – and we'd sit down and eat it together and we'd become the best of friends. And I could once again borrow a little of her light.

But it never happened; she never noticed me. The few times she did pass, she was too busy texting on her phone, or chatting with her awful friend, or later, chatting with her equally awful boyfriend. They deserve each other, Katie and Julien. They never deserved her.

I think of the sad, lonely girl who used to sit six seats behind her in lectures – who remembered the first day she walked into the lecture hall. As with the others, I couldn't decide what I wanted more: to be her, or simply to be close to her. But I could see immediately that neither would be possible. Her friends were nothing like me. None of them were as pretty as she was, but they had the same gloss of cool – even awkward, lank-haired Katie, absorbing some of her allure. They would reject me, as a foreign body.

I had made no impact on her life at all, I began to realise. While she had defined the last few months for me, ever since that interview. So I began to follow her, everywhere. She would – did – call it 'stalking'. I just thought of it as close observation. And when that didn't satisfy, I began to take things. Sometimes items that I suspected were of senti-mental value. Other times things that I knew had high significance – such as the essay she had plagiarised, or the earrings she had stolen. I wore those earrings for a week, the little painted parrots. With them hanging from my ears I felt a little more her, a little less myself, as though they contained some essence of her power, her personality. I actually smiled at baristas in coffee shops, and handed an essay in a day late, and sat in the sun beside the Isis to tan my legs. I waited for her to notice, to challenge me about them. She never did. There was a moment, in the street, when I saw her catch sight of them and stop short. Her mouth formed a small 'o' of surprise. Then she shook her head, as though reprimanding herself about something, and carried on her way, and I knew that she had only seen the earrings. She had not even seen *me*.

That's when I realised that I could force her to pay attention. I could send the items back. I could let her know that it wasn't just her imagination, or that she hadn't suddenly become even more clumsy, more forgetful. Some things though, the most special things, I did not send back. They were my talismans, like the holy relics of a religion. When I carried them about with me, I felt transformed. I became her guardian angel.

She was so careless. Perhaps it was just that she had so many nice things, they didn't mean that much to her. A cashmere cardigan casually discarded on the edge of the dance floor, or a hairband poking out of the top of the bag she left on a café table while she went to the loo, or a heeled sandal after she'd taken them off at a ball and was too drunk to remember where she left them. I was her Princess Charming. I'd return each item with a carefully thought-out note. I imagined the little frisson she would get, knowing that she had a secret admirer out there. It would be better than not having lost the thing in the first place.

I began to dress more and more like she did. I went on a diet, I had my hair straightened and dyed. Sometimes, if I caught a fleeting glimpse of myself in a shop window, it was almost like she was there instead of me. I got a Second, rather than the First my tutors had predicted. But I didn't mind. I'd got top marks in studying, and becoming, her.

I followed her to London. I knew where they liked to

drink, she and her friends, where they went out. The iron-ically divey bar on the high street, and then to the even more divey club on Clapham High Street, Inferno's. And that was where, while I was sipping my lemonade at the bar, Mark approached me.

Of course I knew who he was. At first I was petrified, I thought he'd come to challenge me, ask why I was there. Then he said, 'Can I buy you a drink?' and a whole new world of possibility opened up to me. I suddenly realised that he didn't see me as weirdo Emmeline Padgett. He saw me as a desirable woman he'd met in a club, wearing her Miranda-esque leather skirt and silk shirt. So when he asked me my name, I said, 'Emma.' My favourite Austen heroine, of whom Miranda had always reminded me a little.

Something magical happened. As Emma, I became someone new. It was acting, the same beautiful dislocation from myself that I had known on stage in a school produc-tion, when I briefly managed to become a different person entirely. Emma could be capable and cool, sexy, clever, but not too much so, not the kind of clever that scared people. She would be a social creature, she would be someone without layers, without darkness. She would be everything that I was not.

And I would be legitimately close to her. Would be called, even, a friend.

That bloody photograph. I've thought about it before, many times. Of course I knew it was there, I have an encyclo-paedic knowledge of Miranda's Facebook account. But it wasn't my photograph, I didn't even know the person taking it – so there was nothing I could do about it. I could have reached out, asked him to take it down, but Miranda knew him, so that might only have drawn attention to it . . . It might have been worse than leaving it up. I wasn't tagged in it or anything – of course, no one would have known my name. And I looked so different. You'd have to have looked very hard, and known exactly what it was you were looking for. Why would anyone study a photograph from fourteen years ago, and some thousand photos back? I thought I had been safe. I had been safe.

'It is you,' she says. 'I've always been good at faces.' She shakes her head, as though she's trying to clear it. 'It all makes sense. But wow, you have changed. You've lost weight. You've dyed your hair. But it is definitely you.'

'No,' I say, 'you've got it wrong. It can't have been me. I was at Bath.' I've always prided myself on my game face and my acting abilities, but suddenly everything I say sounds false, sounds like the lie it is. I shouldn't have said that, I realise. I should have just said I didn't know what she was talking about. In denying her accusations I have confirmed that she is right.

I make one more attempt to save myself. 'Oh,' I say, 'perhaps I came up to visit a couple of weekends. I had friends at Oxford, of course.'

But it is all too late. I can hear it in the background like a Greek chorus: *lie, lie, lie.*

It doesn't seem to matter, anyway. It's like she hasn't even heard me. She is saying, 'I can see it all now. The stalker stopped almost around the time you and Mark got together. I thought it was him for a bit – I thought so again recently. He's always had a bit of a thing for me, but then I'm sure you know that. Now, I understand.' She pauses, then says, 'You know I used to feel sorry for you? I thought Mark was just using you, for your passing resemblance to me. Katie pointed it out – I would never have noticed it myself. But it was the other way around, wasn't it?'

'I just want to be your friend.' I know how it sounds – I can hear it. Desperate . . . pathetic. But there's no point in lying. She knows it all now. It might as well all come out.

NOW
2nd January 2019

HEATHER

'What did she look like?' I ask. 'You're sure it was a woman?'

Iain screws up his eyes. He has gone very pale. I hope it's just the pain, not the loss of blood – but I suspect it is the latter. I've seen too many people die in an ambulance from wounds not much worse.

'Iain, what did she look like?'

'Just a woman,' he says. 'Just two women.'

'You must have seen more than that,' I say. 'What colour was her hair? The killer?'

'Don't know,' he says, and gives another groan. '. . . I suppose it was light coloured. Maybe blonde. Not sure. Difficult to see properly. But definitely not dark.' He seems certain of this. The other two female guests – Samira and Katie – have unmistakably dark hair. He might not know the exact shade of the woman's hair, but neither of theirs could be described as 'light'.

And then something else occurs to me. 'Iain, are you telling the truth when you say you didn't take the rifle?'

'Why would I lie?' he groans. 'You know everything else now. Why would I lie about that?'

He has a point. But I don't want it to be true. Because, if it is, she has the rifle. And in coming up here, we've made a horrible mistake.

One day earlier
New Year's Day 2019

MIRANDA

I shove my way out of the cabin. I can hear the clatter of Emma's feet on the steps behind me. 'Miranda,' she says, 'please – please listen. I never meant any of it to upset you.'

I don't answer. I can't look at her, or speak to her. I have no idea where I'm headed. Not to my own cabin, not to the Lodge. Instead I realise that I'm running in the direction of the path that stretches around the side of the loch. I have the dim idea of getting to the train station, waiting for a train. What time did Heather say they leave? Six a.m. That can't be too far from now. I'm aware that I'm still drunk, drunker than I thought, and that there are probably a number of problems with this plan, but my brain is too fuzzy to think of them. I'll work them out when I get there. For now, I just have to get away.

I plunge into the trees. It's darker here, but the gleam of the moon penetrates the branches, flickering over me like a strobe light. *It's a long way to the station*, says a little sober voice, from somewhere deep in the recesses of my brain. I push it away. I could run like this for ever. Nothing hurts when you're drunk.

The only obstacle – I see it looming in front of me – is the bridge over the waterfall. I'll have to be careful there.

And then, suddenly, there's a black figure on the path just ahead. A man. He looks like something that has just uncut itself from the fabric of the night. He has a hood pulled up, like death personified. Inside I can just make out the white gleam of his eyes. Then he is scrambling away from me, up the side of the slope above the path into the trees, disappearing into a little building that is almost hidden there.

I teeter for a second, on the edge of the bridge. Is he going to rush out and attack me? He didn't like being seen, I know that much. I suddenly feel much more sober than before. It's the fear that has done it.

'Manda.'

I turn. Oh Christ. Emma is just rounding the bend in the path. My hesitation has given her time to catch up with me.

'Manda,' she says, breathlessly, walking towards me. 'I just wanted to be your friend. Is that such a terrible thing?'

EMMA

'You were never really my friend,' she says now. 'Friends don't do that to each other.'

'Don't say that.'

'And you were only my friend before because of your connection to Mark. I would never have chosen you as a friend. I've always thought you're a bit dull, to be honest. I always thought you lacked depth. And I always thought you were trying too hard. It all makes sense now.'

There is a terrible pain beneath my ribcage, as if she has reached into the cavity with her bare hands and is squeezing, crushing. 'You don't mean that,' I say.

'No?' she says. 'No – I do.' She is actually smiling. Her face is beautiful and cruel. 'I prefer this version of you. Much more interesting. Even if you are a fucking weirdo.'

That stings. 'Don't call me that.'

'What?' Her manner is playground bully now. 'A fucking weirdo?'

Memories are surfacing from some dark, long-buried place, a classroom, the most popular girl in a year who looks – yes, I can see it now, rather like Miranda. I hadn't realised it before. The two faces: the remembered one and the one in front of me, seem to converge upon one another. Back then I gave that girl a shove, a hard shove in the middle of her chest, and she toppled back into the sandpit.

'God,' Miranda says, 'we call ourselves the inner circle. The best friends – the ones who remained while all the other ones fell away. But those other people were the sensible ones. They saw that the only thing holding us together was some tenuous history. Well, I'm going to get on the train, and start a new life – one in which I don't have to see any of you lot again. Especially not you.'

'Don't say that, Manda.'

'Don't call me that. You have no right to call me that. Can you get off the bridge please? I don't think it's meant for two people at the same time.'

I don't move. 'You can't mean that, Manda. All I have ever wanted is to be close to you, to be part of your life.'

She puts out her hands, as if to fend off my words. 'Just leave me alone, you fucking psychopath.'

That word. It's the action of a moment. I put out my own hands, and grab her neck. She's taller than me, stronger, probably – from all that boxercise and Pilates. But I have the element of surprise. I've got there first.

I don't have any particular plan. I just want her to stop talking, to stop her from saying these horrible things that I know she can't mean. I am so disappointed in her. How can she see those little gifts – the well thought-out notes – as the work of a psychopath?

She's like one of them, one of the adults who tried to

diagnose me, so long ago. Not a psychopath, actually. Personality disorder. That's the 'official' term for what I supposedly have.

But I know the real definition. The feeling behind all that effort. All those little thefts and returns, all that work in tracking her down, in getting Mark to like me, to become part of the gang.

Love. That's all it is.

I don't know when it is that I realise there's no longer any sound coming from her. She has become strangely heavy, limp, in my arms, slumped forward on me so that I am bearing all her weight. It is with a kind of unthinking horror that I push her away from me, with quite a lot of force. Like I once pushed that girl, at the first school – the one who taunted me for dressing like her, for following her back home. No real damage done, just a shattered elbow. Enough, though, for the headmistress to call my parents into the office and for them to announce I was leaving before she could even utter the word: 'expulsion'. Better for everyone's reputation if no one made too much fuss about the whole thing.

Except, that time she fell backwards into a sandpit.

I had forgotten. I swear it. I had forgotten that we were standing on the edge of the bridge, some forty feet above the frozen waterfall. When she fell, her head went back and her limbs were loose like a rag doll's – almost comical, windmilling. Then she disappeared into thin air and there was a long silence.

'Manda?' I called, softly. But I think I already knew there was no way she would answer. 'Manda?'

Only silence.

When I look, there she is. She might almost be sleeping.

Except for the fact that her legs are at funny angles, splayed looking – and she is so graceful, my Miranda. And there is the red bloom around her head where it has struck the rocks – a starburst, a supernova of red – and something else, paler, mixed in with the blood, that I don't want to think about.

I look about me. Has anyone seen? The landscape is completely deserted. There is no one, anywhere. I don't like the look of the little building, perched just above the water-fall. But there is no one in there, of course, it is just the way it has looked all weekend: the dark windows like blank eyes.

The snow continues to fall, like the curtain coming down after the final act. Or a white shroud – to cover the beautiful broken body in the waterfall below. It covers my footprints, filling them as I step away, as though they had never been.

I begin to cry. For her, for myself, for what I have lost.

NOW

2nd January 2019

HEATHER

'Doug,' I say, 'I've got to get back to the Lodge, now. You stay here, make sure he's all right.'

'No chance,' he says. 'I'm not going to let you go haring off to try to kill yourself again. We're going together.'

His choice of words stalls me. Kill yourself. It summons an idea that has been on the edge of thought. Because, when I decided to go up to the Old Lodge, I knew I would be in danger. At that point, I was fairly certain Iain had a gun. I knew that there was a chance I might be killed. I was gambling on that chance. Yes, it was as bad as a suicide mission. And no, I don't want to examine too closely what that means.

Doug helps me to my feet. The sudden movement makes

everything lurch – I'd forgotten about the head injury – and I stagger against him. He wraps an arm about me, to prop me up. I can feel the warmth of his body, even through our clothes. I take a step back.

'What about him?' I motion to Iain.

'He's all right. Let's leave him here to think about what he's done.'

'He doesn't look so good, Doug.' He doesn't – though it's also true that he's not looking much worse. The bleeding seems, largely, to have been staunched by Doug's homemade gauze.

'I'm not,' Iain says. 'I'm not doing so well. Take me with you.'

'If it were that bad,' Doug says, brutally, 'you'd have lost consciousness half an hour ago. You can stay here until we come back to find you, guarding your precious stash.'

It occurs to me that there might be a chance to get a signal on my phone. Every so often, up on the peaks, it flickers into life. I take it out, wave it in the air, turn airplane mode off and on – and finally, with a cry of triumph, I manage to raise a solitary bar.

'Who are you calling?' Doug asks.

'The police.'

Iain shudders, as though someone has just prodded the wound in his shoulder.

In the time we've been in here, I notice, it has stopped snowing. The police helicopter can reach us now. But they are not aware of the new urgency of the situation.

'Please,' I say to the operator, 'put me through to DCI John MacBride. I have something very important to tell him.'

EMMA

Who did you think took that rifle from the storeroom? Me, of course! Tada!

I've become pretty adept at noticing things, over the years. And I have a memory that might as well be photographic. That passcode was stored in the neat little filing cabinet inside my mind from the second that big oaf of a gamekeeper punched it in.

Seriously, what did Miranda see in him? She always did have terrible taste in men.

There is a phone ringing incessantly in the office across the hallway from the living room.

'Why doesn't she pick it up?' Mark asks. 'Or him? It could be something important. It could be the police, or something.'

We wait, as the ringing stops, only to pick up again a minute later.

'I'm going to go and have a look,' I say, 'see what's going on.'

* * *

The rest of the Lodge seems particularly quiet. It is the silence of emptiness. Even before I push open the door to the office I'm sure that the knock I give is redundant. They're not here. Not Heather, not the idiot gamekeeper. The phone is on the desk, still ringing. The sound is so loud it almost seems to vibrate in the silence.

I lift the receiver. 'Hello?'

'Is that Heather Macintyre?' The voice on the other end is almost pre-pubescently youthful. 'DCI John MacBride asked me to give you a call. I've been trying your mobile, too, but it's just going through to voicemail.'

Some instinct now persuades me to say, modulating my voice to a gentle, Edinburgh burr (I told you I've always been a good actress): 'Yes. It's Heather here. How can I help?'

'The DCI is on his way to you, in the chopper.' There is an unmistakable delight in the way he says this, like he's enjoying the drama of it.

'Finally,' I say. 'Well, that's excellent news.' They have no way of tracing it to me, I think. Even if they can work their CSI magic with DNA and fibres – well, I was wearing Mark's coat, and our DNA will be all over one another. There would be nothing strange about Miranda having flakes of my own skin on hers, or my hairs on her person. We've travelled on a train together, eaten together, danced and hugged over the last few days. I owe it to Miranda not to get myself caught, you see. Because I still have my chance to avenge her.

'He also,' the operator coughs. I swear I hear a squeak in his voice as if it's only just breaking (God, if they're practically employing children to man their phones I have even less to fear from these goons than I thought), 'he also asked that you do nothing to alarm the . . . suspect.'

'The suspect?' I ask.

'Yes . . . well, of course' – he's speaking quickly, anxiously now, as though he knows he's made a mistake – 'she won't *officially* be that until we have assessed the situation. But the one you say was seen, that night, with the victim.'

She.

I want to ask him to repeat himself, just to be certain . . . even though I know what I heard. To do so, though, would be to arouse suspicion.

But no one saw. I *just* stop myself from saying it. My shock is a momentary lapse of control. They might be talking about Katie, I think, wildly. Yes – that must be it. Perhaps Julien dropped her in it to save his own bacon, or something to that effect . . .

Except, I'm not sure I can afford to think that way.

It's not prison I'm afraid of. I deserve to pay for what I have done. Though no punishment will be worse than the one I have already had meted upon me, the loss of Miranda: my idol, my lodestar. What I fear is not having time to take revenge on her behalf. Well, I'll just have to speed things up.

KATIE

'Katie,' Emma says. 'Can I have a word, outside?' There's an odd urgency to her tone. I wonder what it was about that phone call she just took. Miranda's death seems to have hit her, if possible, the hardest of any of us. I suppose Julien and I have our guilt to contend with, which complicates things. I haven't yet been able to work out which of the two emotions I feel more strongly: grief, or self-hatred. Somehow, this has all felt like our fault. But Emma has spent the day staring at the floor, hardly saying anything. She rushed to that phone as if she was hoping it was someone ringing to say there'd been a terrible misunderstanding: that Miranda had been found alive, after all – that everything else has been a big mistake.

'Please,' she says, 'it's important.'

'OK.' I get up and follow her. She leads me along the corridor, out towards the front of the Lodge, where the snow lies pristine and white as an eiderdown beside the loch. It has stopped falling, I notice. That's good news, isn't it?

'Who was that on the phone?' I ask Emma. 'Was it the police?'

'Yes,' she says. 'It turns out they have a suspect.'

'Who?' I ask.

'Come over here,' she says. Her face is contorted with some powerful emotion that I can't quite read. She beckons with a hand. 'I don't want one of the others to overhear us.'

This can only mean one thing. It's one of us. *Mark*, I think. I know it can't be Julien – when I woke up from a fitful sleep he was beside me on the sofa, his mouth hanging open. I actually had to double-check he was alive. It has to be Mark. Oh God, that explains Emma's weird expression.

'Emma,' I say, walking towards her. 'Is it . . . is it who I think it is?' He has always been obsessed with her. I warned Miranda, and she laughed it off. She always thought she could handle herself.

Now Emma does something odd. She bends and sweeps her hand through the snow, as though she is searching for something.

'What are you doing?' I ask.

When she stands up she is holding something. It takes me a beat to work out what it is. My body seems to have done so before my mind has caught up: suddenly my limbs are frozen, my spine rigid.

'Emma. What are you doing with that?'

She doesn't seem to register the question. Her entire face has changed. She looks like a stranger, not the woman I have known for three years. 'It's your fault,' she hisses. 'Everything that happened to her. If she hadn't found out about you two, and your disgusting affair, she wouldn't have been so upset. She wouldn't have said the terrible things she did. It wasn't her fault. It wasn't mine. It was yours.'

At first, when I try to speak, I can only form the words silently with my mouth, releasing nothing but a bubble of air. I am aware of a strange thundering noise, staggeringly loud, all around us – the sound of something drumming, *whoomp*, *whoomp*, *whoomp*, like a giant heartbeat. I can't see anything to make sense of it, though. And perhaps, after all, it is only the rushing of the blood in my ears.

'I don't understand, Emma. I don't understand what you're saying.'

'Of course not,' she says. 'Because you're too stupid.' She spits the word. 'You never deserved her for a friend.'

I see something change in her expression; a spasm of pain. I understand. 'It was you,' I say.

She doesn't answer. She just raises her eyebrows, and does something to the rifle, making an ominous clicking sound. It is raised, level with my sternum.

Don't shoot for the head, I can hear the gamekeeper saying. *Shoot for the body, where all the internal organs are clustered together. A shot like that is much more likely to be fatal.*

I see Emma's face as it was after she shot the deer, anointed in gore, marked out as a killer.

I don't have time to do anything before I hear the sound of the report, familiar from before. I feel something shunt into me with terrible force. As I hit the ground, everything goes black.

DOUG

It seems an incredible distance back to the Lodge, much further down than it had seemed, perversely, on the way up. Beneath the snow are tangles of heather that snag at their ankles and threaten to trip them with every step. But it is also the new knowledge they now possess, the new understanding of how dangerous the situation at the Lodge might prove to be. They have made a huge mistake, leaving the guests to their own devices. But knowing what Iain could have done to Heather had Doug not shown up, he cannot be sorry he chose as he did.

Finally they are on the path back to the Lodge. And then above them a vast metal bird begins to descend from the clouds, blades whirring with a deafening throb. For a moment Doug is thrown back nine years to a place of fear and darkness – in spite of the blinding desert light – and the helicopter becomes an instrument of war: an apache circling overhead, trying to pick out enemy positions. He reminds himself that it is the police, that this is a good thing. The great Scots pines are shedding their covering of snow, thrashing in the draught created by the blades.

Then Heather gives a horrified cry and picks up her pace. Incredibly, it is he who is struggling to keep up with her. Now he sees what she has seen. The two women, one blonde, one dark, stand facing one another in front of the Lodge. The blonde is stooping to unearth something in the snow. He knows what it is even before he sees it emerge in her hand. The long, elegant barrel, lethal from some distance – but from three metres, the gap between the two figures: catastrophic.

They have finally reached flat ground. And before he can tell her to stop, Heather is sprinting towards them. Neither of the women sees her, so intent are they on one another. He is running, too, towards the one with the rifle. He is too late. As the gun discharges he sees Heather leap towards the dark-haired woman, knocking her out of the way.

He sees an explosion in a faraway place, that terrible moment – the men, his friends, all dead because of his hesitation. He wrenches himself back to the present. He throws himself down next to her, where the snow is splattered with her blood.

EPILOGUE

HEATHER

When I first came round from an opiated sleep I had no idea who I was, let alone where. The first person I saw was Doug.

'Hello,' he said. 'I hope you don't mind me being here.'

Before the nurse left the room she said, 'You've got a great man here. He's been sitting in that same spot the whole time you were in surgery, waiting for you to come round.'

I looked at Doug. He seemed embarrassed, as though he had been caught out in something. 'I had to tell them we were together,' he said, in an undertone. 'Otherwise they would have sent me away. I hope you don't mind.'

His hand was only a few centimetres from mine, resting on the sheet. I lifted mine, with some effort, to cover his. It seemed miraculously warm and alive. It was the first time I had touched another human being, in any significant way, in a long, long time.

Over the next couple of hours they all arrived after the long drive from Edinburgh: the friends whose happiness and wholeness I have been avoiding for a year. And, of course, my family: my mum repeating that she 'knew that place had something bad in it'. And what I realised was: I am loved. I love. I have lost the great love, the one that for years defined me, that had come to be the sum total of who I was. So much so, that when it was gone, I was certain there was nothing left to salvage.

I'm not sure what compelled me to do what I did. I saw the whole scene playing out before me, as though at half the speed, and I realised that there was time, and that I had the element of surprise. I *could* do something. I didn't even really think about the danger to myself, there wasn't time for it. I didn't even think about it as the bullet entered my abdomen. It was only when I lay on the ground, winded, and the pain arrived in a wave so intense that I was convinced I had to be dying. But now I'm wondering if it was some memory of Jamie always putting the lives of strangers before his own that impelled me.

Iain is all right. In fact, apparently he's on the same ward as me, somewhere. With a police escort, naturally. According to Doug he was in so much pain that he sobbed out his confession when Doug brought the police up to the Old Lodge. It seems he was a cog in a much larger machine: the drugs came from a lab in Iceland. Ingvar and Kristin? Not their real names, obviously. Those backpacks had been filled with something *much* more valuable than hiking equipment. The train guard at the station was paid more than double his own salary to turn a blind eye. A few innocuous suitcases unloaded at the other end, delivered to the boss's members' clubs. And New Year's Eve the best time to do it: everyone distracted, emergency services stretched to capacity.

The one turning these cogs, of course, was the boss. It turned out he and Iain went a long way back. As a young man, Iain had served a long sentence in prison for car theft, and had come out without any options. Finally he had managed to get a job as the bouncer of a rather upmarket club in London. The owner of the club had approached him with an offer: a cushy job, better pay, a new start. The drugs, it turned out, had been the boss's main source of money all along. Not the members' clubs, nor the Lodge – though both had provided a nice blind, and both were integral to the product's journey from Icelandic lab to the well-heeled end users. They caught him sipping an orange juice in the first-class lounge at Heathrow, en route to skipping the country.

Quite a coup for the Fort William police station. A murder *and* a drugs bust, all from the same serene almost-wilderness. A wilderness that, I've decided (and not just because of the murder and the drugs bust), isn't for me. I'll miss my morning swim in the loch, of course. And – a surprise even to me, this – I'll miss my taciturn co-worker. Doug's agreed to come and spend the weekend with me once I've settled back in to life in Edinburgh. I've bought myself a guest sofa bed, which may or may not be used. He has his own stuff to work out first, his own journey to go on. Both of us, I think, have been living in limbo. Both of us running from death, and in so doing fleeing from everything else. Now it is time to get on with the difficult business of living.

KATIE

I'm due to give birth in a few weeks. There was a worry that I might lose the baby, after being tackled to the ground like that – but she was fine. She: I'm going to have a girl. I'm working right up to my due date. I've been working hard, putting in longer hours and operating on less sleep than I should have had in my condition. But it's been a distraction. My whole pregnancy has been tangled up with my grief for Miranda. Yes, grief. I know it might be almost hard to believe, considering what a terrible friend I had been to her of late. And the way she could be with me. It's true, I didn't always like Miranda. Sometimes I positively hated her. But I did love her. That's what happens when you have known someone for such a long time. You see all their faults, yes, but you know their best qualities too – and Miranda had so many of those. No one could light up a party like her. No one would offer her best dress to borrow at the drop of a hat. And there aren't many popular girls of thirteen who will stake all their social credit on the rescue of an outsider. She was, in her way, utterly unique. No one could be a fiercer ally. And yes, no one could be a more formidable enemy.

Apart from, perhaps, one person.

Emma was spectacular at the trial, very contrite and grief-stricken and very – though not *too* – well-dressed. Gone was the resemblance to Miranda, the seductive blonde, the femme fatale. I suppose you don't particularly want to go for the fatale look when you're on trial for murder. Her hair had been dyed back to a very modest shade of mouse, she wore a high-necked, almost Victorian pie-crust blouse: she looked like something between a choir girl and a school-teacher. She wept as she explained that Miranda had started taunting her about her condition, despite her attempts to explain. Oh, she hadn't meant to strangle Miranda, she said. There had been a tussle, yes, after Miranda had said some terrible – unforgivable – things. It was self-defence. Miranda had been drunk and vengeful, had come at her fighting tooth and nail. She'd shoved her away, and then, realising the consequences of the push, had tried to save Miranda by grabbing onto the nearest thing within reach . . . her neck.

No, doesn't sound very likely to me – and the prosecution didn't think so either. It should be impossible *not* to convict on the basis of so much evidence. But we live in a post-truth world. The jury lapped it up. They simply could *not* convict her of murder. Not this well-spoken, quiet, meek person who looked just like the daughter of a friend, or a girl they remembered from school. People like her didn't commit murder. Not proper *murder*. They simply had unfortunate accidents.

The papers compared it to the case of that other Oxford

alumnus, a few years ago, who stabbed her boyfriend with a breadknife. People like them just don't serve time. The defence, meanwhile, gleefully painted a picture of Miranda as an unhappy person: someone whose life was falling apart beneath a glossy facade. A big drinker. A drug-taker – she, after all, had supplied our group with drugs on the first night of the holiday. Emma, importantly, had abstained from taking anything. And Miranda was prone to erratic, bullying behaviour, the defence claimed: the way she'd forced Mark to drink that champagne, coerced me into the freezing loch. Controlling, manic, unstable – she'd been seeing a psychotherapist, hadn't she?

Manslaughter, that was the charge. And a four-year sentence. She – this woman who pushed my oldest friend to her death and who tried to kill me – will be out in four years' time. I try not to think about it.

As for the rest of them – apart from Nick and Bo, of course – I was right in suspecting we had nothing in common. Miranda had really been the link. And history, I suppose: the laziness of habit. I am not here to try to acquit myself. I behaved no better than any of them, and far worse than some. But isn't that just part of the problem? Old friends don't challenge us on our faults. I have not been a good person. I needed something to show me that. I just wish it hadn't been this.

The group has fragmented now. The inner circle has imploded from within. There is no centre to it, no high priestess. Samira and Giles are, I imagine, getting along very happily in Balham with all their NCT-class friends, who don't take drugs or down bottles of champagne, or, for that matter, kill each other.

Nick and Bo are moving back to New York. Mark has

already – make of this what you will – met another almost-but-not-quite Miranda substitute at the agency where he works. Julien's path has been the most radical. He has gone off for a detox in Goa for a month – though with the lithe yoga instructor at the City gym he used to visit, so perhaps there's more to it than a desire to become a Zen master. He's told me he'll be back in time for my due date . . . worse luck. If I could have this baby without ever having to see him again I don't think I'd particularly mind. I'll be for ever linked to him, now. My child's father. Not quite the clean break I would have wanted – from him, and, by association, from the whole group. Still, at least I never have to go on another bloody holiday with any of them.

I'd like, now, to get to know people who know me for *me* – not for who I used to be. Who won't expect me to step back into a role that I don't quite fit into any more. Who won't see me as a project, to be worked on . . . but will see me as whole, fully formed.

Last week, when we concluded our latest case at the firm, I decided to go for a rare drink (elderflower for me) with my colleagues. They actually aren't all that bad – they might even be normal people when they're not inside the fetid air of the office, hamster-wheeling their way through contracts. There is one guy, Tom, from the litigation team, who doesn't actually look all that bad without his crumpled suit jacket, glasses, and the fear of God in his eyes.

Perhaps it's time to make some new friends.

Acknowledgements

To Al – for taking me to the spot that first inspired the book, and for those long walks in the snow plotting and evenings reading . . . Twenty percent definitely earned!

To my dear Hoge – thank you for all your time and wise editorial input. This book would not be the same without you!

To my fabulous agents, Cath Summerhayes and Alexandra Machinist, who were highly supportive of this move to the dark side! And huge thanks to Luke Speed, Melissa Pimentel and Irene Magrelli.

To Kim Young, editor extraordinaire, and her fantastic team at HarperCollins – thank you for all the passion and imagination you are bringing to publishing this book: Charlotte Brabbin, Emilie Chambeyron, Jaime Frost, Ann Bissell, Abbie Salter, Eloisa Clegg.

To Katherine Nintzel, and her William Morrow Stateside dream team: Vedika Khanna, Liate Stehlik, Lynn Grady,

Nyamekye Waliyaya, Stephanie Vallejo, Aryana Hendrawan, Eliza Rosenberry, Katherine Turro.

To Jamie Laurenson and Patrick Walters at See-Saw – I'm so excited by your vision for bringing the book to life on-screen!

A new murder. A new mystery.

Turn the page to enjoy an extract of
the brand new thriller from Lucy Foley

THE
GUEST
LIST

You'd die to be on it...

'Foley is
superb'
The Times

Coming spring 2020

THE WEDDING NIGHT

The lights go out.

In an instant, everything is in darkness. The band stop their playing. Inside the marquee the wedding guests squeal and clutch at one another. The light from the candles on the tables only adds to the confusion, sending shadows racing up the canvas walls. It's impossible to see where anyone is or hear what anyone is saying: above the guests' voices the wind rises in a howling frenzy.

Outside a storm is raging. It shrieks around them, it batters the marquee, whose walls flex and billow helplessly beneath its onslaught. At each assault the whole structure seems to flex and shudder with a loud groaning of metal; the guests cower in alarm. The doors have come free from their ties and flap at the entrance. The flames of the paraffin torches that illuminate the doorway snicker.

It feels personal, this storm. It feels as though it has saved all its fury for them.

This isn't the first time the electrics have shorted. But

last time the lights snapped back on quickly. The guests quickly returned to their dancing, their drinking, their pill popping, their screwing, their eating, their laughing... and forgot it ever happened.

How long has it been now? In the dark it's difficult to tell. A few minutes? Fifteen? Twenty?

They're beginning to be afraid. This darkness feels somehow ominous, intent. As though anything could be happening beneath its cover.

*

Finally, the bulbs flicker back on. Whoops and cheers from the guests. They're embarrassed now about how the lights find them: crouched as though ready to fend off an attack. They laugh it off. They almost manage to convince themselves that they weren't frightened.

The scene now illuminated in the marquee's three adjoining tents should be one of celebration, but it looks more like one of devastation. In the main dining section there are clots of wine upon the laminate floor, a crimson stain spreads across white linen. Bottles of champagne cluster every surface in a testament to an evening of toasts and celebrations. A forlorn pair of silver sandals peek from beneath a tablecloth.

The Irish band begin to play again in the dance tent — a rousing ditty to get things back into the spirit of celebration and many of the guests hurry in that direction, eager for some light relief. If you were to look closely at where they step you might see the marks where one barefoot guest has trodden in broken glass and left their bloody footprints across the laminate, drying to a rusty stain. No one notices.

Other guests drift and gather in the corners of the main tent, nebulous as leftover cigarette smoke. Loathe to stay, but also loathe to step outside the sanctuary of the marquee while the storm still rages. And no one can leave the island. Not yet. The boats can't come until the wind dies down.

In the centre of everything stands the huge cake. It has appeared whole and perfect before them for most of the day, its train of sugar foliage glittering beneath the lights. But only minutes before the lights went out the guests gathered around to watch its ceremonial disembowelling. Now the deep red sponge gapes from within, a mass of crimson and white.

Then from outside there comes a new sound. You might almost mistake it for the wind at first. But it rises in pitch and volume above the wind until it is unmistakable. All chatter ceases.

The guests freeze in whatever they are doing. They turn and stare at one another. They are suddenly afraid again. More so than they were when the lights went out. They all know what it is. It is a scream of terror.

THE DAY BEFORE

AOIFE

The Wedding Planner

Nearly all of the wedding party are here now. Things are about to crank into another gear: there's the rehearsal dinner this evening, with the chosen guests, so in that sense the wedding really begins tonight.

I've put the champagne on ice ready for the pre-dinner drinks. It's vintage Bollinger, eight bottles of it, plus the wine for dinner and a couple of crates of Guinness — all as per the bride's instructions. It is not for me to comment, but it seems rather a lot for the eve of the wedding. They're all adults, though. I'm sure they know how to restrain themselves. Or maybe not. That best man seems like something of a liability — all of the ushers do, to be honest. And the bridesmaid — the bride's half-sister — I've seen her on her solitary wanderings of the island, hunched over and walking fast as though trying to escape something.

You learn all the insider secrets, doing this sort of work. You see all the things no-one else is privileged to see. All the gossip that the guests would kill to have. As a wedding planner you can't *afford* to miss anything. You have to be alert to every small detail, all the smaller eddies beneath the surface. If I didn't pay attention, one of those currents could grow into a huge riptide and sweep everything beneath it, destroy all my careful planning. And here's another thing I've learned — sometimes the smallest currents are the strongest.

I move through the Folly's downstairs rooms, lighting the blocks of turf in the grates, so they can get a good smoulder on for this evening. Freddie and I have started cutting and drying our own turf from the bog, as has been done for centuries' past. The smoky, earthy smell of the turf fires will add to the sense of local atmosphere. The guests should like that. Besides, it may be midsummer but it gets cool at night on the island. The Folly's old stone walls keep warmth out and aren't so good at holding it in.

Today has been surprisingly warm, at least by the standards of these parts, but the same's not looking likely for tomorrow. The end of the weather forecast I caught on the radio mentioned something about wind. We get the brunt of all the weather here. Often the storms we have are much worse than they end up being on the mainland, as if they've exhausted themselves on us. It's still sunny out but this afternoon the needle on the old barometer in the hallway swung from FAIR to CHANGEABLE. I've taken it down. I don't want the bride to see it, to panic. Though I'm not sure that she is the sort to panic. More the sort to get angry and look for someone to blame. And I know just who would be in the firing line.

'Freddie,' I call into the kitchen, 'will you be starting on the dinner soon?'

'Yeah,' he calls back, 'got it all under control.'

Tonight they'll eat a fish stew based on the Connemara fisherman-type chowder: smoked fish, lots of cream. I ate something like it the first time I ever visited this place, when there were still people here. This evening's will be a more refined take on the usual recipe, though – as this is a refined group we have staying. Or at least I suppose they like to *think* of themselves as such. We'll see what happens when the drink hits them.

'Then we'll be needing to start prepping the canapés for tomorrow,' I call, running through the list in my head.

'I'm on it.'

'And the cake: we'll be wanting to assemble that in good time.'

The cake is quite something to behold. It should be. I know how much it cost. The bride didn't bat an eyelid at the expense. I believe she's used to having the best of everything. Four tiers of deep red velvet sponge, encased in immaculate white icing and strewn with sugar greenery, to match the foliage in the chapel and the marquee. Extremely fragile and made according to the bride's exact specifications, it travelled all the way here from a very exclusive cake-makers in Dublin: poor Mattie was tasked with getting it across the water in one piece. Tomorrow, of course, it will be destroyed. But it's all about the moment, a wedding. All about the day. It's not really about the marriage at all, in spite of what everyone says.

See, my job is a profession in which you orchestrate

happiness. It is why I became a wedding planner. Life is messy. We all know this. Terrible things happen, I learned that while I was still a child. They come suddenly, unexpectedly. And they can cut your life in two, guillotine the now from the then into two broken halves that can never be put back together. But life is just a series of days. You can't control more than a single day. But you can control *one* of them. Twenty-four hours can be curated, managed. Just like a wedding day. A neat little parcel of time in which I can create something whole and perfect to be cherished for a lifetime, a pearl from a broken necklace.

Freddie emerges from the kitchen in his food-stained apron. 'How are you feeling?'

I shrug. 'A wee bit nervous, to be honest.'

'You've got this, love. Think how many times you've done this.'

'But this is different,' I tell Freddie. 'Because of who it is.' It was a real coup, getting Will Slater and Julia Keegan to hold their wedding here.

I worked as an event's planner in Dublin, before. Setting up here was all my idea, restoring the island's crumbling, half-ruined Folly into an elegant ten-bedroom property, with a dining room, drawing room and kitchen.

'Shush.' Freddie steps forward and enfolds me in a hug. I feel myself stiffening at first. I'm so focused on my to-do list that it feels like a diversion we don't have time for. Then I allow myself to relax into the embrace, to appreciate his comforting, familiar warmth. Freddie is a good hugger. He's what you might call 'cuddly', which makes sense as he likes his food — it's his job. He had a restaurant in Dublin before we moved here.

'It's all going to work out fine,' he says. 'I promise. It will all be perfect.' He kisses the top of my head.

I've had a great deal of experience in this business. But then I've never worked on an event I've been so invested in. And the bride is very particular, which, to be fair to her, probably goes with the territory of what she does, running her magazine. Someone else might have been run a little ragged by her requests. But I was up for the challenge. I've enjoyed it, even. And we've done it and, if it's not immodest to say it, I'm proud of myself.

Anyway. That's enough about me. This weekend is about the happy couple, after all. The bride and groom haven't been together for very long, by all accounts. Seeing as our bedroom is in the Folly too, with all the others, we could hear them last night. 'Jesus,' Freddie said as we lay in bed, putting his pillow over his head. 'I can't listen to this.' I knew what he meant. Strange, too, how when someone is in the throes of pleasure it can sound so very much like pain. They seem very much in love, those two, but a cynic might say that's *why* they can't seem to keep their hands off each other. Very much in lust might be a more accurate description.

Freddie and I have been together for the best part of two decades and there are still things I keep from him and, I'm sure, vice versa. Makes you wonder how much they know about each other, those two.

Whether they really know all of each other's dark secrets.

THE DAY BEFORE

JULES

The Bride

I'm standing in front of the mirror in our room, the biggest and most elegant of the Folly's ten bedrooms, naturally. From here I only need to turn my head a fraction to look out through the windows towards the sea. The weather today is perfect, the sun shimmering off the waves so brightly you can hardly look at it. I hope it stays like this for tomorrow. Our room is on the western side of the building and because this is the westernmost island off this part of the coast there is nothing, and no-one, for thousands of miles between me and the Americas. I like the drama of that. And the Folly itself is a beautifully restored fifteenth century building, treading the line between luxury and time-lessness, grandeur and comfort. There are antique rugs upon the flagstone floors, claw-footed baths, fireplaces lit with smouldering peat. It's large enough to fit all our guests, yet small enough to feel intimate. It's perfect. Everything is going to be perfect.

Don't think about the note, Jules.

I will *not* think about the note.

Fuck. *Fuck.* I don't know why it's got to me so much. I have never been a worrier, the sort of person who wakes up at three in the morning thinking about something. Not until recently anyway.

The note was delivered through our letter box three weeks ago. It told me not to marry Will. To call it off.

Somehow the idea of it has gained this dark power over me. Whenever I think about it I get a sour feeling in the pit of my stomach. Something like dread.

Which is ridiculous.

I look back at the mirror. I'm currently wearing the dress. *The* dress. I thought it important to try it on one last time, the eve of my wedding, to double check. I had a fitting last week but I never leave anything to chance. As expected, it's perfect. Heavy cream silk that looks as though it has been poured over me, the corsetry within creating the quintessential hourglass. No lace or other fripperies, that's not me. The nap of the silk is so fine it can only be handled with special white gloves which, obviously, I'm wearing now. It cost an absolute bomb. It was worth it. I'm not interested in fashion for its own sake, but I respect the power of clothes, in creating the right optics. I knew immediately that this dress was a queenmaker. By the end of the evening it will probably be filthy, even I can't mitigate against that. But I will have it shortened to just below the knee and dyed a darker colour. I am nothing if not practical. I have always, *always* got a plan, have done ever since I was little.

I move over to where I have the table plan pinned to the wall. Will says I'm like a general hanging his campaign maps. But it is important, isn't it? The seating can pretty much make or break guests' enjoyment of a wedding. I know I'll have it perfect by this evening. It's all in the planning: that's how I took *The Download* from a blog to a fully-fledged online magazine with a staff of thirty in just a handful of years.

Most of the guests will come over tomorrow for the wedding, then go back to their hotels on the mainland — I enjoyed putting '*boats at midnight*' on the invites in place of the usual '*carriages*'. But our most important invitees will stay on the island tonight and tomorrow, in the Folly with us. It's a rather exclusive guest list. Will had to choose the favourites among his ushers, as he has so many. Not so difficult for me as I've only got one bridesmaid — my half-sister, Olivia. I don't have many female friends. It was a surprise to see so many women on the hen do — but then they were largely my employees from *The Download*, or the partners of Will's mates. My closest friend is male: Charlie. In effect, this weekend, he'll be *my* Best Man.

Charlie and Hannah are on their way over now, the last to arrive. It will be so good to see Charlie. It feels like a long time since we hung out as adults, without his kids there. Back in the day we used to see each other all the time — even after he'd got together with Hannah. He always made time for me. But when he had kids it felt like he moved into that other realm: one in which a late night means eleven pm, and every outing without kids has to be carefully orchestrated. I miss having him to myself.

'You look stunning.'

'Oh!' I jump, then spot him in the mirror: Will. He's leaning in the doorway, watching me.

'Will!' I shout, furious. 'I'm in my dress! Get out! You're not supposed to see—'

'Aren't I allowed to have a preview?' He doesn't move. 'And I've seen it, now,' he begins to walk towards me, 'no point crying over spilled silk. You look — *Jesus* — I can't wait to see you coming down the aisle in that,' he says, moving to stand behind me, taking a hold of my bare shoulders.

I should be livid. I *am*. Yet I can feel my outrage sputtering. Because his hands are on me now, moving from my shoulders down my arms, and I feel that first shiver of longing. I remind myself that it isn't as though I'm superstitious about grooms seeing wedding dresses — I've never believed in that sort of thing.

'You shouldn't *be* here!' I say, crossly. But already it sounds a little half-hearted.

'Look at us,' he says as our eyes meet in the mirror, as he traces a finger down the side of my cheek. 'Don't we look good together?'

And he's right, we do. Me so dark and pale, him so fair and tanned. We make the most attractive couple in most rooms. I'm not going to pretend it's not a part of the thrill, imagining how we might appear to the outside world — and to our guests tomorrow. I think of the girls at school who once teased me for being a chubby swot (I was a late bloomer) and think: *look who's having the last laugh.*

He bites into the exposed skin of my shoulder. A pluck of lust low in my belly, a snapped elastic band. And with it goes the last of my resistance.

'You nearly done with that?' He's looking over my shoulder at the table plan.

'I still haven't quite worked out where I'm putting everyone,' I say.

There's a silence as he inspects it, his breath warm on the side of my neck, curling along my collarbone. I can smell the aftershave he's wearing, too: cedar and moss. 'Did we invite Piers?' he asks, mildly. 'I don't remember him being on the list.'

I just about manage not to roll my eyes. *I* did all of the invitations. *I* refined the list, chose the stationers, collated all the addresses, bought the stamps, posted every one. Will was away a lot, shooting the new series. Every so often, he'd throw out a name, someone he'd forgotten to mention. I suppose he did check through the list at the end pretty carefully, saying he wanted to make sure we hadn't missed anyone. Piers was a later addition.

'He wasn't on the list,' I admit. 'But I saw his wife at those drinks at The Groucho. She asked about the wedding and it seemed total madness not to invite them. I mean, why wouldn't we?' Piers is the producer of Will's show. He's a nice guy, he and Will have always seemed to get along well. I didn't have to think twice about extending the invitation.

'Fine,' Will says. 'Yes, of course that makes sense.' But there's an edge to his voice. For some reason it has perturbed him.

'Look, darling,' I say, curling one arm back around his neck. 'I thought you'd be delighted to have them here. They certainly seemed pleased to be asked.'

'I don't mind,' he says, carefully. 'It was just a surprise, that's all.' He moves his hands to my waist. 'I don't mind at all. In fact, it's a *good* surprise. It will be nice to have them.'

'OK. Right. I'm going to put husbands and wives next to each other. Does that work?'

'The eternal dilemma,' he says, mock-profoundly.

'God, I know . . . but people do really care about that sort of thing.'

'Well,' he says, 'if you and I were guests I know where I'd want to be sitting.'

'Oh yes?'

'Right opposite you so I could do this.' His hand reaches down and rucks up the fabric of the silk skirt, climbing beneath.

'Will,' I say, 'the silk—'

His fingers have found the lace edge of my knickers.

'Will!' I say, half-annoyed, 'what on earth are you—' Then his fingers have slipped inside my knickers and have begun to move against me and I don't particularly care about the silk anymore. My head falls back against his chest.

This is not like me at all. I am not the sort of person who gets engaged only a few months into knowing someone . . . or married only a few months after that. But I would argue that it isn't rash, or impulsive, as I think some suspect. That actually it's the opposite. It's knowing your own mind, knowing what you want and acting upon it. Admittedly, the lust I feel for him isn't so rational. It's more of a compulsion. In a way it sometimes feels like a loss of control — and if it weren't so delicious I'm not sure I would like that very much. Sometimes my desire for him almost alarms me, in its power, its voraciousness.

'We could do it right now,' Will says, his voice a warm

murmur against my neck. 'We've got time, haven't we?' I try to answer — *no* — but as his fingers continue their work it turns into a long, drawn out groan.

With every other partner I've got bored in a matter of weeks, the sex has rather too quickly become pedestrian, a chore. With Will I feel like I am never quite sated — even when, in the baser sense, I am more sated than I have been with any other lover. It isn't just about him being so beautiful — which he is, of course, objectively so. This insatiability is something deeper than that. I'm aware of a feeling of wanting to possess him. Of each sexual act being like an attempt at this possession — something that is never quite achieved, some essential part of him always evading my reach, slipping beneath the surface.

Is it something to do with his fame? The fact that once you attain celebrity you become, in a sense, publicly owned? Or is it something else, something fundamental about him? Something secret and unknowable, hidden from view?

This thought, inevitably, has me thinking about the note. *I will not think about the note.*

The Guest List will be available to buy in spring 2020